Praise for *Bearly Departed*

"The first in a new series features a complex plot and red herrings, a perky heroine whose many problems certain to blossom in future installments, and everything you ever wanted to know about teddy bears."
—*Kirkus Reviews*

"Sasha Silverman, the narrator of Macy's entertaining first novel and series launch, runs her family's teddy bear business, the Silver Bear Shop and Factory, in Silver Hollow, Mich., an idyllic small town filled with excellent eateries and eccentric shops—inhabited by quirky, fully developed characters and good dogs and cats."
—*Publishers Weekly*

"Teddy bears and murder may not usually go together, but in this case they make a cute start to the new Teddy Bear Mystery series. Sasha proves to be a delightful protagonist— family-oriented, compassionate, and charming. The mystery is well-plotted, the whodunit not instantly obvious . . . Tours of the factory break up the tension . . . A town full of colorful suspects add to the wit and overall quirkiness."
—*RT Book Reviews*

"Macy, half of the D. E. Ireland team, launches an engaging series filled with charming details about stuffed animals. The appealing, impulsive amateur sleuth, dedicated to the family business, will appeal to fans of character-driven cozies such as Lorna Barrett's 'Booktown' mysteries."
—*Library Journal*

"Information on retail business and, in particular, on

Bear
Witness
to
Murder

Books by Meg Macy

Bearly Departed

Bear Witness to Murder

Published by Kensington Publishing Corporation

Bear Witness to Murder

MEG MACY

KENSINGTON BOOKS
www.kensingtonbooks.com

KENSINGTON BOOKS are published by

Kensington Publishing Corp.
119 West 40th Street
New York, NY 10018

All Kensington titles, imprints, and distributed lines are available at special quantity discounts for bulk purchases for sales promotion, premiums, fund-raising, educational, or institutional use.

Special book excerpts or customized printings can also be created to fit specific needs. For details, write or phone the office of the Kensington Sales Manager: Kensington Publishing Corp., 119 West 40th Street, New York, NY 10018. Attn. Sales Department. Phone: 1-800-221-2647.

Kensington and the K logo Reg. U.S. Pat. & TM Off.

eISBN-13: 978-1-4967-0966-0
eISBN-10: 1-4967-0966-7
First Kensington Electronic Edition: June 2018

ISBN-13: 978-1-4967-0965-3
ISBN-10: 1-4967-0965-9
First Kensington Trade Paperback Printing: June 2018

10 9 8 7 6 5 4 3 2 1

Printed in the United States of America

To my little Sweet Pea

ACKNOWLEDGMENTS

Thanks again to my beary supportive "team"—my daughters, El and Nari; the Empress (my berry best friend) for the Oktobear Fest idea; all the tea ladies; my sisters, Karen, Kris, and Janet for great times away from the laptop; Amy for the antique bears and inspiration; Eleanor (plus Piggy and Stegga) for much-needed laughter; my Little Guy (every writer needs a loyal dog at their feet); my wonderful editor, Wendy McCurdy, and her helpful assistant, Norma; Karen, Michelle, Paula, and everyone else at Kensington; my agent, John Talbot, for great chats about the mystery market; and, last but not least, faithful readers and teddy bear lovers!

I'm always finding a bear around the house I've forgotten I had tucked away, or seeing a few wherever I go—that warms my heart. Gotta love sweet, fuzzy teddy bears.

Chapter 1

"She's so furry! I love her." The little girl hugged the brown bear dressed in a striped orange sweater. "Can I keep her, Mom? Please?"

"We'll see," the woman said with a smile. "You have plenty of stuffed animals at home, remember, and a few teddy bears. Why do you want another one?"

"She told me she wants to come home." The child lifted the bear from its high chair and held it near her ear. "Her name is Daisy. She wants to play with my other teddies."

"Then Daddy will buy Daisy as an early birthday present."

I set a plate of cranberry scones on their table with a smile. Kids and their imaginations could be so precious. "I'll update my list," I said. "Daisy the tan bear to the young lady in the flowered blue dress, table five."

"Thank you, Ms. Silverman," the mom said. "My husband will be picking us up at four o'clock and he can pay you then."

"Of course. And please. Call me Sasha."

"Everyone's friendly here in Silver Hollow. It's wonderful, so charming."

I thanked her and delivered scones to the next table. Thank goodness I'd brought several teddies to sell from the Silver Bear Shop & Factory—which my parents owned, and I managed over the last seven years. My sister, Maddie, who staffed the office, figured a few kids might forget to bring one to the tea party. I checked the list at the front register. Five had sold, a nice bonus. Maddie had also left coupons for fifteen percent off any bear and accessories at each place setting. People seemed to appreciate that.

Things were going well for a busy Saturday on October's first weekend, when people could be attending football games or doing yard work instead. Our event was the kickoff for the village's Oktobear Fest, and we'd been worried. The committee insisted on changing the name to the First Annual Cranbeary Tea Party, despite the flyers we'd passed out last month, but no matter. Tickets sold out within a week. And everyone seemed to enjoy the new Queen Bess Tea Room, housed in the former Silver Leaf Bed and Breakfast.

Owners Arthur and Trina Wentworth, newly arrived from England, had set up tables in the parlors and the adjoining library. Laughter and chatter echoed in each redecorated room. Many of the mothers wore hats along with their daughters; at several tables, dads and little brothers joined in the fun. The children paid more attention to the teddy bears, however, than eating the quiche, salads, scones, and savory sandwiches. Maddie and I poured tea—Lady Grey, Cinnamon Spice, Black Currant, or Cranberry herbal—and waited tables.

Despite my killer sinus headache due to fall allergy season, I was thrilled the tea party was a smashing success. I sneezed into the crook of my elbow. Thank goodness I'd worn the lavender cardigan over a sleeveless dress with butterflies on the skirt. Maddie wore a pale blue cardigan over her floral dress— our makeshift uniforms as temporary waitstaff at the tea room. The Wentworths had yet to hire anyone besides the cook, a young woman from Ann Arbor, who'd prepared the creamy butternut squash soup, sandwiches, and scones.

My best friend, Elle Cooper, smothered a wide grin from where she sat at a nearby table with her young daughters. "I wish Mary Kate could see you as a waitress. The baby got sick this morning, and she feels terrible missing this."

"I wish I could refund her ticket money."

"She won't care. Your nose is all red, Sasha." Elle searched her dress pockets. "I've got an allergy pill. Somewhere."

"I took one. An hour ago." I sneezed again. "Could be the eucalyptus in the vases. Or the goldenrod. But I'm glad the Wentworths bought this bed-and-breakfast. Converting it into a tea room was a fabulous idea."

"I always thought it was too small as an inn anyway, with only four bedrooms upstairs." Elle hooked a thumb toward the back. "I hear they're almost done converting that back closet into a second restroom with handicap access."

"I'm shocked they turned this place into a showpiece so fast."

So much had changed in the short time since "Will's Folly." That's what Silver Hollow residents now called the murder of the Silver Bear Shop & Factory's sales rep, Will Taylor, before Labor Day. Few were sad; Will hadn't been popular with our workers. Still, others had been affected in the aftermath. Murder was a nasty business. Sales at the shop boomed from all the publicity, good and bad, and visitors to the area tripled. But I wasn't proud of nearly getting myself killed by sleuthing. I'd learned my lesson.

In record time, the Wentworths had hired a crew to clear out and clean the entire Queen Anne–style house from top to bottom. Then they brought in a massive black walnut sideboard for the front parlor, plus square tables and chintz-covered chairs in a pink, green, and gold rose pattern. They'd installed teacup chandeliers, four in each parlor and two in the library. Crisp linen cloths in pastel pink or green draped the tables with white lace overlays. Place settings in an eclectic array of teacups, saucers, plates, and flatware added to the charm. Gold-framed landscapes of the English countryside and castles hung on the walls.

I had to admit the tea room was an improvement over the dowdy bed-and-breakfast.

"Celia! Stop that," Elle hissed to her younger daughter, who was dunking a shabby teddy bear's nose into her full teacup.

"Mom, she spilled all over the tablecloth," said her older daughter, Cara.

"I've got it." I mopped the liquid with extra napkins. Both girls wore party dresses and hair ribbons, and I recognized Elle's pale blue dress from a shopping trip we'd taken last spring. "Which of the sandwiches did you like best, girls?"

"The strawberry cream cheese," Celia sang out.

"I like the peanut butter ones," Cara said, "but they need more jelly."

"Jam, not jelly. And no, teddies can't eat or drink," Elle said. The girls giggled at the wet smear on Celia's bear. "Now behave, or we won't be able to come next year."

"I'd better get back to work. Of course I'll bring more scones," I said when the woman at the next table waved me over. "I hope you're enjoying the tea party."

"Yes, indeed. We're planning on a visit to the new toy and bookstore, too."

When she turned to speak to her friends, I noted Elle's discomfort. Maddie, Mary Kate, and I were all worried sick for her and my cousin Matt. Bad enough that people ordered books online instead of visiting small bookstores like The Cat's Cradle. But the competition from Holly Parker's new toy and bookshop, Through the Looking Glass, would draw customers away and cut into their profits. I knew full well that Matt and Elle were barely surviving.

I glanced at the large corner table where Holly sat with a red-haired woman. Holly and I shared a bitter rivalry long ago in high school; she hadn't changed her hairstyle, still wearing it straight and long, although her tortoise-shell glasses looked modern. I tried to keep an open mind about her return to Silver Hollow, although I had to wonder why she chose to open a shop two weeks ago in direct competition. That didn't set well with my family.

Holly looked like an ingénue in a white dress with a row of sparkly rhinestones along the neckline. She'd always favored white, from what I recalled, which set off the natural olive hue of her complexion and tanned limbs. A bright pink jacket with silver bling spelling out THINK PINK was draped behind her chair. That reminded me of her extensive collection of Pink Panther memorabilia. Or perhaps "obsession" was more apropos.

To each their own.

I wasn't pleased reading Dave Fox's *Silver Hollow Herald,* which quoted Holly as saying "Our shop is already number one in sales here in Silver Hollow." That seemed a stretch. Maddie had witnessed her double-parking in the middle of Theodore Lane and getting ticketed by the local police for it, over the weekend when she'd moved into the former Holly Jolly Christmas shop. That reminded me. I needed to ask about some lost merchandise.

"Are you both enjoying the party?" I asked. Holly beamed at me.

"Oh, yes! I'm so glad we got tickets. It's so sweet, seeing all the little kids with their teddy bears. I hope you don't mind that I passed out a few flyers for my shop."

Since she'd already done so, I figured it was useless to object. "Gina Lawson," the red-haired woman said, and gave me a firm handshake. "I'm Holly's shop assistant, marketing guru, and publicity person."

"Nice to meet you, Gina." I eyed her short tomato-red pixie haircut, gelled up in a curved ridge, rocker-style, and heart-shaped face. "Sounds like you know your promo stuff. I've seen a lot of your social media lately. Tweets and Facebook posts about the new store."

"Great."

Gina smiled, a bit slyly I thought, so I addressed Holly. "I should have asked you long before now, but did you come across any of our silver or white teddy bears? Among all the items left behind in the Holly Jolly shop, I mean. We had half a dozen bears displayed there."

Holly looked sorrowful. "No. We tossed broken ornaments, scads of nonworking fairy lights, and empty boxes. It was such a mess cleaning up."

"Well, thanks anyway."

I headed toward my sister, who stood near the front entrance. Maddie snapped photos of various guests. She'd already taken multiple shots of the table settings before anyone arrived. "Isn't Flynn coming?" she asked. "I thought I saw his name—"

"On the guest list? I hope not. I'm shocked Mayor Bloom showed up," I said.

Across the room from Holly and Gina's table, Cal Bloom sat with his wife and ninety-year-old mother-in-law. The Blooms were old friends with my parents. While the mayor's presence in a roomful of mostly women and little girls seemed odd, he appeared to be enjoying himself. His booming laugh caused others around them to join in.

"Mom and Mrs. Davison seem to be having a good time," my sister said.

Barbara Davison, in a bright orange dress and wide-brimmed straw hat, sat with our mother, Judith Silverman, whose teal outfit and fascinator clashed with her friend. The way they giggled like schoolgirls made me wonder if Mom hadn't topped their teacups with a nip of something else. She did love brandy. Barbara clapped a hand over her mouth to stifle a huge guffaw, in fact, which brought on a glare from Mayor Bloom.

"What are they talking about?" I muttered.

"—and I paid a fortune. The restorer used an old fur worn by Alex's mother to fashion a teddy bear," Mom was saying. "And then someone snatched Minky Bear! Right out of the house, under our very noses. I have no idea how."

"Must have been one of the maids," Barbara said. "Did you report it stolen?"

"Yes, but nothing ever came of it."

I noted how both Holly and Gina seemed to be enraptured by their conversation. "What a tragedy," Holly said. "A real mink bear. That must have been precious."

"Yes. And I wouldn't let my girls play with it, ever."

That was certainly true. Not that Maddie or I ever wanted to touch it. Grandma Helen Silverman never let us do anything except sit quiet when we visited her house as children. A teddy bear made of her mink stole didn't appeal to me, especially with its staring beady eyes and those tiny dangling paws. Minky Bear was incredibly soft, but ugh. Bad memories.

After stacking soiled plates, I headed to the kitchen and almost collided with Maddie. She sailed past with a presumably empty teapot in each hand. Skirts swirling, her high heels muted by the carpet, she looked fresh and vibrant. My feet were killing me in flats, and although I spent most of my days standing behind the shop counter, I was exhausted. Maybe I needed to start working out more often. Instead I snitched a crab tartlet.

"Mm."

"Uh-oh. Speak of the devil," Maddie said, and nodded toward the front door.

I peeked around the doorway to see my ex-husband, Flynn

Hanson, waltz into the parlor. He made a beeline for Holly's table. Gina Lawson must have been expecting him, since she rose to her feet, arms folded over her ample chest. They exchanged heated words, from what little I could see after taking a tray of fresh scones across the room. But everyone witnessed Gina and Flynn marching over to the mayor's table before handing him a sheet of paper.

"Mr. Mayor, this is a copy of the court summons I filed on behalf of my client, Ms. Gina Lawson," Flynn said. "This serves as notice of a debt collection complaint against you—"

"And I shall answer with a countersuit," Bloom interrupted. "If Ms. Lawson continues this ridiculous claim, she will lose. I owe her nothing, Mr. Hanson. You could have served this at any time, but here? At a teddy bear party with children present? That's a bit dramatic."

"Whoa," Maddie whispered to me. "Didn't expect fireworks here of all places."

I noticed the very pregnant Lisa Blake, who'd been sitting at a nearby table with her two little boys, rise unsteadily to her feet. She herded the kids toward the door; they clutched their bears, restless and fidgety, ready to leave early. Holly cut off their retreat, however. I kept an eye on them while also watching the exchange between Flynn, Gina, and Mayor Bloom, whose voices had dropped. Cal Bloom snatched the paper from Flynn in disgust and departed without a backward glance. His wife followed, pushing her mother's wheelchair.

Gina and Flynn headed for the farthest corner of the back room. Now that Lisa Blake had departed, Holly waved a hand toward Gina and Flynn. "Hard to believe she's going after the mayor, huh?" she asked me before I could escape. "I've seen the new television commercials, the ones with 'Flynn Wins,' pretty much every morning. He's a pistol, all right. I've heard Hanson's the star of the Legal Eagles team, and they're going gangbusters since he joined them."

"Uh. Yeah," I said and glanced at my sister, now busy chatting with a friend in the back parlor. Maddie was out of range to rescue me. "Yeah, I know all about the Legal Eagles. Excuse me, but we've got to bring out the desserts."

I retreated to the kitchen. Maddie beat me to the doorway, however. Gina and Flynn still had their heads together, and Holly soon joined them. My sister pulled me out of sight beyond the swinging doors. She waved her cell phone in triumph.

"That red-haired woman, Gina Lawson? She's trouble. Mark my words."

Chapter 2

"What?"

"I'll explain later, okay? We've got work to do."

Inside the kitchen, we found Trina Wentworth at the prep table arranging the last plate of iced cookies from Fresh Grounds. She placed a row of chocolate tarts around the outer edge and then waved to the cook who headed out the back door.

"Here I thought you were getting tea cakes from the village bakery," she said. "Pretty in Pink, isn't it? I adore their striped awning."

"The owner's son died several weeks ago." I chose not to go into the details, given how that was all tied in to Will's Folly. "At the funeral, Vivian Grant told us she couldn't handle a special order. Plus she's short-staffed. But we promised to use her bakery for our next teddy bear–themed event. In November."

"I must say, these cookies are brilliant!" Trina bit into an extra. "Scrummy, too."

"Aren't they sweet?" I was pleased with Mary Kate's iced cookie design, shaped as plump tan teddy bears popping from orange pumpkins. "I love these little leaf hats on the bears, too. So adorable."

Trina wore an apron over her rose-print skirt. Her blond bob swooped with every move when she hurried to set cookie plates on all the tables in the tea room. Her tall, silver-haired husband followed behind with two more plates. My sister poked my shoulder.

"Quit sneaking the crumbs and help deliver the desserts."

I crammed the rest of the broken cookie—fewer calories than eating a whole one, of course—and rushed to help. Then I tracked Maddie down in a corner of the library. "What did you mean by Gina Lawson being trouble?"

"Shh! She might hear you."

I grabbed the empty teapot she handed to me and headed to the kitchen again. Everyone oohed and aahed over the tarts and cookies. Relieved, I watched Gina, Holly, and Flynn return to their table, heads together. No doubt they were discussing Gina's lawsuit against Mayor Bloom. What was that all about anyway? My curiosity mounted higher when Flynn stood and headed my way. Uh-oh. I ran for the kitchen and ducked out of sight.

Flynn Hanson had recently moved back to Michigan from Florida. Why had he come today? I knew he hated tea. He also disliked kids of any age—which was the second reason I filed for divorce. Number one? His cheating ways. Flynn actually admitted that he hoped I'd "get over" my desire for a family. As if! I loved kids. The biggest draw to working at the Silver Bear Shop was seeing their joy among all the teddy bears.

I peeked around the doorway. Flynn had stopped to chat with Mom. After she helped him find a huge house west of Ann Arbor, he'd brought her a dozen roses in gratitude. Were they cooking up yet another scheme together? Either real estate or something else?

One of the ladies at a table waved to me, so I walked over with a fresh teapot. "We can't wait to see the Bears on Parade that's part of the Oktobear Fest this month," the woman gushed. "When will they be ready?"

"I believe next Wednesday is 'opening night,'" I said, using two fingers on each hand to suggest quotation marks for emphasis. "My sister is one of the sculpture artists."

"Are they fashioned of resin? If so, they must be heavy."

"Uh, I think it's resin and fiberglass. You can ask Maddie, she's in the blue sweater over there." I swiveled on my heel and then crashed into Flynn's chest. "Ow!"

"Hey, Sasha. Got a minute?"

"Not really."

Pushing him aside, I hurried to the kitchen. Flynn trailed after me, though, as if I was the Pied Piper and only he could hear the tune. With a sigh, I grabbed the last dessert plate and tried to dodge him once more. He grabbed my elbow.

"Hold on. I've got two tickets—"

"What?"

"—to a Red Wings game." Flynn grinned at me, expecting a reaction.

Puzzled, I shook my head. "Sorry. Not interested." I marched over to Mom's table with the plate. "Anyone need a few more cookies or tarts?"

Barbara nodded. "Thank you, dear. I so wanted to take a few extra home for my husband. Could you find a small box?"

"Of course. Should only take a minute."

"Sasha, bring a box for me as well," Mom said. "I'm full to the brim, so dessert will have to wait. Your father would love a tart. Any idea where he went camping this weekend?"

I shrugged. "I'll be right back with the boxes."

Technically, Dad wasn't camping. He was off with Gil Thompson on a trip north to scout a location for another Fresh Grounds coffee shop and bakery, but no way was I rat-ting him out. Mom would be livid about being left behind. She loved stopping in all the boutiques from Petoskey to Traverse City. I had no intention of getting involved in any upcoming battle.

In the kitchen, Trina was busy filling the dishwasher with salad plates. "Do you have any boxes for people to take home desserts?" I asked.

"Look in the stack of cardboard cartons over there," she said promptly. "Don't make a shambles of all the supplies if you can help it."

Flynn had followed me, however. "You didn't let me finish, Sasha. I want to donate tickets to a Red Wings game against Pittsburgh to raffle off at the Oktobear Fest."

"Oh. That sounds great."

Thank goodness he wasn't inviting me to a hockey game. We'd often caught the Red Wings in action while we dated, and he even proposed during a game against the Chicago Blackhawks at Joe Louis Arena one night. The Wings lost in overtime. That should have been a warning bell, but did I listen? Nope. I was over the moon, blind with love, hoping to fulfill my dreams of a happy marriage with a husband, a house filled with kids, and a dog.

Maybe Flynn wanted the tax write-off by donating his tickets. The Wings had faded since their 2007–2008 Stanley Cup season. I remembered the night we attended the playoff finals' first game back then, against Pittsburgh; Detroit lost that one also. Was it coincidence that Flynn chose tickets to a Wings game against the Penguins? Was it a dig at me? Then again, maybe I was reading too much into his generous offer.

"I don't have anything to do with collecting donations, Flynn, but thanks. Maddie will tell the committee, though."

My sister caught my words when she entered the kitchen. Arms pumping, she squealed and twirled around the narrow space as if she'd won the tickets.

"The Red Wings! Wow! Which game, Flynn? Where are the seats?"

"October twenty-third, against Pittsburgh," he said. "Should be a great game, and the seats are great. Right near the Red Wings bench, fifth row."

At last I found the takeaway boxes and pulled them out. I busied myself with figuring out how to fold them properly while Maddie squealed again.

"I'm calling Amy Evans right now. She's in charge of donations and other stuff."

"I heard your design was chosen for one of those fiberglass bears. Congrats!"

She beamed. "Thanks! I'm excited."

"So when is the Oktobear Fest?" Flynn asked.

"Third weekend this month. Two weeks away," I said. "And I'll bet your tickets will bring in a lot of bids."

"People will go nuts," Maddie said. "Amy's been hoping for items just like this, and gift cards for restaurants. Dad and Gil Thompson have donated a few of those."

"Arthur and I will donate a free high tea," Trina said. "Perhaps at Christmastime? We'll be officially open by then. Wouldn't that be lovely to win?"

"Perfect! I'll call Amy right now and tell her." Scrabbling in her skirt pocket for her cell phone, Maddie raced out of the kitchen.

"Great." Flynn flashed another goofy grin at me. "Uh. I better get back."

Arthur brought in a tray of dirty teacups and saucers just then. "Cheerio, then. Hang on, aren't you the chap in that 'Flynn Wins' advert on the telly?"

I kept silent, since in my opinion Flynn didn't need such blatant self-promotion. He'd been a top attorney in Florida. Mark Branson and Mike Blake hadn't been hurting for business, either. What more did Flynn need, unless he wanted an ego boost? Duh! I almost smacked my forehead. Of course that was the answer—Flynn craved attention.

"My publicist thought it would be a great idea," he said.

"Your *publicist?*" I couldn't help the sarcastic twinge in my tone.

"Sure. Gina's a whiz at that kind of thing."

Maddie almost dropped the phone, hearing Flynn and me in the kitchen. "So, the redhead who's doing promo work for Holly's Through the Looking Glass."

"Yeah," Flynn said. "Gina's great."

"She's also Holly's shop assistant, and worked on the mayor's re-election campaign," I said. "Talk about multitasking."

"Gina has lots of great ideas," he said. "Great gal."

"*Great.*" I sounded like the queen of sarcasm today. "So what about this lawsuit she filed against the mayor?"

"Client confidentiality. You ought to know better than to ask."

"But you announced that it's a court summons for debt collection."

He shrugged. I was certain more details would be bandied about in the Silver Hollow gossip mill before morning. Flynn's face and neck had gone scarlet from the roots of his blond hair down to his tight collar. He probably knew that, too.

Maddie waved a hand in dismissal. "Well, we really appreciate the tickets. Cal Bloom donated a signed Steve Yzerman jersey, with a bunch of other players' signatures on it. That will be a fabulous auction package."

"Great." Flynn backed toward the door and bumped into Arthur Wentworth, who howled in pain. "Oh, sorry about that. Stepped on your foot?"

"No worries, mate."

"Good thing we're not officially open. Customers aren't supposed to traipse about in the kitchen." Trina herded both men out the door. "Fetch the teacups, darling."

Once I delivered the boxes to Mom and her friend, I noted

that Gina, Holly, and Flynn all chose to depart at the same time. Hmm. I rushed back to the kitchen and caught Maddie's arm. "So tell me what you heard about Gina Lawson."

First Maddie took over dish duty from Trina. "We're not leaving you with all this to clean up. We can't thank you enough for helping us out today."

Trina laughed. "I'm glad we did, and I'm knackered! I'll go Hoover the rooms while you birds tidy up in here then."

My sister waited until she left. Maddie turned to me but lowered her voice anyway. "You saw that article in the *Silver Hollow Herald,* right?"

"About how Holly sells more than the Silver Bear Shop and The Cat's Cradle combined, when they've only been open a few weeks." I filled the sink with soapy water and washed the delicate cups and saucers while Maddie dried and put them away. "Yeah, right."

"That was Gina's idea, Sash, and it's all smoke and mirrors. She may be a publicity whiz, but Mayor Bloom wasn't happy with her tactics. At all."

"What kind of tactics?"

"He owns the funeral home, remember. Prim and proper like what Grandma Helen would say, but Gina's ads and promo were more suited to a snarky guy with attitude. That's why the mayor refused to pay her fee. Not even half of what she asked."

"Whoa. All I remember is an ad about how he'll be tougher and rougher on crime in the area, and come down hard on all the drugs in the schools," I said. "And something about how parents aren't doing their jobs. Sounds like Gina's marketing made him a big bully."

"She claimed he needed to boost his image." Maddie rubbed her hands with glee. "Given his opponent, that farmer who lives beyond the Richardsons. Tony Crocker got a huge number of people to sign his nomination petition. Could be why the mayor's worried."

"But he'll win again. Cal Bloom's been mayor for fifteen years, and most people don't like change. They also don't bother to vote, except for the mayor's supporters."

"Gina's got a good marketing record, though, from what I heard," my sister said. "I bet that's why Flynn hired her to arrange those commercials. You know he's been dating her off and on for the past few years, right? Abby Pozniak told me, right before she left today."

"Did Abby have any information about Gina's lawsuit?" When Maddie shook her head, I started washing the flatware. The whir of a vacuum floated from the parlor. "I don't see why Cal Bloom won't pay her half her fee and avoid gossip. It's bound to hurt him, whether or not he's a shoo-in to win another term as mayor."

"What did you think about Holly Parker coming to the tea?" She plucked up a towel to dry the spoons, forks, and knives. "Her business is beating our shop, remember, and Matt's bookstore in sales. Odd that she didn't have Gina covering the shop for her."

"Not that odd, since she probably wanted to see Flynn serve the mayor that summons."

Maddie snorted. "You know Holly's carrying Bears of the Heart toys. She never asked us about stocking our bears in her shop."

I shrugged. "People can walk down the street if they want to buy ours."

"It's a popularity contest, Sash, like when the two of you were back at Silver Hollow High. Gina told Holly exactly what to do the minute she returned. Buying a thousand tulip bulbs for the village's garden brigade. Face painting at Richardson's Farms, the same day we're doing our Hide the Bears in the Apple Orchard. Now I've heard she volunteered as Santa's helper at the Bear-zaar next month."

"Wait—what Hide the Bears in the Apple Orchard?"

"Next Saturday. We talked about it back in July." My sister snapped the damp towel at my backside. I flicked soapy water back at her.

"Oh yeah, I remember now. Richardson's will be crammed with people for the usual hayrides, pumpkin picking, donuts, and cider, too."

"Don't forget the haunted maze. Everyone's looking forward to that."

"A haunted maze? What about the haunted house?"

"They change it up every year. A barn one time, and last year's haunted cellar was so gruesome some parents complained," Maddie said. "That's why they're buying our smallest bears and selling tickets for the younger kids to search in the orchard. It's a great idea. Wish I'd thought of it first."

"You do a great job on social media. It's not that hard. I really don't understand why Holly thinks she needs a marketing and publicity person."

"Gina handles the online sales. But I wonder what else the two of them will come up with for Through the Looking Glass. Kip says Holly will do anything to succeed, and I believe it. You ought to know what she was like back in school."

"Whatever. Even if she hires a three-ring circus to perform in front of the shop, people will focus on the Bears on Parade and the Oktobear Fest events this month."

"Ooh, so Holly's return is bothering you. I wasn't all that sure till now."

"Shut up." I twisted the dishrag to squeeze water out and then hung it to dry. "Come on, we've got to get back to the shop. As for Holly Parker, she can go stuff it."

"Didn't she plagiarize your senior English essay? And that's why she was named Student of the Year instead of you?" Maddie asked.

"I couldn't prove I wrote it."

"Then she took away first chair from you in Band. And stole your boyfriend."

"You were in junior high. How do you remember all that?"

"Hey, you were upset, and Mom wasn't very sympathetic."

"Water under the bridge." I waved a hand. "I'm more upset that Holly talked Barbara Davison into renting the Holly Jolly shop before you had the chance to ask. After Mom told her about your plans to open a boutique, too."

"But I'm not ready," she said. "I'm swamped with stuff. Online graphics for a few customers, my bear sculpture isn't done, and I'm teaching Aunt Eve all the new technology. She wanted to do everything by hand, like when she first set up the accounting, but I talked her out of it. Everything's already in the computer."

"It's still not fair."

"My plan for a boutique can wait."

Maddie's cell pinged. She turned around and answered it; I boxed up the extra cookies and taped them shut. My annoyance grew when I recalled my rivalry with Holly. So much for trying to forget all that trouble long ago. I'd expected peace and quiet after our annual Labor Day Teddy Bear Picnic, but that seemed hopeless now.

"Hey, Sasha." My sister pulled me into an alcove of the tea room and waved her cell. "Remember Abby promised to send me information about Flynn and Gina dating."

"Okay, but what about them?"

"You're gonna love this. Every picture tells a story, you know."

I peered at her cell phone, which she'd turned sideways. "What am I supposed to be looking at? It's too dark, I can barely see what it is."

"A hot tub at that bed-and-breakfast, the Waterford Gardens, east of here on Huron River Drive. Swipe to the next photo."

I did and leaned forward with a gasp. The blond guy sure looked like Flynn. Naked as a jaybird—I'd recognize that bare butt anywhere. The memory of how I caught him frolicking with another woman in the buff, and in our bed, soured my mood. The woman with Flynn in the hot tub only wore a thong, and the unnatural size of her chest would give Pamela Anderson pause. The intertwined hearts tattoo on her bare shoulder also caught my eye.

I turned to my sister. "So who is this woman?"

"Wait, you haven't seen the worst."

"Good grief." I realized now my ex had gotten far more than an innocent skinny-dip. "Wait a minute, how did Abby get these photos?"

"Her cousin worked at that bed-and-breakfast before it went out of business."

"So when was this photo taken?" Besides the obvious question of why Flynn would risk having sex in a public place, but I didn't want to go there. I knew too well he loved flirting with danger. "Or did Abby tell you?"

Maddie swiped her phone and held it up. "Yeah, during your marriage. I'm sorry, Sash. But you knew Flynn cheated on you long before you caught him with Angela."

I sighed. "Yeah. So who is this chick in the hot tub?"

"Gina Lawson."

Chapter 3

Trina peered around my shoulder and shrieked at the photo on Maddie's cell phone. "Blimey! They're having it on, aren't they."

"That's Sasha's ex, Flynn Hanson," Maddie said grimly. "Guess he never figured people might be watching while fooling around in a public place."

"Looks a bit chuffed of himself."

"Total egomaniac." I changed the subject, figuring I'd rather not dwell on another of Flynn's conquests during our brief marriage. "Anything else we can do to help?"

"Nothing, love. You two go on," Trina said cheerfully. "We're all set, money-wise, for the food plus room rental. Should I make out a gift certificate for a free Christmas high tea, then? That way you can take it to your friend."

"That would be wonderful," Maddie said. "And thanks again for everything."

"Right-o. Did you know we're booked solid for the month after our official opening? I'm so grateful we decided to wait until after the Oktober Fest."

"Okto*bear* Fest," I corrected gently, "because everything's bear themed. They started doing that a few years ago, I think. It wasn't our idea."

"The committee figured doing that gave Silver Hollow a unique slant on all the other beer-themed festivals in the area. Even the new microbrewery beyond the village limits is getting into the spirit of teddy bears," Maddie said. "Would you like any extra cookies?"

"No," Trina said. "We've plenty of leftover scones. Ta-ra, then."

I grabbed my Simon Miller bucket bag and staggered after Maddie, who half-ran on her high heels out the door. How she had any energy left was a mystery. The tea room had been comfortable, but now I wilted in the last blast of Indian summer heat. A stiff breeze blew, however, with the hint of a chill. I could sense, given my sinus battles over the past twelve hours, that a cold front had to be approaching from the west.

"I'm surprised Trina and Arthur didn't choose a different name for their business," Maddie said. "All those huge pink roses, too! Overkill, in my opinion."

"What's wrong with the Queen Bess Tea Room? Unless you expected an Elizabethan flavor instead of cabbage roses and lace."

"Looks more in line with the Queen Mum."

"Nothing wrong with that. Hey, we forgot the box of extra cookies."

"I'll get 'em." Her cell phone trilled. "Oops, I better answer that—"

"I'll fetch the cookies."

Weary to the bone, I tottered back to the tea room. By the time I returned with the box, holding at least two dozen cookies, I had to fight the urge to sneak another. Maddie was still chatting on her cell with Kip, standing at the curb. My petite sister looked as if she'd never touched a sugar cookie in her life. She took out a bag of peanuts to snack on; due to her low blood sugar, she often needed extra protein or orange sections. I needed to take Rosie for a long walk. Or maybe ride my bike through the village. Anything to resist those cookie carb calories calling my name.

At last Maddie finished her call and pointed down the street. "Looks like Gina's borrowing the boss's car again."

I twisted around, curious. The redhead, clearly identifiable due to her unusual gelled hairstyle, climbed into the blue MINI Cooper hatchback. Gina drove up to Kermit Street and turned right without bothering to stop at the sign.

"So that's Holly's car?"

"Yeah. I wonder if she and Flynn are really seeing each other, or are on the outs," Maddie said. "Abby saw them at Quinn's Pub, having dinner together."

"Maybe they were talking about the lawsuit. And she is his *publicist*."

I didn't want to think about Gina and my ex-husband. She could have him, either as her attorney or lover, and welcome to his narcissist world. Thank goodness I'd gone to therapy after my divorce. It helped me realize the futility of living with Flynn, who craved praise and affection at every moment. I'd nearly lost my mind. Coming home to Silver Hollow had been more of a salvation than an escape. Too bad Flynn followed me here, though.

Maddie studied our new mailbox, her head cocked to one side, while finishing her peanuts. Jay Kirby, a local artist, had carved a realistic brown mother bear standing on a metal mailbox. Quite large, about four feet tall, with two smaller bears playing on either side. I adored it. Thinking of Jay lightened my cranky mood.

"Do you think it detracts from the house's Victorian

look?" my sister asked. "We have gotten plenty of compliments, but maybe we should have asked for a teddy bear instead."

"We have plenty inside the shop. I thought you loved it."

"I do, but Jay could have sold that piece to another client. Does it really fit our Silver Bear Shop? That's all I'm asking."

Eyeing the cleverly carved bears, I disagreed. "It's perfect. I think we need a new sign, though, because it's so weather-beaten. Draw something that incorporates a teddy bear over the name, or else beside it."

"I suppose—"

"Wait, let me guess. Mom hates the mailbox and complained to you."

"I never said that."

I caught her guilty tone. "Ha. You don't have to—and besides, Uncle Ross already cemented the bricks around the wooden post. Too late to change it now."

Maddie frowned. "Okay, okay. Mom's not happy with it."

"Why does she care one way or the other?"

"Probably because Dad refuses to return to Florida. He's having a good time with all his friends. Mom only has Barbara Davison."

"We have enough to worry about without getting involved in Mom and Dad's battles, you know that. But it's true the sign looks battered after a decade of winter storms. We could get a metal sign instead of wood."

"How about neon?"

I glared at Maddie, who snickered, before I realized she was kidding. I'd been drinking in the sight of the turn-of-the-century Victorian home Dad renovated a decade ago that sprawled ahead of us on Theodore Lane. With a corner turret that reminded me of damsels in distress, plenty of gables, a wide covered front porch with several white wicker chairs, plus a dazzling display of colorful chrysanthemums, zinnias, and purple salvia along the front and sides, the shop looked pristine. Except for the dingy sign.

"How did I miss seeing that awful sign the past year?" I mused. "We'd better change it."

"Yep. I second the motion," Maddie said.

She followed me around the addition that housed our offices, now in chaos given the reorganization we planned. I sighed once we entered the house. Onyx the cat didn't blink, but Rosie's tail swished back and forth; she jumped down from her window perch and accepted a big hug. My teddy bear dog loved cuddling, so I took the time to smother her with attention. She ate it up, licking my face and snuggling in my arms.

Maddie and I had two upstairs bedroom suites and shared the downstairs kitchen. We used the former dining room for staff meetings and family game nights; the study held Dad's mahogany desk, a crammed bookshelf, and Kenyan animal statues, plus Mom's collection of knickknacks. Except for a third upstairs suite for my parents, the rest of the house served as our shop with storage rooms, display areas, and a second-story loft playroom for visiting children.

"It doesn't matter what Mom thinks. She doesn't care about the business."

Maddie snickered again, following me—this time in bare feet, her high heels dangling by one hand. "She cares what people say about how it looks, though."

"Ha. You're right about that."

For the most part we didn't mind our parents hanging around Silver Hollow. Dad had quickly settled back into his old routine of daily breakfast with Uncle Ross and Gil Thompson, frequent lunches, and a few nights at the pub. My sister and I knew Mom wasn't happy, but we figured she'd strong-arm Dad into returning to their Florida condo for the winter. Neither of them liked the cold snowy months and gray days in Michigan, from November through March.

Past the covered walkway, its trellis overflowing with vines of clematis and honeysuckle, a stone pathway led to the former carriage house which housed the factory. My uncle supervised production of our teddy bears along with clothing sewed by talented staff. Dad had founded the shop and factory; shortly after opening, he suffered a minor heart attack. Mom insisted he let me take over management duties, since I was newly divorced and had returned to Silver Hollow. My sister and I kept Dad's dream of a successful business alive.

That is, until right before Labor Day. We found our sales representative, Will Taylor, dead at the stuffing machine's base. I shuddered, remembering that horrible night and its aftermath. But things had returned to normal. September was over, and October brought the first changes of color to the village's trees—gold and orange mixed with hints of red. It also brought customers shopping for Halloween costumes for their teddy bears, both kids and adults. Plenty wanted to dress up their bears to complement their seasonal home décor.

I loved the variety we offered, like clown neck ruffs, bat wings, vampire costumes, big and small pumpkin sweaters, along with Christmas-themed attire like angel costumes and Santa suits. Our staff enjoyed the extra sewing, too.

"So what should I do for Rosie this year, at Halloween?" I asked Maddie. "Last year she wore a clown ruff. The year before, she had angel wings."

"I got a big scratch after trying to put those devil horns on Nyx last year. You worry about what to do with the dog. I'm going to a party that night."

The sun sank lower in the western sky, heading toward the courthouse tower. The village clock chimed five times. For a Saturday afternoon, Silver Hollow was too quiet. I followed my sister into the house and kicked off my own flats. Aah.

"Gosh, we need milk and bread, eggs, cheese, juice. Pretty much everything." Maddie shut the fridge and peered into the freezer next. "Meat, too. Today went by so fast. I hoped we'd be done earlier, because I need to scout out a few more thrift shops for an accordion. Used, banged up. Doesn't even need to work."

"Did you check eBay?"

"Yeah, too expensive. Plus shipping is extra, and an accordion can weigh like ten or twenty pounds. I painted my Polka Bear, which took forever to get the dots spaced right. I still haven't figured out how to fasten the accordion straps on his paws."

"I thought Kip was helping you," I said. "He's been calling day and night."

"Swamped with his own bear. That design is giving him fits. It's so hard getting the right paint shadings in such a tricky pattern to resemble a tie-dyed shirt."

"I bet that would be hard."

I'd heard all this before, of course, but listened again to the litany. Maddie droned on and on about the pressure to finish in time. Her sculpture would be unveiled next Wednesday, in between Fresh Grounds and The Cat's Cradle, along with several others around the village. She'd met Kip O'Sullivan, a fellow artist, at the first Bears on Parade meeting back in early spring, but kept their relationship secret until a few weeks ago. Kip had been busy with a summer art project in Grand Rapids, so their relationship grew over texts, Facebook posts, and long phone calls. Since his return, they'd spent a lot of time together whenever possible.

Maddie gushed over his talent. "You should see the collage he did for a big group of heart surgeons. They commissioned it for their offices. Two thousand bucks!"

"Wow, that is great."

"He's pretty livid over Holly competing with our shop and Matt's at the same time. Kip met her a few years ago and said she was nasty."

"Doesn't surprise me. Hey, Rosie. Need a w-a-l-k?" I stooped down to hug my adorable Lhasa Apso and Bichon Frise mix, whose trimmed curly coat made her resemble an overgrown, frisky teddy bear. "Let me change my clothes first. Hang on, baby."

"I'd better check out how Aunt Eve is doing. I left a stack of invoices with her earlier," Maddie said. "Oh, there's Kip again."

She snagged her ringing cell and then headed for the small alcove that served as our office until renovations were finished. I'd hoped everything would be done by the tea party, but that hadn't happened; the contractors took far longer to make all the changes. With our annual Mackinac Island sisters weekend, plus Halloween, we had to get everything moved back and in order before the busy holiday season. I smiled at my sister's excited chatter.

Climbing upstairs to my bedroom, I mused about Maddie's latest flame. Although he had to be eight or ten years older, Kip O'Sullivan possessed the same level of creativity. He taught art classes at the local community college, and worked with several art galleries in the region. Dark-haired, attractive, with playful teasing and a boisterous laugh, he entertained everyone at a family dinner last week. Despite his paint-spattered T-shirt and jeans with multiple holes, which appalled Mom. But Dad liked Kip. That meant a lot to Maddie.

Maddie didn't seem to notice Mom's displeasure, which surprised me. Given the constant exchange of phone calls and texts, her worrying like mad over his projects, and also Kip's clear adoration of her, I figured they had to be in love.

I ought to recognize the signs. Been there, done that. So over it.

After grabbing a pair of jeans from the pile of laundry in my closet, plus a grungy plaid flannel shirt and my beat-up tennis shoes, I rushed downstairs. Rosie waited near the door, the leash in her mouth, her tail wagging.

I had to laugh. "So you've learned how to spell? Okay, let's go."

"Hey, Sash. We need you in the shop, hurry!"

Maddie disappeared beyond the double doors. We kept them locked, usually, as a barrier between the business and residential sides of the shop. Since we'd closed today due to the tea party, they stood wide open. I gathered my blond hair into a ponytail, grabbed a baseball cap from the pegs by the door, but then rehung the leash. Rosie's wagging tail drooped, since she realized we weren't leaving. I dropped to one knee and rubbed her ears.

"Sorry, sweetie, I promise this won't take long. Come on with me."

I led her through the hallway to the shop. Aunt Eve stood near a display rack, her blond hair styled in brushed-out pin curls à la Lauren Bacall; she wore a striped cotton dress with a flared skirt over a rustling crinoline and green leather four-inch heels. Despite suffering major hot flashes, Aunt Eve never went without a white or cream cardigan sweater. She stood near a customer and waved two bears, a small silver in one hand and a larger tan in the other.

"This young woman is trying to decide which bear would look better in a black leather outfit to complement her own."

The customer wore full Goth regalia and looked worlds apart from Aunt Eve. Black lipstick and black eyeliner emphasized the girl's pale makeup; her dark hair, streaked with lavender, fell to her waist. She wore a studded collar, black T-shirt, and low-slung belt with a skull and chains dangling from it, plus leather shorts. Below that, fishnet stockings covered her legs above black ankle boots. I guessed she and Aunt Eve had bonded over their love of furry teddy bears instead of fashion trends.

The girl leaned down to let Rosie sniff one lace glove. "Aww, how sweet. I love dogs, but can't have one right now. There's a cat at the pub, though."

"Yeah, I've seen it a few times," Maddie said. "We don't sell leather outfits for our bears, but you could place a special order if you want."

"Yup. A leather jacket, a black T-shirt with a skull on it, and leather pants," the girl said promptly. "I've got the chains and collar to match mine. I'll pay whatever it costs."

"When do you need it by?" I figured Maddie had wanted my input to squash a big project since we were so swamped. "A special costume for one bear won't be a problem."

"I'm playing in the band two weeks from now, at the village festival. I want a bear with a matching outfit, or close enough."

"How fun!" Aunt Eve snapped her fingers. "That's a great idea. Maybe I'll make a tiny dirndl skirt and blouse for a teddy bear, too. I recommend the larger size bear, Emily. See how he'd fit in the crook of your elbow?" She demonstrated.

"We sell a silver bear in that size if you don't want tan fur," I said. "Here's an order form. Be as specific as possible so we can get the costume exactly how you want it."

Emily spent a good five minutes writing and sketching before she handed a twenty-dollar bill to Aunt Eve. "Down payment, is that enough? I'll pay for the bear and the finished costume when it's done. Can you explain the Oktober Fest? Like, what else goes on that weekend."

Aunt Eve glanced at us. "I just moved back here, so they better tell you. It started long after I divorced Ross."

"It's called the Okto-*bear* Fest," I said. "German beer, food, the dance contest you're playing for, and standing sculptures around the village called the Bears on Parade."

"Cool. What are they made of? Clay?" Emily asked.

"They're cast in a mixture of resin and fiberglass," Maddie said. "I know several of the artists, and one of my designs was chosen for a sculpture in the parade. The bears don't actually parade around, of course, they'll be at certain locations. Visitors do the parading."

"Sounds neat." Emily waved at Aunt Eve, who fanned herself with a manila file folder. "Thanks again for listening, and for all your advice. Not many people understand my situation. It's pretty hairy."

"Anytime you want to chat, drop by. I'll be here with a ready ear."

"I better run or I'll be late getting to my gig."

The young woman rushed out the door. Both Maddie and I turned to Aunt Eve, who raised an eyebrow. "Something wrong?" she asked. "I wanted to make sure you agreed with taking on a custom order. Even a small one like Emily's."

"Sure," I said, "but what did she mean by her hairy situation? Seems pretty young to have it that rough."

"Emily Abbott is a foster kid. Oh, she's old enough to be on her own now," Aunt Eve amended. "Her birth dad died and left her an inheritance. She's never had much in her life, going from family to family in the system, so the money's thrown her off-kilter."

"Sounds like she needs a financial advisor."

"Yeah, I told her that. It's not like a million dollars, but at least half that."

"So Emily plays in a band?"

"At Quinn's Pub. She rents the flat above it."

"How did you meet her?" Maddie asked. "You just moved back a few weeks ago."

"A lot of people avoid her due to all the Goth stuff she wears." Aunt Eve laughed and shook the crinoline under her striped skirt. "I get the same surprised looks."

"Dad says it's good publicity, your unique style." When Rosie gave a loud bark, I had to laugh. "I guess she's getting antsy for her walk. Hold down the fort while I'm gone."

To my surprise, Maddie spoke up. "Wait for me, Sash. I need to change shoes. We've been cooped up all day inside, so I could use a little fresh air. Want to come, Aunt Eve? A walk will do us all good."

"No, you kids go ahead. I've still got plenty to do here."

My sister rushed upstairs. I took Rosie out to the back porch, wondering what was up. Not that Maddie didn't join me on occasion for a bike ride or a swim at the YMCA, but wanting to tag along on a walk seemed odd. I hoped she didn't have something major on her mind. I'd already learned way too many crazy things today.

Chapter 4

Rosie tugged me down the steps to the garden. I paced back and forth, deadheaded a few Shasta daisies, and then dropped them to reseed in the flower bed. Was Maddie worried about her bear sculpture? The Polka Bear sounded sweet, given the painted polka dots and accordion. Maybe she was worried about her relationship with Kip. But why would she confide in me? She'd never shared much about boyfriends in the past. And I hadn't told her much about what I'd dealt with while being married to Flynn.

Once she appeared in ankle boots, we headed out. Maddie had shed her cardigan and dress for a denim jacket and jeans. Rosie sniffed every bush on the way to Kermit Street. We passed Holly's shop, then angled through town toward the Village Green.

"The Oktobear Fest is only a few weeks away," Maddie finally said.

"I can't wait for all this to end." I tugged Rosie away from a discarded potato chip bag in the large parking lot behind the brick building that housed Fresh Grounds, The Cat's Cradle bookstore, and Mary's Flowers. "The Christmas rush will be breathing down our necks soon enough. I need our Mackinac Island weekend to recharge my batteries."

"Um, about that . . ."

"What?" I rounded on my sister so fast, Rosie yelped. Her leash wound around my legs, too. "Sorry, sweetie. You didn't make the reservation?"

"I tried. The Metevier is booked for a wedding. Cloghaun's and Haan's are both booked, but they'll call if they get a cancellation. There's always the Grand Hotel."

"It's so expensive, though."

Maddie shrugged. "We could stay at Mission Point."

"Oh man. It's so far from everything." I yearned for our usual routine and the quiet of Market Street, although many shops closed late in the season. "We'll have to wait and see. There's those west bluff condos, too."

"Talk about being far from everything! And we'd have to wait for the shuttle there and back." Maddie changed the subject. "So. Now that the tea party is done, what else are you going to volunteer to help with for the Oktobear Fest?"

After untangling Rosie's leash, I followed my sweet dog to the grassy lawn past the courthouse. Once I let out the extension to its farthest point, Rosie sniffed around her favorite trees and bushes. Maddie stood waiting, arms folded over her chest.

"What does Amy need help with?" I asked.

"In the beer tent, of course, serving drinks or checking IDs. How about working in the food tent? Handing out German pretzels, sausage, and pastries, that kind of thing."

"How about being a judge for the dance contest?" I was half-kidding, but my sister perked up at the idea.

"I'll ask. Jay Kirby's one of the judges."

"He is? Why not, it might be fun."

"That would be so cute, the two of you together," Maddie gushed. "Did you know Jay's carving a permanent sign for the Oktobear Fest? He came to the committee a month ago with the idea, and we loved his design."

"That's nice."

"Kip and I are getting together with him tonight. You ought to join us—"

"Hey, stop that barking!" I hauled the leash back, since Rosie was growling at a large Doberman. Luckily, the other dog looked amused but reserved. "Stop, or we're leaving."

"Really, Sash. You need to get involved with our committee. You don't do much except work at the shop and walk the dog. That's gotta get old fast." Maddie clapped her hands hard, startling Rosie and me both. "Sit! Good dog. Come along for dinner at the Regency Hotel. It's not really an official meeting, and you need adult time. You like Jay, right?"

"Aha. So that's why you tagged along."

"Oh come on. You ought to know he likes you—"

"I don't need you to set me up on a date with Jay Kirby or anyone else. And everyone knows you love playing matchmaker, so don't try to deny it."

"But you're interested, right?"

I sighed. "I'm too busy right now to date. We need to keep Mom from redecorating the office into what she wants instead of the way we'd planned. Then there's getting Aunt Eve settled into the office routine, plus making sure the five-foot bear for Oktobear Fest's grand prize is finished on time. Oh, and I decided to sew Rosie a vampire cape for Halloween."

"Cute, but that's a lame excuse." Maddie looked smug. "Let Mom do what she wants in the office, who cares? Less for us to do. And Aunt Eve's doing fine. I checked out her progress on the computer's accounting system, and things look solid. As for the grand prize, the bear is finished. The staff only has to make the lederhosen and a hat."

"But Rosie's costume—"

"Get Aunt Eve to do it for you, since you're so busy."

"I'll think about it." I cleaned up after Rosie, using a plastic bag like a glove to scoop her droppings, and then discarded it in the nearest trash bin. "And since when are we putting clothes on this bear? The committee is getting it at cost. That's a big discount already."

"Aunt Eve and I think the bear will look adorable in the costume."

"But we never discussed it!"

"Don't be a spoilsport," Maddie said. "We'll make a pattern if we can't find one to fit the bear, and a hat shouldn't be too hard, either. Uncle Ross and Aunt Eve battled over making a costume until Dad okayed the project. The costume's a done deal."

"Hoo boy. Ever since Aunt Eve hit town, she and Uncle Ross have been at each other's throats. If it's not about production, it's over quality control."

"They're only getting used to each other again. Things will settle down."

"I'm not so sure." I tugged Rosie across the street toward Fresh Grounds. "Come on, baby. I've got a headache, so I think an iced coffee might help. Let's see what Mary Kate's got left in the bakery case, too."

"Forget that," Maddie said. "You're coming to dinner with me, Kip, and Jay. Tonight, remember? We'd better get home and change."

I flexed my shoulder muscles, wishing I could think of a

better excuse. All I wanted was to veg on the sofa. Then again, maybe she was right. I didn't do much except manage the shop and keep Rosie and Onyx company. Maybe I ought to rejoin the book club, or take piano lessons, or sign up for craft classes. I'd been slacking off on feeding my creative juices.

"Fine, I'll go tonight. But that Cran-beary Tea was exhausting."

"Admit it," Maddie said. "You've been jealous of how often I've been meeting with artists. You should have tagged along from the beginning."

"Me? Jealous?"

She laughed and pulled me past Fresh Grounds. "Every time I met with the committee, you started moping around the house."

"How do you know? You weren't home to see me."

"I can read you like an open book, Sash."

"Hmph." I wasn't about to admit that Maddie was right. And I did like Jay Kirby. I was hungry, too, so maybe dinner wasn't a bad idea. "What if you can't find an accordion for your Polka Bear? Cheap enough, not like the ones on eBay for hundreds of bucks."

"Kip said he'll find one. Jay's delivering a sculpture, so the two of them planned to check a few resale shops on the way. But I have no idea if they were successful." My sister stopped to tug at her right boot. "I'm getting a blister. Do you have to walk so fast?"

"I'm keeping up with Rosie. Why did you wear those?" I feigned a look of horror. "Oh, forgive me. Your fashion sense might be scarred for life by wearing sneakers."

"Well, one of us has to look decent around Silver Hollow."

I stuck out my tongue, but Maddie didn't see since she waved madly at Digger Sykes. He waved back while passing in his patrol car, and turned onto Main Street. Now that the sun had vanished behind the distant trees, our shadows stretched long before us when we crossed Kermit Street. Rosie sniffed the air and then led us around the corner of Holly's shop.

The door suddenly swung open, smacking me in the arm before I could stop. Rosie yelped, too, and I crouched down to make sure she wasn't hurt. "My poor baby! Are you okay?" I ruffled her fur and checked her head. She licked my hand.

"Sorry. I had no idea anyone was out here." Holly held a thick stack of flattened cardboard boxes. "That tea party was so nice. The kids sure looked like they had fun, too. I'm going to host one here at my shop, maybe around Halloween."

"You're copying our idea?" Maddie asked in dismay.

"No, I'm going with a Harry Potter theme."

"That sounds great." I rubbed my sore arm. "A lot of kids would attend."

"I think so, too." Holly dumped the cardboard into the Dumpster and let the lid fall with a clang so loud my ears hurt. "We're doing far more online sales than in the shop. Is that normal for business? I figured weekends in small towns like Silver Hollow would be packed. Especially the way the Okto-bear Fest has been scheduled."

Maddie shrugged. "Our Cran-beary Tea was only the first event. Things will pick up after today. Wednesday should be busy with people coming to see the bear sculptures."

"I'd better stay open late that night. Traverse City has had much better success with events, though." She sighed. "Better planning and publicity. It is a bigger town, after all."

"So why did you move here, if it was so much better in Traverse City?"

I elbowed Maddie, whose tone had a biting edge. My sister ignored me. Holly narrowed her eyes, though, as if aware of her borderline hostility.

"For one thing, I have friends here. But it's really none of your business."

Rosie growled low in her throat. "We'd better be going," I said, and tugged my dog away from Holly's shin. "Come on, Mads—"

"It is my business, since you're competing against our shop," Maddie retorted. "Selling cheap bears from a rival company, and what about all the children's books? You know Matt and Elle Cooper have owned The Cat's Cradle on Main Street for almost a decade."

"A little competition doesn't hurt." Holly sounded smug. "But if Silver Hollow is too small for similar shops, then may the best bookstore win."

"Really?" Maddie patted Rosie's head when she growled louder. "Good doggie! Bite the wicked witch of the north."

"That's really mature. As for cheap bears, I can sell whatever I like in my shop." Holly sauntered toward the shop's back door. "Seems things haven't changed around here since high school. Hard to believe, but Mayor Bloom asked if my husband owned this business! Talk about old-fashioned and creaky. Or maybe he feels threatened. He certainly feels that way about Gina, but the mayor had better be prepared to lose that lawsuit in court."

"He had good reason to not pay her," my sister snapped. "He told her he wasn't happy and asked for changes. She ignored him. Why should he pay for something he couldn't use?"

"That shows how little you know." Holly opened the door, but turned back. "And Traverse City is more like Manhattan compared to Nowhere Hollow, USA."

"Then go back! We won't miss you."

The screen door thwacked shut behind Holly. "Good Lord, Mads," I said. "Why did you egg her on? Come on, I need a shower. And a nap."

"No time for that."

Rosie led the way down Theodore Lane. Maddie limped behind, already talking on her cell with Kip, and asking if he'd confirmed their reservation for dinner. I regretted stopping to chat with Holly Parker. Clearly my old rival planned to push my cousin out of business.

After all their hard work, I'd hate to see Matt and Elle lose their bookstore.

Chapter 5

"Hey, guess what I heard?" Maddie waved her cell and limped to my side. "And not just about the election campaign. Abby filled me in on a lot more."

I held up a hand. "I loathe politics. Don't tell me if it's silly gossip."

"It's serious gossip. Mayor Bloom might not be a shoo-in for re-election after all."

"I'd rather not hear it if that lawsuit is the reason."

My head hurt, so I hurried through the garden with Rosie. Loud voices drifted from the covered walkway, and that meant Aunt Eve and Uncle Ross were at it again. Great. Politics was bad enough, but the whole village might be able to hear their argument. His voice boomed; he faced his ex-wife, scowling, and waved a hand in the air. Aunt Eve had both hands on her slender hips, spike heels elevating her to his eye level. I wasn't so sure Maddie was right about them "getting used to each other again."

"We can't throw money around for every cause," Uncle Ross said.

"Alex said we could afford the clothes for that bear! Why don't you admit it," she snapped back. "You're as pigheaded as ever, Ross."

"Oh, brother." Maddie had caught up to me. "I thought this issue was settled. . . ."

She walked over to referee. In the kitchen, I changed Rosie's water, fed her, and then walked upstairs to my room. Dinner at the Regency, hmm. The fanciest hotel in town. Not a date, but sort of, given my sister's slyness. I wondered if Jay knew I'd be joining them. Maybe I'd better go more casual than Maddie would expect. Kip wouldn't be caught dead in a suit, that was certain. And Jay had delivered our mailbox in a sawdust-coated T-shirt and hiking boots.

I chose my best jeans, a maroon shirt, and matching blazer, and then draped a navy and white patterned pashmina over one shoulder.

Good enough.

A touch of lip gloss, a smudge of deep blue eye shadow, and a brush of pink blush over my cheekbones added a little polish. I brushed out my hair and then chose casual flats. My feet still hurt after setting up, serving, and helping the Wentworths clear the tea room after the party. A long Saturday, and I'd been on my feet all week, too. I refused to wear kitten heels. It took a few more minutes to toss my wallet, hairbrush, and other essentials into the deep maroon Coach crossbody purse I adored with its long, braided strap.

I also swallowed two aspirin, hoping it would ease the throbbing at my temples and near the back of my head. And behind my eyes. Ugh.

"Oh! You look—nice."

Maddie had stopped cold in the hallway. Her slinky taupe coat covered a classic little black dress, worn with an eighteen-karat-gold rope necklace, tottering black heels, and a black clutch. Silent, she smoothed a stray wisp of her dark hair and led the way to the car. I could tell she wasn't happy with my outfit choice. We were running late, though, and I didn't want to change. But I insisted on driving, despite the fog of pain blurring my vision.

Not a great start to an evening of fun.

Maddie didn't say a word even when I stopped in front of the hotel. "Go ahead inside and I'll park in the back lot."

My sister slammed the door, which confirmed her mood. Sighing, I found a spot behind Fresh Grounds. Scrabbled in my purse for an allergy pill and came up empty. That aspirin wasn't doing anything. My whole face throbbed. I knew I wouldn't last long tonight.

When I caught sight of Jay Kirby in the hotel lobby, clad in a snazzy dark suit, my heart sank to my shoes. Not that he didn't look great clean-shaven, with his unruly light brown hair slicked back. His wild tie made me smile, though. I recognized the Tasmanian Devil cartoon character holding carpentry tools—what a fun pattern. Although his citrus aftershave was subtle, my eyes burned.

I forced a smile. "Um, sorry about this. Maddie didn't exactly give me much warning about dinner," I said. "She wouldn't take no for an answer about coming tonight."

"Kip railroaded me, too." Jay winked. "Food's good here, even though I'd prefer a burger at the pub. Or a Ham Heaven sandwich. Maybe we can do that some other time. I'd like to show you my studio, if you want to see my carvings."

"I would, thanks. We'd better go in."

Jay escorted me into the hotel's dimly lit dining room with its mahogany tables and tan leather barrel chairs. Very few diners wore casual wear. I felt awkward and out of place. Being a Saturday night, and with so many other women dressed to the nines, I should have turned around and left. Feeling self-conscious, I sat on the chair Jay pulled out for me. Maddie squeezed my hand. That helped. Maybe she wasn't mad after all.

"Hey, Sasha," Kip O'Sullivan said with a welcoming smile. "Glad you joined us. I heard the party was a big success."

"Yeah, but I have a killer headache," I said. "Sorry I won't be much company."

Jay touched my arm. "You're great company."

Maddie looked fabulous, complementing Jay in elegance, while I matched Kip's casual garb of a denim jacket, jeans, and a golf T-shirt. He sported stubble on his jaw as well, which lent him a boyish air. Kip grinned at the waiter.

"Let's start with your best champagne. We're celebrating," he said, although Maddie protested. "Jay's sign is a knockout, and our sculptures will be, too."

"But we don't need a fifty-dollar bottle of champagne." Despite his objection, she insisted on a less expensive Brut. "Once we finish our bears, we can splurge."

"Did you two find an accordion for the Polka Bear?" I asked.

"We did! Score—only forty bucks at a Salvation Army store." Kip leaned back in his chair, clearly pleased. "I say we duct-tape the straps onto your bear's paws."

"You can't be serious." Maddie groaned. "That's bound to look silly."

"It's stronger than anything. Paint it and nobody will notice, trust me."

"At least it works," Jay said with a grin. "The accordion, that is."

"I'll figure out later how to attach it to the bear." Maddie thanked the waiter who finished filling the last flute. "Okay, how about a toast?"

"To the Polka Bear," Kip said. "May it stand long and prosper."

"And to the Hippie Bear," she added with a smile. "You really need to finish the paint job, though. I know it isn't easy making it look tie-dyed, but get it done."

"Jay hasn't even started his," Kip said.

"I have, too. Got the bear and the paint. Just need to finish a carving that's due."

"Never mind," Maddie said. "We'll all get them done on time. Right?"

They clinked their glasses, which sent spikes of pain into my face. While I was glad for the progress on their sculptures, I could only manage a sip and then set my flute down. "Where will your bear be set up, Mads? Remind me."

"Near Fresh Grounds," she said. "I hope Garrett and his staff won't complain about shoveling the sidewalk by hand. The snowplow might not be able to squeeze in between the bear and the shop. Remember those huge Christmas lantern barrels a few years ago?"

"Oh yeah." Jay laughed. "Remember how one barrel turned over?"

"And sparks set the poinsettias on fire in front of the flower shop. Mayor Bloom stomped them out before it spread. Good thing he happened to be there," my sister added.

"I heard the owner of Flambé sponsored a bear." I rubbed the bridge of my nose, aware of a nearby woman's overpowering perfume that wafted my way. "What about Holly Parker? I'm curious if she'll have one displayed in front of Through the Looking Glass."

Kip choked on champagne and coughed hard. "God, I hope not. She doesn't care about the arts. It's criminal how she came here to compete against your shop."

"I wouldn't go that far," I said.

A waitress suddenly appeared. "Is everyone ready to order?"

Maddie chose broiled salmon, while Kip asked for prime rib. When I decided on the lake perch, Jay ordered the same but with mashed, not red potatoes. Over the salad course, the three of them bantered about the Oktobear Fest, volunteer problems, and Amy Evans's frustrations. Once the fish arrived,

I struggled to hide my discomfort. Every burst of laughter in the room sent blistering pain through my head. I couldn't eat much.

"—our next trip up north," Kip was saying. "Last year you caught the biggest walleye, an eighteen pounder. We'll have to go back to that spot again."

"Actually, I'd like to try Long Lake this year," Jay said.

"Too many other fishermen, in my opinion. It's Garrett's turn to choose, remember. Hope he doesn't want to go up to Lake Gogebic. Too rustic for me." Kip pushed away his plate. "Not that I need a fancy cabin, but that one time, a black bear visited our campsite! Digger made it worse when he left out his stupid potato chips on the picnic table."

"What? He only wanted a snack."

"Him and his junk food. Bears can smell seven times better than dogs. I've told him a hundred times to leave all that stuff at home. I swear, we'd all have been dragged out as a main course if not for Matt waving an ax and then spraying that bear. Saved our hides."

Jay laughed. "I had an air horn, too."

"About as loud as your snores—"

Despite joining in the fun, Maddie glanced at me several times in concern. The guys kept trading good-natured insults for what seemed like hours, given my discomfort. I pushed my plate aside. Jay finally touched my arm, looking concerned.

"Are you okay, Sasha?"

"Bad migraine." I rose to my feet. "Sorry, but I need to call it a night."

"That's too bad," Kip said. "Can't you take an aspirin or two?"

"Let her go," Maddie said in my defense. "It's been a long day for us both."

"You've been so nice, Jay," I said. "I'm sorry to ruin the evening."

"No need to apologize. But I'm walking you to your car."

He led me through the now crowded restaurant. I swayed a little on my feet, eyes half-closed against the bright streetlamps outside. Jay noticed and pulled me in the opposite direction instead. "I'm driving you home. My sister Lauren suffers from bad migraines, so I totally understand. Ends up in the hospital if she doesn't get meds in time."

"But my car—"

"Fetch it tomorrow. This way you'll get home sooner. And safer."

"I'll be okay," I said, but glaring headlights speared my eyes. "Ow! Oh."

Jay slid an arm around me. "Come on, we're nearly there." Soon he boosted me to the passenger seat in his truck. I kept my eyes closed while he drove. Jay walked me to the porch, unlocked the door, and then planted a light kiss on my hair. "You need a dark room and some sleep. I'll call you tomorrow, okay?"

"Thanks." I stumbled into the kitchen. Rosie emerged from her crate with a few sharp barks. "Shh! Please, sweetie. Jay's gone already."

She must have sensed my pain. Rosie nudged my leg and stayed by my side, patiently waiting, while waves of nausea threatened. I groped inside the kitchen cabinet for prescription meds, took a dose with water, heated the microbead wrap, and slung it around my neck. Once Rosie returned from a last trip outside, we headed to bed. I stripped and crawled under the covers, grateful that Rosie cuddled behind my back. Her warmth was a comfort. I rode out the worst of the pain until sleep overtook me.

The next morning, I rolled over and checked the clock. Almost seven? A miracle for me to wake that early, although it had to be long before ten last night when I crashed. Rosie didn't budge, so I padded to the bathroom. I looked terrible; puffy eyes, my hair sprouting in all ways, but at least the migraine had receded. I splashed cold water on my face and brushed the tangles out of my hair. Rosie, who was far worse about mornings, stretched and yawned. After donning jeans, a light sweatshirt, and sneakers, I lifted her off the bed.

"Lazybones. Come on, outside with you."

Together we tiptoed past Maddie's suite, where I could hear her light snores. Thick fog swirled beyond the kitchen windows, but Rosie didn't mind. She vanished into the grayness a few feet beyond the porch railing. I blinked in confusion, peering at the empty spot where my car usually stood on the driveway. Dang. I'd forgotten about leaving it behind Fresh Grounds.

"At least Rosie won't mind a walk."

First I filled her bowl with kibble and then raided the fridge for a glass of orange juice. The thought of muffins at Fresh Grounds made my stomach growl, but I couldn't wait that long. A toasted bagel slathered with peanut butter was my breakfast go-to when short on time. Rosie dragged her leash across the tile, so I fetched a doggie doo-doo bag and buckled her harness. She wriggled in excitement. At last we left the house, careful due to the fog.

The village clock struck the half hour while we walked down Theodore Lane. I heard a car's rumbling muffler ahead of us, probably on Kermit, and hurried past Holly's corner shop. Once across the street, Rosie led the way to the Sunshine Café; the fog parted, showing Uncle Ross's vintage pale blue Oldsmobile parked at the curb. He always drove the car in the village Memorial Day and Labor Day parades, chock-full of teddy bears, but never offered anyone a ride if he could help it. My uncle cussed a blue streak if any speck of dirt marred the leather seats, and he routinely checked the polished fenders for any scratches or nicks.

I caught sight of his grizzled beard and cap through the window. Mayor Bloom sat with him at the counter. Dad and

Gil Thompson usually joined them for coffee and the café's popular French toast, but they hadn't yet returned from up north.

Past the half-hidden brick library, I cut through a stretch of blacktop to Church Street. It wasn't easy navigating in the denser fog. Rosie nosed her way through the narrow alley between Abby Pozniak's antique shop and Blake's Pharmacy until we emerged into the mist-covered graveled parking lot. Shadowy forms that loomed in our path turned out to be parked cars, a Dumpster, and a mailbox. I stepped cautiously over the stones.

"Ouch!" I'd hit my shoulder on a lamppost that appeared beside me. I peered at each parked car in the uneven lot. At last I found mine and unlocked the door. Rosie's whining suddenly turned into loud barks. That meant trouble.

"What is it, girl?" She wouldn't budge, so I followed the leash hand over hand.

I found Rosie guarding an inert form on the ground, right beside a blue MINI Cooper. Was it Holly Parker? My heart jumped into my throat. The jacket's hood covered her head. I stood gaping, frozen in place. My brain couldn't register for several minutes. Letters sparkled in the dim light on the hoodie's pale pink fabric. THINK, that was clear enough to read, but PINK was darkened by a mottled brown stain.

So was the knife hilt embedded in her back.

Chapter 6

I sat inside my car, still trembling. Rosie whined beside me. "Sorry, girl. You'll have to wait for breakfast. We can't go home yet."

Panicking, I dialed Mary Kate's number for the second time. No answer again. She might be getting ready for church, or taking a shower, or walking their dog—her one chance for fresh air and exercise. Maybe I should knock on the back door of Fresh Grounds. The weekend staff must be inside, although the music they played while getting ready to open would probably drown out any sound unless I pounded on the door. My hands still shook. I dialed Garrett's cell number instead, and felt better at the sound of his voice.

I blurted out what had happened in a rush of words. "Yeah, called 9-1-1 already—"

"Sasha, listen to me—don't touch anything. I'll be right there."

He hung up. I didn't get a chance to tell him the police had arrived, lights flashing, but without sirens. Thank goodness. My teeth chattered, more from shock than the chilly air. Once I'd cracked open a few windows for Rosie, I met Officer Bill Hillerman in the lot. Digger Sykes joined us, his patrol car blocking access to the street; his navy uniform looked wrinkled, and keys jangled with every step. At barely five-six, he always made me feel Amazonian.

"Figures you'd call this in." Digger smirked. "Where's Maddie?"

"Probably in the shower by now," I said, since the village clock struck eight.

"Sykes, get the crime scene tape." Hillerman directed the younger man to stretch the yellow barrier tape around the parking lot's perimeter, and then walked me over to Holly's body with a long sigh. "Explain in your own words how you came to be here. Keep it simple and straightforward. Take your time."

I drew a deep breath, steadying my nerves, and then plunged into how I'd needed to retrieve my car. "—left it here last night. I usually take a walk with my dog. It's so foggy this morning, though. I didn't see the—this. Not at first. I mean the body," I added, keeping my eyes averted. "Holly Parker. She opened Through the Looking Glass not that long ago, the toy and bookstore. At the corner of Kermit and Theodore."

Wan sunlight cut through the lingering wisps of fog, which increased visibility. While Hillerman jotted in his notebook, Digger sauntered toward the body and then knelt. I stared in shock when he reached for the knife hilt.

"Hey, is he supposed to touch that?"

"No disturbing the crime scene, Sykes," Hillerman barked. "You know better than that. By the way, I called the County Sheriff for assistance."

Digger scrambled to his feet. "Why? We don't need help. I stood right next to Detective Mason at that press conference last month, and he took all the credit for solving Will Taylor's murder. I know as much as he does about how to conduct an investigation."

"I doubt that. You just trampled any footprints."

"Sasha already did that."

Hillerman ignored him. "What time did you find the victim, Ms. Silverman?"

"Sometime after seven thirty. I think."

I watched Digger amble around the lot with restless energy. Hillerman asked several more questions and wrote up everything I said. By the time he finished, a small crowd stood gawking and whispering. Garrett Thompson shoved past Digger Sykes with a sharp word and hurried to my side along with Mary Kate; she draped a light blanket over me and pressed a cardboard cup into my hand. Garrett opened my car's door, grabbed Rosie's leash, and then hand-fed her some kibble from a plastic bag.

"We had to drop the baby off at Elle's before we could come," Mary Kate whispered in my ear. "I knew you'd need your favorite Mint Mocha espresso, too."

"Mmm." I sipped, grateful for it and my friends' presence in the face of another tragedy. Murder, for the second time. I shivered hard.

"Did you call Maddie?" she asked.

"I meant to, but then the police arrived."

"I'll call her. Garrett, check on staff at the shop," Mary Kate added, and then opened her cell phone. "Make sure to bring the officers some coffee, too."

He departed with a nod while Hillerman returned to his patrol car. Digger approached me, wary, an odd gleam in his eyes. "Second time you found a dead body, Sash. This proves you're a magnet."

"That's not fair—"

"Officer Sykes!"

Hillerman beckoned him over. I didn't appreciate the way Digger spread gossip around the village, about me or anyone else. More cars arrived. I was relieved seeing the familiar SUV from the County Sheriff's Department and the burly figure of Detective Mason. Not in uniform, but in a Tigers jacket over jeans and a T-shirt, his light brown hair mussed. He never failed to remind me of an overgrown teddy bear wearing wire-rimmed glasses and carrying a cardboard coffee cup in hand. But he wasn't always warm and fuzzy in his manner.

The detective ignored my halfhearted wave and headed straight for Hillerman and Sykes, who were talking to a rotund man in a golf shirt and twill pants. His light jacket read DEPUTY MEDICAL EXAMINER on the back. Technicians swarmed out of another SUV; one donned latex gloves and snapped photographs of the scene from multiple angles. Two others searched the ground in silence. The onlookers near the alley chatted louder. More people joined them.

At last Detective Mason walked my way, his notebook open, a pencil in his fingers. "Ms. Silverman. We meet again."

"Detective. Too soon, in my opinion."

"I have to agree." He hooked a thumb over his shoulder. "You reported the victim as Holly Parker, is that correct? When did you see her last?"

Surprised by his second question, I thought for a moment. "Yesterday, when my sister and I were walking the dog. We ran into her. Near her shop over there on the corner."

"What time was that?"

"Oh, sometime between four thirty and five thirty. Or six. I'm not sure."

"What kind of shop does she have?"

"Toy and bookstore, Through the Looking Glass. I guess she named it after Lewis Carroll's *Alice in Wonderland* sequel."

"She sells teddy bears as well, from what Officer Sykes told me," Mason said. "You two have been rivals, right? Since high school."

Resentful, I ignored that last question. "Our business has plenty of competitors in Michigan and around the whole country."

He cleared his throat. "Just so you're aware, Officer Sykes believes you have the best reason to get rid of Holly Parker."

"Wait a minute," I sputtered, but Mason held up a hand.

"I know very well he may be wrong. According to him, you and Ms. Parker were 'big-time enemies.' Don't bother to explain," the detective added in a wry tone. "I'm taking what he said with a grain of salt. But Sykes mentioned how your sister 'butted heads' with Ms. Parker yesterday, also in his words. Officer Hillerman confirmed it."

"I wouldn't call it that." I shrugged. "Maddie and Holly disagreed on a few things, that's all. No big deal."

"Good to know." Mason flipped to a new page. "So tell me why you came here this morning. Start with last night."

"Are you saying Holly was killed last night?"

He glanced up at me. "You know I can't confirm that until the autopsy."

"Okay, okay. I had dinner with my sister and some friends at the Regency—"

I stopped, hearing a shout from Bill Hillerman. Mason rushed off to rejoin the policemen and technicians. Despite my curiosity, I had no interest in seeing Holly's body again. I sipped my coffee, surprised that Digger would blow up a minor argument into "butting heads," and rat out one of his good friends. I inched closer to the group, but backed off when a technician gave me the stank eye. And then stumbled into someone who shrieked in my ear.

"Yow! Get off my foot!"

I whirled around and almost fell over in shock. Holly Parker hopped up and down on one foot, rubbing her exposed toes—she wore sandals, black jeans, and a matching sweater. Her face red with fury, she cursed under her breath. Her hot pink baseball cap had THINK PINK written on the brim. A perfect match to the hoodie on the dead body.

"What—then who—who—" I stammered, my cheeks aflame.

"You sound like an owl, Sasha." Her tone dripped sarcasm. "What is going on? Why have the police blocked the whole street off? I had to park at the bank. I can't get to my shop, and I've got orders to fill and deliver to the post office."

"Y-you're not—not . . ." I must have garbled the word "dead." Holly stared at me as if I'd spoken in a foreign language. "Then who's over there?"

"What are you talking about?" she asked crossly.

Dodging around me, Holly stalked toward the group of technicians and policemen who conferred with Detective Mason. They didn't pay any attention to her until Digger turned around and whooped in surprise. Mary Kate rushed back to my side, cell phone in hand.

"I thought you said—"

"Tell me about it. Boy, was I wrong. Big-time wrong," I muttered.

I also dreaded learning the victim's identity, especially given the pink hoodie. It had to be Holly's. Detective Mason threaded through the crowd toward us. He flipped several pages and then skewered his gaze on me.

"I was wrong," I said. "Holly Parker is standing over there. The brunette in the pink hat." I waved in her direction, where she stood beside Digger with a hand on her hip. "Dig—er, Officer Sykes almost pulled the knife out of the body, and he wasn't wearing gloves. Officer Hillerman stopped him in time, though."

Mason glowered at that. "Give me a minute, I'll be right back."

He headed toward Digger, who was now yelling at Holly. "I didn't threaten you. You were double-parked, and that's a ticketing offense—"

"We were moving in our stock! You could have given us more time."

Holly drew back when Mason interrupted to admonish the younger man, stabbing a finger into Digger's chest. I didn't feel any remorse for getting him into trouble. Bill Hillerman ambled over to join them and listened in silence while Digger waved his hands, his voice raised in protest. He deserved being chewed out for bumbling around the crime scene.

"What an idiot," I said.

Mary Kate had returned with two cardboard trays of coffee cups. "Since Will Taylor's murder, he thinks he's an expert. It's not funny, but I heard a few people calling him the next Barney Fife. Remember how Barney kept a bullet in his pocket instead of his pistol? No? Guess I've been watching too much vintage TV."

"I thought you preferred *Sesame Street* and the Disney Channel."

"If I hear that song 'Let It Go' one more time . . ." Mary Kate sighed.

"You don't have to wait with me." I shooed her back toward Fresh Grounds's back door. "Go help with customers. Oh, did you get through to Mads?"

"I had to leave a voice mail. Sorry."

"No worries. Thanks for everything."

Once Mary Kate left to deliver coffee, I realized that Holly had also disappeared. After I finished my drink and tossed the cup, I let Rosie out of the car. She'd been barking for attention. The last thing I needed was anyone getting nipped, however. Rosie sometimes behaved badly with strangers. Now she wagged her tail, so I ruffled her curly head and gave her a smooch on the muzzle. Detective Mason soon beckoned me over to join him. I kept Rosie tight beside me on her leash, although she wriggled with joy.

"Where did Ms. Parker go?" Mason scanned the crowd. "Hillerman, go find her. In the meantime, you'll have to confirm the identity."

I noticed Uncle Ross and Cal Bloom among the group of gossiping villagers. "Election" and "candidates" drifted to my ears, but I turned away. I didn't want to hear their opinions, either on politics or about this latest tragedy. Mason led me toward the technicians. They'd removed the knife and turned the body over, but covered it with a white sheet. One tech leaned down to reveal the face. Not that I needed to see the woman's red hair and wide sightless blue eyes.

"Gina Lawson. Holly's shop assistant," I said, choking the words out.

Digger Sykes whooshed out a breath. "The girl Flynn Hanson's been shacking up with? Whoa. I wonder if he stabbed her—"

"Stop assuming things, for heaven's sake," I shot back.

"Enough, you two." Detective Mason took my elbow and led me and Rosie back to the car. "You never finished telling me how you found Ms. Lawson."

I started my story again, leaning against the car's hood. Rosie sat obediently at my feet. He listened without asking questions; I watched him write in his Moleskine notebook—using the same tiny block letters, with spaces in between paragraphs. I wondered if it hurt his fingers to print so small. He also squinted at the page despite his glasses. Farsighted, maybe?

Was he old enough for bifocals? I chided myself for not keeping my mind on the matter at hand.

A woman had been killed, after all. Murdered.

"So, Sasha," Mason said at last. "What can you tell me about Gina Lawson?"

"Um. Not much." I glanced back at the crime scene. "She works for Holly Parker at Through the Looking Glass. Worked, I mean, as a shop assistant. Maddie said she also did publicity and marketing."

"Maddie? So she knew Gina?"

The snippet of gossip that my sister related suddenly flashed into my head. *Gina told Holly exactly what to do when she got back to Silver Hollow.* But I couldn't tell Mason all that. He was bound to learn it from Holly when he questioned her.

"We both met Gina yesterday for the first time, at our Cran-beary Tea Party," I said.

"Flynn Hanson is her lawyer." Digger Sykes joined us, hands on his hips. "He does all those 'Flynn Wins' ads on TV and radio. Have you seen or heard them? I heard he hired Gina Lawson to do his publicity, too. I bet she helped him with those."

Mason said nothing, only wrote faster before he looked up at me. "Anything else you can add, Ms. Silverman?"

I shook my head. "I don't know much about her."

"Except your ex-husband had a hot fling with Gina, a while back, when you were still married to Flynn," Digger said with a smirk, "and plenty of people said they hooked up again." He looked surprised when Mason glared at him. "What?"

"Flynn and I didn't live in Silver Hollow when we were married," I said. "Don't people have enough to gossip about than digging up old dirt?"

"Oh, come on. Everyone's been talking about Hanson since the minute he moved here. His Florida lifestyle, his big house in Ann Arbor, his commercials. I was at Quinn's Pub when he and Gina talked about that lawsuit against Mayor Bloom. Maybe he killed—"

"Whoa. First of all, who else was there in the pub?" Mason asked. Digger listed half a dozen names and then raced to the patrol car when the radio blared. "Great. Now I've got twice as many interviews than I expected."

"I was at the tea party when Flynn served notice about the lawsuit," I said, "but no way would Mayor Bloom have murdered Gina Lawson. Everyone knows him. He owns the funeral home, over on Quentin Street west of the Village Green."

The detective kept writing in his notebook. "Okay, thanks. I'll look into that."

"And he's up for re-election next month, too."

Mason pointed a finger at Rosie, who'd become restless and circled my legs. "Sit." Her butt hit the ground, and she gazed at him in adoration, head cocked, eyes bright. "High five!" She reached up a paw to meet his palm. He retrieved a treat from his pocket and held up his hand again. Rosie high-fived him a second time.

"Good girl," I said in delight, watching her relish the biscuit. "Peanut butter?"

"What else?" Mason returned to his notebook. "Re-election might be a good motive for murder. Especially politics, even at the local level. You'd be surprised what people are capable of when they're backed into a corner."

I had no answer for that. Mason walked back to the group of technicians, who were finishing their work. First Uncle Ross was a prime suspect last month, and now the mayor of Silver Hollow might top the list. I headed to my car. How crazy. And odd that another murder had happened here, a few short weeks after Will Taylor.

I still felt creeped out in the factory, walking past the closed-off partition that hid our stuffing machine. Silver Hollow seemed different, too. People nodded but rarely stopped to chat, although that could be due to their hectic fall schedules.

I gave up trying to figure it all out, glad to be heading home.

Chapter 7

I parked in my usual spot next to my sister's car and led Rosie inside the house. "Mads? Are you up yet? Where are you?"

My keys jangled when I dumped them into the pottery bowl. Rosie hopped onto the window seat, dislodging poor Onyx. My sister's black cat snarled and hissed, but Rosie settled herself on the padded cushion. Teddy bear dog on guard, alert and ready.

"Stop it, Nyx." I shooed the cat away, since she was swiping Rosie's face with her claws. "It's her turn. You've had the window seat all morning."

The breakfast dishes were piled in the sink—wow. That wasn't like Maddie. She always loaded the dishwasher. Or Mom took care of it, since someone might show up unexpectedly, and God forbid that anything would appear dirty or out of place. I'd hoped to ask Maddie what time she'd gotten home last night, and if she'd seen Gina wearing that pink hoodie. Low voices drifted through the hall. Mom and Maddie must be home after all, then.

Past the double doors, I maneuvered around the plastic-wrapped furniture that cluttered the hallway, along with boxes, file cabinets, shelves, and stacks of books. In the office, the wall between two separate rooms and the alcove that I'd once used for a table and chair had been taken down, making one big area. New plank flooring had been sanded and gleamed in the sunshine, although new area rugs—Persian wool, in elaborate patterns of green, burgundy, and gold—would soon cover most of it. Given the second murder in Silver Hollow, all this chaos symbolized disorder to me.

I forced a smile, however. "The renovation's coming along."

Maddie wiped the last specks of lint from one large window with crumpled newspaper. "Wait till everything's moved into place."

"It's going to look wonderful." Mom rubbed her lower back and groaned, half bent over a large wooden crate. "Ooh! My shoulders. My back . . ."

"You don't have to move furniture," I said. "We hired a crew."

"I know that, but they won't clean before they arrive." She wore rubber gloves and dusty, paint-spattered clothes, although every strand of her auburn hair was in place. "We've handled pretty much everything, Sasha, although we expected that you'd help. What took you so long? I'm assuming you took the dog for a walk early this morning."

"Didn't either of you listen to Mary Kate's voice mail?" Thank goodness I hadn't called. I wouldn't want to hear news about a murder over the phone. "Guess not, huh."

"Nope." Maddie wiped perspiration from her face and neck with a cloth and glanced down at her grubby clothing. "I don't even know where my phone is."

"I was delayed—"

"Did you bring back something from Fresh Grounds?"

Mom interrupted. "Like those delicious chocolate-drizzled scones. Eve said she'd come help, too. Maybe that's her now."

A loud voice had called from the kitchen. Dread filled me. I'd recognized Flynn's voice, so I wasn't surprised when my ex tramped into the room. His blond hair was gelled, and he wore a tight, tailored three-piece suit. A golden arrow pin adorned the jacket's breast pocket instead of a tucked handkerchief, and his red silk tie had a pattern of tiny fox heads. So appropriate for his sly lawyer personality, too.

"Hey, how's it going? Thought I'd stop in for a minute."

"Just an FYI," I said, "but Detective Mason wants to talk to you."

Flynn raised his eyebrows and then let out a long-suffering sigh. "Now what? I've got enough stress. I don't need him on my tail when I didn't do anything wrong."

"You're not the only one who's stressed—"

"Mike and Mark are over the moon about all the extra work I've brought in for the Legal Eagles," he continued, ignoring me. "It's all due to my TV and radio commercials. Some of the other lawyers in the area are so jealous, they're trying to stab me in the back. And I've got to film a new commercial today, too."

"On a Sunday?" I shook my head when he only shrugged. "Well, he has a good reason for wanting to talk to you."

Maddie stopped washing another window. "What's wrong, Sash? What happened?"

"Gina Lawson is dead." I noted shock on all their faces, even Flynn.

"Wh-what?" His anger drained away along with every hint of color in his face.

"Gina's dead?" Maddie looked so pale that Mom slid an arm around her in concern. "How did you find that out?"

"I found her in the parking lot, behind Fresh Grounds."

Flynn looked sick. "What the hell."

"Oh, Sasha! Not again." Mom drew me into a fierce hug, and Maddie joined in as well. "Tell us what happened."

"Rosie found her first. We went to get my car, since I left it behind Fresh Grounds last night. Gina was lying on the ground by Holly's car. She'd been stabbed," I added faintly. "But at first I thought she *was* Holly Parker."

"Why would you think that?" Maddie looked horrified.

"Gina was wearing a pink hoodie. The one with 'Think Pink' on it."

"She always borrowed stuff from Holly." Flynn sounded dazed. "Her car, the phone, even money. Caused a rift between them at times. God, I can't believe Gina's dead."

"Come on, everyone. This has been a big shock." Mom pushed us all out of the office and toward the kitchen. "I'll make fresh coffee. Maddie, see if you can put out cookies on a plate or something. And don't you leave, Flynn Hanson. That police detective can wait, especially if he thinks you're a suspect again. Last time was bad enough."

"Me? I wouldn't have killed Gina! We broke up a while ago. Couple of months."

"I know that, Flynn," Mom said. "No, Sasha, don't you say a word."

"I need my phone."

Maddie rushed out of the room. I was sure my sister would call Kip or her friend Abby to hear any gossip and spread the news. Flynn slid onto a stool at the kitchen island. Mom filled the coffeepot with water and plugged it in, fetched coffee grounds from the refrigerator, and brought out the cream pitcher. She set the sugar bowl near his elbow. Always the hostess, one gene I hadn't inherited. But I was glad. I could use more coffee.

"I suspect Detective Mason wants to talk to you because

you were her lawyer," Mom said to Flynn. "Not because you once dated her."

"Yeah, that makes sense, Judith." He rubbed his face and blew out a breath. "We just talked yesterday about her lawsuit. Oh . . ." His voice trailed off.

"Yeah, I can imagine what you're thinking," I said, "but I doubt Mayor Bloom would have killed Gina."

"Cal Bloom? A murderer?" Mom laughed. "That's ridiculous. I've known him for years, he's a big teddy bear. He wouldn't hurt a fly or a spider. I've seen him catch insects inside his house and carry them outside. Even at the funeral home!"

"Really." Flynn looked impressed. "But Sasha's right. The mayor doesn't have to worry about that lawsuit anymore."

"So you think the police will focus on him as the primary suspect?" My mother looked annoyed. "That's hard to believe."

"How long have you known Gina Lawson?" I asked Flynn, and watched him for any sign of hiding the truth. While Flynn practiced keeping a poker face, he couldn't always keep his physical reactions in check. His face flushed pink.

"We've dated off and on over the years."

"When did you first meet her?" I wondered if he'd acknowledge the bed-and-breakfast hot tub romp, although I had my doubts. "Before we got married?"

"I don't remember."

"What if I told you I saw photos—"

"Stop badgering him, Sasha," Mom interrupted. Flynn looked relieved, since his color had gone from pink to scarlet. "Have I told you how much I love seeing those 'Flynn Wins' television commercials? They're so clever."

"I think they're great, too. Gina helped me write the script. Really, I don't know why Mayor Bloom wasn't happy with the work she did for him. Gina is great. Er, was."

Mom waved a hand. "If Cal Bloom wouldn't pay the woman, then maybe she charged him an arm and a leg. He's notorious for being cheap."

"She also planned more of a snarky image for the mayor, nothing like his 'teddy bear' image." I turned to my ex. "Did Gina want to get married, Flynn? After all, you bought a big enough house. Maybe Gina expected a ring."

"We talked about it, but I told her I wasn't ready to settle." He shrugged. "She knew that long ago when we—well, I meant she was okay with it."

Aha. I figured that was as close to a confession as Flynn would get. He looked guilty for that slip of the tongue. "Digger Sykes has been spreading gossip about you and Gina," I said.

Maddie had overheard that remark on her return to the kitchen. "Digger's worse than an old woman, I swear! Next we'll be seeing the headline 'Lawyer Kills Girlfriend.'"

Flynn's face turned ashen. "But I didn't kill Gina—"

Rosie suddenly jumped down from the window seat, barking joyously. Her tail wagged harder at the sharp knock on the side door. Flynn hunched on the kitchen stool, looking sick with worry, or like the wind had been knocked out of his lungs. I beckoned Detective Mason inside. He'd changed into a shirt and tie under his jacket and entered the kitchen with an indulgent smile for Rosie's eager greeting. That vanished when he caught sight of Flynn.

"I figured you might be here, Hanson. Lucky guess."

"Oh, I doubt that." Mom folded her arms, sounding snarky. "You don't strike me as the type of cop to leave anything to chance."

"It's Detective, ma'am." He glanced at me and then pulled his notebook out of a pocket. "But you're right. I called his colleagues, Mr. Blake and Mr. Branson, who suggested checking here. They thought Mr. Hanson might stop here before his appointment."

"So you want to question me about Gina," Flynn said in a surly tone.

"You've heard she was killed, then." Mason glanced at me with a lifted eyebrow. "From what I've learned, you and Ms. Lawson had an intimate relationship besides her being a client. Is that correct, Mr. Hanson?"

"I didn't kill Gina."

"That's not what I asked." He waited and then repeated the question.

"Yes, but we broke up. Months ago."

Mason interrogated Flynn further, going over when he'd first met Gina, how long they'd been seeing each other, how many times they'd broken up and gotten back together, and why they decided to end it recently. Flynn sounded like a petulant juvenile delinquent, scowling at every query, hesitating before every answer.

"Gina got all mad one day, packed her things, and moved out. That was down in Florida. She moved here, I don't know when. Once I arrived in Silver Hollow, she asked me to represent her. We spent a few nights together lately, but it wasn't serious."

"Where were you Saturday night?" the detective asked.

Flynn gave a flippant shrug. "Out of town."

"Where exactly, and was anyone with you?" Mason jotted notes while he waited.

"At a cabin," he finally said, "with a friend."

"I'm assuming this friend has a name."

Flynn rubbed his hands together, eyes downcast. My own frustration burst. "For heaven's sake, tell him," I said. "Whoever it is can provide you with an alibi."

"Not until I get their permission to name them. I called Gina last night, Detective, but she never answered. I kept getting her voice mail. I wanted to discuss a few more things about the lawsuit against Mayor Bloom, so I left her a message."

"Was this friend a man or a woman?" When Flynn hesitated, Mason sounded cool and calm. "And may I see your cell phone?"

"Why?"

"To verify your calls, although you can refuse my request. If you do allow access, it will help verify your story."

Flynn retrieved it from a pocket, unlocked the device, and then handed it to Mason. He scrolled through the history and then handed it back. "Checks out so far, Mr. Hanson. We might have to ask your provider for phone records however."

"So am I a suspect?"

"I never said you were, sir."

"Good." He perked up. "Sasha told me she found Gina this morning—what, maybe four or five hours ago? I'd like to know where Mayor Bloom was last night."

Mason ignored that comment and opened his notebook again. "Is there anything you can tell me, outside of client confidentiality, that would shed light on their disagreement?"

He cracked his knuckles, a nervous habit from long ago. "Gina wanted the money he owed her for work she'd completed for him. End of story."

"What about—"

"Cal Bloom disagreed with her marketing plan," Mom burst out. "It was all wrong for his re-election campaign. He asked her to make changes, but Gina wanted more money. A lot more. That was shameful if you ask me. And greedy."

I glanced at Mason, busy writing in his notebook. Wow. So much for Mom not knowing the real story. And she didn't hide her dislike of Gina Lawson, either. Flynn sat there, waiting for the detective to continue, cracking his knuckles. But then he offered new information.

"Verbal agreements aren't the best way to do business. I can't tell you much about what Gina was doing Saturday, Detective, but after we served the mayor notice about the lawsuit, at that tea party Sasha and Maddie had across the street, Gina went her way and I went mine. That should convince you I'm not involved."

"We're gathering information at this point," Mason said wearily. "It's early in the investigation, so we have yet to determine any suspects."

"Will you include her boss, Holly Parker?" I asked.

He didn't answer, turning back to Flynn instead. "I'd advise you to avoid any travel out of state, Mr. Hanson, until we know more. Thank you for your cooperation today."

"But—okay, I'll have to reschedule." Flynn must have caught my raised eyebrows. "I'm supposed to sign a vacation rental agreement in Florida. I left all the furniture at the condo, along with the beach chairs, umbrellas, all the towels. Even my bikes."

"I told him to do that," Mom said with a smile. "Pack any personal photos and clothes, but leave everything else. It's bound to be popular with vacationers. Is there anything else we can help you with, Detective Mason? Flynn has that television studio appointment."

My ex jumped off the stool. "I'm running late—"

"I'm not quite finished asking questions." Mason hailed my sister, who hovered in the doorway. "Maddie, how well did you know Gina Lawson?"

I almost laughed out loud at her "deer in the headlights" expression. She stammered a reply. "I never met her until yesterday."

"What about her background?" Mason asked. "Can you tell me, Mr. Hanson?"

"Gina was born and raised in a northern suburb of Detroit," he said.

"Did any of you ever see Ms. Lawson wearing that pink hoodie around the village? The one with 'Think Pink' on the back."

I held up a hand. "Holly wore it at the tea party. And Flynn mentioned earlier how Gina often borrowed her things," I said. "Her cell phone, the car."

"Does anyone know about her working relationship with Ms. Parker? Any arguments? Complaints, problems, that kind of thing."

"They argued about how to organize the shop, but nothing too major," Flynn said. "Gina told me Holly wasn't happy when she didn't refill the gas tank for the MINI Cooper. But she had to deliver packages to the post office or pick up items for the shop. Gina didn't use the car for any personal errands, so she refused to pay for gas."

"Then borrowing Ms. Parker's hoodie wasn't unusual." Mason waited us out, but I didn't reply. Neither did my sister or Flynn. The wall clock ticked for an eternity, or so it seemed, until he sighed. "All right. Let me know if you hear anything else that might be relevant."

Once Mason departed, Rosie looked forlorn. I dropped to one knee and hugged her. "Aw, poor baby. How about a treat? That might make up for your buddy leaving."

"Damn," Flynn said, and kissed my mother's cheek before he headed to the door. "I'll have to do an electronic signature on those rental papers, since the company in Clearwater can't wait too much longer. Thanks for everything, Judith."

I almost choked, sticking my tongue out in mock disgust in my sister's direction, which made Maddie double over in silent laughter. Mom hadn't noticed; she followed him out to the porch and spoke too low for me to hear. I did catch Gina's name, though.

Once he departed, Mom returned to the coffeemaker and filled a mug. She added cream to the steaming brew. Maddie and I sat side by side at the kitchen island. I was suddenly aware of a half-eaten teddy bear cookie in my hand. I glanced at my sister, who folded her arms over her chest and tapped a foot. Mom lifted an eyebrow in surprise.

"What's going on, you two? Cooking up a scheme?"

"Us? You and Flynn are the ones scheming together," Maddie said. "I have a feeling he's hiding something. Didn't you get that vibe, Sash?"

"I always get that vibe." I decided to finish the cookie.

"But he was with a friend last night. Nowhere near where Gina was found," Mom said.

I choked on a crumb. "Did he tell you where he was?"

"Why would Flynn kill Gina? He wanted to make money from the lawsuit, right? I might not agree about suing Cal Bloom, but business is business. And Flynn's the best attorney here in town." Mom sipped coffee. "So are you ready for Wednesday night, Maddie?"

"Oh, no," she said. "Don't change the subject without spilling the dirt on Gina and Flynn. You saw her at the Cranbeary Tea. Did you meet her before that?"

"Yes, at Flynn's house. She's a tramp. Was, I should say. Bossy, too. She wanted him to redecorate, make it cozy for the two of them. He wasn't ready for big changes like that. And Gina demanded an engagement ring."

"Aha," Maddie said with a teasing glance at me. "He wouldn't marry her."

"Why should he?" Mom sniffed. "Gina was greedy. That's why she wanted to sue Cal, and wouldn't consider a smaller payment. A kill fee, that's what Flynn called it. That sounds terrible, but you know more about that kind of thing."

"Yes, it's a freelance term. A fee to kill the project, usually half the original amount agreed upon. I'm surprised Gina wouldn't accept it."

"That's part of the problem with a verbal agreement and not a binding contract," I said. "So who is Flynn seeing now?"

"I don't know," Mom said. "But that detective better not harass Cal Bloom. That would ruin his campaign worse than Gina's terrible marketing plan. If he's a murder suspect, he'd never get re-elected. And like I said, he must be innocent."

"Until proven guilty."

"Then you'll have to find out who killed this woman, Sasha." Mom shook a finger at me. "I won't let a good friend's reputation be smeared. You succeeded in figuring out who killed Will Taylor. You can do the same about Gina Lawson's murder."

I gaped at her in shock, but Mom took her coffee mug and the newspaper into the office. Maddie hooted. "Whoa. Got yourself into real hot water."

"Ain't that the truth."

Whenever Mom expected something, we all gave in. I rested an elbow on the kitchen island, my chin in hand, and recalled seeing Cal Bloom with Uncle Ross. They'd watched the technicians at work for a long time. Didn't killers revisit the crime scene out of curiosity? If only I'd paid more attention this morning.

"So I never told you what Abby said yesterday." Maddie sounded excited. "Not about the re-election, although Abby said the mayor is having trouble getting people to put signs on their lawns. And that was before Gina and Flynn served him notice."

"Like I said, I don't care about politics."

"But you do about Mom and Dad."

"What about them?"

"Abby heard Mom signed up for a forty-hour fundamentals course to get a real estate license. Once she applies and passes the test, Mom has to work for a licensed broker. With all of Dad's and Uncle Ross's friends, that won't be any problem."

"I hope she realizes it's a lot more work than she might expect."

"Yeah, I know. And she won't always get paid for showing a gazillion houses," Maddie said. "But it also means Mom and Dad might be moving back to Michigan."

My jaw dropped. "But what about their Florida condo? Oh—you think they'll rent it out the same way Flynn's doing his?"

"Sounds like Mom gave him the idea, so yeah . . ." Maddie's voice trailed off.

It all made sense now. I glanced at the ceiling, thinking of our parents' suite upstairs. This house seemed to shrink the longer Mom and Dad lingered in Silver Hollow.

Worse, they would seriously cramp our sense of independence.

Chapter 8

"Sorry I had to leave the restaurant early last night, Mads." I filled a mug with hot water, chose my favorite mint tea bag, and added sugar. "What time did you get home?"

"Around ten thirty, I guess." She slathered jam on a crisp English muffin. "You were asleep. I wanted to make sure you were okay, and I wasn't in the mood to party with Kip all night anyway. I keep telling him he's got to finish painting his sculpture. He's so laid-back about getting it done. Too laid-back, given all the trouble he's having."

"I never meant to ruin your evening."

"You didn't. It's an ongoing spat." Maddie bit into her breakfast. "We had a big fight while Jay drove you home."

"What's this about?" Mom had returned and cocked her head. "Are you talking about handling arguments with your boyfriend? Your father and I always talk things over instead of letting things simmer, which only makes things worse."

I bit back a quick retort. Her version of "talking things over" meant she hung on until Dad caved in to whatever she wanted. "Why is Kip having trouble? You told me using acrylic paint would be the best kind given his design."

"Yeah, but making it look like tie-dye is trickier than we thought. We dipped a bunch of shirts to see how the pattern goes, only it takes time to feather and blend the colors. More than he expected. That's why I'm so nervous. I told him to go work on his bear last night, and asked Jay to take me home. He wasn't happy with that."

I wondered if Kip blamed me for Maddie coming home early, and hoped not. I liked him. He had an easy charm and good nature. I didn't want to see Maddie hurt, though, and if it came to taking sides, I would protect my sister. Her well-being came first.

"It won't be long before you're done with both bears," Mom said. "Don't worry."

"I can't help but worry." Maddie sounded unhappy. "At least Kip called me this morning. He acted like nothing happened, too, even though he was furious about my not going to the bar with him last night. Several bars. I never liked pub crawls. You know why."

I did, given the scare she'd once had from a stalker. "He's a college professor. Why not choose a bar and stick to it than go pub-crawling?"

"I always thought it would affect him getting tenure, but Kip doesn't want that. He's happy enough as an adjunct. Claims it gives him more freedom in his artwork."

I stared into my tea, wondering if Kip lacked ambition, but changed the subject instead. "Speaking of getting things done on time, the staff had better start working on that lederhosen for the festival's grand prize teddy bear."

"I found a pattern online and enlarged it." Maddie crunched the last of her English muffin and caught a drip of jam with a finger. "Hilda and Joan are on it. They've worked out a special tooth fairy outfit together, too."

"A tooth fairy outfit?" Mom asked. "For teddy bears?"

"Yeah. Parents can either buy a sparkly dress with wings, or a 'Super Tooth' cape. Their choice." Maddie explained the special pocket in each costume. "It will be much easier to get a child's tooth out and then put money inside. And cheaper than making a specialized bear with a pouch somewhere. We've gotten lots of orders already for both costumes."

"Hey, all, sorry I'm late. How's the office coming along?"

Aunt Eve breezed into the kitchen, looking radiant in fuchsia capris—or pedal pushers, as they called them back in the fifties and early sixties—with a white pin-tucked blouse tied at the waist. Aunt Eve's floral pink scarf covered her blond hair, matching her lipstick and outfit. We all sat up straighter, even Mom. Maybe she was cowed by her former sister-in-law's confident attitude and unique fashion sense, or felt self-conscious in sweats.

"The office is a royal mess," Mom said ruefully. "Are you sure you want to help? You'll get as filthy as I am, Eve."

"A little dirt doesn't hurt anyone. I know projects take time," she said, "and I'm eager to move out of that little alcove near the cash register. I don't like people watching me work while they shop. Or listening to my conversations every time I answer the phone."

"All right then. Let's get to work."

Mom led Aunt Eve down the hallway. "Like I said, let them do what they want," Maddie said in a low voice. "Helping them will take our mind off the murder."

I held up a hand when she rose from her chair. "Wait, wait. So if Jay drove you home, did you happen to see anyone in the parking lot behind Fresh Grounds? Like Gina, wearing Holly Parker's pink jacket. Remember it has 'Think Pink' spelled out on the back."

"So that's why you thought she was Holly?"

"Yeah. She'd been stabbed in the back."

"Stabbed? Whoa." Maddie gulped coffee. "Must have been terrible finding her."

"You got that right. I know Holly always loved the Pink Panther, but does she sell them in her store? I'm curious to check out what she does carry, given the name she chose."

"I'm sure it's chock-full of Alice in Wonderland stuff."

"I suppose. So did you see anything in that parking lot or not?"

Maddie sighed. "I was tipsy after all that champagne. Unless someone crashed into Jay's truck, I wouldn't have noticed anything. And I was so worried about you."

"I felt great this morning until I found Gina. Even Digger thought she was Holly at first, and then he started in with the 'dead body magnet' again."

"Sometimes he can be a real pain."

"He threw you under the bus." I explained how Digger had reported our encounter with Holly to Detective Mason. "Took everything way out of context, too. Figures. So what are we going to do about Mom and Dad?"

"What do you mean?" Maddie asked. "They didn't know Holly or Gina."

"I meant about them moving back here. If that's true, I'll find an apartment or a house to rent. I'm thirty-one. I love working here, but I need my own space."

"Yeah, but I bet Mom will get Dad to buy a house or a condo. Close enough so he can meet the guys for breakfast or lunch. Mom does not want to live above this shop. She'd rather sell it. Barbara Davison probably put that idea in her head."

"Maybe I ought to buy them out. And your portion of the inheritance," I added.

Maddie laughed. "No way could you afford it. But once things settle down after the Oktobear Fest, I'll set a goal and business plan for my boutique. You know I've got your back, Sash. Even if I don't work here."

I squeezed her hand. "Yeah. And thanks."

"I'm glad Holly rented the former Christmas shop, if you want the truth. It's too close. I'd rather be next to Abby's antique store on Church Street."

"What about the Time Turner? Now that Cissy Davison is officially engaged, I'm betting she'll close her business."

"Maybe," Maddie said, her eyes bright. "That would be a great spot. Hey, did you know Gina worked for Cissy before she started working for Holly?"

"No. Maybe we should ask her why Gina quit."

"Abby told me Cissy fired her, but don't quote me on that." My sister scratched her nose, thinking. "You know, the Time Turner would be perfect with that nice little flat above the shop. But Barbara Davison charges a lot for rent, from what I've heard."

"Maybe Mom can finagle a better deal for you," I said. "We'd better get to work with her and Aunt Eve, or we'll never hear the end of it. Oh, good, the moving crew's here. No way could I haul furniture back and forth until Mom's satisfied."

Once I coaxed Rosie into her crate, Maddie let the trio of workers inside and herded them into the hallway. My sweet dog growled and barked while the young men unwrapped each piece of furniture and muscled them around. Mom and Aunt Eve changed their minds several times, as I'd expected, but the guys took it in stride without complaint. Maddie ended up outside, chatting on the phone with Kip, for the most part. After the crew left, we started unpacking.

For the rest of the afternoon we filled the shelves and file cabinets with paperwork and books. My back and shoulders screamed for mercy. And when I jammed my index finger on a crate, sharp pains shot through my hand, wrist, and up to my elbow.

I danced around, cursing in my head, while Aunt Eve rushed to get ice. "Ow, ow, ow. Oh, man. Can't we finish the rest tomorrow?"

"Stop whining, Sasha, you're not five years old." Mom wiggled my fingers and thumb. "Doesn't seem to be anything broken."

"Hurts like the devil," I said. "I hope we're not out of ice."

Aunt Eve hurried in with a cold plastic bag, twisting around every so often to argue with my uncle, who followed her. "I can't believe you didn't confirm that order, Ross."

"I'm pretty sure we did," he grumbled.

" 'Pretty sure' isn't good enough, especially when they're one of our best customers. It doesn't make sense that different items on the bears were missing. One didn't have spectacles, another didn't have the hat. And one uniform was missing the belt."

"For our Teddy Roosevelt bears?" I asked, and pressed the ice bag on my thumb. "Whoa. That sounds like an error with the sewing staff."

"Well, shipping should have caught all that. But I was busy training Tim Richardson," Uncle Ross said, "so maybe we didn't check all five hundred bears going to South Dakota. We'll ship the missing items tomorrow, first thing in the morning."

"You do that," Aunt Eve said. "We ought to photograph every single specialty bear we make. Then laminate the photos and post them above the crates, so whoever fills orders can see what each bear should have. Or put the photos in a three-ring reference binder."

"Oh, brother. Overkill," he grumbled.

"Great idea, Aunt Eve. I prefer posting them above the crates, and I'll take the photos." Ignoring my uncle's dramatic sigh, I checked my thumb. Only a slight bruise. "Make sure those items are shipped off, and add extra bears to make up for the mistake."

"What?" Uncle Ross slapped his cap against his knee. "No way."

"Yes, Ross," Aunt Eve said sternly. She grabbed my bag of ice and pressed it against her face. "Oh, these hot flashes! In fact, make it half a dozen bears. We have to keep our customers happy, or they'll stop ordering specialty bears."

"I've got a tour tomorrow at one," I said. "I'll take the photos after I'm finished with the church group. They're seniors, so it might take me a while."

"I promised Kip I'd help him finish painting his bear, so I can't cover for you behind the sales register." Maddie looked guilty. "Sorry."

"I can do it," Aunt Eve said. "Just give me a quick lesson on working the register. All these fancy tech gadgets, I tell you. I feel so old."

"Have to admit the office looks good," Uncle Ross said. "Need any help?"

"Ha. Where were you three hours ago when we needed a hand moving furniture?" Her tone dripped with sarcasm. "Such great timing, like during our marriage. But you're right. It does look nice. With a few more touches, we'll be done."

"Hmph. I'm catching a burger at the pub."

"You ought to order a salad."

"Rabbit food. I starved whenever you cooked," he said, and stalked out the door.

Maddie chuckled. "For eating so many greasy burgers, fries, and donuts, how can he be so skinny? I bet you didn't really starve him."

"Meat and potatoes, every night," Aunt Eve said. "Beef or chicken, fried fish. Wouldn't touch anything green. But listen, I made a tuna macaroni salad this morning for us. I figured we'd be too tired to cook after doing all this work."

"Oh, yum. I love your tuna and mac salad." Maddie grabbed my arm. "Come on, let's finish everything so we can eat and relax."

I loved the drastic improvements. Will Taylor's masculine office, with its sleek metal and wood furniture, was gone; the large room now had a door leading to the parking lot, and looked far cozier with the white-painted brick wall and comfortable chairs in a sunny yellow fabric grouped around a rustic, round wooden table. Teddy bear magazines and a basket holding Silver Bear Shop & Factory flyers filled a shelf nearby, along with several custom-order bears.

Facing that "consultation" area, a long counter served as Aunt Eve's desk that attached to the floor-to-ceiling hutch. Cubbies were filled with a printer and other supplies. That also gave her a measure of privacy from the rest of the office. A pale robin-egg blue lampshade and an orange chair added a fifties touch. So did the muted graphic bird-themed wallpaper surrounding the windows. Oddly enough, I noted her wedding portrait on the desk. In it, Uncle Ross looked so funny with long dark hair, a beard, and his mustache.

Maddie had hung a row of her annual teddy bear cartoons, framed in white, in the long hallway leading to the shop. I'd staked a claim to one corner of the office, using my weathered table as a desk. Not that I'd have time to sit here, but I did have a window view now. And my hanging spider plant loved sunshine. Dusty olive green shutters folded against the beadboard wall. The aged teddy bear on my floral-patterned chair looked familiar.

I walked over and picked it up. My hands ran over the corduroy arms and legs, the faded and worn nose and dull eyes. "This was one of Grandpa T. R.'s bears."

Mom smiled. "Dad found it packed in a box down in Florida. Ross played with it first, and then gave it to him. We figured you might appreciate it. So you like the changes?"

"Absolutely, and thanks. But what's in this?" I waved to the huge armoire, also painted the same green as the shutters, that stood against the opposite wall.

"Open it!" Maddie shooed me over to it.

Inside the double doors, I found rolls and pads of paper, jars of paintbrushes, cases of ink pens and pencils, all stored in wicker baskets. Bottles, tubes, and jars of paint filled one cubicle. Several drawers held reams of printer paper and forms.

"Wow. This is really cool," I said. "So you're still working in the shop."

Mom stepped forward. "We figured she could use your table whenever we need a design for the shop. I'm so glad you like this storage cabinet, Maddie. Your father thought it was too expensive, but I insisted. It'll serve for now until you open your own business."

"Like I said, a million times, I'm not ready to decide on anything," my sister said.

"We understand. Dad and I are fully behind whatever you want, whether it's a boutique or a graphic design company. No pressure."

Maddie met my gaze with pursed lips. I had a hard time keeping a straight face, too. We knew the real story on that score. No pressure from Mom?

Yeah, right.

Chapter 9

My curiosity got the better of me within the hour. I fetched my bicycle and pedaled down the lane, thinking up an excuse to stop in at Holly's shop. Did she have an Alice in Wonderland theme going on in her décor? And if so, what did it look like? Given all the work we'd done in our office and for the Cran-beary Tea, I never had a chance to check it out. I leaned my bike against the former Holly Jolly's picket fence. I heard voices beyond the screen door, although the porch supports prevented me from seeing who was visiting Holly.

Until I recognized Detective Mason's gruff tone. Oh boy. Where was his SUV? Maybe he'd parked it around the corner. I climbed the steps and then hesitated. He wouldn't appreciate me showing up during an interrogation.

"So Ms. Lawson borrowed your jacket without permission."

"She often did, yes." Holly sounded perturbed. "Bad habit—although we had discussed it and Gina apologized. Really, we were more like sisters. Not just employee and boss."

Ha. The insincerity in her voice didn't surprise me in the least.

"So Ms. Lawson was not your business partner."

"More of a personal assistant. She took care of things I didn't have time for. Errands, checking inventory, handling online inquiries. That kind of thing."

Arms folded, I surveyed the window display of stuffed bunnies, cats, teddy bears, and a variety of zoo animals in wicker baskets. A fanned-out display of books took up one corner, mostly Disney princess titles, but here and there Holly had tucked in other small items—a White Rabbit clock, a Mad Hatter top hat, and an Alice in Wonderland Barbie doll in the original box. Must be why her online sales exceeded any shop purchases. I had to wonder, though, why Holly hadn't kept her shop specialized to the theme. Why throw in teddy bears and unrelated books into the mix? Unless that was a deliberate dig at us and at The Cat's Cradle.

Then again, she had to have a few Pink Panther items. The shop bell jangled when I walked inside. I stared at the huge antique gold-framed mirror on carved legs that blocked the passage into the shop; its wavy glass distorted my image, stretching me long and thin in an unnatural way. I'd always wondered what I'd look like being so skinny, but this didn't look right at all. My fat head didn't jive, and my legs looked like sticks. Until I shifted and the image reversed. Now I had a pinhead on top of a huge body. Ugh.

It seemed to fit with my memories of Holly's personality. Sweet to your face, but ready to change in an instant or stab you in the back. I shivered when I recalled Gina facedown on the graveled parking lot in that bloodstained hoodie.

"Since you have a customer, I'd like to check for anything Gina may have left here," Mason said. "I'll start in the back."

"Thank you, Detective." Holly used her "people voice"

with him all right, her words dripping honey. "Anything to help you resolve who killed my assistant."

I couldn't see her or Mason, since a large bookshelf stood beyond the mirror and blocked any view of the counter. A row of pink striped Cheshire Cats, the Disney tags showing, lined the top; vinyl Queen of Hearts figurines, with huge heads on tiny bodies, filled another shelf. Other movie tie-in merchandise was displayed as well. A huge cardboard cutout of the twins, Tweedle-dum and Tweedle-dee, loomed near the bookshelf. Beyond that stood two racks of blue dresses with white aprons, costumes I assumed, in both children's and adult sizes, plus a third rack with a variety of other costumes.

The shop looked so different from the Holly Jolly Christmas shop's arrangement. I hadn't known what to expect. Especially not the six-tier rack of teddy bears, all in costumes, with Bears of the Heart tags. Plus a huge variety of children's picture books arrayed on a bookshelf.

I met Holly's surprised gaze. "What are you doing here?" she asked.

"I wanted to extend my condolences about Gina."

"It's not like she was family," Holly said with a dismissive wave. "I'm sorry she's gone, of course, but I'll manage. Digger said you replaced some staff after they quit."

"Retired, actually," I said, wishing Maddie's friend would find something better to do than gossip. Like doing his job. "So you do have a Lewis Carroll theme going on here. People love shopping for collectibles."

That seemed to erase the suspicion in Holly's dark eyes. "Yeah, they do. It's my favorite Disney cartoon, and the movie was fabulous. Did you see it?"

"With Johnny Depp as the Mad Hatter? Yeah." I thought the actor's character portrayal was pretty wild, but it hadn't surprised me given his weird version of Willy Wonka. I preferred

Gene Wilder, hands down. "I loved the actress who played Alice."

"Mia Wasikowska. Oh, I forgot to put on the music."

Holly turned to push a button on her open laptop. Strains of the Danny Elfman and Tim Burton movie soundtrack began, with its building crescendos and subtle undertones of racing to adventure. While I'd enjoyed the movie, hearing the score in this shop unsettled me.

"I have a White Queen costume and makeup," Holly said, and waved to a photo on the wall. "People say I look as good as Anne Hathaway."

"Cool." In my opinion, her image looked ghostly in that white wig and pale skin, with dark brows and dark red lips, plus dark nail polish. Not that I would ever admit that. More power to her if she enjoyed a little cosplay. "What unusual teapots."

They sat inside a locked glass cabinet to the left of the counter. One was squat and four-sided, topped with the Mad Hatter holding a teacup; another teapot had a White Rabbit shape, with his pocket watch dangling from the spout. A snow globe caught my eye, encasing the Mad Hatter's tea party with all the participants. Next to it, a second glass ball showed Alice holding her flamingo golf club. I walked over to view several framed posters on the far wall. One was a classic illustration I recognized from the book my Aunt Marie had given me.

"I always wondered who did those illustrations," I said.

"Sir John Tenniel," Holly said promptly. "He did satirical cartoons for *Punch* magazine for over fifty years, too, but he's best known for his artwork in Lewis Carroll's books. I have a rare edition, but not one of the original two thousand printed by the publisher. Tenniel demanded the book be reprinted and those first copies trashed. They're worth millions now."

"You really know your stuff—"

"Ms. Parker? I'd like to show you something." Holding a

cardboard box, Detective Mason walked from the back room but stopped when he caught sight of me. "Ms. Silverman."

"I came to offer my family's sympathy," I said. "For Gina's death."

"Perhaps you could help identify an item or two in this box."

"Where did you find that?" Holly sounded panicked and pushed me toward the door. "Sasha's not a customer, so she'd better go."

"Wait, hold on. I think she could help."

That puzzled me. I watched Mason set the box on the counter. Still in his limp shirt and tie, he looked weary as if he'd battled a heavy storm. A cobweb glistened in his mop of sandy hair, and he pushed his glasses farther onto the bridge of his nose. I glanced at Holly, who bit her lip. The detective pulled on latex gloves, lifted an object from the box, and uncoiled the loosened bubble wrap. I gasped in shock at the furry teddy bear he'd uncovered.

"Minky Bear," I said. "Someone stole it from our house in Ann Arbor. That had to be at least fifteen years ago, though."

"Why would it be in a box in my shop?" Holly asked. "Unless the former owners left it here. We tossed out a bunch of junk, but never finished clearing all the boxes out. But maybe it's not the same bear that you owned."

"A professional artist fashioned Minky Bear out of my grandmother's fur stole. Mom still has the papers. Here's the tag," I added, "and that's the artist's name."

Holly shrugged. "Then maybe Gina bought this off of eBay. We do buy unusual items and resell them. Usually Alice in Wonderland items, but other stuff on occasion."

"Perhaps you could look in your files," Mason said. "If Gina bought it, she ought to have kept an invoice or a sales receipt."

I could tell Holly hadn't thought of that by her furtive

glance. She walked halfheartedly toward a cabinet and made a show of riffling through the contents. My gut instinct told me she wasn't willing to admit how Minky Bear ended up here, hidden in a box.

Mason drew out a small carved bird next, and a scrapbook. "I bet Flynn would know if any of this stuff is Gina's," I said. "What's that big roll in the box?"

He retrieved it while I opened the scrapbook and scanned the pages. It looked like a sample for a paper products company, with beach-themed stickers and paper. Photos could be pasted or inserted into slots, and several pages had dotted lines for text. Mason unrolled a canvas painting, oil or acrylic by my guess. It didn't have the subtle hues and washes of Maddie's watercolors. Smudged evergreens lined the shores of a wide deep blue lake, with a thunderstorm approaching in the distant sky.

"Looks unfinished, though. No signature." I pointed at the bottom edge.

"I have no idea if Gina painted it or bought it," Holly said. "We couldn't possibly sell an unsigned work of art."

"I think the artist intended to fill in more detail on the trees in the foreground," I said. "From what I've seen of my sister's work, I mean. Maddie starts in the back and works her way to the front, adding in all the details."

"Did your mother file a police report about this mink teddy bear?" Mason asked.

"No idea. But I do remember that Mom didn't realize it was gone for a while. She always invites a lot of people over in December, before and after Christmas. She finally realized it was gone long after New Year's Day. My sister had a birthday party, and Mom wondered if one of the kids took it home. She asked, but no one had seen it."

I recalled how frustrated Mom had been, questioning all the girls' mothers. Dad had not allowed her to round up my sister's friends who attended the slumber party that January. I'd been grumpy since they disturbed my rereading of the latest Harry Potter novel.

Not a great memory.

I watched Mason return all the items to the box. "Thanks so much for cooperating, Ms. Parker. I'll take these items as evidence—"

"Is that necessary?" Holly interrupted. "I mean, you don't know for certain if they have anything to do with Gina's murder. Do you?"

"But it's possible. I'd like to check for fingerprints, too."

She looked stricken by that remark and her pale face turned red. Holly flashed an angry look at me, as if this was all my fault. I wondered where she'd been last night. Had Mason asked her that yet? Too bad I hadn't come sooner to hear the answer.

"Thank you again, Ms. Parker."

The screen door clanged shut after the detective. I hung back, hoping I'd figure out how to ask without seeming nosy. "That was awful, finding Gina this morning," I began, and then explained how I'd gotten a ride home after dinner. "That's why I had to retrieve my car this morning. I was so shocked to see your 'Think Pink' hoodie jacket."

"Yeah. And you thought somebody knifed me."

I should have been prepared for Holly's snide tone, but only shrugged. "I didn't know Gina borrowed that much stuff from you."

"One thing is sure," Holly said. "You wished it was me, lying there dead."

"I wouldn't wish that on anyone."

"Why don't I believe that?" She slammed the file cabinet shut. "I'm closing up, so buzz off. You didn't come to buy anything."

I changed tactics, hoping to find some common ground.

"Listen, we've had our problems in the past, but that's all water under the bridge. We're both business owners in the village. Any type of tragedy affects us all."

"I suppose that's true." Holly narrowed her eyes. "You've been through this before with your sales rep. I hope Gina's death won't affect my sales."

"It might, at first—"

"Even bad publicity is good, I suppose." She shoved me around the corner and all the way to the door. "Like I said, buzz off."

"I don't suppose you were here all last night," I said, half outside.

"No. But since you asked, I was visiting my mother."

Holly slammed the door in my face. I stood on the porch, wondering at her strange obsession with Alice in Wonderland, and her clear pride in portraying the White Queen. She acted more like the selfish Red Queen in my opinion.

Using her mother as an alibi seemed convenient. I had to wonder whether Mrs. Parker would cover for her daughter. If my mother ever thought I'd committed a crime, she'd turn me in without a shred of guilt. And claiming Gina bought the mink bear off eBay also seemed fishy. No doubt Holly knew a lot more than she was willing to tell. Minky Bear's reappearance was an odd coincidence, turning up in the back of Holly's shop. Or was it?

It certainly threw a wrench in the works.

Chapter 10

Sunshine bathed the factory floor on Monday afternoon. Wishing I could grab another cup of coffee for sustenance, I gathered the large tour group of seniors and led them away from the sewing machines. Hilda Schulte seemed relieved. I knew she didn't like anyone watching her work. She'd recently joined our staff and already chafed under Flora Zimmerman's strict training rules. That might be why she'd bonded with Joan Kendall, who was more relaxed about visitors trooping through the area.

"We have to move on," I called out. "Ladies, rejoin the tour so we can continue."

Trying to keep them together was almost impossible, unlike the schoolchildren who followed directions. Not that the adults ignored me on purpose, but their curiosity seemed insatiable. Like mine, I suppose, so I couldn't complain. But this wasn't their first tour of the Silver Bear Shop & Factory. I kept my impatience at bay. Their enjoyment over seeing every little thing was refreshing along with their camaraderie.

"May I ask you a question, Ms. Silverman?"

I nodded, although I could barely hear the older woman's quavering voice. These local seniors knew my parents well, attended the same church, and always bought teddy bears and accessories as gifts for grandkids, nieces, or nephews. My father's mantra echoed in my brain—"Questions lead to opportunities, so always engage with the customer." I figured he'd adjusted that phrase from his former job as an attorney.

I got the gist of what the woman asked when she gestured to a door marked PRIVATE. Uh-oh. I knew they all knew what stood behind that door. They all wanted me to answer why we'd closed off our stuffing machine from display. I sidestepped the issue.

"Employees only, I'm afraid. Let's continue—"

"You had a new room built?" a bearded man asked, his fedora at a jaunty angle.

"Walter, please. We all know what's in there," another woman said.

"Ross Silverman told me after church, Shirley," he said. "He hired that young Kirby, the carpenter. Everyone knows what happened to Taylor, so why hide the stuffing machine?"

"Sorry, it's no longer included in the tour," I said stiffly.

"You showed us how the bears are sewn, but you're skipping how you stuff them?"

"Come on, Walter," another gentleman said. "It was murder—"

"Mur-der?" One woman had drawn out the syllables, mimicking a character in a Pink Panther movie with Inspector Clouseau. Everyone laughed. "Did you say mur-der?"

Fake gasps arose from some of the other ladies. Taking a deep breath, I figured this could go on forever if I didn't put a quick end to it. "Yes, Will Taylor was murdered. It isn't funny in the least, though. His death started a chain of consequences. Many people suffered in the long run, including our staff here at the factory."

Shirley nodded. "We understand that, but—"

"We will not satisfy anyone's thirst for gore," I said firmly. "There's too much of that now in the world."

"But some of us have never seen the stuffing machine."

I shook my head. "I'm sorry. My father says it's off limits."

"We know there's a time and a place for humor," Walter said, "and never meant to poke fun at what happened. I mean, yes, it was a real tragedy."

"Sometimes joking takes the edge off a very nasty truth." The elderly lady who'd first asked about the room nodded wisely, her hands as shaky as her voice. "I read this somewhere, and it's true. 'There is a thin line that separates laughter and pain, comedy and tragedy, humor and hurt.' I love that quote."

"Who said that, Hannah? William Shakespeare?" Walter asked.

"Erma Bombeck," she said. "You should know, you gave me that book!"

The seniors all laughed. "I've got a better one," Walter said. "'Learn from the mistakes of others. You can never make them all yourself.' Groucho Marx."

He waggled his eyebrows and pretended to flick a cigar. I smiled in relief when the group followed me to the shipping department. I twisted around to walk backward, pointing to Deon Walsh. He rocked to music on his headphones and shuffled his feet.

"We store finished bears in bins where our staff can easily access them, wrap them in bubble wrap, and box them for delivery. Say hi to our newest employee, Tim Richardson." The group waved to the young man, who smiled. I continued on. "Our office staff prints shipping labels and staples them with the order forms. Deon and Tim fill orders, attach the labels, and set them in this crate for UPS pickup. Okay, let's move on."

Uncle Ross's voice boomed over mine, however, from the

doorway. "How can we be behind on filling orders? Two weeks behind!"

"Because we need to hire a third person," Aunt Eve said, and stabbed her pencil on the clipboard she held. "I'll start interviewing. Now sign this order, please."

"Wait just a minute—"

I hurried their way. "Keep it down, you two. I'm giving a tour, remember."

The seniors walked slowly past with sly smiles. Uncle Ross scowled, but Aunt Eve whispered so only I could overhear. "Listen to me, Ross. Sales have jumped and we've got to keep orders going out on time. We can't be backed up like this."

"Can we discuss this later?" I asked.

My uncle sighed. "Okay, okay. By the way, Sasha, we're going to need more of that green corduroy. Joan and Hilda had trouble cutting out the pattern for the lederhosen."

"Oh no! I hope we can find matching fabric—" I stopped, aware that everyone in the tour group had twisted around to listen. "Okay, everyone, move on! Retrace our steps."

Asking my aunt and uncle to whisper had drawn more attention to them. Aunt Eve looked sleek in a red plaid pencil skirt with a large ruffle at the hem, black spike heels, and a white blouse. She slid her reading glasses down, flashed a bright smile at the group, and then walked back toward the office, heels click-clacking on the tile floor. All the men ogled her.

Even Uncle Ross.

"Stupid prize bear," he muttered to himself, stalking off. "I knew it would be more trouble than it's worth."

I let out a long breath. "Nothing more to see. Or hear. Let's go."

"Why can't we see the grand prize giant bear?" Walter asked.

"That way we can tell everyone about how wonderful it

looks," Shirley said. "A bit of free publicity for your shop and the Oktobear Fest."

"Great idea," I said, relieved to get them away from office drama. "We have to take the stairs in the shop, but there's also an elevator. Follow me."

While we walked beneath the honeysuckle-covered trellis between the factory and the house, a fit of sneezing hit me. "Only my allergy, go on. I'll catch up."

I groped for a tissue and waited for the stragglers. At last we all gathered at the Silver Bear Shop's front porch and slowly climbed the steps. Walter helped Hannah up the long ramp near the end. I thanked him since I hadn't washed my hands.

"Head straight through the shop," I said. "The elevator's next to the Rotunda, but it will only hold five or six people. I'll lead whoever's able to use the stairs."

It took forever for the seniors to climb the circular steps, since they oohed and aahed at each acrylic display box holding a custom teddy along the way. We all met near the waist-high crate holding a five-foot tan bear wrapped in plastic.

"Our staff is sewing a costume for this adorable bear," I said. "The dance contest winners last year donated their bear to a children's hospital."

"I believe it was a dark brown bear, wasn't it, dear?" the frailest woman asked.

"Yes, and next year's bear will be silver, like Mr. Silver sitting beneath the photo of my grandfather. We change the donation every year."

"Is there any chance the same dance contestants might win again?" Walter asked.

"I don't know. It hasn't happened yet." I waved an arm. "You're welcome to look around the rooms for as long as you like. Take turns heading downstairs on the elevator. Don't try the stairs. I'd rather not take any chances of falls."

The seniors all agreed. "Walter did a number last month while he was doing a rumba," Shirley said. "He's one of the best dancers, too."

"You're far better than I am, and you know it. We ought to enter that dance contest." The old man winked at me. "Good to see T. R. again, even in a photo. I remember him handing out the bears he made by hand. I wasn't one of the lucky ones, though. Dad wouldn't allow us to have toys. We worked in the fields—"

"From dawn till dusk, yes," Shirley teased. "Summer and winter, no time for school. Walked ten miles, uphill, both ways."

Others razzed Walter and Shirley both. I thanked the seniors for coming, which brought on a chorus of cheers that warmed my heart. Apparently they didn't hold it against me for not showing them the stuffing machine. My nerves were shot, though, after stumbling upon another murder victim. Alone this time except for Rosie. Thank goodness for my friends Garrett and Mary Kate, who'd come to my aid.

I hooked the chain across the stairs, hoping it would remind them to use the elevator, and headed back to the factory. I felt pressured to make up for lost time after spending more than two hours with the tour. Using my camera phone, I snapped photos of all our bears—white, silver, beige, tan, brown, and black—before the specialty models. Career bears in the proper attire, such as nurses, doctors, and teachers; nationality bears like the German, Japanese, or Scottish bears; holiday bears for Valentine's Day, Halloween, or Christmas; character bears like President Teddy Roosevelt and A-bear-ham Lincoln, Shakesbear, Queen Eliza-bear, the Three Muske-bears, Napoleon Bear-naparte; and literary bears like Scarlett O'Beara, Hucklebeary Finn, and Bear-lock Holmes. I walked back to the office to print them.

At the front sales counter, I stopped in surprise. Maddie

chatted with Kip, who wore a paint-spattered shirt and jeans. "Hey, where's Aunt Eve? I thought you were busy and couldn't cover for me."

My sister smiled. "We made progress on our bears."

"Yeah," Kip said. "This is my light day for classes, too. We managed to get the accordion attached on the Polka Bear's paws. That was tricky."

"I think it looks kind of lame," Maddie said. "That duct tape might be strong, but anyone could pull it off."

"No way." Kip shook his head. "Plus we'll seal it."

"I wanted to wrap the leather straps with carbon fiber and then use Goop."

"Not strong enough, babe. I bet people will want to play the instrument, and only duct tape will keep it in place. Besides, they won't care how it's attached."

"But—"

I whistled shrilly. "Time out, you two. You can always fix it if the straps get loose."

"Hello?" Walter suddenly appeared, holding two tan bears. "Sorry, folks. We wanted to buy these for my grandkids." Shirley smiled beside him.

"I helped him choose them before the tour. I found this blue Cinderella dress, isn't it darling? And the baseball uniform comes with a tiny leather mitt."

"Plastic, actually," I said. "Pretty realistic, though."

"Aren't you two artists for the Bears on Parade?" Walter asked Maddie and Kip. They nodded. "I thought I saw you in the photo with a write-up in the *Silver Hollow Herald*."

"I can't wait to see the sculptures," Shirley said. "I saw Chicago's Cows on Parade a long time ago. I'm thrilled the committee came up with bears for Silver Hollow."

"They raised a lot of money for charity with those cows," Kip said. "I heard only a few of the Bears on Parade will be auctioned off, though. A majority of the artists found private donors to pay for their sculptures, who will keep them. Like Alex Silverman."

I hadn't known that, but wasn't surprised. Walter winked at my sister. "Are you nervous with all the people coming out on Wednesday night?"

"Should be a great turnout." Kip slid an arm around Maddie. "You have no reason to be nervous, babe. The Polka Bear is almost done."

"Don't forget it still needs sealer, and that will take time to dry."

She looked annoyed by his quick shrug. Even Walter and Shirley seemed to sense a hint of trouble. I stepped in to reassure Maddie. "You'll get it done by Wednesday night. If you need help, let me know. I'm good with a brush. Sort of."

"So what's the order for the Bears on Parade?" Shirley asked.

"Wednesday is when the first few are unveiled on Main Street, including Maddie's," Kip said. "Then more on Saturday, and the final ones come the following Wednesday before the Oktobear Fest. Mine's in the last group. A few artists are having trouble, like me."

"What kind of trouble?"

"Zoe Fisher tried a glue that wasn't clear enough for her Bling Bear," Maddie said. "She had to gouge it all off and start over. And Jay Kirby is doing a Lumberjack Bear. He needs help with the costume, Sasha, so I told him you'd help."

"Uh, okay."

Amazed that she'd volunteered me without asking, I was at a loss for words. I disliked being put on the spot, but she left to help Aunt Eve. I had no chance to refuse.

Kip laughed. "Jay's panicking, so he'd appreciate any advice."

More seniors arrived to purchase items for their families,

so I helped them choose bears and accessories. I didn't get a chance to ask Kip if Jay really needed my help or if it was another ploy to throw us together. At last the final customer paid and departed. Sighing in relief, I closed the register drawer. Oddly enough, Kip rose from the bench by the front door. He looked uneasy, shifting on his feet and wiping his hands on his jeans.

"Hey, Sash. Can I ask you a question?"

"Um, sure."

"First, I should apologize. About not understanding that migraine you had on Saturday," he said. "Maddie explained how they're not like regular headaches. I had no idea."

"No problem."

"Sometimes I get a little carried away. Like ordering that expensive champagne."

"It's okay." I sensed genuine concern in his tone. "Stress-related headaches hit without warning. It's been pretty crazy over the last month."

Kip gave an odd shake, shoulders, arms, and head, as if quivering in revulsion. "Yeah, Maddie told me what happened. That must have been pretty grim."

"Very." I hesitated before posing a question. "Can I ask what you did after Maddie left with Jay Saturday night? Did you go on a pub crawl without her?"

"Nah. I called it a night. Whatever."

"You didn't see anyone—a stranger, or someone you knew," I said, "maybe hanging around the parking lot in back? Behind Fresh Grounds."

"Nope, but I didn't go that way. My car was parked over by the Village Green." Kip planted his elbows on the front counter, chin in one hand, his warm brown eyes meeting my gaze. "Do you know how serious Maddie is, and whether she's ready to settle down? Maybe it's too early to expect that, but I'm crazy about her."

"We haven't had a chance to talk much. What with renovating the office, and all the work she's been doing for the Bears on Parade committee—"

"Yeah, I get it. I have to be patient. I'm not so good at that," he said with a laugh. "Okay, but don't tell her I asked. She'd probably think it's too weird. I've never fallen so hard for a chick before now. Maddie is really special."

"I agree." I matched his smile. "I really hope things work out for you both."

"She's so down to earth. So genuine. I really dislike women who fake things, play games, and pretend they know so much." Kip breathed deep. "Just so you know, Sasha. Jay's into you. We could try again for dinner, the four of us, if you're up for it. If you feel the same about him. Not trying to push you, but think about it."

"Okay, thanks." Unwilling to share my thoughts, I started cashing out. "I'll see you Wednesday when Maddie's bear is unveiled. What time does it start again?"

"Six o'clock." Kip flashed his boyish smile and then lumbered toward the door. "Jay will be there. You can ask him then about his bear's costume."

Hoo boy. I flipped the CLOSED sign and locked the door after him. While Jay's bear sounded adorable, I wished he would have asked for my help instead of relying on his friends. Unless he'd intended to ask me Saturday night and never got the chance, given my migraine. Or maybe Kip and Maddie jumped the gun, asking me without his knowledge. Still, I couldn't help resenting Maddie's matchmaking. Kip, too. He'd definitely been fishing.

I tiptoed past the office, ignoring Maddie's and Aunt Eve's voices. Rosie stood by the back door, leash in her mouth, her tail wagging. I laughed. "Yes, you sweet baby. Let's go."

Due to the tour, I'd worn my Chacos for comfort. Getting out into the fresh air and bright sunshine helped lift my mood.

With so many things to deal with all day long, plus the tour, the day had sped past. Now I could relax and avoid thinking about my job, family, and any future relationships. Even Gina Lawson's murder.

Rosie padded eagerly down the sidewalk, claws clicking. I glanced inside Through the Looking Glass's windows, open but without any browsing customers. Holly Parker shelved some books near the front door. Silver Hollow residents had been sad when the Holly Jolly Christmas shop had to close; I certainly enjoyed seeing all the sparkling trees and ornaments, year-round. Holly had added an ironwork fence around the wide yard that faced Kermit, with a locked gate. Inside, a metal butterfly chair and a resin play structure with wood chips spread underneath gave kids a chance to play while parents shopped inside.

I opened the door and stuck my head inside. "Hi, Holly. Do you know if Gina's family will have a funeral or memorial service? I know the police have to do an autopsy."

"She was an orphan, and an only child," Holly said. "So who knows if there'll be any services at all."

She vanished around the corner, leaving me to get another look inside the shop. The new books below the Disney collectibles had been crammed in helter-skelter, nothing at all like the tidy shelves at The Cat's Cradle. Elle insisted all the books be in alphabetical order by author and within categories—picture books, early readers, chapter books, YA—and then within various subcategories like bedtime, adventure, mystery, etc. I wondered if Holly carried any first editions of Lewis Carroll's books, or various versions of the author's biography.

Losing Gina was a big disadvantage, given her marketing skills, but Holly would survive. She always had in the past.

"So what do you really want?" Holly asked, returning with another box.

"You said Gina uploaded listings, and handled online sales, right?" I asked.

"Yeah. I'll have to teach myself how to do all that now. She said writing the summaries was the hardest part."

"We hired Tim Richardson to help with shipping. Maybe one of his sisters could help you out here, part-time, until you find a permanent replacement."

"I need someone with experience, not a farm hick. Gina knew accounting, marketing, how to organize things, everything about running a small business," Holly added. "We planned everything for this shop when we worked in Traverse City."

"Really?" That was news. I wondered if Maddie had learned that before. "It still boggles the mind, how she happened to be wearing your jacket."

"You keep saying that, so you must have hoped it was me killed. Don't try to pretend. Everyone in Silver Hollow knows we hate each other's guts."

"I may not like you," I said slowly, "but I've never hated you."

"Ha." Holly opened a lethal box cutter and then scored along the closest sealed box's top. "I wanted to open a shop in Ann Arbor, but Gina convinced me to come back here instead. Flynn told her this shop was for rent, and that it was a great location for business."

I fought to hide my shock. First Holly accused me of being coldhearted, but learning my ex had betrayed me again was too much. Had Mom mentioned it to Flynn? She must have, if he'd turned around and relayed the information to Gina, who then told Holly.

"Why would Gina have bought those items off eBay?" I watched for her reaction. "The ones Detective Mason found in the back of your shop."

Holly hadn't been paying attention to me while she unpacked a second box of books, but nearly dropped the box cutter. Her cheeks pink, she faced me.

"I have no idea. I'm busy, so get off my back. You and your dog."

Holly slapped a leather-bound book on the counter with a bang. I knew she disliked being questioned, especially when odd things happened—like back in high school. When all my oboe reeds had been split, she'd easily won first chair. Nobody admitted to doing the deed, but that drama seemed silly now. Murder topped old resentments and rivalry. At least in my book, if not Holly Parker's. She slammed things around, still angry.

Rosie and I dodged the screen door before it banged shut behind us. "Good luck finding someone to help you," I called.

Holly didn't reply. Not that I expected an answer.

Chapter 11

Despite my disgruntled mood after that encounter with Holly, I didn't want to cheat Rosie out of her walk to the Village Green. She sniffed every bush, tree, mailbox, trash barrel, plus anyone's hands when they reached down to pet her along the way. A few people she knew and greeted with a wagging tail. Several strangers asked for directions to Blake's Pharmacy or the park. Once past the courthouse, I let Rosie's leash extend to its full length. She barked at another dog that resembled a beautiful golden Labrador, but with the oddest blue eyes. Jay Kirby waved, holding on to the Lab's similar retractable leash.

The large dog raced over to give Rosie the universal greeting. I smiled at Jay. "Hi. Didn't know you had a dog."

"Yeah, this is Buster."

Casual in blue jean shorts, a shirt flecked with bits of sawdust, and fisherman sandals, he hauled back on the dog's leash. Rosie took off in another direction as far as she could. Jay ordered his dog to sit, so I scratched behind Buster's silky ears and under his muzzle.

"What kind of mix is he? Such beautiful eyes."

"Husky and Lab," Jay said. "Call him a Hubrador or a Lab-sky. Your choice."

I laughed. "Rosie's a mix of Lhasa Apso and Bichon. I get her groomed to make her look like a teddy bear."

"She's a beauty. Love the curly hair."

Jay was only a few inches taller than me. His friendliness and easy manner, plus the way he listened, put me at ease. I glanced around the grassy expanse. A few couples strolled along the sidewalk; one mom pushed a double stroller while she jogged. A group of teens gathered at the farthest corner closest to the school. Rosie's leash wound around a slender tree, so I retrieved her and untangled the cord. I led her back to rejoin Jay and Buster, who sat with his tongue hanging out, calm and cool. Rosie lowered herself to the grass, panting hard.

"Honestly, I am the worst dog owner," I said. "She's the alpha, I'm a wimp."

Jay chuckled. "I rescued Buster, so I had to learn how to control him. He's eight years old now, more mellow. Nice evening to be out."

"Yeah." I hauled Rosie in by her leash when she started to chase a squirrel. "It is." I'd run out of things to say, though, and glanced up at the dazzling sunset.

"I'd love for you to come out to my studio," he said. "See my latest projects."

"Uh, sure. But I won't have time till after the Oktobear Fest."

"Okay." Jay shifted his feet and sounded awkward when he changed the subject. "Sorry we didn't get much of a chance to talk Saturday night. I meant to ask you—well, about helping me. With my sculpture for the Bears on Parade."

"Maddie and Kip mentioned that."

"They did? Well, my Lumberjack Bear needs a costume."

I nodded. "Okay. What did you have in mind?"

"I should have called you and asked, before Maddie and Kip did." He sounded uncertain. "But I was afraid you might turn me down."

I grinned at his sheepish expression. "You don't know me well enough. Tell me about your Lumberjack Bear. Are you thinking of a flannel shirt and jeans? Maybe you should get a knitted wool cap for his head, too."

"Great idea. If I can find one to stretch," Jay said. "That head is pretty big."

"My aunt would make a hat if you give her the measurements. She's a fast knitter and loves those kinds of projects."

He rubbed his jaw. "Really? That would be so cool. My bear is one of the last to be displayed because I had to finish a carving project. Maddie's Polka Bear is ready, and Kip's should be done by the weekend. I haven't even come up with an official name yet."

"So it's not the Lumberjack Bear?"

"I said that, but the committee thought it was too lame."

"Hmm. How about the Paul Bunyan Bear," I said, "or the 'I'm a Lumberjack and I'm Okay' Bear, from the Monty Python skit. Or the Jack Pine Bear."

Jay had cracked up over the Monty Python suggestion and caught his breath. "Wow. Good one, but I like Jack Pine better. Done! We could add suspenders to the costume, too."

"I love that idea."

"Thanks so much, Sasha. The committee asked for another bear on Roosevelt Street when one artist dropped out. That's the only reason I was asked. To be honest, I'd rather carve a bear than use that resin sculpture. But I'm stuck with the rules."

"So what about shoes or boots? He can't be barefoot. Er, bare paws."

"Bear paws, ha. I chose boots, so I split a pair in half. Size sixteen, the biggest I could find on eBay, and glued each half on with industrial adhesive. I almost passed out from the toxic fumes. I'd rather not use that stuff again."

"You need Velcro," I said promptly. "Top of the line, not the stuff you can buy at a craft shop. Duct tape won't work, although Kip might not agree."

"I know. It's his favorite go-to."

"He might say anyone can rip the clothes off if we use Velcro, but not if you spray on sealant. We'll have to make sure the seams aren't that visible. That way people won't know Velcro is keeping it all together."

"Maddie said if anyone could figure out how to do it, you would. Thanks so much."

Jay's smile was on the shy side, not flashy or fake like my ex-husband. I tried to forget Flynn's plastered smile on those TV commercials, and focused on Jay and his bear.

"Do you have enough flannel for the shirt? And denim?"

"I found a bunch of plaid shirts in the same pattern," he said, "at all those resale shops when we searched for Maddie's accordion. And I bought at least three pairs of jeans, the biggest sizes I could find. Would that work?"

"We'll have to cobble together what you have," I said. "Sew them to fit around the bear's body, and try to make it look natural. We'll do the same with the shirt front, and that way we won't have to deal with buttonholes. I hope it won't look pieced together like a quilt."

"Yeah—" Buster lunged suddenly and almost dragged Jay off, chasing another dog. Rosie wasn't interested—a real miracle. Jay apologized multiple times when he returned. "Stay, for pity's sake." He hugged his dog, who still squirmed. "I won't mind if it's all pieced together. Anything to get it done on time. My mom and sister never learned to sew. Maddie said you learned, though. Did you take classes at some point?"

I nodded. "Remember how I bailed on Wood Shop back in high school? I took sewing instead that term. Turned out to be an easy A, since I could read a pattern and figure out the machine. Our industrial machines aren't so easy, but I'll manage. I'll need exact measurements for this costume to work, though."

"Yeah, I've got all that."

"How about you bring the shirts and jeans tomorrow night," I said. "We can sew Velcro on the edges and see how it all works."

Jay rose to his feet. "Great. And then you can come out to the studio and help me fit them on the Jack Pine Bear."

"That name does have a nice ring to it. Okay, and don't forget to buy the Velcro. I doubt if any shops here would carry it, but I bet you can find it at a home improvement store. Try over in Ann Arbor or up in Brighton."

"Thanks. I really appreciate this, Sasha."

"By the way," I said slowly, "did you happen to see anyone Saturday night? In the lot behind Fresh Grounds. When you drove Maddie home, I mean. Like a stranger, or Gina Lawson, maybe with someone?"

He looked puzzled. "No, I didn't. After I dropped off your sister, I went home to my apartment. North of here, so I didn't go back toward the village."

"I was just curious." I smiled. "See you tomorrow."

"Sure. Good night."

"I hope you don't mind how Maddie's pushing us. Into being friends, I mean."

"Not one bit. I hope we'll be more than friends."

Jay grinned and led Buster toward Mark Fox's vet clinic, where his dust-coated truck sat on the street. My cheeks burned as I walked Rosie in the opposite direction. Maybe he didn't mind my sister's matchmaking, but it embarrassed me to no end. Flattered by his interest, I still hoped Jay wasn't planning on rushing into a relationship. I had too much going on in my life.

I waved frantically at Ben Blake, who was locking up his drugstore. "Hey, wait! Got a question for you," I called out, and hurried to catch up to him. "How's it going with Wendy, by the way? Will I see you two at the Oktobear Fest?"

Ben flashed his million-dollar smile. "Yeah, we're helping staff the beer tent. Checking IDs and serving up pitchers, in costume. I am not looking forward to wearing lederhosen."

"Aw, why not?" I couldn't help laughing at his sour look. "Wendy will make a fetching barmaid in a dirndl and corset. Where are you getting your costumes?"

"Probably online. So what's up?"

"Do you know if your sister-in-law was friends with Holly Parker? I saw them talking at our tea party. Poor woman looks ready to give birth any day."

"Yeah, Lisa can't wait. I think they used to hang out back in high school." Ben scratched Rosie's head and ears. She ate up the attention, licked his hand, and stretched on the ground so he could rub her belly. "My brother didn't like Holly, though."

"I don't remember that." I hadn't paid that much attention to Holly or her friends, since I'd avoided her on purpose as much as possible. "I can't remember a whole lot from high school. In fact, everything before my divorce is pretty fuzzy."

He chuckled. "I get that. Mike thought Holly had too much influence on Lisa."

"Lisa didn't graduate with us, right?"

"She's a few years younger, like your sister. I do know this much," Ben said. "After Lisa started dating Mike, Holly gave her an ultimatum. Their friendship or her boyfriend. Guess what Lisa decided. She married him, after all."

"I'd say she definitely made the better choice."

"I gotta run. Wendy's expecting me at the pub. See you later."

Once Ben vanished around the corner, I led Rosie toward Theodore Lane and home. Maddie and Mom sat at the kitchen table with Aunt Eve and Uncle Ross. Rosie padded toward her drinking bowl, lapped up half of it, and then lay down in her crate with her toy bear. I longed for peace and quiet, too, given my hectic Monday. Alone time with a good book and a glass of wine wasn't going to happen with so many relatives around. After I washed my hands at the sink, I fetched a bottle of water from the fridge.

"Help yourself to the salad bar, Sasha," Mom said. "There's a second loaf of fresh bread in the bag. Leave some chicken for your father, because he should be home any minute. At least that's what he texted me from the freeway."

"Dad *texted* you?" That surprised me. "He has an old flip phone."

"He upgraded to a smartphone. I have no idea what he was doing up north," she added, "and I'm not sure I want to know. Gil Thompson had better not have talked him into another hare-brained investment scheme. We lost too much money the last time."

I piled chopped greens, chunks of apple, walnuts, and dried cherries on a plate. My stomach rumbled, smelling the still-hot mesquite chicken strips I laid on top. Then I grabbed a can of chow mein noodles from the pantry, popped the lid, and tossed a handful over all. A river of spicy red French dressing helped balance the healthiness factor. Mmm. If only I could add some crumbled cookies. Maybe I could use that as an ice cream topping for dessert.

After tearing off the crusty bread loaf's end, I sat next to my sister at the table. "So what did Dad invest in a while ago?"

"Oh, brother," Maddie said under her breath. My question set Mom off on a long rant about fishing and hunting trips, dilapidated lodges, and campgrounds.

"He poured five thousand dollars into that dump of a hunting shack on Bass Lake, and what did we get for it? More repair bills when the ceiling caved. I told him not to listen to that snake of a Realtor up there." She smoothed back her freshly tinted auburn hair, styled in a new shorter bob. "Why men need to hunt or fish is a mystery anyway."

Uncle Ross snorted. "Because we like to eat what we kill. Why do women get a weekly manicure, or buy a new outfit? You can't eat any of that."

"Weekly manicure?" Aunt Eve waved a hand in the air. "I do my own, thank you. And I'll have you know, Ross Silverman, that I only bought a new dress for the holidays, if that, when we were married. But a professional pedi is pure heaven. You ought to try it. There you go, bah-humbugging everything I say. How did we stay married more than a month?"

"I love that Christmas dress you showed me in your closet," Maddie said. "We'll have to host a party at the shop in December."

"The red velvet one is darling, isn't it?"

My sister turned to me, although I'd just taken a huge bite. "It's deep red, with a tiny belt at the waist, sleeveless, and a large collar. Aunt Eve wears her pearls with it."

"Ross gave me that necklace long ago," my aunt said. "Imitation."

"Authentic and you know it," he growled. "I gave you the certificate to prove it. They're genuine freshwater pearls from Hawaii."

The screen door slammed shut when Dad breezed into the kitchen. "Stop bickering, you two, or I'm going back to Traverse City. You act like teenagers."

Grinning wide, his duffel bag in hand, he set down multiple paper and plastic bags on the floor and waved me back into my chair. The minute he'd walked in the door, Mom rushed to concoct a salad for him and set it down at the table's only empty spot. Dad sank down with a grateful sigh and tucked a napkin into his plaid shirt collar.

"Ross called me about what happened. A second murder,

wow. I'm sorry I wasn't here again, Sasha." He accepted the piece of buttered bread Mom handed him. "Gil and I had to check out a few more places up north."

"So what did you invest in this time?" Uncle Ross asked.

"Nothing. Gil wanted my opinion on some coffee shops there. He's getting new ideas for Fresh Grounds, I guess. He wants to liven things up."

"What do you mean?" I set down my salad fork, worried for Garrett and Mary Kate. "It's always crammed from morning to night, so why would he want to change things? It's cozy with all the wood and the seating arrangements, too."

"Gil wants to set up a display of tea canisters, and sell coffee beans to grind at home, but that means they'll have to expand their sales area."

"But that means fewer tables for people to sit with their coffee."

"Might be a good thing." Dad shrugged and took a huge bite of salad. "People sometimes spend hours there."

"Amanda Pozniak writes her blog and freelance articles at Fresh Grounds. When she's not working in the antique shop, that is," Maddie said. "I think taking away tables would hurt getting repeat customers in the long run."

"I'm not running their business."

"What if Mr. Thompson wants Matt and Elle to move out of their bookstore?" I asked, horrified. "Dad, can that be true? No way would Garrett and Mary Kate agree. They love having The Cat's Cradle open to the coffee shop. People browse all the time through both shops, and everyone loves that arrangement."

"All I know is that Gil wanted some new ideas," he said. "So while we were there, we scouted a hunting cabin one of his friends offered him to rent."

"I knew it," Mom said in disgust. "Hunting is all you men ever think about come fall. Unless it's football, or the World

Series if the Tigers are in it. If you're going hunting with Gil and a bunch of his friends, then I'm taking a trip as well."

Dad wiped his mouth with a napkin. "Fine with me."

"All right. Eve and I will spend a weekend on Mackinac Island."

I choked on a walnut piece. Maddie pounded me on the back and leaned forward near my ear. "Let's hope it's not the same weekend we'll be there," she whispered.

"Are you okay, Sasha?" Mom asked.

I nodded, unable to speak, and coughed harder. Mom and Dad turned back to Ross and Eve, continuing their argument about hunting and fishing up north. Maddie handed me my bottle of water and waited until I swallowed several times.

"Okay, now tell me about Jay and his bear costume," she said.

I limited my answers. Maddie seemed pleased that I'd accepted the task, although she questioned using old clothing for the bear's outfit. Aunt Eve overheard our chat and quickly agreed to knit a cap for the head.

"Piece of cake. I've got red, green, and navy blue yarn, so I'll start right away."

"Go with navy blue," I said. "But nothing fancy."

"With a rolled-up brim," my sister added. "Did Jay ask you out to dinner, Sash?"

"No."

"Why not? He's really in to you."

"Jay and I haven't even dated yet—"

"What?" Mom shifted her attention from Dad and Uncle Ross. "Wait a minute, you don't mean that boy who carved our bear mailbox?"

"He's not a boy, Judith," Dad said.

"Yes. Jay Kirby. He's the same age as Sasha." Maddie poked me with her elbow. "Such a hottie. You two would be perfect for each other."

"Stop trying to set me up."

"Come on, admit it. You crazy about him."

"He's nice," I said, my cheeks hot. "We're friends for now."

"I hope that's all, for heaven's sake." Mom sounded offended, as if she'd discovered a nefarious plot. "It's long past time you and Flynn got back together."

My jaw dropped. "What? No way."

"What the hell, Judith." Dad banged a fist on the table. "You can't be serious."

Maddie looked shocked, too. "Why would Sasha marry that jerk again!"

My gratitude rose several notches when Aunt Eve added her two cents of protest also, her face red. Either from anger or another hot flash, I couldn't tell. Only Uncle Ross didn't bother, although he'd waggled his shaggy gray eyebrows my way. That was our private signal back when I first started managing the shop seven years ago, which meant I was doing fine. Mom seemed genuinely surprised by all the negative reactions, however.

"What's wrong with wanting a happier ending? I've always liked Flynn. And he's a wonderful son-in-law—"

"What about his cheating?" Aunt Eve asked. "From all I've heard, he's the last man Sasha should have married. Why let him ruin her life a second time?"

My mother turned to Dad, who drew a finger across his throat in warning. "I know you don't believe me, but Flynn's changed," she insisted. "He bought that house, didn't he? And he told me yesterday he wants to get married again."

"Mom," I said, trying to remain patient despite my urge to scream. "Flynn refused to marry Gina Lawson, remember?"

"He was never interested in that tramp."

"Don't believe everything Flynn tells you." I rubbed my forehead in suspicion. What game was this about? I didn't need this right now, especially among family. "He always leaves important things out. And it's too late to get Gina's side of the story, since she's dead."

"I take it Gina is the woman who was killed Saturday night?" Dad asked.

"Or early Sunday morning," Uncle Ross said. "I'm not a suspect this time, thank God. Flynn loves to show off his money. Like that big house he bought, and now he's driving a snazzy car. Whoa, baby."

"Look who's talking about a snazzy car," Aunt Eve teased.

"Flynn has a great income. Why shouldn't he buy a gorgeous house?" Mom sniffed in disdain. "I don't blame Flynn for wanting someone better than Gina Lawson."

"So who's investigating the murder?" Dad asked. "Digger Sykes?"

"That same hard-nosed detective," my uncle replied. "Mason, from the Dexter County sheriff's office. Looks are deceiving in that one."

"He's very good at the job." I understood his underlying resentment due to the tough questions Uncle Ross had endured after Will Taylor's death, but turned to Mom. "Why would you think Flynn wants to marry me again? Seriously."

"Think how you could help his career."

"Flynn doesn't need help, not with those TV commercials," Maddie said.

"He claimed his colleagues are jealous," I added. "I doubt that."

"Blake and Branson?" My father's eyes rolled heavenward and then glanced my way. "I'd have to agree. They're benefiting plenty, from what I've heard."

"You're all wrong." Mom stood, her eyes flashing with anger. "Especially now that Gina's out of the picture, he needs you, Sasha. Wait and see."

She stormed through the kitchen toward the stairs. I blinked several times, totally stunned by her words. What did she mean?

Now that Gina's out of the picture . . . Maddie grabbed my arm and hauled me outside to the porch.

"Did you hear what I just heard?" She wiggled an ear. "Or did I dream that?"

I only shrugged. "You heard what Flynn said about people stabbing him in the back. It's kind of creepy, given what happened to Gina."

"Well, yeah, but Mom—" Maddie clapped a hand over her mouth. "I mean, no way could she kill anyone! But why would she say that? 'Now that Gina's out of the picture?'"

"She's a trip and half, but don't you remember how someone pulled a knife on Dad in New York City, right in front of her? That traumatized Mom for months. She couldn't even cut up her meat for dinner."

"I'd forgotten that, yeah," my sister said. "Wow. You're right. It's still weird."

"If anything, Flynn's hiding something," I said. "I'd like to know who he was with, for one thing. But Mason will have to figure it out."

Mom's idea that Flynn wanted to get married again threw me. So did her fit of temper. And she would certainly flip out if she knew I hadn't started finding evidence to prove that her friend, Mayor Cal Bloom, was innocent of Gina's murder.

Things had certainly gotten complicated.

Chapter 12

After an early Tuesday morning lap swim at the community pool, and a busy day working in the shop, my stomach knotted tight. I'd been too nervous to eat lunch. Jay Kirby was coming tonight. My confidence had plummeted, however, since I'd promised to help sew the Lumberjack Bear's costume. Would Velcro be strong enough to work? What if Jay didn't bring enough material to fit a five-foot-tall resin sculpture?

I rubbed sweaty palms on my jeans. I wore a maroon T-shirt instead of my usual silver logo one, plus a gray cardigan, jeans, and knee-high boots. My necklace's tiny charms tinkled whenever I moved; I'd bought it at an art show, drawn by the glass bottle of sand, a gilded pinecone, curved shell, a piece of beach glass, and a Petoskey stone. They all represented the state of Michigan's natural wonders. People had complimented it all day in the shop. And I loved supporting unique artwork. I'd agreed to help Jay for that reason, too.

But how would we manage fitting a costume on his fiberglass bear?

Suddenly I snapped my fingers. Mr. Silver—our giant bear—

could be a mannequin. Jay's sculpture wouldn't have the same give as a stuffed toy, but it was better than nothing. I glanced at the clock. Almost closing time, thank goodness. Since two customers browsed in the next room, I dialed my sister's cell. Maddie was working in the office alcove, designing brochures for our holiday sales.

"Hey, Mads, can you cover for me? I need to do something."

"Sure, but wait five minutes. Aunt Eve is tearing her hair out over a new online order. The company changed their mind twice. She's trying to get a firm decision."

"Soon as you can, then."

My sister arrived within ten minutes, looking adorable as usual in the T-shirt that she'd designed for the Bears on Parade. The committee had been selling them all month. I loved the image of a line of upright bears, touching paws to shoulders, marching in a rainbow of colors across the white shirt with black letters spelling out OKTOBEAR FEST and then SILVER HOLLOW, MICHIGAN, below that. I was so proud of her amazing talent, and glad she'd taken up art again instead of the shop's office grunt work.

"I wish I'd bought a second T-shirt," I said. "Mine's in the laundry."

"Want me to get you an extra one?" Maddie grinned. "Ten bucks, half-price. We've got plenty to sell in the next week or so. I hope we don't get stuck with 'em."

"Okay, cover the register. I'll be right back."

I raced upstairs to the loft and grabbed Mr. Silver from his spot. Stuffing him into the small elevator was real fun, along with dragging him through the office to the side door. Aunt Eve, in a flared white dress with tiny strawberries all over it, didn't look up from her desk. She peered close to the laptop screen through rhinestone-edged glasses, similar to the ones

Marilyn Monroe wore in *How to Marry a Millionaire,* and then banged a fist on the desk.

"Honestly, people. It's not that hard to decide—"

I lifted the bulky Mr. Silver and carried him out the door and toward the factory, avoiding the covered walkway. Despite that, I bumped into a support post. Then I trampled a bed of chrysanthemums and nearly dropped the bear.

Crash.

The large pot of petunias I'd knocked over hadn't broken, thank goodness. I shifted the bear over my shoulders back-pack-style. Oof. Awkward to say the least. A flashy sports car pulled into the parking lot, a dark blue Jaguar. I should have guessed the owner.

"Hey, Sasha! Still playing with toys, I see."

Flynn climbed out of the car, grinning as usual, wearing a dark three-piece suit. His tie was blue paisley today, with a silver tiepin and cufflinks, plus a maroon handkerchief tucked in the suit's breast pocket. He also wore exotic black leather boots.

"What are those?"

"Croc. Lucchese brand, seven hundred bucks, handmade. Really comfortable."

"What do you want now?" I had to admit I sounded cross to my own ears, but the last person I wanted to see was my ex.

"What's the deal with you lately? Even your mom thinks you've been treating me like I've got the plague." Flynn squinted hard. "Sun's in my eyes, hang on. Move to the left a little. A little more. Perfect."

I'd shifted without thinking, and then mentally kicked my-self. "Why aren't you wearing sunglasses? Like Gucci, or Tom Ford."

"I left them in the car. Now you and Mr. Silver are block-ing the light, so it's cool."

I moved back to the original spot to annoy him. "Why do

you expect everyone else in the world to revolve around you, Flynn Hanson? And by the way, I bet Detective Mason is going to track you down for more questions."

"Why?"

"For more information on Gina."

He shrugged. "My schedule is so tight, he'll have to wait."

"The cops don't wait for whatever time's most convenient for people," I said. "They'd never solve a case if they did that. Why are you here if your schedule's tight? And why is Mom sticking to you like a burr on Rosie's coat?"

"We're good friends."

"Friends."

"We always had a great relationship. Nothing wrong with staying friends even though you divorced me. Judith's great. Very supportive, unlike you."

"Seems she has a lame-brained idea that you and I are getting back together." I hadn't meant to blurt that out, but there it was. Flynn didn't laugh, which stunned me more. In fact, he looked serious and inched toward me. I backed away. "That is a joke, right?"

"Sasha, you were the best thing that ever happened to me—"

"No way, no how," I cut in and shoved Mr. Silver into his arms. "I know you're dating someone else, so don't even go there. And think how that will look to people around here. You and Gina break up, and now you've got a new conquest."

Flynn waved a hand. "Let me finish what I was saying. I think getting remarried is a great idea, and so does your mom. In name only, if that's what you want." He had that petulant tone, like a little boy who might not get his own way, which I'd heard so often before. "Lots of people make a mistake the first time around. Why not give it a second chance?"

"In name only? Your new girlfriend would love that."

"Why do you keep bringing her up?"

"Because unless she's totally nuts, she would never buy that kind of arrangement. Plus you had Angela on the side, and Gina Lawson, and who knows how many others. I'm not at all interested in your wacky ideas about marriage."

I turned on my heel and headed to the factory. Flynn followed with the bear. "Come on, Sasha. I came back to Michigan and bought that house—it's everything we've always wanted. Remote, lots of land, a pool, a neat layout. It's great. Your mom thinks it's great, too."

"She would." I couldn't believe what I was hearing. "Mom can move in, then, if she likes it so much. And there's no 'we' in wanting all that. You never listened when we were married, and you're not listening now." I stopped at the factory's door and snatched Mr. Silver from him. "I never wanted a house that big, or a pool in the backyard, or a fancy Jaguar."

He ignored me, plunging on. "Judith is over the moon about my commercials. We could be in them together, as a family—"

"Have you both lost your minds?" Stunned, I almost laughed at the thought of appearing in a commercial with Flynn. And my mother. My long necklace caught on the giant bear's fur and nearly strangled me. "It's a ridiculous idea."

"The producer thinks it's a great." Flynn straightened his tie. "It's not just a marriage of convenience, you know. It would help both of our businesses."

"Never." I shoved Mr. Silver into his arms, unhooked my necklace with its jangling charms, and pocketed it. "Our business doesn't need help, and neither do you."

"What if we announced we were getting back together, made the commercials, and then broke off the wedding at the last minute?"

"Listen to me, Flynn." I smacked my forehead, wondering what it would take to get through to him. And my mother, who ought to know better. "This conversation is over. Any chance of marrying again is nonexistent. Not even pretending. Forget it."

"Okay, okay!" He looked downcast. "You don't have to be so negative."

"I'm stressed to the max, my mother is driving me batty, and you're—"

"Am I interrupting something?"

I glanced over to where Jay Kirby stood outside the open door, carrying a stack of large boxes and a canvas tote over one shoulder. "Nope. Flynn's leaving. Ready to start?"

"Start what?" Flynn asked, his tone sour.

"None of your business." I grabbed Mr. Silver out of the flower bed where my ex had dropped him. "Good-bye."

Jay nodded. "Hanson."

"The wood-carver, right? The one who did the mailbox." Flynn arched an eyebrow, as if considering what to say. "Great work. Okay, Sash, but I'm hoping you'll meet Judith and me for dinner tonight. Eight o'clock at Flambé. My treat."

"No."

He looked surprised. "Oh, come on. Why not?"

"She's having dinner with me." Jay flashed a sudden grin when I blew out a breath in relief. "For helping me with my Jack Pine Bear."

"Oh. Then tomorrow night."

"No. Maddie's bear is being unveiled at the Bears on Parade," I said, reining in my temper. "I'm not going to dinner with you or my mother. Not tomorrow, next week, next year. I'm not interested in being in any of your TV commercials. Or in anything. Period. End of story, except I'm going to find out who you were with the night of Gina's murder."

Flynn stammered. "I—I didn't kill her. I swear it. The last time I saw Gina alive was at Quinn's Pub on Thursday. I was nowhere near Silver Hollow Saturday night."

"Okay, whatever." I turned to Jay. "First I've got to check with my sister. I'm supposed to close the shop at six o'clock."

"Maddie sent me over here," Jay said. "She's closing up, and said to go ahead with the project. She'll hang around, too, in case we need her help."

"Okay, great."

Now I sounded like Flynn, who'd stalked off toward his sporty car. If only he would tell Mason where he'd spent Saturday night, or who he was with. It would give him a solid alibi, but he'd fallen back on stubbornness. His usual smoothness had cracked, though.

I brushed dirt and a few stray leaves off Mr. Silver and then entered the factory. That whole crazy TV commercial idea, and Mom's eagerness, puzzled me. He'd been so adamant about not killing Gina. What had he said just now? *The last time I saw Gina alive . . .*

I stopped in the hallway. When Jay bumped into me, we both almost fell over Mr. Silver. Somehow I managed to catch myself, but the top box tumbled off his stack; he swung around in a valiant effort to keep the middle one from falling. But his heavy canvas tote knocked me flat on my behind. We both laughed our heads off. Jay pulled me to my feet.

"Sorry about that. Are you all right?"

"Yeah, but it's my fault. I was thinking about what Flynn said."

"Joining him for dinner?" Jay teased. "He's persistent."

"Thanks for saving me, and yeah. He's more stubborn than my dad and Uncle Ross put together. You know how people get the seven-year itch in a marriage? I can't figure out why Flynn has an opposite seven-year itch going. Marriage in name only. Ha."

"Maybe because you're fun to be around, super nice, brainy, beautiful—want me to keep going?" He'd been ticking off each trait on his fingers with a wide grin. "Even if your sister did play matchmaker, I've been wanting to ask you out for a while. Hope you don't mind it came about this way. With the bear sculpture, I mean."

"Hey, boss. We're heading home," Joan called out. She, Hilda, and Evelyn blocked our way, sweaters and purses in hand. Embarrassed again, figuring they must have heard Jay's list of compliments, I swallowed hard. "Need help with anything, Sasha?"

"No, we're good. Thanks," I said, hating that fake cheerfulness in my voice.

Jay retrieved his boxes and tote bag. I dragged Mr. Silver past the staff into the large room. Flora Zimmerman examined a bear alongside Jessica North, who was new to the sewing staff. A petite blonde with bright blue eyes and a wide smile, she had a lively energy that gave Flora fits. Despite Jessica's background in sewing costumes for a university theater program, Flora always lectured the younger woman. I could tell Jessica was bored.

"Hey, J. J.! What are you doing here?" She laughed at Jay's obvious surprise. "Didn't you know I work here now? Huh."

"Glad to hear it." He sounded uneasy.

"What's in the boxes?"

"A project for the Oktobear Fest."

"Oh. A costume?" Jessica glanced at me with a broad smile. "I could have helped you, all you had to do is ask. You must be carving a lot lately. Haven't seen you around."

Jay nodded. "Yeah. Lots of commissions."

Flora marched out, clearly peeved that her advice had been cut short. While I lugged Mr. Silver over to the window, Jessica asked Jay several rapid-fire questions, which answered, friendly but reserved. He didn't explain much about his Jack Pine Bear, too. That was odd. And why hadn't he asked Jessica to sew the costume, given her experience? Hmm.

I thought back to the day Maddie showed me Jessica's application. We both figured she'd be a good fit for our staff, given how she broke a leg—a spiral fracture, the worst kind—in a skiing accident over the winter. With debts racking up, both medical and living expenses, Jessica decided to postpone pursuing her master's degree and took the job here. She also promised not to leave us short-staffed without giving at least a month's notice.

Self-conscious, I poked a stray strand of my long hair behind an ear. Jessica's natural wheat-hued pageboy cut perfectly framed her face. I really ought to get a new style at the local salon, and maybe even some highlights.

I stopped myself. Brother. I felt off-kilter, due to Holly Parker's return to Silver Hollow and a second murder, but those were pitiful excuses. While a trim wouldn't hurt, I didn't need to compete with any woman Jay had dated in the past.

"—at the Bonstelle, but the ski accident really messed me up," Jessica was explaining to Jay. "My parents didn't want me to go on that trip back in February. Said I'd have to figure out how to pay my bills and foot the rest of my degree's tuition."

"Wow. Sorry to hear that."

"Yeah. I guess I'd better go. We ought to get together sometime."

"Maybe so."

"I can show you all my photos from the last production I worked on at the Bonstelle. *Man of La Mancha,*" she added. "All those Spanish costumes! That was a ton of work."

Jay listened in silence while she rambled on about the skirts, the ruffles, the satin, and velvet. At last Jessica realized I'd checked the clock more than twice. With a smile for Jay, and a friendly wave at us both, Jessica headed for the door.

"Good luck."

Once the door shut behind her, Jay turned to me in relief. "Oh man. Sorry that took so long. I had no idea she worked here at the factory."

"Can I ask you something?"

"Sure."

I felt uneasy and hoped for an honest answer. Jay had relaxed since Jessica's departure, but I had to know why. "What happened between you two? And why didn't you ask her to sew the costume? Jessica has a lot more experience," I rushed on, preventing him from interrupting. "She could do it with her eyes closed and one hand tied behind her back."

Jay spread his hands in dismay. Large hands, I noted, with calluses and a few scars on one palm. "We dated last year. You heard her talking my ear off, and that was the problem. It was all about her. She craves attention."

"Really? All I know is she wants to be an actress."

"Yeah. And nothing else matters." He hunched his shoulders. "She wore me out, totally. It's hard being in a one-way relationship."

"Don't I know it," I said with a sigh. "Okay, I get it. Flynn's world doesn't include much besides his needs, his wants. So Jessica's the same?"

"You got it." Jay glanced at the framed photos of Grandpa T. R., my dad, Uncle Ross, and staff members lined up along the wall. "When I delivered the mailbox, I saw you with your sister and parents. Family means a lot to you. I can relate to that."

I smiled. "So you're close to your family, too."

"Yep. Dad spreads the word about my carvings, along with my sister. That's led to a lot of freelance jobs. You and Maddie have done the same."

"We've gotten such positive feedback on our mailbox. People love the mother bear and her cubs, so of course we tell everyone who carved it."

"Thanks. You've done a great job managing this shop for your parents. I figured we could share pointers. While we're getting to know each other, of course. If that's okay."

"Sure. But it's getting late, and this project might be trickier than I thought."

"Let's get rolling."

Jay opened the boxes first. I had to admit he'd found a nice haul at the thrift shops. Taking the largest pair of jeans, I marked with chalk where extra material needed to be added on either side of the front zipper fly and leg seams. Then I did the same to the red plaid flannel button-down shirtfront; extending the collar to fit the bear's thick neck would be difficult if not impossible. We measured Mr. Silver's fluffy neck and compared the numbers to the fiberglass sculpture's measurements. Wow. Not as far off as I'd expected.

"Now to sketch out a plan." I measured and drew pattern pieces, allowing for extra in the seams. The front door's buzzer startled us both. "That can't be Maddie, she has a key."

I rushed to the hallway and yanked the door open. Detective Mason stood there, hands in his pockets, in a rumpled suit, shirt, and tie. "Your sister said I'd find you both here."

"Come in," I said, although my heart sank. What did he want with me? Or had he come to question Jay? "I haven't heard anything more about Gina."

"I have a few questions for you and Kirby." He lumbered ahead down the hall. Dread filled me when I followed. Mason gave a thumbs-up when he spotted Jay on a stool by the worktable. "Hope I'm not interrupting something important."

"We're making a costume for his Bears on Parade sculpture," I said quickly.

Mason pulled out another stool. "Gotcha. I asked Maddie to join us. She had something to take care of first, so we'll wait. Shouldn't take too long."

I glanced at Jay, who shrugged. After a few minutes of awkward silence, Maddie strolled in with two large paper sacks from La Mesa, the local Mexican hole-in-the-wall. The tempting scents of refried beans, melted cheese, and seasoned ground beef wafted my way. We unpacked the Styrofoam containers of tacos, burritos, quesadillas, chips, and salsa. Maddie also brought four bottles of water from the house.

"I know Sasha didn't have lunch. Please join us, Detective," she added.

Mason flipped through his notebook. "Thanks, but I'm not hungry."

Maddie pushed a container his way. "There's plenty."

He gave in, devouring a taco in two bites. "Wow. Not bad. Okay, here's the thing. I heard about a fishing trip, up north near Traverse City. Were you there, Kirby?"

Jay nodded. "Yeah. We take an annual trip over Memorial Day. Four or five guys."

"So how exactly did Officer Sykes lose or misplace his knife?"

Jay glanced at me, clearly puzzled. "Oh. We figured he dropped it in the lake. Digger had it on the boat. I remember seeing him with it, cutting his fishing line."

"So when did he claim it was gone?" Mason asked.

"No idea. The next time Digger needed it, he couldn't find it."

"Wait," I said, my suspicions aroused. "Are you saying Digger's knife was used to kill Gina? No joke?"

"And how do you know for sure it's his knife?" Maddie asked.

The detective shrugged. "No initials are carved or stamped on it, if that's what you mean. But he identified it as his."

I did a double take. "Maybe that's why Digger almost grabbed it, early Sunday morning, before we stopped him."

"And the only prints we found on the weapon belong to Officer Sykes."

Chapter 13

My sister choked. "Why would Digger kill Gina Lawson?"
"I never said he did." Mason drank half a bottle of water.
"Office Sykes admitted he'd recognized his knife, and almost interfered with evidence at the crime scene."

"Maybe someone is setting him up," Jay said, "although that seems a stretch. He lost the knife back at the end of May. That's a while ago."

"I'm taking that into consideration." He poised his pencil on the paper. "Who else was with you on this trip? And where in Michigan?"

"Lake Leelanau. Me, Kip O'Sullivan, Digger, his brother Larry, Matt Cooper—"

"Our cousin Matt?" Maddie cut in. "I didn't know he likes to fish."

I choked back a laugh. "He doesn't. Matt uses it as a convenient excuse. Elle complained about that trip in June. Her family had a reunion that weekend, but he chose to join the guys up north. Boy, did that set off fireworks. Elle had to take both girls on a plane by herself to South Dakota. That wasn't easy. Matt was in the doghouse for weeks."

"I didn't know that," Jay said. "Garrett Thompson also joined us. And Sean Jones. The seven of us went fishing. Sean fished with Digger, then Kip and me, and Larry was with Garrett, who has the most patience of all of us."

"Larry sweeps floors at the Quick Mix factory," I said to Mason, hoping he'd understand the sensitive situation. Mason kept writing without comment. "He's very sweet, but he doesn't always understand things. Larry is very aware of things people might miss, however."

"He's a whiz with baseball stats," Maddie said with a smile. "He can reel off a ton of them better than the TV or radio announcers."

"We met a few other guys from the area," Jay added. "They'd rented a cabin, while we had tents. Sean Jones is a volunteer fireman here, by the way. He works at the Quick Mix factory full time, too."

I finished my burrito. "So anyone could have taken that knife. But why would whoever took it set up Digger for suspicion of murder?"

"There you go again, jumping to conclusions," Mason said. "What I need are hard facts. By the way, Kirby, where were you Saturday night?"

Startled, Jay repeated what he'd told me—not word for word, but close enough. The detective wrote it all down and then rose to his feet. "Okay. If you learn anything else, let me know. Here's my card, one for each of you. And thanks."

Once the door swung shut behind him, Maddie pounced on Jay. "So what happened on that fishing trip? I bet Digger thought Larry took his knife, didn't he?"

Jay looked pained. "Yeah, that's true. Gave his brother hell, but the poor guy kept saying he didn't touch it. Come to think of it, Matt lost his knife on the same trip."

"Whoa. Two knives went missing?" I wiped my clammy palms on my jeans. "That can't be a coincidence. Maybe you should have told Mason."

"I forgot until now. It does seem suspicious."

"It's crazy that someone would take a knife over Memorial Day weekend, save it over the summer, and then use it to stab Gina Lawson," Maddie said. "I mean, she didn't start working for Holly until last month."

I pointed in Jay's direction. "Mason's got you on the suspect list for going on that fishing trip. Now he'll ask everyone else for an alibi, too. But maybe whoever took that knife didn't know it was Digger's and just happened to use it. Out of convenience."

"Hey." Maddie snapped her fingers. "Remember how Digger gave Holly Parker a few parking tickets while she was moving stock into the new shop. So what if Holly killed Gina, and she used that knife so he'd get the blame?"

"But how would she get his knife?" I asked. "Holly didn't go with them over Memorial Day weekend. Right, Jay?"

He laughed. "No way. No wives or girlfriends allowed."

"Like Mason says, let the cops figure things out." I waved a hand at the worktable. "So let's get back to the clothes for Jack Pine Bear, or we'll never get finished."

Jay helped Maddie and me when we cleared the empty food containers and dumped them into the trash. "What do we do first?" he asked.

"Cut." I fetched the scissors. "First the pattern, and then the fabric pieces. Are you sticking around to help, Mads?"

"Only if you need me."

"Okay, you're in charge of pinning."

I took a deep breath and cut the pattern shapes. Jay fetched a dozen packages of Velcro from the canvas tote; Maddie searched the sewing area for a box of pins and then fastened the cut pattern pieces to fabric. Next she basted the shirt while I worked on the jeans.

"We can always take in any extra material," I said. "But we can't add more if we don't plan for it. Let's hope Jay brought enough clothing."

A cell phone rang. "That's Kip," Maddie said, and dug in her pocket. "Hey—right now? Okay, I'll be right over. Yeah, sure. No problem."

I laughed at her guilty look. "Go on and help him. It's okay."

"He's freaking out over a mistake he made painting the bear's back. Says it doesn't look right. I'll have to help him fix it. Good thing he's using acrylic."

"Tell Kip I'll beat him getting my bear done," Jay said. "That should egg him on and make him work faster."

"He's had so many distractions. Prepping for his classes, teaching, and students coming around asking for help." Maddie sighed. "I have no idea if the Hippie Bear will ever get done. But I won't worry if he's not worried."

"You sound worried," I said. "I know that tone of yours, and that little furrow between your eyes. And the way you're sitting, all tense and hunched over."

"Okay, I am worried. Kip won't listen. He keeps saying he's got plenty of time, but only the bear's front is done. And he's on Saturday's schedule."

"Is he painting the arms and legs brown, like fur? That would be pretty cool."

"Yeah, but it's already Tuesday and it takes a few days to seal it." Maddie waved a hand. "My Polka Bear should be dry by now. It's in the back here. Why not use it and see how Jack Pine's clothes fit together? It would be better than using squishy Mr. Silver."

"Good idea. Thanks."

Once my sister left, Jay took over basting—with an occasional muffled curse. Once he finished, we walked past all the bins of bears, around the long tables Deon and Tim used to box and ship orders. Metal shelves held flattened boxes, rolls of paper for stuffing around items, bubble wrap, plastic bags, mailing tape, labels, and other miscellaneous items. Maddie's Polka Bear stood half-hidden behind the tall crate where we stashed our largest bears.

I almost shrieked in delight, seeing the rainbow of polka dots over the standing bear. The accordion hung between its outstretched paws. "Aww, this bear is so adorable." I moved the bellows while lightly fingering the keyboard, which produced a loud wheeze. "Cool!"

Jay held up the basted shirt pieces. "Ready?"

While I slid the buttoned shirt front around the body, he stretched the back pieces to meet mine. We could have used a third pair of hands to mark how we needed to fit them, but somehow managed. We had a harder time wrapping the arm pieces and staying clear of the accordion.

"Maybe we should roll up the sleeves," I said.

"That might be the answer," Jay said. "I can paint tan-colored fur on his arms that way, make him look more real."

"You'll have to do his face to match, though. That's a lot of work. And you can't be too picky like Kip, because Maddie's right. Time is really short."

"Yeah, but it will look better in the long run."

"Let's do the jeans now."

I handed him the front piece, with the zipper fly, and then repeated the same mark-up on the denim sections for the sides. The backside with its pockets proved harder; Jay lost his grip several times, or I did, while we figured out where to join the material around one leg of the bear. I finally gave up, trusting to instinct. My arms ached, and so did my fingers after I pinned the Velcro strips to the thick material's edge.

"Finally ready to sew." I straightened my stiff shoulders.

"Uncle Ross told me Velcro is a combination of velvet and crochet. Doesn't that sound wacky?"

Jay retrieved his phone. "Hmm. I'll google it."

He followed me back to the industrial machines. I sat down, hoping I didn't look or act as nervous as I felt, and began sewing seams. Each time I came to a pin, I slid it out and fed the material with its Velcro strip under the machine's needle. I had to sew each side, however, which took time. My eyes hurt from concentrating so hard.

"So I guess it was invented by some Swiss guy," Jay said.

"When he was walking his dog, my uncle said. The guy saw burrs stuck over his clothes and came up with the idea. I bet he made a fortune."

"He did." Jay held up his cell to show me. "George de Mestral, a 'Swiss engineer and amateur mountaineer,' filed a patent in nineteen fifty-five."

"Wish I'd thought of it. I'm sorry this is taking forever." I peered closer at the machine while the material inched forward. "I'd rather not break a needle. I'd be done for then. I've never figured out how to replace one on these things. Anyway, I bet George's dog had plenty of burrs, too. Rosie always gets them."

"The only idea I ever came up with was a coffee bag. Like a tea bag but with coffee, back when I was a kid. My mom loves tea, but Dad drinks coffee—so I thought it might be easier, you know? Few months later, my mom found 'em for sale at the grocery store."

"Too bad. A lot better than instant coffee, I bet."

Jay opened the next package of Velcro and handed me the strips. "Now I can see why Maddie's so worried about whether those duct tape straps holding the accordion will last. They do look fragile on the paws."

"Yeah. Some of the paint's flaked off, too, and I hope nobody will notice. But people are bound to try playing it." I set aside the finished piece and selected the next one. "Maybe Mary Kate and her staff at Fresh Grounds will keep an eye on the bear, and tell Maddie if the straps come loose."

Jay stepped up, helping to guide the fabric toward the needle and not let it get bunched up while I sewed. "We'll see what happens tomorrow night."

"Yeah, the big reveal."

I couldn't wait to see what other artists had created. This month seemed to be flying by, with the Cran-beary Tea Party, the first night of the Bears on Parade, and the Hide the Bears in the Orchard event this weekend at Richardson's Farms. Gina's murder added to the craziness.

The machine whirred while I thought about other possibilities. Had Digger met Gina at some point, and she'd rejected him? What if he'd taken revenge? I'd heard Maddie mention how he often acted desperate with women. But Cal Bloom might be desperate, too.

"What if Mayor Bloom didn't want to face that lawsuit in court—"

"What's that?" Jay interrupted. He'd scrambled to retrieve a few fallen pins.

I laughed. "Sorry. Talking aloud to myself. But I can't help wondering where the mayor was on Saturday night. My mom thinks he wouldn't hurt a fly."

Jay rubbed his neck. "I have a hard time believing anyone would resort to murder."

"You and me both." I sighed and started sewing the shirt pieces. "Have you ever hunted deer in the fall? Bow or rifle?"

"Nope, not into that. Just sport fishing. Golf, too." He tested the bear's denim pants, pressing the Velcro strips together and then tearing them apart with a satisfying *r-r-rip*. "Looks like these will hold together. I'd say the costume will look amazing on my bear."

"But not without this!" Aunt Eve strolled into the large

room, waving a plastic bag in one hand. She pulled out a huge, bulky, navy blue knitted cap. "The pièce de résistance. So you're Jay Kirby, the carpenter and wood-carver?"

"Pleased to meet you." He walked forward to shake her hand. "Thanks for helping."

"You're so welcome!"

I introduced my aunt. "Eve Silverman, formerly married to Uncle Ross. And none of us in the family blames her for divorcing him. That hat looks fabulous."

"I'm happy to help out any way I can. I love the shop's mailbox," she said to Jay. "Tell me all about your wood carvings. I've heard you do commissions."

They chatted while I worked on the shirt, a little faster this time since the material was easier to feed under the needle. "Okay, you two," I said when I finished. "Let's use Maddie's bear and see if we need to adjust anything. Come on."

They followed me to the shop's back. Once we dressed the Polka Bear—sort of, since the jeans proved a little too generous in fabric, and we had a struggle in rolling up the flannel sleeves—we stood back to admire our handiwork. The sculpture's polka dots looked odd, but Jay and I fist-bumped our success. The shirt fit almost perfect.

"I could sew another strip of Velcro on the jeans, and we could move the seam over to fit the legs better. I doubt if anyone would notice the bulk," I said.

"Or maybe I could find a belt instead of making you do all that extra work."

"You could use twine," Aunt Eve suggested. "I doubt you'd find a leather strap that long anyway. A frayed rope. That would add to the rugged look."

I clapped my hands. "I love that idea! Let's try the hat."

The knitted cap slid sideways off the bear's slippery head. Every time I adjusted it, the hat slithered the other way. We all laughed.

"Maybe I should have included holes for the ears," Aunt Eve said.

Jay leaned back. "I can always glue it on, like I did the boots. Looks like we might have to roll up the jeans or tuck the extra material into the boot tops. I expected the pants might end up too short, but that's not the case."

"The height is mostly from the waist up, that's why," I said. "Good thing there's extra material around him, because I forgot about the tail. Do you want me to cut a hole for it?"

"Nah. It looks fine."

"How about fastening an ax into the bear's hand—or paw?"

"I had an ax in the original design," Jay said, "but the committee rejected all weapons. Can't say I blame them. There's a log or two around the barn at my parent's house. I could attach a chain to one end, and then stretch it over one arm down to his paw, like he's dragging it. That might be rejected, too, so I'll ask first."

"I think you'd better undress that bear," Aunt Eve said. "It's long past midnight, and I'm going to bed. High time you both called it quits."

"Can I pay you for knitting the hat?" Jay asked.

"No, no. That was fun, and I didn't have any other plans for the yarn. Good night!"

"And I've got an early meeting." I winced at the Velcro's ripping sounds when we took the shirt off. The stitches held, however, even at the fabric's worn spots. Both items of clothing came free without any damage to the seams or to Maddie's bear. "I wasn't so sure about this one area. The flannel's so faded and threadbare. Thank goodness it didn't fall apart."

"I won't have time to look for any matching shirt fabric, so I hope it holds."

"So I heard the artists had to find a sponsor to pay for the sculpture, right? My parents paid for Maddie's. How much did the bears cost, if you don't mind me asking?"

"Twelve hundred bucks." He laughed at my shocked expression. "Fiberglass isn't cheap, which is why they mix it with resin. My dad paid for Jack Pine, because he wants to display it at my brother's lumberyard near Chelsea."

"That's how you got the idea for a Lumberjack Bear, then."

Jay nodded. "So how about dinner on Friday night?"

I folded up the clothing, fetched the unused Velcro, and packed it into a box. "Tomorrow works better, or next week. You've got to seal the costume's seams, remember. I'll be out at Richardson's Farms on Saturday. There's hayrides, face painting, a pumpkin patch, all the usual stuff for fall. We're doing an event for younger kids with teddy bears."

"My sister volunteered to help. Last year she was a zombie in the haunted cellar," he said with a wry grin. "Lauren's younger than Maddie."

"I've never met her."

"She's not around much. Studying to be either an EMT or a paramedic, although she might change her mind again."

"Nice." I handed him the empty tote bag. "I had fun tonight."

"Me too. And thanks again."

Maddie met us in the hallway on our way out, panting for breath. "We're done," I said. "How did it work out with Kip's bear?"

"Don't ask. See you tomorrow night, Jay."

"Sure thing, and good night."

We walked Jay out to the parking lot and then headed toward the house. His truck's headlights shone bright, and he waited until we were safe inside. The kitchen was dark, with only a dim light over the sink. I turned to my sister.

"Do you think there's any chance Digger knew Gina Lawson? Before she moved here to Silver Hollow, I mean. Maybe at college?"

"He graduated from a criminal justice program at Wayne State. Oh!"

"What?"

"Abby told me Gina worked at Wayne State for some professor. What if they had met?" Maddie chewed her thumb. "I know he's afraid Mason will arrest him."

"What's this about an arrest?" Mom loomed in the doorway, one finger holding her place in a hardcover book. I let Maddie explain what Detective Mason told us about the fingerprints. "Great! That means Flynn's innocent. I told you so, Sasha."

"I wouldn't say he's in the clear," I said, "but Mason's suspect list tripled in size."

Mom looked confused, so Maddie explained next about the fishing trip and the group of friends who had access to Digger's knife. "Not that anyone swiped it on purpose," she said, "but Mason will have to find out what happened, if he can. Who knows how that knife ended up in the hands of the murderer."

"Well, Flynn wouldn't have taken it." Mom sniffed. "People have been accusing him to his face that he killed Gina. He's worked so hard to become the area's top attorney. He doesn't deserve such abuse."

I snorted. "He just moved here. How can he be the area's top attorney?"

"You're so biased, you wouldn't believe anything I said about Flynn. As for Jay Kirby, he doesn't impress me at all."

"Because you don't like the mailbox he designed?"

"No, that's not why, for heaven's sake." She shrugged. "I don't see much potential in someone who carves wood for a living, compared to Flynn's career."

"Jay and I are friends, Mom. Why don't you work on getting Uncle Ross and Aunt Eve back together," I suggested. "And let Flynn worry about his career."

"Your father doesn't think much of that carpenter, either." Mom marched upstairs.

Puzzled, I turned to Maddie. "Why would she say that about Dad? Did he mention Jay to you since he got back from up north?"

"Mom's yanking your chain, Sash. Forget it. I already let Rosie out, too."

With a tired wave, my sister climbed the steps. It burned me that Mom was so defensive of Flynn, so eager to help him. For some odd reason, she'd taken his side. But Dad? He always thought the best of people, even Will Taylor. He'd given our sales rep chance after chance, and in the end Will's betrayal had stung. My poor father had shrugged it off, though. Unwilling to let such things haunt him. Unlike me.

Maybe Maddie was right. Mom was crazy, and trying to upset me. It didn't take much.

Rosie wagged her tail at the top of the stairs, whining a little, ready for bed. I joined her and followed to the bedroom. Opened the window farther, slid under the covers, lay there and contemplated why I couldn't be more like Dad. Shake it off, I kept telling myself. It doesn't matter. Jay was sweet, and he wanted a relationship. That had to be a good thing.

But I wasn't happy.

Chapter 14

"What's it supposed to be?" My mother stared at the fiberglass bear which stood near the Time Turner shop, painted a deep navy and covered with white stars.

"'The Starry Night Bear,'" I read aloud from the glossy flyer the committee had printed for the event. "'All the constellations and zodiac signs are related to the universe and time.' So that must be why they chose this location for it."

Mom waved a hand in dismissal. "Where's the next one?"

Dave Fox popped up from behind the sculpture. "Excuse me." He snapped a photo of the Starry Night Bear with his Nikon professional camera and then hurried off.

I scanned the large crowd across the street. "Let's head to Fresh Grounds. Maddie's sculpture will be unveiled in about twenty minutes."

"It's too crowded over there." Mom shaded her eyes from the sun sinking lower toward the west and then walked in the opposite direction. "I want to see the Legal Eagle Bear at the courthouse. Flynn should be there, too."

Sighing, I followed. Why was I surprised by that? I saw

Mark Branson, Mary Kate's brother, standing beside Mike Blake and a man with frizzy gray hair and a beard. By his T-shirt, emblazoned with DETROIT ARTISTS MARKET, I figured he must have painted the Legal Eagle Bear. He wore thick black-framed glasses, sandals, and cargo shorts, and used his hands a lot while talking. He also had a boisterous laugh that made everyone around him smile.

"Mom, watch out!"

A car barreling down Archibald Street almost hit her. Oblivious to danger, she stepped onto the curb and smoothed her auburn hair. I wished I'd caught the license plate number. The cops should have closed this area of the village to traffic, for that matter, given the groups of people standing on every corner. Everyone strolled casually back and forth across streets, too. Despite that, most cars didn't slow down.

Dave Fox arranged the artist beside the Legal Eagle Bear and took several photos, and then motioned for Blake and Branson to stand on either side for more shots. The crowd gathered around to admire the fabulous paint job with a cartoonish bent; the bear "wore" a three-piece suit and a gold chain across the vest, plus wing-tip shoes. The light brown paint on its head simulated an Ivy League haircut with a side part. But real spectacles perched on the bear's nose and a tan leather briefcase had been attached to one paw.

I read aloud again from the flyer's inner page. " 'The Legal Eagle Bear by Jim Perry. A nod to fashionably suited lawyers who must uphold the rule of law, suitable or not.' Oh, that's good. I like this guy and his work."

"Perry's a jerk." Kip O'Sullivan had startled me when he appeared at my shoulder. "So what if he's a big-shot painter? I think Maddie's Polka Bear is ten times better."

"Perry teaches at Cranbrook and the Birmingham Bloomfield Art Center, plus at Center for Creative Studies near the DIA. He's won a lot of awards."

"He's full of hot air. Worse than Holly Parker," Kip added, and then flicked his nose a few times with a thumb. "Saw her a few minutes ago, brown-nosing Mayor Bloom. I heard she might be running for village council in November."

"That's true," Mom said. "Barbara Davison heard the same thing."

I barely heard them, too busy admiring the Legal Eagle Bear. I didn't care what Holly did or how jealous Kip was of Jim Perry. I liked the paint job and subtle dig at lawyers' professional ethics. My dad had never manipulated the law like many of his colleagues, who benefited from shady deals. He'd left after a particularly stressful time, helping to uncover a decade of political corruption that ran amok at multi-county and state levels.

Dad regained his sanity and purpose after founding the Silver Bear Shop.

"Hey, thanks for coming tonight!" Maddie joined us, in a white lace sundress, sky blue cardigan, and long silver earrings that swayed with every move, her short hair sleek. "Don't you love this bear? Jim Perry has paintings displayed in several Detroit galleries."

"What did he say about your bear?" I asked.

"Kitschy, but I don't mind. It's meant to be that way."

"You wouldn't recognize an insult if it slapped you in the face," Kip said, frowning.

"He didn't insult me—"

"Sure, sure. And I'm Vincent van Gogh."

"You should be working on your Hippie Bear," Maddie retorted. "Every day you come up with a different excuse not to finish it. Maybe you're doing it on purpose."

When she flounced off, Kip raced after her. "Come on, babe. I didn't mean it."

Uh-oh. Sounded like trouble in paradise to my ears. I groaned aloud, since Mom stood chatting with Flynn, Mike

Blake, and his pregnant wife. Lisa looked more uncomfortable than she had at the Cran-beary Tea Party last Saturday. She headed to a bench and sank down, clearly tired, and checked her cell phone.

Before I could join her, Holly Parker wove her way through the crowd and parked beside her with a thud. "I've been on my feet all day! I bet you're twice as miserable."

"I've got another month." Lisa slid her phone in a pocket. "Last baby, for sure."

"Give me running a business any day than being chauffeur, maid, and cook."

"It's not so bad."

"Bite your tongue," Holly chided her. "You always wanted to be the little mother and housewife. Not me. I can't stand the idea. My career is too important."

I turned away and saw Dad walking toward Fresh Grounds with Gil Thompson. In my rush to overtake them, the breeze fluttered my skirt, à la Marilyn Monroe over the steam grate. I grabbed a handful and held the fabric tight against my thigh.

"I knew I should have worn jeans. Dang."

Dad and Gil joined Maddie near her bear, still covered with a white cotton sheet. Amy Evans, petite at five foot two with her dark hair pulled into a bun, wore a navy pantsuit and a name tag spelling out EVENT COORDINATOR. She stuck two fingers in her mouth and gave a high-pitched whistle. Once the crowd fell silent, Amy adjusted the earpiece wired to a voice amplifier stuck in her front pocket. She fiddled with a button while flashing a broad smile.

"Our second-to-last reveal tonight is Madeline Silverman's Polka Bear. Please do not touch the musical instrument on this bear, or any other sculpture's props," she said. "Thank you for your cooperation. All right, is everyone ready?"

Kip and Maddie must have resolved their spat. He slowly drew aside the cotton fabric to reveal Maddie's bear on the sidewalk between The Cat's Cradle and Fresh Grounds. The colorful polka dots glistened in the sun. My sister beamed at the crowd's enthusiastic clapping. Once Dave Fox arranged a photo for his *Silver Hollow Herald,* Mom rushed over. She hugged Maddie and praised the paint job and accordion. Dad squeezed her hand.

"So proud of you, Mad-a-lean, my little Jumping Bean."

"Aw, thanks."

"It's wonderful, Mads." I crushed my sister in a big hug.

"Family photo op," Dave Fox called. He snapped a picture of us gathered on either side of Maddie and shooed my sister away. "Go talk to your fans."

She gave a nervous laugh and walked over to the knot of people with questions. After a few minutes, I plucked the sleeve of Dad's white golf shirt and beckoned him away. We had to retreat past the beauty salon before we could hear each other. Dad's gaze darted around the crowd, so I waited several minutes until he focused his attention on me.

"What's up, Alley Bear?"

I felt like a kid, repeating my mother's words last night, but I'd been fretting all day. Hearing Dad's pet name for me didn't help, either. "I thought it sounded odd. Maybe she didn't mean to let it slip—"

"Sasha, stop." He clapped his large hands on my shoulders. "You ought to know me better than that. Jay's a decent guy. Your mother and I never discussed Jay or even Kip, for that matter. You girls have to decide for yourselves, and I trust your judgment. As for your mother, I've given up trying to figure out why she says or does certain things."

"I wish she'd give up on Flynn."

"Tell me about it." Dad let go and nodded to several villagers passing by before he spoke again. "Judith complained all summer about his cheating ways, and how unfair that was to you. But now she's done a three-sixty and acts like his biggest fan."

I laughed, my relief washing all my self-doubt and vulnerability away. "Maybe Mom is dying to take part in those 'Flynn Wins' TV commercials."

"Are you kidding? Good Lord." He rubbed his face with one hand. "That could be why she's looking to buy a house near his. Anything else bothering you?"

"Gina's murder, for one thing."

Dad nodded. "Yeah, Cal Bloom told me all about the detective questioning him about where he was Saturday night, over and over."

"So is the mayor a suspect?" I asked, but he shook his head.

"Linda and Cal had invited another couple over to play cards. They all stayed up till long past midnight, so that seemed to satisfy Mason. Good thing, too."

"Why is that? Because he didn't pay her what she wanted?"

"That's only part of it," Dad said. "Cal admitted threatening her, and his staff overheard him. Not the kind of thing you want on record, but he lost his temper. Said he'd never give her a red cent, and she deserved to rot in hell for being so greedy. Or something like that."

"Wow. That does sound ominous."

"Remember, there's no such thing as privacy. Someone's always listening."

No wonder Mason put the mayor on the hot seat. I folded my arms over my chest. "I do remember when Mom's Minky Bear was stolen from the house, and how the police couldn't find any evidence of a break-in. Or fingerprints on the shelves or anything. But Mason found Minky in a box, stored in the back of Holly's new toy and bookstore."

"Really? I can tell you one thing. If it has anything to do with this murder, Detective Mason will figure it out. He's sharp. Now come on, let's get back to the Polka Bear."

We walked arm in arm toward Fresh Grounds. Maddie stood with Kip, Mary Kate and Garrett Thompson, plus a few other friends. Jay waved at me, looking pleased, in his usual casual jeans and dusty T-shirt.

"—twice the number of people coming in today than yesterday," Mary Kate was saying, "and I bet more people will come by to see it all week. We're proud of you, Maddie, and happy the Bears on Parade committee chose this spot near our shop."

"I bribed Amy, that's why," Maddie said with a laugh. "Since there's no music store in the village, she agreed polka music might fit with a quirky coffee shop."

"We've been playing polka tunes off and on all day, piped through the speakers," Garrett said. "I thought people would figure out why after they read the flyer. But no, we've had to explain the reason multiple times."

"Elle is sorry she couldn't be here," Mary Kate explained. "It's Meet the Teacher Night at Cara's school, and Matt's covering the shop for her."

Amy Evans gave another shrill whistle. "Let's go on to the next bear, which will be unveiled in"—she glanced at her wrist watch—"ten minutes. Over by Quinn's Pub. The Fish Bear, by an artist from Plymouth, with a fisherman in a boat painted on the bear's back. Follow me if you want to see the unveiling!"

She race-walked down the street. Most of the crowd trailed after her, although a few stragglers remained behind. Mary Kate, jiggling her restless toddler in her arms, stepped closer to the Polka Bear and pointed out the dots.

"See, Julia? Look at the pretty colors. Red, blue, green, orange. I love the accordion, Maddie," she said. "Is it true you found it at a resale shop, Kip?"

"A Salvation Army store, actually." He drew Maddie close. "I told you it would look terrific, babe! Taping the straps worked."

"One edge is already loose," she said, and pointed it out.

"You can have that toxic stuff I used for my bear's boots," Jay said. "Wear a mask, or even a scuba diver's oxygen tank. Lethal, I tell you."

"I don't think it's gonna come off." Kip sounded stubborn, but he must have noticed my sister's unhappiness. "Okay, I'll do it if you really want me to, but I've got classes tomorrow and Friday. It can wait until after that."

Maddie shrugged. "Sure, whatever."

She exchanged a meaningful glance with Jay. I knew that look. Maddie had no intention of waiting for Kip, and she also broke free of his possessive hold around her waist. That was another certain sign of trouble. What was going on? I'd have to ask her later.

"You really should get back to your bear," Maddie said to Kip. "I'll come later to help once things wind down here."

"First I'm going to see the Fish Bear. I parked down by Quinn's," Kip added. "Catch you later, Jay. Congrats, babe, because yours is the best sculpture today."

He planted a kiss on her and then strolled off, hands in the pockets of his ratty jeans. Jay avoided my questioning look. And Maddie was busy greeting Abby Pozniak, who arrived to admire the Polka Bear. My curiosity would have to wait.

"Way cool, Mads," Abby gushed. "I love that accordion."

"A bear with polka dots. How—quaint." Holly Parker appeared behind Jay and eyed the tall sculpture. She pushed hard against the accordion's bellows. The instrument wheezed. "Oh, too bad it's off-key."

"People aren't supposed to touch the sculptures," I said.

"I didn't. Just the accordion." Holly's sly smile aggravated me, and she fixed her gaze on Jay. "I hear you're one of the artists in the Bears on Parade tonight."

"Actually, not till next Wednesday." He sounded aloof.

"And you'll be at Richardson's Farms, Sasha," she said

next, swiveling to stare at me. "A teddy bear giveaway, or something like that."

"Good luck with the face painting." I turned to Jay. "Ready to go?"

"Sure."

He led the way down Main Street to the corner. Before we crossed at the light, we heard a prolonged wail from the Polka Bear's accordion. I twisted around, but Holly had vanished. The instrument now dangled by one strap.

"What the—"

"I've got it, Sasha!" Mary Kate had rushed out of the coffee shop and waved to us. "I'll have Garrett wire it back into place until Maddie can fix it."

"I am so tempted to pull Holly's arm out of her socket," I muttered.

"Temper, temper." Jay laughed. "I don't blame you, though. I'd pull her other one out, and break her nose for good measure. But my parents taught me girls were off-limits."

"Oh?" I flashed a teasing smile. "In that case—"

"Ha. Not that way." He drew me into a tight hug, right in front of the tiny Mexican diner, and brushed his lips against mine. "There. I didn't get a chance to thank you last night. I owe you a lot more than that, too."

I'd felt a spark at his kiss, despite its short duration. "All this success is going to your head, Jay Kirby. Is your new Oktobear Fest sign ready?"

"Yeah, finished it Monday. The committee wants to install it this Saturday, too."

"How about carving a new sign for our business? I'd love to come and watch you work on it at your studio." I poked him in the chest. "So is dinner on the menu tonight? Too bad Ham Heaven's closed. How about a burger?"

"Yeah, I'm starving." Jay nodded toward the pub across

Kermit Street, where the noisy crowd milled around the Fish Bear. "We'll have to run the gauntlet, though."

"Eyes on the prize, like Quinn's terrific onion rings."

We threaded our way around the surge of people still chatting with the artist, including Kip, who didn't seem in any hurry to get home and finish his own bear. Twilight descended, which sent most of the crowd home. Jay led me to the pub; loud music blared the moment he opened the rustic door. My eyes had trouble adjusting to the dim interior. My ears throbbed, too, from the pounding rhythm. In a far corner, the rock band's drummer and a screaming singer churned out a Bob Seger song. I recognized Emily Abbott on bass by her Goth attire.

A gum-snapping waitress led the way to a booth in another room, although we could still hear the music. Jay raised his voice. "Kinda hot. Must be from all the people."

I laughed, since this area was almost empty. "They must have turned off the A/C."

"Want me to come back?" the waitress asked.

"Burger with Swiss, well done. Onion rings, and—a Pilsner," I added.

Jay waved a finger. "Same burger, fries instead, and a Midwest IPA."

Once she departed, I watched a willowy young woman emerge from the restroom. Her slinky Hawaiian-print dress swished with every hip wiggle when she passed our table. She wore four- or five-inch designer heels, a row of silver and gold bangles on one arm, and had flowing black curls rippling down her back. She slid into a booth. The man with her straightened, his cell in hand, his blond hair unmistakable. My jaw dropped.

"Something wrong?" Jay tapped my hand. "You look like you've seen a ghost."

"Not exactly. Now I know who my ex, Flynn Hanson, is

dating." I hooked a thumb in their booth's direction. "Why does she look so familiar?"

He twisted his head for a quick look and then whistled low. "I've seen her on one of the local TV channels. Isn't she a weather forecaster?"

"You're right! Cheryl Cummings, I think that's her name. Maybe they're—" I stopped, since Flynn leaned over to kiss her. "Hmm, more than friends. He must have been with her the night Gina was killed. I bet she wants to avoid getting involved in any way."

"Yeah, it might affect her job at the station."

I wondered what Mom thought of Cheryl, or if she even knew about her. Then again, if she didn't, that crazy idea of resurrecting my marriage, in name only, might make sense. Had Cheryl refused to give him an alibi? Maybe Flynn was lying. What if he'd met Gina on Saturday night and argued about their breakup? Had he lost his temper? I couldn't picture him with a knife in his hand, though. He couldn't be that desperate.

And he'd never been violent with me. Flynn couldn't stomach the sight of blood. But Gina would not have been happy, finding out he'd dumped her to be with Cheryl. Drop-dead gorgeous, arm-candy in style and social grace, worthy to host parties and dinners at the huge, elegant house in Ann Arbor. Gina might be talented and "great," but Flynn had refused her demands for an engagement ring. She hadn't been good enough to marry.

Yet Gina wouldn't let Cal Bloom off the hook. Being her lawyer, Flynn was a party to it and knew how far she'd intended to go to make him pay. What if Gina had threatened Cheryl? Would Flynn risk everything to protect his new flame? I'd never understood the way his mind worked, and his ego ruled him in every way. Maybe my ex had taken a fateful misstep.

If so, Mason would nail him to the wall.

Chapter 15

On Saturday morning, Maddie drove east along River Street out of Silver Hollow. "At least it's not raining," my sister said. "It's going to be hot, though—"

"Hey, slow down a little. I want to see something. Thanks."

Keeping a tight grip on my Mint Mocha from Fresh Grounds, I leaned out the open window. The brick Queen Anne–style house with its front gable, etched glass windows, and a large porch came into view. I'd always wondered why Mike Blake and Mark Branson chose it as the Legal Eagles' offices, being so far from downtown. Jay's carved sign was off to one side so it wouldn't detract from the architecture. But it certainly had the wow factor.

"Look at that huge eagle! Jay did that."

"Yeah, I've seen it before. Nice."

"Nice? Is that all you can say?" I rolled up the window, given the dust cloud that spiraled up after we crossed the wide cement bridge. The dirt road leading to Richardson's Farms beyond the village limits needed grading. Every bump and rut jarred my sister's small car. "You don't sound that impressed."

"Jay's very talented. Everyone knows that, but Kip thinks he should move to Ann Arbor, or Chicago. He'd get more jobs and make a ton of money. No, don't start arguing with me— it's his opinion. Not mine." Maddie slowed the car again and avoided a huge pothole. "I'm hoping for your sake that Jay sticks around. It's high time you got laid."

"Gee, thanks."

"Are you sure we have the right number of bears?"

"You didn't give me the order till last night," I said crossly. "I stuffed all of them into separate plastic bags this morning while you overslept. Now we need more?"

"Aunt Eve forgot to give me the invoice until Thursday, and I forgot to give it to you. The last few all-nighters with Kip have really worn me out." Maddie turned onto the road that led to the large parking lot. "Maybe we have enough, but we're late."

"It's only noon! Our event doesn't start until four o'clock."

"They changed it to three."

I groaned. "Why didn't you tell me before now?"

"I left a voice mail on your phone. At least I think I did. Maybe I should have texted, sorry." She laughed when my head lolled against the bucket seat. "So have you dated Jay yet? An official date, I mean."

"We went to Quinn's Pub Wednesday night."

"And?"

"We had a burger together. Hey, I saw Flynn there with a TV personality. She's on one of the big stations in metro De-troit."

"Oh, brother. Why can't you stick to what's important? Forget Flynn! And forget about who he's dating, and all this murder business," Maddie said. "Honestly, it's like you're not interested in having a relationship. Ever again."

"That's not true."

I wasn't about to share any details about what Jay and I did after Quinn's. Maddie didn't share details with me about Kip. I smiled, remembering Jay's spine-tingling kisses and warm hands. That led me to wonder about other warmer parts. . . .

The truck in front of us skidded to a stop. I yelped when Maddie braked so hard, the car fishtailed a few times. We ended up sideways on the road. Good thing I'd set my coffee into the console cup holder a few seconds before.

"I really hate that," she grumbled. "And yeah. I was tailgating, so shut up."

"I didn't say anything. But it is always crowded on fall weekends."

Maddie righted the car and followed the line of visitors into the wide graveled parking lot. I collected the boxes stuffed with our smallest bears and another with five of our larger bears. An invoice for sixty bears made a nice crinkling sound in my pocket. The Richardsons charged two dollars per child—two to eight years of age only. They never took a loss from extra events like these, earning far more from sales of fresh cider, donuts, and apples.

They also made a huge profit by charging admission for the haunted house—an old run-down building on one corner of their large property, newly renovated into an animal shelter—haunted cellar, or this year the haunted maze. Open every weekend until Halloween, too.

We walked past a row of stacked straw bales that surrounded a large slide. The top had a huge piece of painted plywood shaped as a grinning jack-o'-lantern. One man with a toddler on his lap emerged from the mouth and slid down the gentle slope. A woman waiting at the bottom snapped photos with her cell phone camera. The child gurgled in glee.

"Aww, how cute. I don't remember them having that slide last year," I said.

"It's new. Are you going into the maze?" Maddie asked.

"You always chicken out of the haunted attractions. I don't blame you for last year, though. Pretty gruesome."

"I don't like clowns, or hanging dummies, or fake blood." I trudged over the rutted path toward the buildings, grateful I'd worn sturdy sneakers. "That's such a cool skeleton in the tree branch over there. Look at the skeleton dogs barking at him. Funny."

"Did you know the Richardsons are selling hard cider now? Kip says it's really good. He was here last month with the new microbrewery owner. I forget his name."

"What microbrewery?"

"Over on Baker Road, somewhere. That's where it's made."

"Don't they need a liquor license to sell it here?"

"No idea. I don't envy people in the food business. I'll stick to boutique items, if I can ever get to that point." Maddie sounded frustrated.

Since Mom had already been bugging her on that subject, I sent her ahead of me. "You take the box of bears out to the orchard on the handcart. I'll find Emma. She can't pay us until she gets the invoice, and then I'll come out to help hide the bears."

"Okay."

Maddie skirted the barn, rolling the handcart and trussed boxes over the bumpy ground, and passed families gathered in the picnic table area. A huge red-and-white-striped tent offered shade or protection from rain. I entered the first low building, which held the bakery and sales rooms; wooden bins lined the walls and signs spelled out the varieties of red and green apples like McIntosh, Jonathan, Ida Red, Honey Crisp, and Granny Smith. The adjoining room had long shelves filled with apple peelers, jars of fruit preserves, and recipe books, plus a display table stacked with kitchen placemats, napkins, tablecloths, and aprons.

I followed the scent of fresh donuts to the next room. Emma Richardson left the counter where she'd been selling popcorn, cones of spun sugar, plus candy and caramel apples. I had to worm my way around people lined at the tall counter who ordered cider and other snack foods. The aroma of fresh fried dough, plain or dipped in powdered or cinnamon sugar, nearly made me swoon. My mouth watered.

Calories, schmalories. Cider season was only once a year.

"Here you go!" Emma handed me a cinnamon donut. "I saw you drooling."

"Mmm," I mumbled, my mouth full of yeasty, sugar-coated cake. "Mmmph. Um, here's the invoice for the bears. Sorry it's a little wrinkled."

"And here's your check. We sold all the tickets, and I want to keep the kids corralled in the orchard. We changed the time to three o'clock because of tonight's Bears on Parade. We figured people would want to get back to the village."

"No problem." I folded the narrow check and stuffed it deep into my jeans pocket. "I'd better get out there and help Maddie."

"I've got someone to help you, too." Emma scanned the room and then waved at a slim girl with long silvery blond hair, who stopped clearing the cluster of tables in one corner and ran over. "This is Lauren Kirby, Sasha. Lauren can help hide the bears in the orchard."

"I'd love to! Aren't you dating my older brother?" Lauren tucked her plaid shirt into her jeans. "Jay's talked about you a lot."

"He told me you were studying to be an EMT."

"Yeah, I'm finishing up. Gotta take a CPR course and then the certification exam, but I'm picking up a little extra money here and at the Sunshine Café." Lauren followed me out to the farm area. "Emma said I could help Holly Parker with face painting, but—she's such a prima donna. Told me to get lost, basically. The kids are running wild, though."

"You mean over there?"

A troupe of kids chased each other behind the large pumpkin slide. Toddlers wriggled, jumped up and down, or wailed despite their parents' attempts to calm them. Paints and a jar of dirty water stood on a side table, along with a plastic plate for mixing colors. Holly Parker was perched on a chair, brush in hand, leaning toward a child who squirmed on a camp stool before her. She frowned when the little girl erupted into giggles.

"Wow," I said. "Is there a different way to get to the orchard?"

"Nope."

Lauren took hold of my arm and strode in that direction. Kids of all ages surrounded us, swaying and hopping in excitement. Holly chatted with the mother while she filled in a butterfly on the child's plump cheek with purple and pink dots.

"—poor thing. So Gina borrowed my phone, my car, my clothes. She didn't always ask permission, but we were like sisters."

Holly had told Detective Mason the same thing, but I still doubted it. She'd embellished stories in the past. Lauren stopped to chat with Janet Johnson, another waitress at the Sunshine Café, who held her little boy on one hip. A few moms asked questions of Holly, in vague terms given the kids present, but others looked uneasy.

"I haven't heard anything on the news yet," Holly said, "But I did hear the mayor might be involved. Gina was suing him to get paid for work she did on his re-election campaign."

"What about that lawyer she was dating?" someone asked.

"Flynn Hanson, of the Legal Eagles here in Silver Hollow." Holly pushed a strand of dark hair behind an ear. "He does those cheesy 'Flynn Wins' commercials on TV. Talk about a huge ego. I hear he calls himself 'Sexy Beast' in the mirror."

I swore she'd caught sight of me in the crowd by her sly smirk. But I kept my eyes on the kids, who ran pell-mell in all directions. Too bad I couldn't shut out her voice. Lauren and Janet compared their schedules at the café. I hoped they'd be done talking soon.

"Isn't that an adorable butterfly?" the mother said when her child slid from the stool. "How much are you charging, Ms. Parker?"

"It's free, and my pleasure to help at the Oktobear Fest events. Who's next?" Holly raised her voice so that I'd be sure to hear, along with everyone else. "Did you know that the cops identified the fingerprints on the k-n-i-f-e."

All the women gasped at the news. "When was this?"

"Sasha, why don't you explain?" Holly beckoned my way. "You're chummy with the detective on the case. Tell everyone here what you've heard."

"Sorry, but I don't know anything new."

The last thing I wanted was to "out" Digger Sykes as a murder suspect. That would start a panic in the village. Plus she'd already bad-mouthed both Flynn and Mayor Bloom.

"Why can't they explain what really happened?" one mom asked.

"They will, in time," I said. "Detective Mason solved Will Taylor's murder."

"That's right! Your company's sales rep was killed," Holly said, a shade too gleeful. "And now Gina Lawson, who dated your ex-husband. I'd say you're bad luck to be around!"

Lauren gasped. "That's not fair—"

"Aren't you Jay Kirby's little sister?" she interrupted with a catty smile. "He'd better be careful about getting too friendly with Sasha."

"Gina was your shop assistant," I snapped back, "so don't talk about bad luck."

My sour tone didn't go over well with the crowd. Holly must have sensed blood in the water, in the same way she'd gotten to me long ago. She swished her paintbrush in the jar of water and then boosted the next child onto the stool.

"Gina had bad luck, not me. Cissy Davison fired her, didn't you know? She worked at the Time Turner for less than a month. Then Gina blew Mayor Bloom's marketing campaign. He wanted a small-town image, but she had all these other plans and didn't listen. They fought pretty hard over what she came up with, and then he refused to pay her."

"I don't blame the mayor," Janet Johnson said. "It's not what he wanted."

"But he could have paid half the fee after she did all that work. The mayor risked a real scandal," Holly said. "Only now, he isn't. Gina's dead. Convenient, huh?"

I changed the subject. "By the way, Holly. Remember you said Gina bought those items off of eBay, the ones the police found." In spite of her blank stare, I noted how her face flushed dark pink. "How else would you know her box was stored in your shop's back room."

"I didn't know."

"Odd that my mom's mink bear was in that box."

Holly's outline of a tiger on the boy's hand looked scraggly. "Gina must have thought it would fetch a good price as a collectible in our shop."

"Then why not show it to you? Why hide it?" I asked. "And the other things in that box didn't look like collectibles."

Holly dabbled her brush into orange paint next. "Maybe they meant something to her. Like personal items. How would I know?"

I wondered if those items meant something to Holly instead. She'd often projected her own feelings, good and bad, onto friends back in high school to avoid taking the blame when trouble arose. I persisted, wanting to dig for the truth.

"What would a carved bird, a scrapbook, an unsigned oil painting, and a mink bear have to do with one another?"

"We'll never know." Holly's self-satisfied smile dug in deeper.

"Too bad your 'Think Pink' hoodie is ruined."

"I'm so mad about that. But I already ordered a replacement."

After noticing everyone's surprise at her venomous tone, Holly focused on the task at hand. I knew I'd cracked her composure. The tiger head had suffered, and while she tried adding white to fix the mistakes in the stripes, Holly finally shooed the boy off the stool. The woman who sat down next shifted her infant to one knee and whispered close. They both smiled, as if sharing a secret. Holly glanced over her shoulder at me.

"You're right about that. How about a tiny pumpkin on the baby's hand? The paint's washable if she doesn't like it."

"Cute! I wish the police would hurry up and solve the case," the mother added.

Janet Johnson stepped forward before Holly could reply. "You can't expect them to snap their fingers and boom, the case is solved. I work at the café, owned by Captain Ross and his wife. Digger Sykes and the other officers work hard to keep this village safe."

"Digger couldn't catch a dead rabbit on the Village Green," Holly said. "He's totally incompetent. He'd botch his brother Larry's job, sweeping floors at the Quick Mix."

That hushed everyone. "That's a terrible thing to say." Janet sounded incensed. "I doubt very much that you and Gina Lawson were like sisters. The mayor said Gina always complained about how you stole her marketing ideas—"

"She stole ideas from me," Holly cut in, "and she wouldn't

listen to any advice! I told her the mayor wouldn't like her campaign ideas. Gina resented how I was right about that, too. But none of this is your business, anyway."

Miffed, Janet Johnson marched off with her little boy. The others' silence must have signaled that Holly had overstepped the bounds. Several mothers grabbed their kids and followed Janet. I felt a twinge of satisfaction, since Holly's reactions verified her lack of compassion. Especially when it came to Digger Sykes and his brother Larry. Silver Hollow residents felt protective of him and supported Digger's loyalty to family.

"All right, who's next?" Holly tried to move on, a fake smile pasted on her face, but sounded shaken. She'd quickly finished the tiny pumpkin on the baby's hand and cooed at the next toddler. "How about a kitty? A white one?"

I drew Lauren away. "We're late, let's go."

Jay's sister followed me past several fields of tall corn toward the distant orchards. I tried to forget Holly and her annoying remarks, and hoped people recognized her phoniness. She seemed to top me at every turn, however, striking like a snake. But this time Holly had sunk her fangs into the wrong targets—Digger and Larry Sykes.

We finally reached the lowest-growing apple trees where a small section had been roped off. Maddie looked upset. "Where have you been? I thought you got lost."

"Ran into Holly Parker," I said with a groan. "Lauren's helping us, though."

"Hey, thanks." My sister smiled at Lauren. "Did Jay get his bear finished for tonight's unveiling at the Village Green? I hope the clothes worked."

"Yeah, but he had trouble lacing the boots after the sealing coat dried."

"Quick, hide the bears," I said, my voice low. "People are heading this way."

Maddie set up the big sign spelling out FIND TEDDY BEARS

HERE on a post at the entrance. Although most of the apples had been harvested, foliage remained thick on the trees. We took bears out of the plastic bags and perched them amid clumps of grass or in Y-shaped forks on the low branches. Lauren even hung one large bear upside down, hidden by leaves.

"Hope some kid finds this one. It's supposed to rain tonight."

"Every bear has a plastic bag, so we'll know if there's any missing," Maddie said. "Let's hope kids without tickets won't show up, expecting we might have extra bears."

We finished with ten minutes to spare. Emma Richardson began collecting tickets from adults in line. Toddlers ambled around their parents' legs, and older kids jumped up and down in excitement. I loved seeing their eager, happy faces.

"—about what happened?" a woman asked. "I never expected two murders in a small town like Silver Hollow."

"Tough break for Holly Parker," another said. "She's here, doing face painting."

"Wow, that's awfully nice for her to volunteer," a third added. "It's only been a week since it happened, too. Talk about dedication."

"It's great that she put the community ahead of her own shop."

"I heard Gina doesn't have family, so Holly's taking charge of the funeral arrangements. Once the police are done, of course, with an autopsy."

"Wow. Good for her."

Oh, brother. I ignored the rest of their gossip exchange, knowing now I'd been wrong. People had not seen through the mask Holly put on for the public. Whether or not she had an audience, her true nature remained well hidden.

I pushed Holly out of my mind. Focus, on everything but her.

Chapter 16

"Hey," Lauren said, breaking into my thoughts. "Once this event is over, I'd like to show you something. Believe me, you'll love it."

"Sure, but what is it?"

"I'd rather surprise you. Trust me, it's fabulous."

Her friendly enthusiasm cheered my spirits. My sister chatted with Emma Richardson while parents and grandparents lifted kids to find bears in the trees. Lauren handed bags to those who found their bears. I watched with delight, enjoying how kids compared bears or traded for a different color fur. At last everyone seemed satisfied, adults and children. They soon headed off toward the next event of the day.

"I'm glad that's done." Maddie touched my arm. "You're going to see Jay's bear tonight, right? I'm stuck helping Kip again. I swear, if we don't finish tonight, I'm giving up."

"I'll ask Lauren for a ride, and that way you can take the car," I said.

"Thanks, Sash. Tell Jay congrats for me."

Maddie headed to the parking lot. I caught up with Lauren, who retrieved candy wrappers and other trash. Together we collected litter and tossed it in the nearest trash bin.

"So what's this surprise you want me to see?"

"The haunted maze? This way, come on!"

I balked. "Uh—"

"Jay carved something," she said, coaxing me. "You gotta see it."

"For the maze?"

Lauren nodded and half-dragged me along. I loathed horror-related things, but also hated to act like a coward. It couldn't be that bad. Not in full daylight, although the sun sank toward the west; long shadows stretched over the uneven ground. I stumbled on in growing dread. We'd be in and out before dark, right? I had nothing to fear. Except fear itself—where had I heard that before? Probably in history class. Either Theodore or Franklin Roosevelt said that. Silver Hollow had a few of their quotes on plaques around the village.

"Did you know that detective questioned my brother Thursday?" Lauren asked. "Along with Matt Cooper and Kip O'Sullivan. Plus some other friend of theirs."

"Jay didn't tell me," I said. "We talked on the phone yesterday—"

"Here we are!"

Lauren waved me on toward the corn maze entrance. Rats. I'd hoped to take a peek at Jay's carving and then skip going through it. The carving had to be inside somewhere. A breeze rustled the dry cornstalks and sent a shiver down my spine. Nothing at the entrance was scary, at least. They'd set up a cute sign—DON'T GET CORN-FUSED—STAY ON THE PATH—with a benign scarecrow. Lauren greeted a boy, who added straw to the figure's legs.

"Hey, we want to see my brother's carving. Won't take long."

"Sure, Lauren," he said, "but don't touch anything."

She pushed me into the long web-covered tunnel. Cotton tube socks dangled every few feet from the pallets overhead, weighted down with softballs, and covered with fake plastic spiders. I dodged one that swung, but another hit me in the cheek. Ow.

Lauren lowered her voice to a whisper. "We have to go through to the end, where they installed Jay's carving. They paid him big money. I bet they'll use it every year."

"Maybe we could go around to that point." I jumped when a huge feathery creature slid across a wire overhead. Ugh. Also fake, but Lauren giggled.

"It's faster to go through the maze. Come on."

She screamed, more from excitement than horror, when we turned a corner between the stiff cornstalks. I stared at the swirling chiffon "ghosts" with white masks that dangled before us. Not as bad as that spider, at least until a creepy zombie with fake blood and a decent makeup job thrust his hands before my face. Startled, I dodged and fell to one knee. Lauren hauled me to my feet with a cheerful laugh. We plunged onward around a few more bends.

Lauren pointed to the large boxing glove nailed to a board, with a sign THIS WAY—BEWARE THE PUNCH. "Cheesy. Look at the punch bowl."

"There's a plastic cup attached to a string, so I bet it's rigged."

"Maybe whoever tries to take a drink gets doused with water?" She pointed upward, and craned her neck. "Or maybe they're still setting it up. Whatever."

"How about a water pistol," I asked, "or those Super Soakers?"

"Yeah, those things hurt." Lauren entered the next tunnel with two-by-fours hammered together in a wide lattice frame. Blown-up surgical gloves, attached to long coat sleeves, thrust through several openings. "Pool noodles. I helped staple the fabric around them. I didn't know they put those silly gloves for hands on the ends, though."

She screamed when a real arm and red-stained hand touched her shoulder. "Sorry," someone called out. Dan Russell, the police chief's son, poked his head around a curtain. "Hey, Lauren. I'm not supposed to touch anyone, but it's hard to see how close people are."

"We came to see Jay's carving," I said, and pushed Lauren forward.

"It's so cool! I helped him set it up last night."

Dan disappeared. I had no idea if we neared the end, and wanted to get this over with soon. We passed beneath another wood pallet tunnel with thicker spider webbing. Some of the spiders looked real and sprung out on long coils. At last we emerged from the network of tunnels to see a metal shelving unit, draped with flimsy netting, and holding jars of preserved heads. Lauren pointed to several, naming the people's ghostly faces.

"First they posed for the photos, their eyes closed and mouths shut, like they were dead. Then we printed them in a sepia tone and put two side views on either side of the head-on view. Being in the water makes the faces look creepier."

"It does look weird," I admitted. "So where's the carving?"

"We might be only halfway through. For ten bucks, people expect a good scare or two. Come on."

I followed her between the tall cornstalks, giving in to the inevitable. Might as well enjoy the experience. Especially after another zombie, with tattered clothing and fake blood, carrying a small chainsaw, blocked our path. He moaned and fumbled with the tool's pull cord. It didn't start. Lauren patted his arm in sympathy.

"It's okay, Tim. Doesn't he work for you at the factory, Sasha?"

"Hi, boss." Tim grinned sheepishly. "Guess I'm not very scary, huh? Last year my crazed clown was better. I need more practice starting this thing."

"Maybe it needs oil," I suggested.

"Great makeup job. You've got time to figure out how to start the chainsaw," Lauren added. "See ya later at the Bears on Parade, if you make it."

"Yeah," Tim said. "Maybe we can round up some people and go to Sushi Town."

"Ooh, sounds good. Or make our own," she said. "Come on, Sasha."

I walked onward, smiling at their easy camaraderie. Luckily, only a few dead ends here and there had chicken-wire ghosts or more scarecrows. We easily retraced our steps back to the main path. The head and upper body of a skeleton protruded from the ground at one point, holding a lantern in one arm. That was clever. I would have chosen to step over the skeleton and continue, but Lauren took the path through an open coffin serving as a doorway.

A mannequin in a white hospital gown and a long black wig was posed climbing out of a fake stone well. A stone-faced teen in a similar costume emerged from a side path. Lauren's shrill scream hurt my ears.

"Get out—before it's too late," he moaned.

I drew Lauren away, weary of all the fake figures, the dried brown puddles—probably animal blood—on the ground, and the creepy clown's head that sprang up from a black painted trash can. What was it about haunted houses—or cellars, or mazes—that people loved? The scare factor, of course, but beyond that. It wasn't my idea of fun.

I screamed this time when a girl with long blond hair, wearing a bloody dress over jeans and sneakers, ambled our way in the maze. Lauren admired her pasty white face and the black squiggly streaks below her kohl-rimmed eyes.

"Awesome makeup job, Jordan."

The girl didn't say anything, merely stared up at us with a malevolent sneer before she retreated back into hiding. I breathed deep. I might be over my fear of haunted houses and this maze, but I couldn't help my body's natural reactions. My heart throbbed, and I rubbed sweaty palms on my jeans. Lauren crept forward on the path, and jumped when a fake corpse slid out on a wooden board, and then slowly withdrew again.

"Yikes!" Lauren beckoned me forward. "Come on, we're nearly through. I'm coming back a few more times. This is awesome."

I disagreed. The innocent fun that teens relished had vanished the minute I'd come across Will Taylor's body last month. Seeing Gina nearly a week ago magnified the reality of violent death. Corpses, fake or not, weren't on my list as entertainment.

Lauren looked disappointed when we came upon a cauldron hanging over a pit. "This is supposed to have flames coming up, not real ones. Special effects. I guess they haven't turned it on yet. We must have taken a shortcut and missed a few things."

"No problem," I said under my breath.

I did appreciate the artistic creation of a "skele-crow" hanging overhead. The burlap face grinned to show a few rotten teeth, empty eyes, and a hole for a nose. We finally stepped out of the maze into a clearing. A large post stood between two gnarled apple trees.

"Here it is," Lauren announced. "Isn't it amazing? Okay, I am biased."

She held out her hand with a flourish, Vanna White style, over the carved bear's head emerging from the post. With an open jaw, the pointed teeth looked ferocious. One hairy arm and paw extended outward, complete with sharp claws.

"Wow. That is seriously fabulous."

Jay had brought a realism to the piece, with its darkened etched "fur," narrowed angry eyes, and a blackened nose. I fingered the claws and teeth, noting how they looked sharper but had blunt edges—good thing. I figured ticket buyers had to sign a release form before entering the maze, agreeing not to hold the farm liable for injuries, but Jay had been careful with this piece. He had a true gift, seeing an animal or object hidden within wood, and then bringing it into clear focus with such talent and skill.

"I can't wait to see his other pieces at the studio."

"I know, right? Jay's self-taught," Lauren said proudly. "He took a few advanced classes in carving right after high school, and since then, it's been practice, practice, and more practice. Jay could teach, you know. He's wonderful, patient with kids and adults. I've seen him helping people learn to use all kinds of carving tools."

"You ought to write his résumé," I said. "I wonder if Kip O'Sullivan could put in a good word for him at the community college."

"Jay asked, but Kip keeps 'forgetting' to do it. Great friend, huh." Her angry tone faded when she placed a hand on the bear's head. "Maybe Kip's jealous. Unless Jay needs a bachelor's or master's degree to teach? That might be it."

"I don't know."

Maddie could tell me whether Kip had a degree, and that could be why he was only an adjunct, not a full-time professor. I was more surprised that Kip had failed to help. I thought he and Jay were good friends.

"Nice meeting you, Sasha, but I gotta run," Lauren said. "I don't want to miss being there when they show his bear sculpture. You are coming tonight?"

"Yes, but only if I can hitch a ride back to the village with you. Maddie drove today, and she needed the car. You can drop me off near the park, and I can walk home."

"Sure, no problem. I gotta get my purse," she said, and then pointed. "Take this path to the right and you'll end up in the parking lot. I'll meet you there."

I trudged for what seemed like five miles, through orchards with taller apple trees, past fields of pumpkins, and finally reached the parking lot. Lauren ran toward a sporty low-slung Saturn coated with dirt, waving madly. Somehow I managed to squeeze into the front, my knees near my face. I hadn't thought of pushing the seat back.

"I didn't think I was that tall."

"Sorry, there's a box on the floor behind you, and it doesn't leave much room up here. This is a hand-me-down car. My older brother Paul's head hits the ceiling with every bump in the road," she said with a laugh. "Jay had the engine replaced before he gave it to me. Besides the usual repairs, like the brakes, oil changes, fuel pump."

"Jay knows how to fix cars?"

"Simpler jobs. Otherwise, we take it to Randy's Garage behind the pub."

"How many brothers and sisters in your family?" I asked.

Lauren explained how Paul had a wife and two kids. Her younger brother, Drew, was still in high school, and her parents lived in the two-story house her grandfather built. They'd sold the majority of the acreage to a neighboring farmer; Mr. and Mrs. Kirby both had jobs in Ann Arbor at the medical center, as therapists. Jay had moved out a few years ago to the apartment complex north of town, close to Silver Lake.

"Even though it's brand-new, there's problems with the air-conditioning, water leaks, and other horrors." Lauren sped down the road, gravel and dirt spewing behind the car. "Mom keeps bugging him to come back home. His studio is the old barn on our property, and she said he can convert the loft into living space. Jay thinks it would cost a fortune."

"He needs a tiny house, like the ones on HGTV," I said.

"Great idea, but he prefers being on his own. Wish I could be. That will be a while, with school and all."

She chattered on about her boyfriend, who planned to enter med school, and their dream of renovating a farmhouse near Chelsea. Lauren insisted on driving to the Silver Bear Shop and gushed over the mailbox with the mother bear and its two cubs.

"Wow! I wanted to see this ever since Jay mentioned working on this piece."

I shut the passenger door. "Thanks again for the ride. See you tonight."

Lauren sped off, so I hurried inside and let Rosie out into the yard. Poor baby, waiting all afternoon to go out. I glanced at the clock. Too late for a long, hot shower. I'd heard the village clock chime six times. The Bears on Parade event had started, so I rushed upstairs for a quick rinse, dried my hair, and stood in front of my closet. I chose rust-colored slacks and a cream sweater, a chunky wood necklace, tweed jacket, and my flats. Comfort over fashion. The last time I'd worn ankle boots with this outfit, I'd gotten two blisters.

Rosie wasn't happy being left behind again. I hugged her tight, fed her, and tossed a chew stick in her crate. "I'll be back soon, baby. Promise."

Then I hurried off to the village. Cars lined Kermit Street and both sides of Roosevelt Avenue. Good thing I hadn't bothered to drive. Being a Saturday, twice as many visitors had come tonight than Wednesday. I joined the throng around the

Park Bear, unveiled earlier. Painted green for the most part, the bear had multiple oval vignettes on the front and back, each showing tiny figures flying kites, enjoying a picnic, playing football, baseball, or soccer. Dave Fox posed the shy female artist next to the bear.

Amy Evans, in her usual navy suit, waved people down the street. "Twenty minutes before we unveil the next bear on the Village Green!"

"Hey, Sasha!" Lauren joined me, still in jeans and the T-shirt she'd worn to the farm. A woman bumped into her from behind and sloshed half her coffee over them both. "I sure am glad I didn't get dressed up tonight."

"Sorry, I didn't see you," the woman said. "The lid wasn't on tight, I guess."

"It's okay, really. You didn't get any on you, Sasha?"

I'd already checked and shook my head. Lauren and I walked down Archibald Street and then past the Regency Hotel. The Starry Night Bear had a steady stream of admirers in front of Cissy Davison's Time Turner shop. A larger group of people milled around Maddie's Polka Bear. Tonight wooden barriers blocked traffic to the main downtown area, and Officer Hillerman sat in a police car by the courthouse.

"I wonder why they chose the Village Green for Jay's bear," I mused.

"The committee added it at the last minute, along with the waiter bear on Theodore Lane. The one in front of the restaurant." Lauren shook her damp coffee-stained shirt, as if hoping the sun would dry it. "Did you know the Legal Eagles lawyers paid Jay a thousand bucks for that carving in front of their office? Mr. Richardson paid five hundred for the bear in the maze."

"Plus the Oktobear Fest hired him to do a new sign."

"Jay is thrilled doing it, too. Oh, there he is! Hey," Lauren called out, jumping up and down. She reminded me of the kids earlier at the farm event, her excitement contagious.

I laughed at the Animaniacs tie Jay wore this time with his suit. He hugged his sister and then pulled me closer for a brief kiss. "Hey, people might get the wrong idea," I teased.

"I hope they do. How did it go out at Richardson's Farms?"

"Fine. I saw your carved post in the maze," I said. "We'd better print out a contract for our new shop sign, since you're getting so swamped with commissions."

Jay gave a rueful smile. "I'm not complaining, but I've got enough work to last through winter. Let's get over to my Jack Pine Bear. After that, they'll unveil the Honey Bear in front of the Sunshine Café. Turns out Pet the Bear isn't done yet, so that's coming next week."

"It's not tonight?" Lauren wailed. "Oh, man! I'm working all next week, and I so wanted to see it. I heard it's painted with cats, dogs, and birds."

"It won't be going anywhere," I reminded her. "I wonder if Kip's done with his Hippie Bear. That's where Maddie is tonight. She's sorry to miss your unveiling, but boy, is she worried. I hope they do finish soon."

"Me too." Jay squeezed my hand. "I wonder where Amy Evans is—"

"Over there, talking to Mayor Bloom," his sister said. "Don't forget to ask Sasha about the box. It's really important."

"What box?" I glanced between them, puzzled.

"The one you mentioned to Holly Parker. Out at Richardson's." Lauren fidgeted with her shirt again, clearly nervous. "The box with stuff Gina Lawson supposedly bought on eBay, or so Holly claimed. But I bet she's lying through her teeth."

"Lauren called me from the orchard," Jay said, taking my hand as we walked to the Village Green. "What did the carved bird look like?"

I caught my breath, wondering for a moment, before answering. "Pretty crude, blond wood. With a streak down one side, I think." I tried to recall when Mason had held it up to the light in Holly's shop. "It might have been a natural flaw in the wood."

"Outlined darker, right?" Lauren sounded triumphant. "It has to be yours, Jay!"

He nodded. "Back in high school Shop class, I carved a bird for a project, and I promised Lauren could have it after school let out for the summer. But it went missing."

"Wow." I glanced at Amy Evans, who was marching our way. "Uh-oh, show time. I had a feeling that bird wasn't a collectible from eBay."

"That crude, huh." Jay laughed at my dismay. "Don't feel guilty for dissing my first carving. I planned on using it as a prototype for a few more, over the summer. Stashed it in the locker I shared with a friend. Only Holly was dating Ron at the time. I didn't even realize the carving was gone until I was supposed to turn it in for a grade."

"So you think Holly stole that bird?"

Lauren broke in before he replied. "It has to be Jay's carving!"

"Are you ready, Mr. Kirby?" Amy joined us, along with three or four dozen people. "Next up is the Jack Pine Bear. This way, please."

Jay's covered sculpture stood in the middle of the Green. The laced boots peeked beneath the white sheet; I'd failed to notice how each bear was mounted on a square platform, painted white. I wondered if metal or wood rods inside the legs aided in the sculpture's stability. I'd have to ask Maddie or Jay later, since admirers surrounded him. At last Amy signaled for the sheet's removal. Everyone clapped with enthusiasm when Lauren drew it aside.

"The Jack Pine Bear symbolizes Michigan's lumberjack

history," Amy read from the flyer. "Jay Kirby usually carves bears, but he was gracious enough to take part in our event. He'll be available to answer questions about his design. Just remember, in half an hour, we'll be heading on to the Sunshine Café to reveal the Honey Bear."

Jay's bear, in his knit cap, rolled-up jeans, and red plaid flannel shirt, held a heavy chain over one paw that led to a rough bark-covered log behind him on a wooden sled. I was glad he'd managed to add that element. And proud that my sister and I helped bring the costume to life. Jay had washed a light tan stain over the bear's exposed face, paws, and neck, and then added tiny brushstrokes in a darker brown to simulate fur.

I listened to him answer questions and checked the clothing from all angles. It wasn't too obvious from a distance where we'd added extra fabric. Dave Fox waved Jay closer to the bear sculpture and snapped several photos.

"I had a lot of help from Sasha and Maddie Silverman," Jay said. "Their aunt knitted the hat, and my sister Lauren helped me seal the bear's boots and fashion the sled. I'm thankful to the other artists who participated in the Bears on Parade project, too."

"Did any of you work together on your sculptures?" someone asked.

"No, but we met several times over the summer to discuss how we wanted to interpret our designs. Some artists chose only paint, others utilized props or other . . ."

"Ms. Silverman?" Detective Mason looked professional tonight in a suit and tie. "Have you got a minute?"

"Sure. I heard you questioned my cousin Matt Cooper," I said. "Along with the others who took that fishing trip back in May."

"Yes. Mind if we head over where there's fewer people?"

I followed him away from the crowd surrounding Jay. "I've

been wondering about the knife used to kill Gina," I said once we reached a clear area. "How can Digger know for sure it's his? I mean, you said it didn't have any initials or markings."

Mason shook his head. "That's not important. I do think you were right about the victim from the get-go."

"Uh. I don't understand."

"Whoever killed Ms. Lawson thought she was Holly Parker."

Chapter 17

Numb, I leaned against the closest lamppost. "Because of that hoodie."

Mason waved a finger in the air. "And it was dark that night. Foggy."

"But why would anyone want to murder Holly?"

"Why else? For money, love, revenge. Officer Sykes is on desk duty for now, because Ms. Parker believes he's targeting her. He did ticket her several times over the past two weeks, and you witnessed his attempt to tamper with the crime scene."

"Digger doesn't like her, but it doesn't mean he'd try to murder her." I folded my arms over my chest. "But on the other hand, Holly wasn't happy that Gina kept borrowing her stuff, and who knows what really happened while they worked in the shop. I doubt they were all that chummy, 'like sisters,' no matter what she claims."

"About as weak a motive as Digger's, but I have other suspects," Mason said. He must have noticed my raised eyebrows. "Your cousin threatened Holly Parker."

"What?"

"News to you, huh? Your sister's a witness, and so is Officer Sykes."

"When was this?" I demanded.

"Two days before Gina Lawson was killed," Mason said.

"But why would Matt want to murder Holly?"

"She's stiff competition with her toy and bookstore. Cooper admitted his business has suffered. And someone used Officer Sykes's knife to throw off suspicion. Your cousin was on that fishing trip, after all."

I spread my hands in disbelief. "That was months ago, over Memorial Day weekend. And Matt's knife disappeared on the same trip."

"So he claims."

"This is ridiculous. Where is he? At the station for questioning?"

"He's being detained as a person of interest."

"But he's not under arrest," I said quickly.

"Not yet. I don't have time to argue," Mason added, cutting off my protest. "I thought you might be interested to know your theory is being considered. That's all."

"Gee, thanks. And business competition as a motive? Then you ought to be investigating me, because she competed with our shop. I suppose you're going to search The Cat's Cradle for evidence, too. Why not come to the Silver Bear Shop while you're at it."

"I might."

The detective strolled off without another word. Good thing. I wanted to pummel my fists against his chest, which would have landed me in jail for assaulting a cop. Instead I stalked in the opposite direction from the Village Green, fuming with every step.

I didn't acknowledge anyone I passed, strangers or friends,

or pay attention to any street signs. When my blind haze of anger cleared, I found myself by the gate-enclosed side garden of Holly's shop. Thank goodness she wasn't in the yard or on Theodore Lane. But a group of angry people stood in front of the Italianate's porch, along with Officer Hillerman. I knew Holly had closed the shop, since she'd been at Richardson's Farms all day, but she wasn't among them.

"I'll file a report," Hillerman said to the crowd. "Ms. Parker has already contacted us about this matter. It's time to disperse. Go on home, folks."

"She doesn't need this," someone said loudly. "Vandalism's a crime."

He climbed into his squad car and slowly drove off. I overheard muttered complaints from the few people who lingered by the shop's front steps, and recognized two women who'd been at Richardson's Farms that afternoon.

"I feel so sorry for Holly. The cops haven't figured out who killed her assistant, and now they won't do anything except file a stupid report."

"Who would paint such nasty graffiti?"

"I can guess who did it," one woman said with a furtive glance in my direction. "Let's go. Holly will call us once she buys razor blades to scrape off the paint."

Once they all left, I slowly walked around the corner and stared at the large black scrawls on Holly's shop windows. The letters spelled two messages, the first being GET OUT OF TOWN and beneath that, YOUR NINE LIVES ARE OVER. Soapy water dripped down the glass to the siding below. Puddles dotted the sidewalk as well. Holly must have tried to wash off the graffiti, but failed. She'd need a ladder as well as razor blades to reach the highest parts. It looked like spray paint to me, which had to be acrylic. I hadn't noticed anything earlier today.

How odd that the second phrase referred to "nine lives." I

stopped cold. Matt and Elle owned The Cat's Cradle. Oh no. Neither of them would have defaced property. Someone had pointed the finger in their direction, though. The murderer?

I hurried home, unwilling to consider that. Rosie's whining worried me before I could unlock the door. My sweet dog rushed past me and through the yard to her favorite spot. My cell needed charging, so I plugged it in and dialed Maddie.

"Why didn't you tell me about Matt?" I asked, before she could say hello.

"What about him?"

"He's being questioned at the police station, and might be arrested—"

"What?" Maddie sounded as angry as I did. "No way!"

"How come you never told me that Matt threatened Holly? Mason said you witnessed it, along with Digger Sykes."

"It wasn't a big deal. It happened when Holly was moving in, when Digger wrote out those parking tickets. Matt happened to drive by, and he said a few words to Holly about her competing with The Cat's Cradle. Digger blew it all out of proportion."

"Someone painted graffiti on Holly's shop windows," I said. "And anyone with half a brain would put two and two together and blame Matt. One message said, 'Your Nine Lives Are Over.' How crazy is that?"

"Oh. Em. Gee." Maddie groaned. "I am never speaking to Digger again. Matt was angry, but he didn't *say* he'd kill Holly. Only that she'd be sorry one day."

"Things have gone from bad to worse. I'm going over to Elle's right now. Are you still pulling another all-nighter at Kip's?"

"Yeah, he had to get more paint. I'm waiting, but I'm so tired. Kip's got to finish tonight. He needs to put sealer on and give it enough time to dry."

I snapped my fingers, half-listening to her. "I wonder if Holly painted the graffiti herself. What do you think? Possible or too far-fetched? I mean, it looked like spray paint, and maybe she did it before she came out to the farm today for face painting."

"But why would she—no, don't answer that. We both know Holly's crazy enough, and she must have heard about Matt being a suspect. Go to Elle's, and let's worry about all this tomorrow. Maybe the cops let Matt go already. Should you call over there first?"

"Nah, I'll take Rosie with me. That will make a good excuse, letting the kids play with her. In case you're right and Matt's already home. I sure hope so."

I hung up. Next I texted Jay a brief message about why I'd left early. After grabbing the dog's harness and leash, I searched for car keys in my purse. Dang. Not in the ceramic bowl by the door, or my upstairs bedroom, or the office. I grabbed two small bears, stuffed them into a logo bag, and left a note for Aunt Eve about gifting them. But where were my keys?

The screen slammed shut behind me. I stood on the back porch and stared at the empty spot where my car usually sat. Oh. I scanned through the contacts on my phone for Mom's cell number. "Hi, did you or Dad borrow my car?"

"Yes, we're driving home right now," Mom said. "We wanted to scout out a few condos around the area. Have you talked to Flynn? He called you three or four times today, why didn't you answer? He's inviting us to dinner so we can all talk—"

"I'm not going to dinner with him."

"Honestly, Sasha. You've got to let him explain."

"There's nothing to explain," I said. I so did not have time for this, but tried not to lose my temper. "Flynn's dating a weather forecaster. I saw them together at Quinn's."

"You know he's such a flirt—"

"Flynn and I are done, Mom. I've moved on, I'm dating Jay Kirby. But I need my car to get over to Elle's house. Right now."

"All right! We're parking outside."

I punched off the phone, shielding my eyes from the flash of headlights, and whistled for Rosie. Harness and leash on, we dashed out to meet my parents at the car. Dad coughed hard, one hand on the hood, and then doubled over to breathe.

"Sounds like you need a treatment." I snatched the keys from his hand. "Hey, Matt's going to need a lawyer. He's been detained at the station and might be arrested."

"What for?" Mom grabbed Dad's arm. "Good heavens, not murder."

"Just call Mike Blake or Mark Branson and have one of them go over there. I'm going to see Elle right now. She's probably freaking out over this."

Dad gave a thumbs-up sign. "Sure, honey. We'll take care of it."

"Come on, Alex. Into the house, let's get that treatment started." Mom supported him all the way to the porch. "We'll call the Legal Eagles."

"Maddie's helping Kip tonight, by the way," I called out, and boosted Rosie into the car. "Come on, baby. We've got to spread some good doggie cheer."

I rammed the gas pedal to the floor, my stomach clenched tight. I'd forgotten to eat. Again. My tires squealed when I backed the car onto Theodore Lane. Rosie hung her head out of the window, tongue lolling. I passed the group of Holly's friends, who were scraping paint off the windows in the light of several electric lanterns. Not an easy job. Where was Holly, anyway? The least she could do was help them, but I didn't care.

I headed west on Kermit Street. Once past the Quick Mix

factory, I turned right and headed to Franklin Street. At last I pulled into my cousin's long driveway. No sign of the girls playing behind the house in the large yard, so that wasn't good. Rosie jumped out the minute I opened the car's door and gave several sharp barks.

"I bet you're looking for your favorite friends." I raised my voice louder. "I wonder if Celia and Cara are in bed already. Where could they be, Rosie?"

"Here we are, here we are!"

Both girls had burst out of the house and raced to hug Rosie. I waited for Cara to open the backyard's gate while Celia twirled in excitement. Cara unhooked Rosie's leash and handed it to me; she took that job so seriously every visit. I watched the kids play for a few minutes with my dog, chasing her around the fenced-in yard, before I climbed the porch and walked into the bungalow. The acrid smell of burnt toast hit me hard.

Elle sat in Matt's battered recliner in the living room, hands covering her face, weeping. Her shoulders shook, and she'd curled up into a ball. I set my purse and the logo bag on the sofa and walked past her, into the kitchen. I couldn't tell if the police had searched the house. Maybe, but I thought Elle would have managed to tell me that much. For now, I'd let her emotions run their course and focus on menial tasks.

I gathered plates with uneaten, cold scrambled eggs, macaroni and cheese, and blackened toast crusts, dumped the food scraps in the garbage, and soaked a dishcloth with hot water. Dark crumbs coated a sticky trail of honey across the table. After I scrubbed it down, then washed and dried the dishes and flatware, I warmed the rest of the macaroni and cheese in the microwave. Beggars couldn't be choosers. Not half bad, either, although my mother would be aghast. She'd never resorted to boxed products, not even from the Quick Mix factory.

I parked myself on the back porch's top step. The girls rubbed Rosie's belly and rolled on the grass, trying to evade her slobbery kisses, which was hilarious. My dog loved these kids and would let them do pretty much anything; Celia hugged her neck tight, although Rosie shook free and then chased the ball Cara threw toward the fence. It bounced, and my dog caught it midair. The girls both squealed with joy. They all raced around the yard again, tumbling once or twice, and scrambling up to start over. All three would soon be worn out. I hoped.

The porch light flickered on, probably on a timer. A few pesky mosquitos buzzed around my face, so I swatted them away. My cell phone pinged. I read Jay's text reply with relief. *Hang in there, family first.* I'd felt so guilty leaving without telling him in person. That took a huge weight of worry off my mind. What a keeper.

At last I heard the screen door squeak. "Hey." Elle sniffled and blew her nose.

"You all right?" I glanced at her when she dropped beside me on the step. "Um. Maybe that's a dumb question. Did the cops search the bookstore?"

"Yeah, and they came here. They took Matt's laptop. Some papers." She wadded the tissue in her fist. "What am I gonna do, Sasha? What if they do arrest him? Matt's never hurt me or the kids. He'd never kill anyone."

"I'm going to prove he's innocent. That's a promise."

"How can you—"

She dissolved in tears again. Elle rested her head on her knees, face turned away from me, and rocked back and forth. I hugged her. Mom expected me to clear the mayor's name, and now I'd have to help my cousin. But I felt like I'd been spinning my wheels.

I had no idea who might want to kill either Gina or Holly.

The girls followed Rosie up the porch steps, so I shooed them inside. Elle crept back to the recliner once more; I handed her the box of tissues. Cara and Celia stared at their mom, not able to understand why she wasn't functioning. I clapped my hands.

"Time to get ready for bed!" I summoned a cheerful smile. "You'll have to take a bath tomorrow night, okay? Let's go."

"But we're dirty," Cara said. "Mom always gives us a bath."

"You can wash up at the bathroom sink."

Although my skills with little kids were practically nonexistent, I somehow managed to wash faces and hands, get them into pajamas, comb out and braid their hair, before I supervised them brushing their teeth. Then we headed to the bedroom. Celia stuck a foot in the air.

"Really dirty. See?"

"Whoa! Back to the bathroom. What did you do, run around without shoes all day? I'm not sure, but this—might—just—tickle!"

Celia shrieked while I scrubbed the soles of her feet and ankles with a soapy washcloth. Both girls squirmed and giggled until we finished. I was sweaty and exhausted after they finally tumbled into bed. We chose five books, and I read the last one twice.

"Daddy always skips pages," Cara said, "but Mommy doesn't. You're a better reader with all the funny voices. Read another, please?"

"We agreed that *Piggie Pie* would be the last one. Give Rosie a kiss! No, she can't sleep overnight. I should have washed her paws, too, before she jumped on the bed," I said. "Kisses! Hugs! Wait, I forgot my surprise for you."

I retrieved the shop's logo bag from the living room, gave the small pink bear to Celia and the white one to Cara. They hugged them tight. "What are their names?"

"Mine is Pinky," Celia said. "I love her, love, love, love her."

Cara thought for a moment. "My new teddy bear is Lily."

She tucked the toy under her chin, pulled the blanket over it, and closed her eyes.

"Thank you, thank you," Celia chanted, bouncing up and down.

"You're welcome, settle down now. Good night, sleep tight—"

"Don't let the bedbugs bite!"

Celia gave one last bounce and snuggled under the covers. I turned off the light, sighed in relief, and then headed back to the kitchen with Rosie. Found a bottle of wine, opened it, poured two glasses, and carried them into the living room. Elle took one with a grateful sob.

"Thank you, Sasha. So. Much."

"Hey, you'd do the same for me."

"But I didn't. Last month when Will Taylor was killed, I didn't come around. Or call." She gulped back more tears. "Matt and I both should have helped you and Maddie."

"We don't keep tally marks on a board," I said. "It's not a contest of who does more. Mary Kate would win that hands down, anyway. You've got two beautiful girls. Caring for them takes most of your time, plus staffing the bookstore when Matt works overtime at the factory. How you both manage everything, I don't know."

Elle rose wearily from her chair. "He's exhausted when he comes home, poor guy. And Matt drops Cara at school whenever Celia is too much for me to handle in the mornings. He was home, here with me and the girls, last Saturday night. He told that Detective Mason, over and over again, on Thursday afternoon."

"I'm sure Matt's repeating his story again at the station, too."

"I don't know what we can do, Sasha. This is horrible."

Elle paced the room, bare feet slapping the hardwood floor. I knew Matt sank most of the profits from the bookstore back into expenses—paying for supplies, inventory, and taxes. Then juggling their schedules between work, family, finding time for dinner, doing laundry, cleaning, and grocery shopping. Both Elle and Mary Kate had their hands full. I had it easy with only the shop to manage. Even with the busy seasonal events.

Rosie plopped down beside me on the worn sofa. I stroked her curly fur and glanced around the room, taking in the framed family photos on the walls, the small television monitor on a wobbly stand in the corner, the tubs of blocks and other toys near the front window. I counted my blessings. A healthy bank account, a trust fund, and the perks of living above the Silver Bear shop, with cleaning and gardening staff. But I'd trade Elle in a heartbeat for Cara and Celia.

Not that she'd give them up, of course.

My poor cousin. I couldn't understand why Detective Mason would grill Matt because of a meaningless threat. Benign, by the sound of it. What had Maddie said? Something about Holly being sorry one day. I'd probably said the same thing a few times in our rivalry.

"Did Matt leave at any point Saturday night? On an errand?" I asked.

"I did send him out." Elle stopped pacing and turned to me, her dark eyes fearful. "Oh, my God. For milk! Just ten minutes, to the grocery store and back. Maybe it was fifteen or twenty minutes. But that's all."

"That could be why he's being held." I rubbed my forehead. "Mason will need proof, though. That knife won't be enough to make a murder charge stick. So when did this all happen today? I was out at Richardson's Farms."

"We'd planned on coming, but then Matt called. Around three o'clock, and he had to close the store. Even though customers were browsing, because the cops had a search warrant. They took Matt to the station, too, by the time the Bears on Parade event started." She finger-combed her dark hair away from her face. "Gossip is already so bad around the village."

"It'll get worse." I explained about the graffiti spray-painted on Holly's shop windows. "Matt couldn't have done it if he was at the shop, and then at the station. You've been with the kids all day, too."

"Yeah. How strange, that reference to nine lives."

"That must have been deliberate, to point the finger Matt's way, but there's not much we can do about it. Drink your wine, try to relax. I haven't told you about the box Mason found in the back of Holly's shop, because that's just as weird."

After gulping some of the too sweet Chardonnay, I launched into the story. Elle had stopped crying. Getting her to focus on anything but poor Matt, who was no doubt cooling his heels at the police station, helped. I hoped Dad had called a lawyer, since he'd do anything for Aunt Marie's son. I explained about the various items in the box, but Elle's jaw dropped open when I related how Holly might have stolen Jay's carved bird.

"Unbelievable, but not really. She's a piece of work, and I bet Holly did it on purpose. And that mink bear! I remember how upset your Mom was back then. But how could Holly have taken it, if she'd never been to your house?"

"I don't know. But Mom didn't keep Minky Bear or any of her Madame Alexander dolls locked in a curio cabinet back then—"

"Hey! Maybe Holly's a kleptomaniac," Elle interrupted. "She took Jay's carved bird, sort of like a keepsake. Or a trophy."

"That's as good an explanation as any." I rubbed the bridge of my nose. "I wonder if Holly and Mayor Bloom have any bad blood between—"

The phone rang, so Elle rushed to answer. I mused over how Jay and I could get a look at that carved bird. If Mason had stashed that box at the Silver Hollow police station and not the county building, that is. Maybe we could ask Bill Hillerman.

BEAR WITNESS TO MURDER

"Oh, thank you! Tomorrow? What time?" Elle thanked the caller again and hung up. She turned to me, her face glowing. "That was Flynn Hanson! He promised to get Matt home by tomorrow morning at the latest."

"Uh. I wonder how—never mind," I added. Why upset Elle all over again, although the police could detain Matt for up to forty-eight hours. "Good news."

I should have known Mom would insist on getting my ex involved, even though I'd asked Dad to call Mark Branson or Mike Blake. Huh. Mom always got her way. I was sure she'd grill me about getting on the ball proving Cal Bloom innocent. I hadn't found out for sure if Flynn was with Cheryl Cummings or someone else the night Gina was killed, either. Or why he'd said "the last time I'd seen Gina alive." Rosie shifted closer, sensing my worry. I ruffled her ears.

Some things were out of my control.

Chapter 18

The next day, I relaxed after church. I needed a lazy afternoon without any further troubles, without worrying about murder, and without running around asking questions of people who didn't want to answer. I did hear a few snippets of gossip after the service, however. The graffiti had been scraped off Through the Looking Glass's windows; police cars patrolled the village streets last night until well after midnight, both downtown and in the neighborhoods; and Matt had been released at six in the morning. Elle had texted confirmation, too.

I shared my relief with Mary Kate and Garrett, who planned on visiting the Coopers. That let me off the hook. Now I sat in the parlor watching a favorite Sandra Bullock movie, *Miss Congeniality*. The talent scene, where her character demonstrated self-defense, always made me laugh. A cool breeze wafted through the open window. Squirrels raided the backyard for peanuts I'd thrown out earlier. My parents had gone to brunch with Uncle Ross and Aunt Eve, and planned to check out a few condos.

Maddie filled a mug with coffee. After an all-night marathon with Kip, she looked bleary-eyed and pale. "Why did I even offer any help?"

"What's wrong?" I asked.

"I'm going back to Kip's, that's what. It's wrong."

"So the Hippie Bear isn't done, I take it."

"I think it looks great, but he's such a perfectionist." She slammed the refrigerator door and tucked an apple and string cheese, along with a package of trail mix, into her bohemian ecru macramé purse. Maddie gulped more coffee. "I can't get through to Kip that it's gotta be done by Wednesday, and he should let the committee be critical."

"Who sponsored his bear? Maybe that's why he's being so nitpicky."

"Abby raised money for it, using GoFundMe or something. She's hoping to auction the bear for charity during the Oktobear Fest."

I smiled. "Anything vintage is sure to draw a lot of money."

"I know, but Kip is being such a pain. I had the backside done," Maddie said, "but he got mad and painted over my work."

"Really? You should let him crash and burn, then."

"I don't think he realizes how bad it would look if that happens, that's why I can't. He's a college instructor! It's crazy."

I straightened up and joined her in the kitchen. "Yeah. Look at all the attention Jim Perry got for the Legal Eagle Bear, and so did Jay last night."

"Maybe Kip thinks his design isn't up to par with theirs? What do you think?"

"Me? I'm no art critic."

"It's no worse than mine for the cheese factor." Maddie plopped down sideways on a chair, her bare legs hanging over one arm. I paused the DVD player and brewed a latte, waiting for her to continue. She did before I finished. "So when I told Kip I wouldn't touch his bear again, he got mad at that! He wants me there, giving him advice, but then he rejects anything I've said. He's so hard to figure out sometimes."

"Sounds like you need some space. Stay away for a day or two."

"That won't solve the time crunch problem, Sash."

"You need a sanity break," I said. "Like me. Take it easy today. You can always go back tonight, if you have to, but give yourself some time."

"Maybe you're right."

Maddie scrambled out of the chair and returned everything to the refrigerator. She padded back and curled on the sofa, flipping through a *People* magazine. Tossed it aside. Fetched a Sudoku book, then set that down to watch the final few minutes of the movie. When the Kenny G ringtone trilled on her cell phone, my sister jumped to answer.

"Hey, Kip—"

I smiled, figuring she'd give in sooner than later. Within ten minutes, Maddie waved on her way out, wearing paint-spattered clothes, all smiles. She couldn't resist an artistic challenge. I burrowed into the pages of my latest book. I'd heard so much about the Broadway musical that I finally bought the biography of Alexander Hamilton. Heavier reading than my usual cozy mysteries, but interesting. Until I yawned. Rosie snored beside me. I curled up for a nap, my dog cuddling in my arms, for almost an hour.

Jay called around four o'clock. I took the time to explain Matt and Elle's situation, but begged off catching a pizza together. Maddie might not need space, but I did given this past week. Things were bound to get crazier, too. Instead, I took a leisurely bike ride around the village before I headed home. While scrambling eggs for supper, I couldn't help worrying about my sister's confusion over Kip. She'd never acted so wishy-washy before with a guy. I added some feta and spinach, slid the mess onto a plate, and ate while thinking.

Scrubbing the skillet eased some frustration over my lack of progress.

Mom and Dad finally returned after dark. "Signed a purchase agreement for a new condo," Dad said after kissing my cheek. "We'll be out of your hair in a month."

"You haven't been in my hair," I said, "and where's this new condo?"

"Only ten minutes away, a bit west of here," Mom said. "Ross bought one last month, only he never told us till now. It's lovely. Almost as nice as our Florida condo."

I dogged my father when he climbed the stairs to his suite. "Hey, Dad. Have you talked to the mayor lately? I'm wondering how his re-election campaign is coming along."

He squinted, one hand on the bedroom doorknob. "Not that great."

"Is it because of Gina Lawson's murder?"

"Could be." Dad sounded weary and loosened his tie. "He mentioned how Detective Mason questioned him, several times, about the court case. But Cal said if the judge had decided to rule against him, he would have paid. Linda isn't happy with him, wishing he'd avoided all this trouble. Neither of the Blooms expected Gina would be murdered."

"Do you know if he ever threatened her?"

"Leave the investigation to the police, Sasha. Remember the last time."

He shut the bedroom door behind him. That signaled the end of the conversation, even though I'd started to ask another question. Apparently, Mom hadn't told him how she'd asked me to prove the mayor's innocence.

I wandered back downstairs, recalling Cal Bloom's friendly and outgoing personality, hefty build, and how he always hugged or shook hands with whomever he met, stranger or village resident. The mayor even acted pleased to see Jack Cullen, the cantankerous old man who'd once owned a house before the village council condemned it; Jack blamed Cal Bloom, in fact, for allowing my father to pave the Silver Bear Shop & Factory's parking lot in its place. Bloom tolerated Jack's accusations with his usual good-natured disposition.

He would never risk his political campaign by murdering Gina. And how would the mayor have gotten Digger's knife? Lost or not. That whole scenario seemed ludicrous.

I sighed. "Come on, Rosie. Outside."

Her claws clicked over the kitchen tile. I let her out and stood on the porch, shivering in the chilly night air, thinking of my parents living in a condo. I'd gotten used to Dad hanging around. Despite Mom's faults, she often cooked dinner on weeknights. Now Maddie and I would have to take turns again or order carry-outs. Privacy came at a price.

If Maddie was serious about Kip, though, she'd need space and privacy without parents hanging around and checking on our coming and going. I had yet to consider how things would develop with Jay. Slowly, at first, before getting into an intimate relationship. I'd made a huge mistake marrying Flynn too soon, and didn't want to repeat that. Rosie followed me upstairs and jumped on the bed, right in the middle.

"I bet you won't like anyone else sharing your spot," I said. She closed her eyes without bothering to answer. Ha.

My dreams that night shifted several times, in crazy directions. I woke up late, trying to figure out why I'd stuffed a wad of cash into a lawn mower. Clearly not for safekeeping, since the machine spewed bits of money all over.

"Why not the bank? A lawn mower, of all things," I said with a laugh, and topped my coffee mug. "That's crazy, all right. Does it mean I'm wasting money? Hmm."

I headed to the shop. Aunt Eve waved at me, already at

work behind her laptop in the office. She looked spiffy in her black blouse with a white stand-up collar, a black-and-white-striped skirt, and red spike heels. The phone rang, but she pointed toward the front room.

"An early customer is already waiting on the porch."

"Whoa. Thanks!"

I rushed faster to unlock the door. On a Monday? We never had people coming early, unless they'd arranged a tour. I yanked the door open. Lisa Blake stood there, smiling, pregnant, but alone. She rested one hand on her rounded stomach.

"Hey, Sasha. I hope this is a good time to stop by," she said. "I have an appointment at the doctor's, so my mom is watching my youngest this morning. Are you open?"

"Sure, come on in."

Lisa Blake walked past me into the shop. Petite and blond, she reminded me of Reese Witherspoon, the actress—with a baby on board, of course. Her husband, Mike, looked a lot like his brother Ben, tall, dark, and handsome, but his smile wasn't as broad and cheerful. Together Lisa and Mike seemed a perfect family with their two boys. I wondered if Lisa yearned for a girl. Another boy would make it easy in terms of hand-me-down clothes and toys, though.

"Are you shopping for a teddy bear for the new baby?"

"Um, no. I need to talk to you." Lisa sounded nervous. "It's important."

"Have a seat." I gestured to the benches by the door. After the recent senior tour, I bought padded cushions to cover the hard wood. "Make yourself comfortable."

"Thanks." She sank onto one and clasped her hands together, avoiding my gaze. "I'm hoping this baby comes fast like the others. They popped out like toast!"

We both laughed, although I wasn't sure how funny that was in reality. To me it sounded downright scary, but what did

I know about childbirth? She smoothed her maternity dress with a manicured hand, looking smart with styled hair and makeup, even false eyelashes.

"Can I get you some coffee or tea?" I offered. "Water?"

"No, but thanks. I'm glad Deanna Walsh is managing things at The Birdcage. My doctor wants me to rest up these last few weeks. Borderline diabetes, you know."

I didn't, but only nodded. "So business is good at your shop?"

"Winter will be better. More people feed wild birds out-side." Lisa shifted, clearly not as comfortable, and focused on the counter, the barrels of small teddy bears, anywhere but my face. "Mike told me about your cousin's arrest."

"Matt was detained, not arrested. He was released yester-day." I figured she'd get around to the point. Eventually. "Not all that fun for the family."

"Yeah. I'd hate for my kids to hear about that kind of thing when they get older."

I only nodded, wondering again why Lisa had come to visit. We didn't know each other that well. She rubbed her belly, shifted again, examined her fingernails. Patient, I waited her out. Finally Lisa glanced my way.

"I'm here about Holly Parker. She's cracked, Sasha. I want you to know that."

"Uh. I don't understand." I knew she was right, but wanted Lisa to explain. It didn't take long for her to launch into the full story. But I was surprised by her rush of emotion.

"She's been driving me nuts," Lisa said, dabbing away a tear when it rolled down her cheek, "calling and leaving voice mails, plus texting me all the time. Like it doesn't matter that we haven't seen each other since high school! Holly expects us to be close friends again, I guess. But I've changed. A lot. I'm busy with my shop and kids."

"I can see that." I nodded, as encouragement to continue.

"We don't have anything in common now, too. And Holly has to be first in everything. That's why she came back to Silver Hollow." Lisa sniffled and drew out a tissue. "Holly found out how successful you've been. She told me she planned it all out a few months ago. How to take you and your family down—"

"Wait, what? Take us down?"

"She's so jealous! I told you, Holly's got a screw loose." Lisa stopped me before I could say anything. "Remember back in high school? She knew Maddie was my friend. She asked me about you both all the time. I don't know why I listened to her so much. Mike's ready to go to the police, but I don't want any trouble. She might get even crazier."

"Holly? Like how much crazier?"

"What if she targets my kids? Or Mike?" Lisa shifted on the bench, wringing her hands. "I'm telling you she's obsessed. Holly will find out and then take revenge on us."

That sounded totally whacked, especially this early on a Monday morning, but I took a deep breath. "I'm glad you're telling me this," I said. "I mean, after someone painted that graffiti on her shop windows, and killed her shop assistant. It's beyond crazy."

"Yes! Exactly. Holly said she knows who painted her windows." Lisa leaned forward and lowered her voice. "She said Maddie did it, not your cousin Matt. See what I mean? Your sister wouldn't do anything like that! But she's telling everyone."

"Holly thinks Maddie—"

"Yeah, and that's why Mike convinced me to come here today. To confess."

"Confess?" Now I really was confused. "What do you mean?"

Lisa rushed on, her words tumbling over one another. "About what I did for Holly. Back in high school, and her rivalry with you. She won't let it go, trust me. And yes, I'm going to the police and telling them. But I had to warn you. Holly's capable of anything."

I hoped no other customers walked in on us. I dreaded anyone overhearing this chat, especially one of Holly's sympathizers, but I steeled myself. Patience wasn't my strongest suit, but I had to clear up a few things.

"Do you think Holly is capable of murder?" I asked. Lisa blinked a few times but didn't reply. "She might have killed Gina because she kept borrowing her stuff."

"I suppose it's possible. Like I said, Holly takes revenge. She's very careful planning things. Like having me do stuff for her, because she never wanted to get caught."

"You mean back in school," I said, cautious.

Lisa nodded. "Why can't she forget all that? Holly's jealous of your parents, the house you lived in, and now this shop. She hates her own family. Her parents divorced a long time ago, and her mom's an alcoholic. Holly hasn't visited her in years—"

"Wait. I'm pretty sure Holly told the police she was with her mom last Saturday, the night Gina was killed," I said. "It's supposed to be her alibi."

"I'm sure that's a fat lie." Lisa stretched sideways and massaged her lower back. "Holly swore long ago that she'd prove she was better than you."

"Better than me and my family."

At last I had the answer. Holly's anger and resentment had built over the years, whether or not I'd ever done anything to deserve it. I couldn't remember doing anything, that is, directly to her—I hadn't even accused her of plagiarism. I'd mourned privately, and hadn't involved my parents. They'd have fought for me, but I never wanted that. Holly and I had never been friends. Never shared many classes together, either.

How odd that she'd focused on me as a target.

"Holly wanted to be like you, Sasha. Everyone liked you," Lisa said, which surprised me. "All your teachers, the band director, even the Study Hall monitors. You worked so hard to get good grades. But Holly made it her goal to take your place at the top."

"But I wasn't at the top," I protested. "Not like Brittany and Ashley. They were more popular. Rivals for Prom Queen and all that rot. They dated the football jocks, not me."

"Yeah, I know that. And you know that. But Holly didn't see it like that. She needed you to suffer, so she took your boyfriend away, and beat you for first chair in Band. But you always bounced back. It didn't seem to affect you at all. Holly's been stewing about that for years. She's determined to turn people here in Silver Hollow against you. And your shop."

Stunned, I had trouble thinking. "That is crazy."

Lisa rubbed her swollen belly with a frown. "All these years, I've felt so guilty over what I did to help her. That's why I came here today."

"How did you help her?"

"I stole that mink teddy bear, and I am so sorry. I took it during Maddie's slumber party." Lisa straightened her shoulders. "I hid it in my sleeping bag."

"And then you gave it to Holly," I said. "Wow."

"Yes. I thought it was yours, and she was thrilled to have it. But after the Cran-beary Tea Party, Holly called me. She found out then that the mink teddy bear actually belongs to your mom. She was so mad!"

"That's why Holly saved it all these years." I tapped a finger on the bench's wooden arm. "Do you know if Holly stole anything else? Like Jay Kirby's carved bird?"

Lisa nodded. "I refused, so she had to do it."

"But why?"

"Holly got mad at Jay when he laughed at a mistake she

made in math class. She started dating his locker partner, so she could get close, and stole Jay's carving. Then Holly dumped the guy. Just wait. She'll soon find out you and Jay are hooking up."

I didn't want to think about that. "So she collected trophies. Minky Bear and then Jay's carving, but what about a scrapbook? Or an oil painting?"

"Holly knows lots of artists, but she never told me about stealing a painting," Lisa said, biting her bottom lip. "She co-owned some kind of stationery store with a friend, though, up north. I hope you can forgive me. For taking your mother's teddy bear."

I squeezed her shoulder. "It turned up, so Mom's happy. And once Detective Mason figures out who killed Gina, this will be over."

"I'm so worried Holly will find out I came here." Lisa stood up, awkwardly, and plucked a bear from the nearest bin. "I'll have to buy one from her shop, too, or she'll flip. This is really silly, I know, but whatever works."

"Okay, if you really think so." I rang up the sale and nestled the small brown bear in a layer of tissue, then handed her the bag. "Tell Holly you wanted to get two different teddy bears so your boys can each give the new baby a present."

"Good idea," Lisa said with a shaky laugh. "I'll have to stop by her shop after my doctor appointment, though. I'm running late."

I walked her outside to the porch. "Thanks so much for explaining everything."

"Sure. Thanks for listening."

Lisa walked to her car in the parking lot. I didn't blame her for being so afraid of Holly Parker. The fact that she'd been hounding Lisa with constant phone calls and texts, when the poor woman had two sweet kids, a shop to run, and a baby on the way, seemed bizarre.

I returned inside and sat on a stool behind the sales counter.

Propped my chin in one palm and stared out the window, thinking over everything. Maybe it wasn't such a stretch after all, if Holly found someone else to set up Digger Sykes for Gina's murder. According to Lisa Blake, she was capable of anything. A real loon. What if she'd befriended one of the guys Matt, Jay, and Kip saw up north? And talked him into stealing Digger's knife? Hmm.

I plucked up the ringing phone near the cash register. "Silver Bear Shop, how can I help you?" I said automatically. "We're open until six, Monday through Saturday. Sure."

My coffee tasted cold and bitter. Dang. I considered contacting Detective Mason and relating what I'd learned from Lisa Blake, but he might dismiss it without merit. Despite my vow to avoid trouble after Will's Folly, I'd become entangled in another dangerous mess. Ever since finding Gina's body, my world had tilted like a polar bear on a drifting iceberg.

What about Jay? I wanted to tell him, for sympathy if nothing else. Short of quitting Silver Hollow and moving away, I had no idea how to free myself of Holly Parker. And that was out of the question. My family and I were not the problem.

I rubbed my face and eyes with both hands, trying to clear my head. "It's so insane, who would believe it? Stranger than fiction, for sure."

One thing was certain. Given Holly's close proximity to the Silver Bear Shop, I'd have to tread carefully. She might be watching my every move. I sounded paranoid, but it wasn't funny in the least. The bell over the door jangled. I put my worries aside, since several customers walked through the door. Maybe things would settle down. Maybe Mason would solve the case. Maybe Gina had been a random killing, in the wrong place and at the wrong time.

"Good morning," I said, but my voice sounded as hollow as my hope.

Chapter 19

While Monday proved a slow day at the shop, Tuesday more than made up for it. After dealing with the last wave of customers, I felt frazzled. Once I replenished accessories in the racks, and laminated the photos printed out for the shipping bins, I headed to the factory. Deon agreed to post them, so I checked on the grand prize bear's lederhosen costume. Uncle Ross had come through, making certain the patterns were accurate, although Joan had insisted the muslin shirt needed embroidery. I examined the intricate floral pattern with interest.

"I found a template to follow," she explained, "and that made it much easier. It was worth the extra work, although I had to keep changing the bobbins."

"Looks fantastic," I said. "How about the hat?"

"Waste of time," Uncle Ross growled. "Don't bother, in my opinion. Plus I'm starved. I'm ready for a burger."

"At Quinn's Pub?"

He gave a noncommittal shrug. "Or Ham Heaven, whatever Eve wants."

I exchanged furtive looks with several other staff members, but put a finger on my lips. After the door clicked shut behind Uncle Ross, we all snickered. I'd wondered how long his "old codger" persona would last after my aunt's return. Some rough edges had clearly softened.

"We should start a pool," Joan said. "When will wedding bells ring again? We can make a grid, and whoever comes closest wins."

Even Deon laughed at that suggestion. "Ross keeps his cards close to the chest, though. Hasn't said much to me. But he doesn't complain as much."

"He hasn't bickered with Aunt Eve, so maybe he's given up trying to win." I held up the embroidered billowy shirt. "Let's see if the costume fits the prize bear. Bring it down from the loft, Tim. Use the elevator."

Once he returned with the enormous bear, we all held our breath while Hilda, Joan, and Evelyn stuffed the giant toy's arms and legs into the outfit. "What a relief it fits," Jessica said. "Good thing, too. There's no time to do alterations."

Evelyn held up a finger. "Don't forget we still have to make the hat. We ordered felt, but it hasn't come in yet. At least we have a pattern."

"Don't worry about it now," I said. "Go on home, everyone. It's late."

"Did Ross tell you about my sewing machine?" Evelyn asked. "It's been giving me fits, no matter how often he brings in the repairman."

"Yes, we discussed it and we're ordering two new machines." I eyed the sewing area, wondering where we might put them. "We can't afford any more downtime if one goes on the fritz. With sales booming, I'm not going to complain about the cost."

"And Christmas orders haven't started coming in yet," Joan said.

I nodded. "Don't remind me."

A month ago, Will Taylor bemoaned lagging sales. Our sales rep's murder made the local and state newspapers, and orders started pouring in from all around the country once Mason solved the case. Online orders boomed as well. Maddie had scrambled to hire replacements for the staff members we lost, and I hoped we could find seasonal help. Maybe Aunt Eve could deal with that problem after the Oktobear Fest.

I also hoped my sister had succeeded in helping Kip to finish his bear. But I hadn't heard from Maddie since Sunday night, when she'd come home exhausted yet pleased. I guessed they had made some progress, although I didn't want to ask.

Deciding against a bike ride, I collected Rosie's leash and harness. That started her tail wriggling. I'd forgotten to use sunscreen on Saturday, so I took the time to smooth aloe vera gel on my peeling nose and cheeks.

"Every Saturday football game at The Big House at UM, fighting traffic in Ann Arbor, I never missed wearing sunscreen. I'm getting old and forgetful, Rosie."

She only thumped her tail and led the way outside. To avoid Holly's shop, we walked in the opposite direction, past the Davisons' home, the Queen Bess Tea Room, and Flambé, to the end of Theodore Lane. The scraggly picnic area was empty, although traffic rushed by on Main Street. Coming this way meant walking past the shuttered theater—an old opera house from the early nineteen hundreds, designed for stage plays—and La Mesa, with its tantalizing scents of frying tacos and refried beans. The Fish Bear stood in front of Quinn's Pub. Late afternoon sunshine glinted off the colorful paint.

I walked to Kermit Street and passed by Fresh Grounds, still busy with customers. The accordion strap on my sister's Polka Bear had been repaired, although kids clustered around the sculpture; they poked the bellows and laughed at the wheezing sounds. I crossed over to The Birdcage and glimpsed Deanna

Walsh behind the counter. Rosie rushed to sniff the base of the Starry Night Bear in front of the Time Turner shop, her nose working overtime.

"Hey, Sasha. Got a minute?"

Cissy Davison stood in the doorway. Her straightened platinum hair, worn with a side sweep over half of her face, fell below her shoulders; bright red lipstick matched her dazzling fingernails. She teetered on leopard high heels below black skinny jeans.

"Sure. Can I bring Rosie inside with me?" I could tell by her hesitation that she wasn't so keen on the idea. "I can't leave her out here alone with so many people walking around to see the bear sculptures. She's not great with strangers."

"I guess, since this won't take long."

Cissy smoothed her leopard print top when I walked past the small wooden cart beside the door. Her shop carried books of all sizes, mostly paranormal topics from astrology to psychic interpretations, dream interpretation manuals, plus tarot card sets. A faded sign by the register read PSYCHIC READER MONDAYS. Two wreaths graced the brick on the far wall, one studded with Queen Anne's lace and dried flowers, the other a mess of metal wires, glittery stars, and tiny fairy lights. The wicker seat in a corner needed a teddy bear, in my opinion.

A virtual mishmash of tchotchkes, glass bottles, exotic jewelry, even hats and scarves filled the shelves. Racks of chiffon-layered dresses and fringed shawls stood by the long polished counter. Rosie lay down by my feet, disinterested. I didn't blame her. The stuffy air gave me a sense of claustrophobia.

"Has the Starry Night Bear brought in a lot of customers?" I asked.

"Browsing, but not many buyers." Cissy shrugged. "Fall is for college kids setting up their dorm rooms with cheap junk. Christmas is on the way, though. People will start thinking of buying gifts once the Oktobear Fest is over."

"That's true."

"How many more sculptures are coming?" she asked.

I had to think through what was already installed. "Four or five. I think."

"Nice." She sounded bored, actually, but I didn't reply. Cissy fiddled with a diamond ring on her left hand. She smiled when I complimented the setting. "Gus is spoiling me. He wants me to sell the shop, even though the wedding's not till next year. I haven't decided what to do. I'm swamped with planning everything."

"Congratulations again," I said, and meant it. "How's Debbie? I should call her and see if she has more honey to sell from her hives."

"I don't know. She's had a lot of trouble with bees this year."

"By the way, Maddie mentioned that Gina Lawson, the woman who was killed a week ago, worked for you earlier this year."

"Yeah, for a bit." Cissy hesitated. "I let her go when it didn't work out."

"Too bad. Holly said Gina was like a sister to her."

She reared back as if I'd slapped her. "You're kidding, right?"

I shrugged. "That's what Holly told the detective."

"They weren't that close. But I'll tell you what happened," Cissy said, glancing around as if anyone might be listening. "I let Gina go when I caught her snitching a few items here and there. 'Borrowing' is how she termed it. Unacceptable on my terms, though."

"Wow."

I knew Holly had the same problem with Gina about borrowing. Cissy's ringtone, a lively Italian tarantella, interrupted before we could continue our chat. She dodged behind the counter and snatched up her cell. No doubt Gus Antonini was on the line, since Cissy kept murmuring "mm-hmm" every so often. She ended the call within a few minutes.

"Sorry about that. Gus is thrilled about the Maître D'Bear going up in front of Flambé. He wanted to make sure I'd be there Wednesday night. Now, what were we talking about?"

"Gina Lawson."

"Oh. Isn't it a shame what happened to her?" Cissy flipped aside her hair with a dramatic twist of her head. "I was surprised Holly hired her—for marketing at first, and then as a shop assistant. You must have heard Gina worked for Mayor Bloom on his re-election campaign. While she worked for me, in fact. Always making excuses about being on the phone or checking her laptop, another no-no."

"I don't know much, but she filed a lawsuit against him," I said.

"Gina was mad he wouldn't pay her. He insulted her in front of a lot of people, too," Cissy added. "She'd posted social media stuff, on Twitter and Facebook, setting up events. That all takes time, which is why I wasn't happy."

"Some people think the mayor killed her, to avoid scandal."

"Oh, brother. Cal Bloom's as old-fashioned as the sauerkraut and horseradish sauce they'll serve at the Oktobear Fest," she said with a laugh. Cissy tapped her long fingernails on a display case's glass surface. "That's not what I wanted to talk to you about, though. Don't take this the wrong way, Sasha. Okay?"

The hairs on the back of my neck prickled. Her words sounded more ominous than what Lisa had shared yesterday morning. "What do you mean?"

"I wanted to warn your sister, actually, but I haven't seen her much."

Startled for the second time, I knocked over a jeweled trinket box shaped like a cluster of blackberries. Cissy set it aside on the counter. "Warn Maddie? What about?" I asked.

"About the guy she's dating." She glanced toward the front window of the store. A few people had stopped on the street, perusing the Starry Night Bear, so she waited until they walked away. "Kip O'Sullivan used to live and work up in Traverse City, you know."

"Okay." My sister hadn't told me much about him, but I never asked about his past. "So why is that important?"

"Gus saw him around the city when he worked at the Grand Traverse Resort and Spa." She sounded proud of her fiancé, adding, "He moved on to work at the Capitol City Grille in Lansing. I'm only relating what Gus told me. About Kip."

I waited, impatient, and had to prompt her. "So what did he say?"

"That Kip's had financial troubles. He never finished some major commissions. Word got around, and his reputation tanked. Debbie took beekeeping classes at North Central, so she heard the same stories," Cissy added. "Kip filed for bankruptcy, too."

"Wow. Then he must have known Holly Parker," I said. "I think she lived there."

"She owned some shop up there, selling stationery. My sister witnessed a big fight, too, between Kip and Holly at one of his gallery shows."

"Really. What that was about?"

"No idea. But Kip did well at first. Sold a lot of artwork, taught classes, and he even bought a big house with a studio out back." Cissy plucked an imaginary thread from her jeans. "You ought to warn Maddie that Kip could be trouble."

I knew that would be tricky. When my sister took on a "cause"—either for charity or to help a friend—she remained stubborn in her loyalty. Maddie wouldn't give up unless she chose to on her own. What a shame about Kip's past. I really liked him, despite the troubles he and Maddie were having.

Then again, maybe most of this was rumor and not fact. I'd rather ask my sister before believing any story. I thanked Cissy, nevertheless.

"You're welcome. Gus and I were surprised to hear that Kip walked away from his house and studio," Cissy went on. "Packed up and let the property go into foreclosure. He didn't pay back the commissions he'd taken on, either. I'm so afraid Maddie will be hurt. She's got so much talent, and deserves better. I've always liked her."

I blinked in surprise. Her phone trilled again, so I turned toward the door. Since when had Cissy paid that much attention to either of us? Debbie was closer in age to Maddie. I gave up trying to reason it out and left the shop.

Relieved to be outside, Rosie shook her curly fur. I breathed in the fresh air, just as glad. After a few laps around the Village Green, stopping by each of her favorite trees, Rosie led the way toward home. A car's blaring horn startled me. I'd been thinking about Kip and his troubles, and nearly tripped over the cement curb in a scramble to get out of the way. Holly's blue MINI Cooper sped down Kermit Street. I picked up my trembling dog and hugged her.

"What a witch," I muttered aloud. "Come on, baby."

The wind blew dry leaves past us, I shivered in the chill air, wondering if Holly would have dared run me down. I couldn't be sure given what Lisa Blake had said. Rosie wriggled free of my arms and tugged at her leash, eager for supper. I felt better once we rounded the corner and passed the toy and book store. Too bad I couldn't snoop around inside, since Holly had gone on an errand. I'd have loved to dig up more secret trophies.

I surveyed the Dumpster behind the shop. Had Holly painted the graffiti herself? Maybe I'd find a can of spray paint. I walked over to the hulking metal bin, lifted the rubberized lid with a grunt—ugh. I jumped back, holding my nose, and winced from the strong stench.

After I caught a few deep breaths, I stood on tiptoes to peer over the side. Flattened cardboard boxes, some with crushed sides. Loose papers. Metal pipes. Junk food wrappers, milk cartons, and plenty of other trash. No paint cans, spray or gallon-sized.

What a shame.

Chapter 20

Wednesday after work, I changed into a deep green dress and my knee-high leather boots. Jewelry? Hmm—layered chains would have to do, plus big hoop earrings. I grabbed a pair of sunglasses and a leather jacket, then headed to the village.

Officer Hillerman braced himself against a car parked on Kermit Street, writing out a ticket. Another good reason to walk. Jay had texted earlier about meeting on River Street, past the bank and the market. I enjoyed the sunshine, the cool breeze, and the drifts of colorful leaves underfoot. Autumn was fading fast. November's gray skies and bone-chilling wind would soon arrive. Halloween in Michigan was always a toss-up in terms of weather, from balmy warm to rain-soaked, or even a blanket of light snow.

"Sasha! Over here," Jay called.

I rushed to meet him. "Nice tie, Kirby. A carrot-chomping Bugs Bunny. You've also got a kinship with bears, the way they look so real."

He laughed. "So I guess you like this carving?"

Mounted on wheels, the sign had huge carved wooden letters spelling out OKTOBEAR above the much larger FEST on the bottom. Two realistic bears on either side were poised in the act of climbing onto the top. One had a mischievous grin, reminding me of something.

"Hmm. I wonder where Yogi's hat is," I said. Jay looked sheepish.

"You nailed it. Does that bear really resemble the cartoon?"

"There's a slight similarity in the expression. I admit I loved watching old cartoons on VCR tapes and DVDs when I was a kid. But how often did you go camping at Jellystone Park in Frankenmuth? Or maybe the one near Grayling."

"South Haven, actually." He grinned and drew me into a hug. "So we both love Looney Tunes, good. I'm glad you're early. Remember how Holly tore off the accordion strap on Maddie's Polka Bear?"

"We didn't actually see her do it, though."

"She hasn't been the only one fooling around with the sculptures. Lauren heard someone was hanging around Jack Pine Bear. When a police car drove by, they took off on a bicycle. I didn't think vandalism was possible in a small town. Everyone knows everyone else."

"And people are always looking for fresh gossip—"

I stopped, since Amy Evans, Mayor Bloom, and the rest of the Oktobear Fest committee walked toward us. Barbara Davison, my mother's best friend, and Mary Monroe, who owned the flower shop, crowed in delight at the sign; Tom Richardson, plus Mary Walsh of Ham Heaven, all chimed in with praise as well. Amy, wearing her trademark navy suit and flats, this time with a navy and gold scarf, spread her arms wide.

"That sign is so worth the money we spent."

"Absolutely," the mayor boomed. He shook Jay's hand with enthusiasm, and grabbed mine next. My teeth rattled. "Congratulations! We hope to see many other successful events for our future Oktobear Fests. Don't forget to vote next month."

Dave Fox suddenly ambled over to the group. "Get around the sign, all of you. This is going on the front page of the *Herald,* all about the Oktobear Fest."

"Wait, wait." Cal Bloom adjusted his suit jacket and tie. Some of the women fluffed their hair before Dave snapped several photos, checked his viewfinder, and then waved.

"Thanks, all."

"Time to head over to the vet clinic," Amy said, and checked her wristwatch. "First up is Pet the Bear, and then the Bling Bear over on Kermit Street near the ice cream shop."

"What about Kip's bear?" I hissed at Jay before we followed everyone. "Isn't it on the schedule for tonight? In between the vet and the Silver Scoop?"

"Not finished." He pressed me closer and whispered that in my ear. "Pet the Bear's artist was supposed to be up last Saturday, remember. Amy told Kip he'd better get the Hippie Bear here by tomorrow night. Don't say a word to your sister. She's—"

"I know. Ready to blow a gasket."

"Something wrong, you two?"

We whirled around to see Cal Bloom, his tanned face a mass of wrinkles when he smiled. Almost a constant occurrence when he met people, although he acted somber at the funeral home he owned. David Richardson, Tom's son, managed it for him along with his wife Leah; visitors and newcomers to Silver Hollow had trouble understanding the tangled connections between families and friends in the various businesses.

"Hope you're not gossiping about the election," the mayor joked.

I didn't laugh. "We're heading off to see the next bear."

"Like I said, Kirby, you did a great job on that sign."

"Thanks."

Cal Bloom glanced at me and then clapped Jay on the shoulder. "Alex told me he's hiring you to redo the Silver Bear Shop's sign next. Nice to have an in with the family."

I winced at that obvious hint. "My sister and I hired Jay. Not my dad."

"Right."

His condescending manner rankled me worse. "By the way, what's going to happen to that lawsuit regarding your marketing campaign?"

"Listen, Sasha," he said. "I'll set the record straight. I had nothing to do with that young woman's murder. We each had our own version of the story, and I was willing to abide by what the judge ruled in court. I didn't expect Gina to take it that far. She should have come to me in private. We could have settled it on our own, without lawyers."

"Do you think it's going to hurt your re-election?" Jay asked.

"I hope not. But people are wrong if they think I'd hurt any woman. Or man, for that matter." Bloom let out a long sigh. "It is what it is, or what it will be. My hands are tied, but I'm not giving up until the last vote's counted."

"Where were you the night she was killed?" I asked, and watched for any change in his facial expression. The mayor didn't bat an eye.

"Home with the wife, where I belong. Linda told the police that." He cocked his head to one side. "Your mother promised that you'll help clear my name. Is that true?"

"Are you a suspect?"

"That detective has me on his list, along with Matt Cooper, and heaven knows who else. Neither of us would have any reason to murder anyone. We grew up here, people know us. It's downright ridiculous, if you ask me. But the police don't seem to care."

Bloom lumbered off down the street. I glanced at Jay. "I

wonder if he's going to lose this time. Who's running against him? Some farmer?"

"Tony Crocker. He bought out my parents' farmland. Quiet, doesn't say much. And he's too cheap to put up lawn signs or send flyers around."

"So maybe if I do clear Mayor Bloom, he'll win again," I said.

Jay shrugged. "Good chance of it. Let's go."

While we walked, I pondered what Mayor Bloom had said. "Hey. Does everyone around here think my dad's in charge at the factory?"

"Don't let his remarks bother you, Sasha," Jay said. "The mayor's old-school. Look how Gil Thompson still lords it over Fresh Grounds. Even though Garrett and Mary Kate do all the work, and own half of the business."

"It's true the mayor doesn't give women much credit. A lot of women own businesses in Silver Hollow." I started counting. "Cissy Davison. Mary Monroe. Abby Pozniak. Vivian Grant. Lisa Blake. Holly Parker—and Chief Ross's café is managed by his wife. Oh, and the hair salon owner, Karen Olsen."

"His daughter owns the Silver Scoop, remember."

"Kristen co-owns it with Isabel French. That leaves Quinn's Pub, Fresh Grounds, Ham Heaven, and the Queen Bess Tea Room run by couples. Only Blake's Pharmacy, Flambé, and Jackson's Market are owned by men alone."

Jay smiled. "Don't forget the hotel, the bank, and the Quick Mix Factory."

"But even so, Cal Bloom needs to update his thinking. Maybe that's another reason why he's not a shoo-in for re-election this year. Younger voters and women don't like him."

"You could be right. Is it true Holly Parker is running for a council seat? Imagine her speaking for the rest of us 'slack-tivist' people."

"Ugh. Besides, we're not slacktivists. We're involved in stuff."

"I'd love to see Holly battle it out with Cal Bloom over issues," Jay said, "but I doubt I'll have time to attend any meetings. If they're open to the public. Maybe it's just a rumor. Who knows if she missed the filing deadline to be a candidate."

The thought of Holly Parker taking part in decisions that affected Silver Hollow and its businesses disturbed me. Especially after Lisa's warning. What kind of mischief could she cook up against the Silver Bear Shop as a council member?

The weather soon reflected my mood's downturn. A bank of dark clouds piled up in the northwest, so Jay and I rushed to join the crowd around the sculpture near Mark Fox's vet clinic. We missed most of Amy Evans's introduction. The images painted on the shiny fiberglass bear included cats, dogs, birds, and reptiles, along with ADOPT, DON'T SHOP! in bold letters.

"Bring your pets to us, no matter how you get them," Mark Fox added. Everyone laughed at his shameless plug. "What? We're the best vet clinic in the area."

"You're the only vet in the area," Abby Pozniak said, to more laughter. I hadn't noticed until now that Maddie stood beside Abby and her sister. "We don't have a choice unless we want to drive all the way to Ann Arbor."

"That's right—we save you money and gas mileage." Mark grinned.

Amy Evans waved a hand. "On to the next bear. We have a tight schedule tonight!"

She headed across Roosevelt Street. Most of the crowd followed her over the Village Green to the shops farther away on Kermit. Jay and I linked arms with Maddie, whose face flushed deep red. We all slowed down, keeping our voices low.

"I'm so angry at Kip, I could choke. He should have brought

the Hippie Bear last night, and then put the sealer coat on after tonight's unveiling," she said. "It would have been fine. But no, he insisted on touching up a few spots first. Now Amy's threatening to cut his bear from the event. I don't blame her one bit."

"Not good." Jay looked uncomfortable. "Pet the Bear was done, but the artist couldn't get it here on time due to a hauling problem."

"I know! Everyone knew the rules. And Kip promised me Sunday he'd finish."

"It's not your fault, Mads," I said.

She turned to me, close to tears. "I shouldn't have believed him. And now today, no bear. I'm so done with his excuses. And Kip. I told him it's over. I mean it, too."

That surprised me. Now was not a good time to explain what Cissy had informed me, though, given her bad mood. It would have to wait, along with everything I'd learned from Lisa. What a crazy day. At least it was nearly over.

Jay squeezed her arm. "Give him a second chance, Maddie. I'll make sure we deliver it tomorrow at the latest. Okay?"

"It's got to be tomorrow. Friday won't work," she said, "because all the food vendors will be arriving to set up. It's bound to be a madhouse."

"Got it. I'll call Kip," he said. "We'll make it happen."

I caught sight of my cousin Matt with Elle and the girls. Cara and Celia both wore shirts with unicorns in a rainbow of colorful rhinestones. They had stopped a block away from the ice cream shop. Leaving Jay and Maddie behind, I hurried to catch up to them. Celia squealed in excitement and jumped into my arms.

"Oof."

"We're gonna see a bear tonight," she yelled in my ear.

"Settle down, baby, or we'll have to go home," Elle said in warning. "Tell Sasha you're sorry for screaming, too."

"It's okay." I set her down and patted her pink bear. "The Bling Bear?"

"Yeah! It's pink, too."

"Does she know what the word means?" Jay had joined us and smiled at Elle and Matt.

"Bling, bling, bling," both girls chanted.

"Oh, you bet they do," I said. "They're really into bedazzling all kinds of stuff. Glitter, sequins, sparkles, you name it. It's a huge market trend. So how are you doing, Matt? Recovered from the weekend?"

My cousin shifted on his feet, clearly embarrassed. "Sort of, yeah. People suspect me of painting that graffiti on Holly's shop. Doesn't seem to matter that I didn't. And The Cat's Cradle will close if we don't get any customers. Bankruptcy might be the only solution."

Elle gasped at Matt's morose announcement. "Dad will help you get through this," I said. "Our sales were nonexistent after Will's murder, but we recovered. You will, too. Dad can loan you whatever you need to help pay rent, bills, or payroll. Families stick together."

"Thanks, Sash. Hey, you two little monkeys—"

Both Matt and Elle hurried after the girls, who'd slipped between adults to get a closer look at the unveiling. The sculpture stood between the Silver Scoop and the Pretty in Pink bakery, both popular shops with visitors. Amy Evans had already removed the cotton sheet; the Bling Bear, painted bright pink, also wore a white satin gown worthy of the Oscars' red carpet. Sparkling blue crystals had been glued to simulate a waterfall over the fabric. Everyone oohed and aahed, pointing to the blond wig styled in an updo covering the bear's head, topped by a tiara. False eyelashes and painted red lips on the face brought more life to the sculpture.

The artist, Zoe Fisher, balked at a photo, however, despite

Dave Fox's persuasive hints. He finally posed a group of children with the Bling Bear instead. Celia and Cara hammed it up, posing to show off their unicorn shirts, sparkly bracelets, and teddy bears.

"That design is so cool, Zoe," Maddie said. "I thought you were covering the bear itself with crystals. Kip told me you glued a heart shape on the chest."

She nodded. "I did, but the rhinestones kept falling off. Hot glue wasn't gonna cut it. That's why I used the dress, but it's so heavy! I never thought I'd get it over the bear's head. It took three of us to manage."

"I love the wig. And congratulations," I said. Zoe thanked me and turned to another admirer who had a question.

After Maddie, Jay, and I examined the sculpture from all angles, we made our way west on Kermit Street to Main. Past La Mesa, the crowd threaded through the small patch of birch trees to reach Theodore Lane. Jay eyed the weathered picnic table and crumbling cement.

"Didn't the council want to open this street up to through traffic?" he asked. "Now that there's a restaurant, it might help. Two of them, if you count the tea room."

"Yeah, I wish they would. An easy fix, too," I said. "People wouldn't have to turn around and drive back to Kermit Street."

"Wasn't this restaurant a former carriage house?"

Maddie nodded. "Dad tripled ours in size to make the factory when he renovated. Flambé was rebuilt from the foundation last winter and opened in early May."

The restaurant's floor-to-ceiling windows faced the street. Brazilian cherry hardwood covered the floors, reflecting light from the Tiffany-style chandeliers. A French-Canadian chef, Christophe Benoit, had established a menu based on Provençal cooking. Despite its small size, the restaurant proved a big success. My family had dined there recently, and everyone loved the food. I'd enjoyed the fresh flatbread studded with olives most of all, plus the array of honey and pear tarts, chocolate ganache macarons, and butter cookies.

Amy Evans stood chatting with Benoit now along with his sous chef, Gus Antonini. Both men had muscular builds, dark curly hair, and mustaches. Benoit's aquiline features set him apart from Antonini, however. Cissy Davison parked her car on the street; four-inch heels clattering, she rushed to join her fiancé. She looked like a movie starlet in a sexy black dress and a wide-brimmed beribboned hat.

"—need a bigger parking lot," Benoit was saying, "especially now that the tea room is near. They close at three. We open at four, so there's not much overlap."

Holly Parker appeared at his elbow and poked up her glasses. "I heard the Queen Bess's owners will offer Sunday brunch. That's gonna cut into your business."

His left eyebrow raised an inch. "That is news, indeed."

"Can't be true," Gus Antonini said with a frown. "I spoke to Arthur Wentworth three or four days ago. He never mentioned hosting a Sunday brunch."

"They're booked solid for a month," Maddie said. "I doubt they'll want to open on a Sunday, since they're so busy the rest of the week."

"Booked solid?" Holly scoffed. "I doubt that."

"You're wrong. You shouldn't spread rumors—"

"The waitress told me that today," she interrupted my sister. "You'd think one of their employees would know the latest plans. Not some neighbor selling teddy bears."

"Okay, ladies, chill." Amy Evans raised her voice. "We're ready to unveil our last sculpture in the Bears on Parade."

"Minus the Hippie Bear," Maddie muttered under her breath.

"The artist who came up with the original design could not clear his schedule to undertake the work. Zoe Fisher, who had already undertaken the Bling Bear, was gracious enough to help at the last minute. The Maître D'Bear signifies service and hospitality."

Amy signaled Gus, who pulled the cotton cover with a snap of his wrist. Dressed in a black tux and tie, the bear had painted dark hair and a tiny mustache; a silver tray balanced on one paw, and a white towel was draped over one arm. The bear's feet had also been painted to resemble shiny black shoes complete with laces and white reflections. Everyone clapped, and Zoe gave a little bow before she stepped back. She refused to be photographed again.

"It's wonderful," Maddie said. "Congrats, Zoe!"

Dave Fox posed the two chefs in front of the bear for a camera shot. Cissy draped herself along one side, mugging as a sultry vixen. Holly snorted in disgust.

"Talk about stealing the spotlight, when it's all about the bear."

I ignored her and turned to Jay. "I'd like to see more of Zoe's work. She's so talented."

"The gallery's listed in the Bears on Parade flyer," Maddie said. "Zoe started working on this bear first, thinking it would be easier, but those shoes took a whole week to paint. Those reflections are tough to get right."

"Wow, two bears," I said. "That's a lot of work."

"Mayor Bloom's her uncle," Holly said with a smirk. "That's why they asked her. No other artists are related to any of the committee members."

I changed the subject. "Have you found anyone to replace Gina?"

"No. But Flynn Hanson replaced her." Her acidic tone stung. "Fast work, dumping Gina, and then dating a television weather girl."

"A weather *forecaster*," Maddie shot back.

"What do you know? That Polka Bear was so lame, I'm

not surprised someone cut a strap on that accordion," Holly said, her eyes gleaming. "Bet you think I did it, Sasha."

"Did you?"

"I don't care if she did." Maddie turned her back on Holly. "Jay, are you really going to Kip's to see if his bear's ready?"

"Yep, planning on it. Come on, let's go."

Jay, Maddie, and I skirted the crowd and walked toward the Silver Bear Shop & Factory. I kept quiet, listening to them chat about the hard work they did for their bears, and breathed a sigh of relief once we reached our driveway.

"What is with Holly Parker?" Maddie suddenly asked. "It's not enough to bad-mouth Zoe, so then she starts in on Flynn!"

"I only hope Cheryl keeps him out of my hair," I said.

Jay slid an arm around my waist. "I have to agree. How about we meet at Ham Heaven tomorrow, after Kip and I deliver the bear. I'll text you."

"That sounds good. They close at eight, remember."

He kissed me and headed to his truck, parked by the bank. Maddie tugged my sleeve; we both watched Holly speed-walk in the direction of her shop. Head down, arms pumping, she let the door slam behind her. My sister dissolved in giggles.

"Too funny. She looked like the Red Queen, didn't she?"

"Never mind her." Once I let Rosie out, I pushed Maddie onto the porch swing and sank beside her on the padded seat. "I hope you won't shoot the messenger, but I'd better tell you what Cissy Davison said. About Kip."

Maddie listened, eyes widening, while I explained everything. She let out an audible "huh" before lapsing into silence. The swing creaked back and forth while I waited her out.

"I figured you might want to know," I finally said. "I'm sorry. I really like Kip—"

"Yeah, I know. So do I." She squeezed my arm. "The red

flags were there, in plain sight. Maybe I've known all along that something was wrong, but couldn't put a finger on it."

"You need to give him a chance to explain. All that information was unsettling, and some of it might not be true."

"Yeah. I don't know if I should drop all this on him tonight, though," Maddie said, and stood. "But I'm dying to know if that's why he can't finish the Hippie Bear. Plus I've got to make sure that Jay succeeds. Abby's my friend. She's counting on that sculpture, and so is everyone who contributed to the GoFundMe account."

My sister stooped to plant a kiss on Rosie's muzzle and then headed to her car. Squinting against the last rays of sunlight, I watched her drive to the corner of Kermit Street. A solitary bicyclist pedaled, chain clanking, across Theodore Lane. Once Maddie's car vanished, I headed inside for a late supper. Crackers and string cheese, since we had yet to do a grocery run. Rosie wolfed her kibble and then watched my every bite. I held up a sliver of mozzarella.

Rosie sat up, paws waving. "Aww! Here you go, baby."

She scarfed it down. I switched the TV on for a *Monk* rerun, loving his idiosyncrasies, from even numbers to phobias, and the little details he picked up that seemed oblivious to everyone else. That reminded me of something. About Gina.

Before I could wrestle with that, my cell's ringtone jangled with the *Peanuts* theme. Uh-oh. "Hey, Mads. Everything okay?"

"It's gone!" My sister sobbed, hysterical, and gasped for breath.

"What's gone? What do you mean—Kip's bear?"

She garbled something I couldn't make out and then hung up. Another call beeped on my phone. Maddie's phone must have lost the signal and she'd redialed. But instead, Mary Kate's voice blared in my ear.

"Sasha? You'd better get over here to Fresh Grounds."

Chapter 21

What was going on? Mary Kate hung up before I could reply. My worries shot into overdrive. I glanced at Rosie, who was calmly chowing down the rest of my crackers and cheese. Onyx meowed, arching her back, her silky black fur all aquiver.

"Oops."

I dumped a can of wet food onto a plate for her and raced out to the parking lot. Rushed back to snatch my car keys from the ceramic dish by the door. Then I drove, tires squealing, all the way to Main Street. Stomped the brakes in front of The Birdcage. The vintage lamppost's globe was broken. When had that happened? Shadows stretched everywhere except around the bright lantern Mary Kate held in her hand.

"Where's Mads?" I asked.

"Inside, with Garrett. Take a look at what she found."

No wonder Maddie had lost it. I stared in horror at what was left of the Polka Bear. The accordion lay on the ground, keyboard smashed, taped straps still attached to its broken paws. Parts of the bear's head, the arms, torso, and legs were scattered on the sidewalk, between the building and the street's curb, the fiberglass pieces shiny with brightly colored polka dots. The base remained intact with jagged bits of the bear's feet.

"We already called the police." Mary Kate's apron had streaks of white flour across the black fabric. She pushed a strand of her reddish blond hair behind one ear. "I was in the kitchen prepping for tomorrow's bread. I had the music on loud, so I didn't hear anything."

"I wonder how they—"

A squad car screeched to a halt across the street. Officer Hillerman climbed out, the radio microphone in his hand, answering the dispatcher. Officer Adam Shook, the village fire chief's son, stalked over to the smashed bear.

"What the hell?" he said. "I knew fiberglass cracked easily, but this is totally smashed."

"That's why we called." Mary Kate moved the high-beam lantern closer. "I hope you can figure out who did this, and if someone saw or heard them."

"We'll try, ma'am," Officer Shook said, and started searching the area.

Mary Kate eyed me, mouth open in shock. " 'Ma'am,' " she hissed. "I feel eighty all of a sudden. We can't be that much older than him."

"At least six years."

Hillerman brought a camera from the squad car and snapped photos of the damage. Too restless to stand idle, I crossed the street and examined the Starry Night Bear in front of the Time Turner. It looked untouched, its white stars dim. I crossed back and searched the cement around the flower shop, the hair salon, The Cat's Cradle, and Fresh Grounds. Nothing caught my eye. Heartsick, I fetched a flashlight from my car and started over.

"Damn. Something's gotta be here."

I circled around the row of shops to the parking lot where

I'd found Gina's body. The crime scene tape was long gone, and none of the lamps here had been smashed; pools of light illuminated the rough gravel. I searched behind each shop, wondering why the local police hadn't conducted regular patrols of all the bear sculptures. But Silver Hollow didn't have the same level of crime as larger towns, though. And the cops had enough to do.

At the corner of Archibald and Main, I spied a trash can. I inched my way forward, checking the sidewalk, and then glanced inside to view the contents.

"Jackpot."

Using a scrap of corduroy fabric I'd tucked inside my purse, a sample of what we had bought for the prize bear's lederhosen, I retrieved a long metal pipe that had been tossed into the trash can. Marked with several scrapes and dents, too.

Then I flagged down Officer Hillerman. "Over here! And look at this." I pointed to a crumpled pair of latex gloves on the ground. "I hope there's fingerprints on the pipe, even if they used those gloves. Or maybe there's skin cells or a hair left inside."

"Probably not, but thanks," he said. "Our lab isn't that technical anyway, like on TV. Too bad we didn't get a photo of the pipe inside the barrel."

I bristled at his subtle reprimand, but let it go. Hillerman took the metal piece over to Officer Shook, who whistled low. They conferred for a few minutes, heads together; I marched into Fresh Grounds, not willing to wait. Garrett mopped the floor in back. The scent of bleach almost overpowered me, but I held my breath until I could tolerate it. Muted music played overhead. It seemed odd being in here without the usual fragrances of coffee and pastries.

No crowd, either, except for Maddie, Mary Kate, plus Abby and Amanda Pozniak, who all gathered at a back table.

Amanda pulled out another chair for me. My sister let out a long breath, shuddering a little. I felt horrible for her.

"I'm so sorry, Mads. I don't know what to say."

"Yeah, this sucks." She sniffed. "It's art. I mean, I know kids can be mischievous, but they took it way beyond that."

"Malice, pure and simple," Abby said. "They waited for the right time, when all of the shops were closed. Broke the street-lamp, too. Probably didn't know Mary Kate was in here, too, but that was pure luck."

"But why?" Maddie kept shaking her head. "Why my bear?"

"The police will find out," I said. "I found a pipe they must have used—"

"Hey, we heard some loud bangs earlier," Amanda cut in, and nudged her sister. "We thought a truck backfired on the street, remember. I peeked outside to see if a delivery truck had left something at Mary's Flowers, or The Birdcage."

"We didn't see anything, though," Abby said. "The noise had stopped by then."

"Did you happen to see someone on a bicycle?" I asked.

"I did, yeah. Out the front window, after we checked the back door. We saw him ride past on the street. And about five or ten minutes later, Maddie called us over here."

"Damn. I might have seen that guy, too," I muttered to myself. "We'll have to wait and see if the cops find any evidence."

Maddie wiped her eyes and sniffed. "I can't redo the Polka Bear, it's too late. Completely worthless. All that money wasted, too."

Both police officers entered the shop. "We have a few questions for you, Ms. Silverman," Hillerman said. "And your friends, of course, but let's start with what time you arrived, and what you saw first. Take your time."

They all took turns answering, while Hillerman wrote the

information. Officer Shook questioned Garrett in the kitchen. My mind kept returning to the bicycle. Jay's sister had seen someone skulking around the Jack Pine Bear before riding away. Could it have been the same person? What if he'd smashed the Polka Bear, hopped on his bike, and tossed the pipe in the trash? Then rode around to Church Street, where Abby saw him through her shop window, and down Kermit. Crossing the road where Maddie waited in her car.

I'd seen him, too. Or was it a woman?

I kicked myself for not watching where the cyclist had gone next. Why would a teen have targeted only Maddie's bear? They could have damaged multiple bears around the village. But Holly Parker had good reason to take revenge.

"Did you check all the other bears?" I interrupted Hillerman, who shrugged, and then turned to Abby. "Can you describe the person you saw on the bicycle?"

"Sure." She laced her fingers together. "Dark coat. Jeans. White sneakers, I think. They caught the light, that's why I noticed. And a hat. Baseball cap."

"Man or woman?"

Abby shrugged. "Could have been either, I guess."

"Wearing glasses?" I asked.

She closed her eyes, clearly concentrating. "I couldn't tell. Head was down, and he or she rode fast along the street."

"What bicyclist?" Hillerman waited, his notebook ready.

"The one who probably smashed my sister's bear," I said. "Even if he or she's innocent, they were around, close enough, when it did happen. So they might be a witness."

"I suppose you'll want us to ask everyone in the village if they own a bike," he said, his sarcasm clear. "Not everyone registers them. Or buys a license for their dogs."

"Then send everything to the county lab. That pipe and the gloves."

"Yeah, we will. Even if it's a hopeless case."

A truck's tires squealed outside. Kip O'Sullivan surged through the coffee shop's doors, his face red, as if ready to burst a blood vessel. Maddie jumped to her feet. He rushed over and folded her into his arms, hugged her tight.

"What the hell happened? I couldn't get here right away. Babe, shh." Kip murmured against her hair, rubbed her back. "Who would smash it like that?"

Maddie gulped back her tears. "It's okay."

"But your Polka Bear. What's being done about this?" Kip turned to the policemen, his voice raised in anger. "I hope you're taking this vandalism seriously. It's not like spray-painting a freeway underpass, you know. Anything over a thousand dollars is a felony. And it's clear that all the bears in the village are at risk."

"We're doing the best we can, sir." Officer Shook sounded defensive, but Hillerman waved him back to the kitchen.

"It might take some time to investigate."

"You better find who did this." Kip drew my sister toward the door. "Mads. I need your help with the Hippie Bear's highlights."

She twisted away. "I can't leave! They're still asking questions."

"I can't finish without you, babe. You're the only one I trust." He turned to Hillerman. "You're done here, right? She can go."

Abby, Amanda, and I exchanged shocked glances. How could he drag Maddie off to help him with his bear, after being dealt such a blow? Talk about selfish. I could tell Abby looked ready to tell him off, and struggled to control herself. My gut churned. I hoped Kip would think twice before pushing harder. But no. He kept the pressure on.

"It won't take much time, just a few more touches. Then Jay and I can seal it."

"Just seal it, or it won't be dry by tomorrow night," she

said wearily. Tears dripped over her cheeks and off her chin. "I can't help you any more than I have already, Kip. I'm so tired, don't you understand? Your bear's done. Seal it, let it dry, and bring it in."

Kip whispered low, his eyes darting to the rest of us and back to her. I couldn't hear what he said, but she shoved him when he tried to clamp hands on her shoulders. Officer Hillerman took a few steps, but Maddie signaled for him to stop.

"I'm going home, and so is Kip."

"Mads—"

"No. I'm done, totally done. Abby doesn't expect perfection, Kip! She asked a whole slew of her friends for money to buy the sculpture," Maddie said. "I'm tired of fighting about this. I don't want to see you anymore. Especially since you keep badgering me."

Kip rubbed his unshaven jaw, avoiding everyone else's eyes, and ran a hand through his dark hair. "Come on, Maddie. You don't mean that."

"Your bear's fine the way it is. Mine is trashed. If you can't understand how that's affected me, then forget it."

Maddie retreated to stand between Mary Kate, Garrett, and me. Abby and Amanda closed ranks around her as well in protection mode. Kip stewed over that in silence, glowering at us all. At Hillerman's signal, Officer Shook led him outside. The door swung shut with a hiss.

"Well, we're done here, too," Hillerman said. "If we find anything, Ms. Silverman, or have further questions, we'll be in touch."

My sister collapsed into a chair at the table. Her friends joined her, although Mary Kate and Garrett drew back to the kitchen; I trailed after the policeman. I knew Maddie was hurt, and scared, and needed time and space to recover. She'd also get over breaking up with Kip faster than mourning her Polka

Bear. I toed the shards on the sidewalk that the cops hadn't bagged, hoping to find anything we'd missed.

Jay's truck pulled to a stop on the street while Mary Kate and I collected the Polka Bear's shattered pieces. Garrett dragged the heavy bag inside Fresh Grounds. Jay walked over, disbelief clear in his eyes.

"Kip told you what happened, I take it?" I wiped my dusty hands on my jeans.

"So what all happened?" Jay asked. "Or would you rather tell me tomorrow."

"I'm too wound up to go home yet."

Plus I'd indulged in a cup of coffee, and knew that would keep me awake for a while. Jay led me over to his truck; he listened in amazement while I explained the whole story, about the vandalism, my theory of the bicyclist. Even Kip and Maddie's heated exchange.

"Wow. I don't blame her, not one bit," Jay said. "He may be under stress, but he did it to himself. Kept putting things off, and now it's crunch time."

"Unbelievable. How could he expect her to help after what happened?"

"His bear's done. Been done, probably for a week." He thumped the truck's fender. "I've told him that, Maddie told him over and over. Kip wouldn't listen. He kept saying it needed a few more details. That I didn't understand."

"Yeah, but your Jack Pine's finished! Even though you waited till the last minute."

Jay shoved his hands into his pockets. "I'll wrestle that damned bear out of his hands," he said. "I had to meet with a client tonight, or I'd have forced him to seal it. Maddie's right. He owes the sponsors."

I nodded. "Okay. Let me know what happens."

Once Jay's truck rumbled off, I drove my car a block over to

Abby's shop. Compared to the clutter inside the Time Turner, the Pozniaks' antique shop looked pristine. My sister perched on a chair, her feet tucked under her, china teacup in hand, eyes focused on the steaming brew. Until I cleared my throat. Maddie blinked.

"Remember earlier," I began, "when Holly talked about Flynn. How she called Cheryl Cummings a weather girl? And you said she was '*a weather forecaster.*' That could be why she may be behind the vandalism. With the pipe."

"But we can't prove she smashed my bear." Maddie set her cup aside.

I didn't reply. Wishing Holly Parker was guilty didn't make it true, even if my theory made sense. But I believed Lisa Blake. Holly had it out for my family, and destroying Maddie's bear seemed to fit.

"I saw a few pipes like that one in the Dumpster behind her shop."

"Too bad the village council rejected the idea of installing cameras around the village," Abby said. "Gina would still be alive if they had. But listen. Both of you go home, take it easy until the Oktobear Fest."

"Jay will make sure Kip brings the Hippie Bear in tomorrow," I said.

"Doesn't mean we're getting back together, though." Maddie hugged both of her friends, and then drew me into their circle. "Thanks for coming to my rescue, all of you."

I followed her car around the block, barely paying attention to the traffic signals or other drivers on the way, discouraged to the max. My sister trudged upstairs to bed; I'd never seen her so dejected. And never felt so awful when I tossed and turned for most of the night. Rosie snored beside me, content with her doggie dreams. Morning dawned, and soft sunlight crept into the room. I dozed for a few hours but finally gave up, hit the shower, and dressed.

What else did Holly have in mind to plague my family? Maybe I was wrong. Maybe someone else had shattered the Polka Bear and crushed Maddie's spirits. But my gut instinct told me otherwise.

Chapter 22

Carrying a cardboard tray with Maddie's favorite coffee, plus a Mint Mocha for me and a bag of scones, I let Fresh Grounds' door bang shut behind me. Being a Thursday, the shop wasn't too crowded. By tomorrow afternoon, the line of customers would stretch halfway down the block. Mary Kate had hired three college students to handle the excess, in fact, and help turn out all the various baked goods for the Oktobear Fest.

I sighed when Flynn's electric blue Jaguar stopped at the curb. He climbed out and stared at the spot where the Polka Bear's square base remained. I noticed a few shards I'd missed last night on the ground, but my hands were full. They'd have to stay put for now. Flynn walked toward me, clearly puzzled. He straightened his silver cufflinks.

"What happened to Maddie's bear? Judith texted me—"

"At seven thirty in the morning?"

"Sure." Flynn waved a hand. "So what happened?"

"Vandalism. Pretty obvious to anyone."

"Cops on the case?"

"Of course. And whoever did it, if they're caught, will be charged with a felony." I set the tray on top of my car. "So I hear you're dating Cheryl Cummings."

"I see her from time to time."

"Oh, come on. I saw you both at Quinn's Pub. Anyone would think you're more serious than just casual dating. Are you bringing her to the Oktobear Fest this weekend?"

Flynn barked a laugh. "No way. She's not into corny stuff like that. We have tickets to see *Mamma Mia!* at the Fisher on Saturday. Cheryl talked me into it. She loves musicals. Said we get to participate in the show, too."

For the life of me, I couldn't see him enjoying that kind of play. That vague something, about Gina, kept bugging me— what was it? Was it something Flynn had done? Or said?

"When did you and Gina break up?" I asked, since he hadn't made a move to leave.

He cocked his blond head. "Things cooled down when she talked about filing that lawsuit against Mayor Bloom. Wouldn't have looked right. So we broke up."

"I thought you balked when Gina wanted an engagement ring."

"Judith told you that, I suppose." Flynn shrugged. "Whatever."

"I'm surprised Gina didn't ask one of your other team lawyers to take the case," I said, "since it sure seems like a conflict of interest for you."

"She trusted me. And I have more experience in that kind of lawsuit." He opened his car door and leaned on it. "Plus I handled another case for her a while back, and won. She expected to win again. Bloom owed her a lot of dough."

"But you didn't see her the night she was killed?"

Flynn shook his head, but I could tell the question flustered him. His face flushed red the same way it had a few nights ago back at the factory, when Jay and I planned to work on the costume for Jack Pine Bear. And that's when I remembered what Flynn *had* said.

"By the way, what exactly did you mean by 'the last time I saw Gina alive'? Remember you stopped by Wednesday night, when you wanted me to go to dinner—"

"I told you I talked to Gina at Quinn's Pub, on Thursday."

"You said, 'The last time I saw Gina alive'—that's an odd way to phrase it." I caught that wary gleam in his eye and felt triumphant. "You did see her Saturday night. Maybe after she was stabbed? Am I right?"

His face turned ashen and then flooded scarlet again, from his neck to the roots of his hair. "Listen, Sasha. I didn't kill her. I swear."

"I didn't say that. But you saw her, after she was dead?"

Flynn rubbed his face with both hands. "Okay, I'll explain. I spent Saturday night with Cheryl. Her family has a cottage out on Portage Lake, but her parents are strict. Greek, and Catholic. We can't let on about how we're fooling around. I left around five o'clock Sunday morning. I had that appointment at the studio to do another commercial, but I drove through Silver Hollow on the way. Stopped for coffee."

"What time?" I asked, relieved he'd finally come around to being truthful.

"I don't remember. I pulled into the parking lot behind Fresh Grounds. Not in front of the building, but I wish I had," he said in regret. "I wanted to check my phone messages, and I had trouble with all the fog. But then I saw Gina in that stupid pink sweatshirt thing."

"Wait a minute. I thought she was Holly—oh." I caught my breath. "You covered up her red hair, didn't you? Pulled the hood over her head." Flynn shuffled his feet and refused to answer. "How could you do that? And not call 9-1-1?"

"I did. Once I got to my office." He held his hands up in surrender. "I'd first checked my messages, but my battery ran out. By the time I called, the dispatcher said they'd already been notified. She took down all the information anyway. Mason can verify that."

"Yeah. And where the call originated. I bet he already knows."

"Okay, then."

"You better explain all this, as soon as you can. Not whenever you happen to run into him," I said. "Gina was murdered, and you knew her better than anyone else around. I bet Mason hasn't crossed you off his suspect list, either."

"I'll talk to him." Flynn dodged me and opened the coffee shop's door. "I'm late getting to the office, and I'm booked solid all day. But I will tell him."

I walked to my car, wondering if he really would follow through. Flynn soon drove his flashy Jaguar past me, leaving a black skid mark on the street, and his squealing tires hurt my ears. Brother. I mulled over the past twenty-four hours on my way home, hoping Maddie and I could get a breather. Especially with the Oktobear Fest tomorrow.

I set my sister's coffee on the kitchen island, removed a scone from the bag, and then perched on the window seat next to Rosie. She lifted her head for a moment, eyes on the trees outside, guarding against any rogue squirrels.

"Yeah, it's hard work. But some dog's gotta do it—"

"What?" Maddie stood in the doorway, hair spiked every which way, in a bathrobe. "Gaah. I feel terrible. I hope that's my coffee."

"Have at it. So you and Kip are no longer an item."

"Do we have to talk about it now?" she groaned.

"No. But remember how Cissy Davison mentioned a spat between him and Holly, up in Traverse City," I said, "so I'm curious. How well did Kip know her? Maybe Holly's taking some of her anger against him on you. By way of the Polka Bear."

"I suppose that's possible." Maddie curled up in an armchair with a scone and sipped her coffee. "But we don't know who smashed it. Not yet."

Rosie's head jerked up. She panted and then jumped to the tile floor, claws scrabbling, and whined at the back door. I grumbled, following her out and watching her trot down the porch steps and out to the lawn. Sipped my coffee—I'd left a half-eaten scone inside, and wanted to finish it. Or crawl back into bed. My head throbbed. The sleepless night would not make the day easier, given a tour with out-of-town Red Hat Society ladies this afternoon. I couldn't take Rosie for a walk during lunch. And Uncle Ross and I had to deliver the grand prize bear to the village, after preparing for the weekend's special sale.

I walked through the garden. Where was Rosie? She usually didn't take this long to tinkle in the morning. "After the Oktobear Fest is over, baby, we'll go to the dog park—"

"What a silly name. The Okto*bear* Fest," a voice sounded from over the hedge. "Every other festival is 'Oktober.' But because of your teddy bear shop, the whole village has to kowtow to whatever the Silvermans want."

Heart in my throat, I peered through an open space in the shrubbery. Holly Parker stood on the sidewalk, hands tucked into the pockets of a green sweatshirt. The early morning sun burnished her dark hair with a reddish glow.

"What do you want?"

"Just being neighborly."

"At eight in the morning? Or maybe you were heading off on a bike ride."

She drew in a quick breath, as if she'd caught my underlying meaning. "Maybe. I've seen you bike around the village. It's good exercise."

"Yeah. Tough to hide a length of metal pipe while you're pedaling, though."

Holly poked up her glasses. "I don't know what you're talking about."

"I think you do," I said, anger bubbling up into my voice. "Did you know my sister's bear was vandalized last night? Not just a broken accordion strap this time."

"Why do you keep blaming me for whatever bad luck your family suffers?" Her tone held more than a hint of spite. "You've got a problem, Sasha, being so suspicious. Kids will do anything for attention. Look how they painted graffiti on my shop windows."

" 'Your nine lives are over'? What kid would paint that as a message on anyone's shop window? You came up with that to point the finger at my cousin and The Cat's Cradle."

"I didn't do it," Holly snapped. "I'm not that desperate."

"Some people will do anything for attention," I said.

"Ha." She tossed her ponytail over one shoulder and headed back toward her store. "Better watch out. Some kids might fiddle with the gate latch, and your little dog would get loose. The way people drive around here, she might get run over by a car."

That sounded like a threat. If only Maddie had overheard Holly. Damn. I rattled the gate, making sure she hadn't tampered with the lock, and whistled for Rosie. Inside the house, I felt better. My dog jumped up onto the window seat again. Maddie sat at the kitchen island, far more awake, and drained her coffee.

"Hey. Thanks for getting this, and the scones."

"I got Aunt Eve's favorites," I said, trying to forget the encounter with Holly. "Did you want me to pick up our costumes for tomorrow?"

"Nope. Got everything under control." She bit into a second scone, chock-full of plump blackberries. "Wish I could figure out how to make these. Then we wouldn't have to keep running over to Mary Kate's."

"I tried once, but they came out tough and dry. Not like these moist, delicious gems." With a sigh, I nibbled the rest of my scone. "Mary Kate said there's a trick to getting the dough just right. Some people have the knack for baking. Some don't."

"You make wonderful cakes," my sister said. "And that buttercream icing. Maybe you ought to take lessons in decorating from Wendy Clark."

"Sure! I'll squeeze a class or two in between everything else I do. No problem." I laughed at Maddie's stuck-out tongue. "I'm more than willing to pay for cake, or cookies, or whatever else they want to make. Saves me the trouble—"

A choking sound caught our attention. Maddie twisted around and pointed to Rosie, who now stood on the rug by the back door. Her paws splayed, she heaved several times.

"Poor thing! What's the matter, baby?"

I rushed to her side and pried open her jaws, praying she hadn't eaten a baby bird, one of my garden gloves, or a half-chewed golf ball like the last time. Rosie choked again, and twice more, until a lump of something small and green-hued fell out of her mouth.

"What in the world is that?" Maddie had crouched down, but jumped back in horror.

"Call the vet clinic. Tell them I'm bringing her in."

Rosie's breathing came in short pants. That scared me. I lifted her head when she went limp, and my heart melted in sympathy at her whimper of pain. In between hacking sounds, she barfed up another wad of greenish scum. I panicked at the streak of blood.

"They don't open until ten," Maddie called, waving her cell. "I'll call the emergency number on the fridge magnet."

Once we followed their directions, I wrapped Rosie in a towel. Maddie handed me the greenish barf she'd scooped into a plastic bag. While I carried my dog to the car, she searched the lawn and bagged several more green chunks.

"Go on, I'll open for you and cover the register," she said. "Forget the tour, go!"

I barely paid attention to anything but the drive, via Baker Road, to the vet hospital. Traffic grew heavy closer to Ann Arbor, and I chafed at the delay. Rosie lay still on the seat, her head down, eyes closed. That worried me worse than anything. I fought back tears.

After I rang the after-hours buzzer and waited, heart in my throat, a tech quickly arrived to unlock the door. I barged past, rushed to the room where he directed me, and laid my dog on the examining table.

"Here's what I caught her eating." I handed the plastic bags to the tech. "I can't tell what it is, though, or why it was on our lawn."

"No problem, ma'am. If you prefer, you can wait outside in the lounge."

Ma'am, again. Now I understood how Mary Kate felt. The tech looked fifteen with barely a trace of a beard. Mark Fox was around my age. I should have called him at home and begged him to open his clinic early, offered double his fee, but I didn't have his private number. I stayed by Rosie's side, since she seemed calmer with my presence. Once the vet, a Dr. Garvey, arrived and shook my hand, she did a quick checkup and then murmured to the tech.

"We'll give Rosie IV fluids, with vitamin K, and some meds to settle her stomach," she said to me. "Looks like she purged the worst of it. Good thing." Dr. Garvey spent several minutes massaging Rosie's abdomen. "Do you keep rat poison around the house?"

"Rat poison?" I stared at her, horrified. "No way."

"That stuff looks like chunks of bromadiolone. Yellow or green, comes in a bucket or box. Common use is for killing rats. You found it on the lawn?"

I nodded. Not long after Holly visited, too. She'd ruined Maddie's bear, threatened to run over my dog, but instead tried to poison her. Things had gotten way out of hand. My hands wouldn't stop shaking, and I left Rosie in Dr. Garvey's capable hands. Pacing in the hallway outside the room, I dialed my cell and waited on hold. The calming classical selections helped to calm my angry mood. But I seriously needed sleep. Or more coffee.

Dr. Garvey finally came out to the hall. "I think you'd better leave Rosie here overnight, or at least for the day. We'll let you know how she's doing later this afternoon. With the IV and medication, she should recover nicely."

I juggled the phone to my other ear, still waiting out the taped music. "Do you think the poison affected her?" I asked. "Permanently, I mean."

Dr. Garvey smiled. "No, you acted quickly. If you'd waited, she might have been too far gone. Rosie will need to rest, though, for a few days."

"All right, and thank you so much."

"No problem. She's a beautiful dog. I love her teddy bear grooming, too."

I nodded and headed to the lobby. At last the receptionist spoke in my ear. "Hello? Yes, I'd like to make an appointment. Sasha Silverman—with Mike Blake, thanks," I said. "As soon as possible, please. Tell him I spoke to his wife, and I have a similar situation. Yes, it's urgent. That would be great. See you in a few hours. Thanks."

Out in my car, I called Maddie and updated her on Rosie. "I've got an appointment with a lawyer. Rosie was poisoned—"

"What? You're not kidding, are you?"

"It's true, and I think Holly did it. I'm meeting with Mike Blake."

"Whoa. Listen, we've got customers," Maddie said. "I'll see you whenever you get back. Do what you have to do, Sash."

I pocketed my phone, relieved by her supportive words. We both knew it was long past time to take drastic steps. We needed help. Especially since the cops didn't seem to be making much progress. Mike Blake would understand.

We had to end Holly's devious plans.

Chapter 23

"Poor sweet baby. How are you feeling today?" Aunt Eve rained kisses on Rosie's head. My dog ate up the love, her tail wagging, while perched on the kitchen window seat. "You are the sweetest thing! Yes, you are. Such a good girl. Did you eat any breakfast?"

"She did," I said with pride, "and kept it down, too. I'm glad she didn't have to stay the night at the hospital. The vet said she bounced back quicker than expected."

"But you gave her what, kibble?"

"A touch of rice with a little cooked chicken mixed in."

"Aww! I bet you were hungry, Rosie." Aunt Eve straightened her back, her posture better than anyone's in my family. "I sewed her costume, you ought to see how darling it is! Those factory machines are much nicer than my old Singer."

"Thanks," I said and hugged her. "I'm glad you had fun with it."

"I sewed that poodle skirt for my teddy bear, too. So easy! I ironed on an appliqué, and then embroidered a little leash." She patted her hair. "Emily Abbott's bear costume is finished, too. I hope she has time to pick it up today, but her band is practicing."

"I'd better get ready for customers. Maddie could barely handle everyone who came in yesterday. I bet we'll be swamped again today."

"Ross called from the Sunshine Café. He waited twenty minutes to get a seat!"

"For the counter? Wow, I'm surprised he didn't leave." I ruffled my dog's curly coat. "Who's a smart girl. Next time, don't eat anything in the yard, okay?"

Maddie carried in two plastic hanging bags and laid them on the parlor sofa. "She might have suffered weeks before the end came," she said. "A slow and painful death, according to Mark Fox. If Holly did toss that rat poison in our yard, she's seriously sick in the head."

"What is the matter with people nowadays?" Aunt Eve said with a sigh. "I'd better get to the dry cleaners right now and pick up Ross's blazer. He wouldn't let me buy him a costume, so I had to improvise. I can't wait for you girls to see him dressed up."

"So are you coming tonight?" I asked.

"No. Ross thinks we need more practice for the dance contest."

Maddie clapped her hands. "Wow! A samba, or the jitterbug?"

"It's a surprise, so you'll have to wait till tomorrow night."

Cheeks pinker, Aunt Eve rushed out the door. I turned to Maddie, suppressing a laugh. "I'm thinking love is in the air again for those two," I said. "So which costume is mine?"

"This one." Maddie pointed to the dark green dirndl dress. "Isn't that the cutest little deer pattern? I couldn't find this in my size, so you get to wear it."

"Gee, thanks." I plucked up the frilly blouse, so short it stopped below the bust. "Let's hope the dress will cover where it ends, but couldn't you have found a regular one?"

Maddie tossed a beige silk ribbon my way. "Don't make fun, have fun. Tie the sash at the waist in a bow. Jay's lederhosen and hat are a matching dark green, too."

"So yours is the blue one, I take it."

"Yup." Maddie's dirndl was far simpler, with a black, laced corset over her ruffled blouse and a plain sky-blue skirt. She held up two short pigtails, decorated with beads, and twirled them. "I'm off to the salon so Karen or Lynn can clip in these extensions. Jay said he'll pick us up at four o'clock, so be ready."

"I put a notice that we're closing at two o'clock today," I said. "Joan Kendall asked to cover the shop all day tomorrow. She needs the money. Time and a half, so I agreed."

"Got it. Why don't you braid your hair?"

"Why don't you tell me whether Jay and Kip delivered the Hippie Bear last night? I had to pick up Rosie, remember."

"Yes, they did." Maddie looked happy at that. "Finished at last, and it's even sealed."

I hated to burst her bubble, my curiosity wouldn't rest. "Did you ever ask Kip what happened in Traverse City?"

"Abby found out." Maddie hesitated, fluffing her dark pixie hair with a sigh. "When he first moved there, the local art galleries loved his work. All that sudden success went to his head. That's why Kip bought that house with the studio, and a brand-new car. Got in debt, and then he couldn't get enough commissions to pay it all off."

"Like Flynn, huh? He revels in showing off around town."

"Yeah, maybe. You know how it is in the art world. The spotlight shifts to the next big trend." She sounded wistful, as if empathizing with his fading career. I knew Maddie had taken a few hits over the years as well. "Kip scrambled to get his pieces shown, and spent a lot on high-end marketing, open houses with wine and food. Gina Lawson's idea, actually."

"Really. She worked for him, too?"

"Just a onetime deal. It didn't work, he admitted failure,

and left it all behind. Kip blamed himself. Told me he came here to start over, right after we met."

"Never mind, Mads. Go to the salon or you'll be late." I hadn't meant to worry her. "I'll hang these dresses in our rooms."

My sister rushed out, grabbing her phone and keys. "Don't forget, four o'clock!"

Once I returned from upstairs, I let Rosie outside and stood guard. I wasn't about to take any further chances. I couldn't prove that Holly put the rat poison in our yard, but she'd worn a green sweatshirt. That was too much of a coincidence.

"No, no, stay away from there." I guided Rosie clear of a thick bush. After pushing aside the shrubbery to check, I breathed easier. Nothing hidden beneath. "My precious baby. You rest this morning, okay? Keep Nyx out of trouble."

I carried Rosie up the steps and into the kitchen. The cat stared balefully at us both from her perch atop the tower. Apparently, Onyx had already conceded the window seat. Rosie curled up in the sunshine with a happy sigh. I'd dragged out the wooden stairs from an upstairs storage room last night, so my dog would have an easier time getting up and down.

Now I kissed her on the muzzle, poured more coffee, and headed to the shop. Aunt Eve was right. Customers had already lined up outside the front door, ten minutes early. Steeling myself, I plastered on a smile and unlocked the door.

"Happy Oktobear Fest! Welcome to the Silver Bear Shop and Factory."

"Are there any tours today?" one woman asked.

"Yes, one at noon. Only a few spots left."

"So you're closing early today?" someone else asked. "How about tomorrow? My sister is off on Saturdays, and she wants to buy a silver bear."

"We'll be open our usual hours, ten until six." I turned to answer more questions. "Yes, the grand prize bear will be on display at the courthouse. The vandalism incident is still under investigation. We haven't heard any updates from the police, so I can't tell you more. Feel free to browse through our bears, the accessories, and clothing items. We have special bears dressed in dirndls and lederhosen for sale. Over on the far side, the middle shelf."

The morning hours rushed past. I'd added an extra half-dozen people to the tour, which proved difficult for the staff trying to work; they made the best of it, given the long line of curious visitors trooping through the factory. By the time I returned to the shop, I couldn't move past all the people lined at the register. Maddie had changed to her costume already, chatting with women holding bags of merchandise from other shops in Silver Hollow.

"We wanted to display the Polka Bear in the garden here," my sister said, "but that's not possible now."

"What a shame. I wonder who would do such a terrible thing," one said.

"They ought to be thrown in jail, for sure."

Maddie handled their comments and sympathy with grace. At last she locked the door and then glanced at the clock. "Whew, three o'clock. You'd better get dressed."

"Sounds like people want you to do another Polka Bear," I said. "Too bad the fiberglass is so expensive."

"Dad wanted to buy another sculpture, but my heart wouldn't be in it."

"I'm on your side. Better to get over it." I hurried to the office. "Aunt Eve, are you sure you don't mind keeping company with Rosie tonight? If you need to go practice, put her in the crate in the kitchen. It's her safe spot."

"We'll practice here, and she can watch. Ross rented a DVD for afterward, so we'll settle in for a quiet evening. I'll make some popcorn."

"No treats for the dog, remember! Her stomach is still healing."

Before I rushed upstairs, I gave Rosie her meds and fed her the rice and chicken mixture again. Before I reached my bedroom, I heard Jay's truck in the parking lot. I brushed on powder, blush, a touch of eye shadow, then tied two short braids on either side of my ears with green ribbon. My dirndl had hooks in front instead of lacing, which made it less easy to adjust, so it felt a little tight. Too many cookies. I'd been stressing out about Rosie and indulged.

"Pockets. Thank goodness."

I heard a ding for a text message. Maddie—with a frowny-face emoticon. "Yeah, yeah, I'm coming! Sheesh." Slipping the phone into my skirt pocket, I rushed downstairs.

My sister was breathless with excitement. She looked adorable, tiny and cute in the sky-blue dirndl, embroidered apron, and puffy-sleeved blouse. I probably resembled a hefty Viking Brunhilde, minus the horned hat and steel chain mail.

"You be good for Aunt Eve." I fluffed Rosie's blanket in her crate, retrieved her from the window seat, and placed her inside. "You're safe, sweetie."

"I'm so glad she's better," Maddie said. "Come on, we're late."

We rushed outside to meet Jay, who slid out of his truck. I burst out laughing when he struck a pose, one arm bent to show off a muscle. He tipped his green feathered hat at a jaunty angle and lifted one leg to display knee-high stockings; his short green britches buttoned up on either side, attached to H-shaped suspenders with an embroidered band over his chest. Jay scratched his chest with a wide grin.

"Kind of itchy. So are these wool socks. You both look great, by the way."

"Thanks. I think." Being bustier than Maddie, I kept tugging up my blouse in a futile effort to hide my cleavage. The dirndl skirt swished with my every move. "Doesn't 'lederhosen' mean 'leather' in German?"

"Yes, but don't even go there," Jay said. "These are bad enough."

"I dunno. Leather might make a real statement," Maddie teased.

"You're hot, even without leather. Hot as in hottie." I kissed Jay, which ended up longer than intended. "Thank goodness for flats, because we'll be on our feet all night."

My sister used the truck's bumper for balance and shook out a piece of gravel from her shoe. "No kidding. Now I wish I'd found boots."

"I hope we won't get cold after dark," I said, "especially if any one sloshes beer on me. Are you all ready to go?"

"How's Rosie?" Jay asked.

Without waiting for me to explain, Maddie plunged into the story while Jay drove to the bank parking lot reserved for volunteers. "Who else but Holly would do it?"

"I bet Mason won't help," he said. "Nothing's been done about Gina's murder."

"Speak of the devil. Er, the detective."

I gestured toward the county SUV, which pulled into the lot as well. Mason parked and then strolled over to join us. Casual in scruffy jeans, a dark green MSU sweatshirt, and a baseball cap, he blended in with the other tourists. I frowned. Tomorrow afternoon's showdown between the state's two top universities always drew fierce competition.

"I take it you're a Sparty fan?" Jay asked.

"Alma mater," he said with an upraised thumb. "They'll beat the Wolverines."

"Not the way UM's playing," I retorted. "We've won almost every game so far. Brian Quinn is setting up a huge outdoor monitor so people won't miss the game."

"He's showing the Red Wings game tonight, too. I wish the beer tent was closer to that screen," Jay said. "I'd love to see them play the Hurricanes."

"So, Sasha. I heard about your dog being poisoned," Mason said. "We'll look into who may have bought the stuff at any local shops, here or in the area."

"I already called The Birdcage. They don't carry it." I glanced at Maddie. "Whoever did it could have gotten it anywhere. With cash."

"Yeah," the detective said. "Proof—a necessary evil. Well, enjoy your evening, folks. I'm working another case in Ypsilanti. Can't stay long tonight."

He loped off toward the village with a casual wave. Maddie snorted in disgust. "Gee. Thanks for nothing."

"He's right, though," I said. "The police can only do so much."

"First Maddie's bear, and then your dog." Jay hugged me tight, clearly worried. "What if Holly targets you next, Sasha?"

"She's a coward at heart, and doesn't want to be caught in the act. I doubt she'll try to pull anything else with so many people around. Come on, we'd better go."

Jay escorted us down Archibald Street. We had to stop several times to pose for selfies with tourists who begged us. I tried to be a good sport about all the attention until a rowdy group of teenagers jostled against my sister. They hooted with laughter.

"Hey, watch where you're going," Jay said. "You'll wrinkle my hosen."

"Sorry, man!" They rushed off toward the park.

I laughed. "Wrinkle your hosen, ha. I bet you didn't expect volunteering meant serving beer in costume, or judging the dance contest tomorrow. You're taking all this in stride."

"It's all in good fun." He let out a deep sigh, though, and slipped an arm around me. "I've got news. I hope you'll take it in stride, too, because in a way it's bad timing. I couldn't tell you until I signed the contract."

"Contract?" Maddie's voice rose in pitch. "Hey, congrats. For what?"

"Thanks. I'm teaching chainsaw carving starting in a few weeks," Jay said. "November through February, east of Gaylord. That's about three or four hours north of here. My parents will take Buster for me."

"How wonderful." I hugged him, but fought a wave of disappointment. "Your reputation has grown, and what a great opportunity! Maddie and I have a trip planned for Mackinac Island. Then there's Halloween, the Bear-zaar, and the Christmas rush. I'll be so busy, and you will be, too."

"For sure we'll spend the holidays together." He kissed me soundly. "No way am I gonna miss ringing in the New Year with you."

"It better be less murderous."

"Listen, you two. Stop smooching and get to the beer tent," Maddie called out, and ran ahead. "It's almost half past five!"

"I want to see all the decorations first," I yelled back. "Especially if we'll be stuck serving in a tent all night."

Banners had been draped across shop fronts, or attached to lampposts, spelling out SILVER HOLLOW'S OKTOBEAR FEST in bright orange letters. Each had Maddie's logo of an adorable tan teddy bear in lederhosen and a hat. On the way to the beer tent, we checked out Kip's Hippie Bear. I thought it looked fabulous with its tie-dyed shirt, peace patch, and a triple strand of beads. A long-haired wig fastened to the bear's head streamed behind the sculpture, and a tie-dyed headband was tucked over the forehead. Below the bear's nose, a thick mustache had been attached as well as a beard on the chin and jaws.

"I glued all that on after Kip sealed the paint," Jay said. "He didn't want to bother. He's too bummed about Maddie breaking up with him. I hope he leaves her alone for a week or two. He's patrolling the bears with a few others to avoid any more vandalism."

"I'm glad Amy Evans is taking steps to prevent any more trouble." I noted the strips of duct tape that held the John Lennon–style round glasses on the nose. "Abby and all the people who donated money will be thrilled if someone bids on this bear."

"I heard the Legal Eagle Bear already found a buyer," Jay said. "Saw the article in the *Silver Hollow Herald*. Hanson, Branson, and Blake made a deal with a law firm in downtown Detroit. Then they donated the money to charity."

"I bet for a tax break, and Flynn's idea. Anything to get out of paying the IRS."

We threaded through crowds strolling around the sidewalk sales tables in front of the Time Turner, The Birdcage, and Mary's Flowers. Even the salon had a display with nail polish bottles, hair products, and accessories.

"Wow, that band sounds good." I stood on tiptoes, peering at the musicians on the steps of the courthouse. Huge speakers flanked them, booming out the lively "Flyer Song" with plenty of *La La La La La*'s and *Schwimm, Schwimm, Schwimm*'s. "Who are they?"

Jay grinned. "The Bavarian Burgermeisters. They're playing all night. Oompah-pahs, waltzes, marches, polkas, all kinds of music. Although some people don't think Polish polkas really fit in, but hey. Why not? 'La Bamba' is just as popular. I think a local band's playing for the dance contest tomorrow night."

The courthouse looked festive as well. A large banner on white canvas, strung on wires, waved in the light breeze between two flagpoles. Below it, a line of small teddy bears in a rainbow of colors, each clipped to a rope, stretched overhead.

"That was a nice order a couple of years ago," I said to Jay. "One hundred and fifty bears, at a discount of course, but they've had to replace a few every year. They're so cute."

"Look at the line already." He held open the beer tent's back flap. When I ducked inside, someone handed me a stiff white apron. "Hey, how come I don't get an apron?"

I snapped it at Jay's backside and then tied it around my waist. "Get busy, Herr Kirby. Thirsty people are impatient people."

"*Ja wohl,* Fraulein."

We spent the next three hours filling beer steins. Despite the growing dark, the crowds swelled to a huge number of people. I couldn't tell what was happening out on the streets. The pavilion's flaps blocked much of our view, and we couldn't see the Red Wings game either. Too bad we hadn't volunteered to man the food tent—delicious smells of sausage, sauerkraut, and baking pretzels made my stomach grumble. Tall stacked lights that stood on almost every corner of the downtown streets helped illuminate the Village Green.

Wendy Clark, Mary Kate's assistant at Fresh Grounds, appeared in a dirndl and apron to pass out free samples of cinnamon apple scones, fried donuts, and muffins from a tray. "I've got coupons, too, good for tonight and tomorrow."

"I wish I could grab one of those. I'm starving." Jay groaned. "Maybe we should have stopped by Fresh Grounds before we started working in here."

"Half an hour until our shift ends." I handed a full stein to a customer. "Try to hang in there and then we'll indulge."

"Fill 'er up," another man said.

"No token, no beer," I said cheerfully. "Only three drinks per night allowed."

"How about I give you thirty bucks, and you fill it up anyway?" he suggested.

Jay stepped over with a frown. "Rules are rules. We don't want anyone driving home intoxicated, sir. The local cops are on the lookout, too. Fair warning."

Thankfully, the guy shrugged and tried his spiel on someone else. Didn't work, either. At last Jay and I finished. Once I turned my apron back in, we raced each other to snag grilled bratwursts in plump hoagie rolls, slathered on mustard and spiced cabbage, and then carried them over to his Jack Pine Bear. Some kids straddled the log like a pony; they whooped and hollered in fun. We stood to eat, since all the picnic tables on the Village Green were occupied. People sang along to the Bavarian Burgermeisters' rendition of "Born in the USA," followed by "We Are the Champions" and "Sweet Caroline."

They started playing "The Donkey Song" next, which I loved, about a donkey who refuses to go home and waits to see his sweetheart. But I froze at the sight of Holly Parker on the other side of the Village Green. She passed out flyers, smiling to those who took them. Beneath a pair of unauthentic suspenders, her white blouse showed off way too much cleavage; her bosom nearly popped out when she bent over. On purpose, since a horde of guys ogled her layered petticoats. Her frilly red embroidered dirndl resembled a miniskirt.

Talk about tacky and tasteless.

"Oh, Sasha! You'd better take one of these." Holly flashed a sickly sweet smile and then shoved a flyer into my hands. "I'm running for mayor this November."

"Mayor?" I stared at her huge glossy photo and campaign slogan—*Mayor Holly Parker for Progress*. "You can't run against Cal Bloom."

"Shows how little you know. People have been so supportive since Gina's death, and they've all promised to vote for me."

"You filed back on August eighth, the deadline at the county clerk's office?" Jay looked incensed. "So you waited to promote running against the mayor until after he became a suspect in Gina's murder."

Holly narrowed her eyes. "Are you accusing me of arranging it?"

"Wait a minute," I said. "How could you get your name on the ballot without enough signatures on a nominating petition?"

"I paid the fee instead." Smug, she leaned close and lowered her voice. "And after I'm mayor, you're gonna be sorry, Sasha Silverman. Your shop will suffer, too."

I stepped backward and ran into Jay's chest. "Think again, Holly Parker. This is the third time you've threatened me and my family."

"What a load of crap! I never threatened you."

"Maddie's bear was smashed, my dog was poisoned—oh, don't act so innocent! A chunk of bromadiolone happened to be on my lawn, right before you walked by. And now this. Jay's a witness. I filed for a personal protection order against you, and one of the lawyers from the Legal Eagles is handling it. Expect to receive notice any day."

"You can't prove anything." Holly stalked toward a group of revelers with a pasted-on smile. "Having a good time? Great! How about making sure Silver Hollow doesn't go stagnant? Mayor Bloom is a murder suspect—you haven't heard? Let me tell you all about it."

Jay shook his head in disbelief and muttered a curse under his breath. "Now, now, no name-calling," I said, and shook a finger. "Don't descend to her level."

"So Flynn came in handy after all, helping you with a PPO."

"Mike Blake, actually. He filed one for Lisa, too."

"Why did she need one?"

I explained how Holly had sent Lisa text messages, dozens of them, plus badgered her with phone calls and voice mails. "That's stalking, non-domestic. It takes two incidents in order to file for a PPO. Mike doesn't want Holly visiting the hospital when Lisa delivers, too."

Jay hugged me close and kissed the top of my head. "I'm glad you took action. I won't worry so much while I'm gone up north."

Proof or not, the less I saw of her, the better. I was satisfied, puncturing Holly's self-satisfaction. And ego.

Chapter 24

Early Saturday morning, since Mary Kate and Wendy were swamped at Fresh Grounds, I baked a double batch of muffins. Popped them into the oven and then brewed coffee for the family. Set the table, poured orange juice, and started cracking eggs into a bowl while bacon sizzled in a skillet.

I'd slept better after several restless nights of worry over Rosie. She acted like herself again, tail wagging, with more energy and agility jumping from the bed or onto the window seat. I would have been a total wreck if my dog hadn't survived. But the thought of Holly Parker presiding as mayor at every village council meeting gave me a sick feeling in the pit of my stomach. Not that it was a given. The election wasn't until early November, but I hadn't made any progress proving Cal Bloom's innocence.

Then again, I didn't have time to worry about that now.

Once I plopped the cinnamon apple muffins into a towel-covered basket, I called at the bottom of the stairs, "Breakfast, everyone!"

Uncle Ross and Aunt Eve breezed through the back door.

"Just in time, I see," my uncle said. "I'm surprised Alex and Judith aren't up yet."

"We are," Mom said, snapping the last button of her housecoat when she entered the kitchen. "How nice of you, Sasha. You even used the good china and linen napkins."

Dad sat at his usual spot. "Thanks, Alley Bear. Smells great."

Maddie rushed down in sweats. "I'm the unlucky one. Someone spilled beer on me last night," she said, "and I wasn't even near the pavilion! I sponged my skirt clean, but I need to iron it. I hope I'm not late for my noon shift."

I set the platter of bacon and the crock of scrambled eggs on the table. While we ate, we discussed today's dance contest, the extra police brought in from neighboring towns to handle the crowd, and how the new microbrewery owner had set up a tasting booth. Eric Dyer was young, a go-getter according to Mayor Bloom, and planned to offer hard cider and a variety of brews for all the local restaurants after production began.

"Dyer needed the committee's approval first, of course," Dad said, "but Cal Bloom managed to convince them."

"By the way, is there anything new to report?" Mom asked me. "You promised to prove the mayor is innocent in this murder business."

"I didn't promise anything," I said. "You assumed that."

"Did you hear that Holly Parker is running against him in the election?" My sister pushed her plate away. "I saw a flyer she was passing out last night."

"What do you mean? How can she run for mayor?" Mom set her coffee cup down so hard, it clanked on the saucer. "She just moved back. There must be some rule that you have to be a resident for the past few years, or something like that."

Uncle Ross plucked another muffin from the basket with a derisive snort. "I saw those flyers, too. Heard what she was telling people about the mayor."

"And wearing a scandalous costume," Aunt Eve said.

I didn't say anything, since I'd seen my aunt in several family photos wearing hot pants, a miniskirt, or a bikini. How soon people forgot their own fashion choices. I didn't care what Holly wore, as long as she stayed far away from me, my dog, and our shop.

"She grew up in Silver Hollow," Dad said mildly, "so I suppose Holly Parker has as good a chance as Tony Crocker. He's never attended council meetings, that's what Cal said. Crocker's more of a farmer than a politician. At least she owns a business."

I snitched another crispy slice of bacon, wishing I could forget Holly and all the trouble she'd caused. "I've got to get to the village. See you all later."

"Wish us luck in the dance contest," Aunt Eve said. "But be fair—"

"I'm sure Amy Evans will want different judges when your turn comes up," I said. "That way it avoids any bias."

Upstairs, Maddie handed me my dirndl on a hanger. "Don't forget, you have to fill out a grading sheet for every dance group you're assigned to judge."

"A grading sheet? Wow, that sounds complicated."

"It isn't. Write down the group name, what type of dance, and then rate them from one to five. Be honest. I mean, cute is all well and good, but someone's gotta win. On technique, of course. And costumes. Oh, and how the audience reacted."

"I'll do the best I can," I said. "I can't even do a line dance without getting all confused. And every dancer looks good to me."

"Pretty sure you and Jay are judging with Isabel French and Lacey Gordon, who works for an insurance company somewhere around here."

"Hey, did you notice something different about Aunt Eve?" I asked. Maddie finished ironing her skirt and unplugged the cord. "I couldn't figure it out."

"Oh! Oh, I might know—"

She raced out of the bedroom. I followed, too curious to stay behind, and heard Maddie's whoops of joy before I reached the kitchen. Uncle Ross stood beside Aunt Eve, who flashed a large diamond ring on her left hand.

"You're getting remarried?" I asked, dumbfounded.

"I think it's marvelous," Mom said. "I can't wait to plan the wedding."

Dad shook his brother's hand. "I never thought you two would patch things up."

"Nothing has been decided yet," Aunt Eve said. "Ross proposed last night, in the most romantic way possible. He'd rented *Time After Time,* the movie we both love. About H. G. Wells following Jack the Ripper from London to modern San Francisco, and falling in love."

My uncle didn't say anything, but his face turned scarlet. Maddie and I exchanged wide grins. I had little trouble envisioning Ross Silverman wooing Eve, a year younger, back in the mod seventies-style clothing. She seemed to regress over the years, though, wearing a bouffant sixties hairdo for their wedding, and favoring the vintage fifties crinoline skirts, white blouses, and knit cardigans now. Even Uncle Ross had cleaned up lately, shaving every day, but he hadn't given up his sailing cap and deck shoes.

"Come on, Ross. We've got to practice before getting into our costumes." Aunt Eve shook out her napkin. "Sorry I can't help with the dishes, Judith."

Once they departed, I took Rosie outside on her leash. Maddie and Mom had already cleared the table before I fed the cat and changed the water in the dog's crate. Rosie curled up with her teddy bear, content.

Onyx lay full length on the sunny window seat. "You'd better not chew on my sandals again," I scolded. "I found teeth marks on the straps last night!"

"You shouldn't have left them out, Sasha." Mom held up a rose-hued, full-skirted dirndl on a hanger, with a white blouse and striped green apron. "How do you like my costume? I've got a flower crown, too. But your dad refused to wear lederhosen."

"Bring a shawl. It's going to be colder tonight." Her dress had a tiny rose pattern on the fabric, but with buttons up the front instead of hooks or lacing. "Hope you have a petticoat to go underneath. Time to get ready!"

After an invigorating shower, I French-braided my wet hair and then added silk flowers where I'd pinned the ends at the base of my neck. I'd gotten used to the dirndl, although I still wished Maddie had brought me a full-length blouse. After tying the silk ribbon around my waist and slipping my feet into flats, I hurried downstairs. Mom fussed over Dad, who looked smart in a forest green brass-buttoned wool blazer, long trousers, and a feathered hat.

"Does it look real?" He tugged at a fake handlebar mustache under his nose. "We're on crowd control duty tonight. And checking out each bear sculpture, too."

"We'll wait for Eve and Ross," Mom said. "You two go on ahead."

I walked out to the car with Maddie, fluffing my skirts again once we parked in the bank lot. My sister checked her hair extensions in the side mirror, retied one ribbon, and then shooed me across the street toward the courthouse.

"Have you heard anything from Kip?" I'd been afraid to mention his name, and couldn't gauge her mood today. She only shrugged.

"He's called a few times. Left messages. I did text him back, since he said he's meeting with someone who wants to lease his bear."

"Lease the Hippie Bear?"

"Yeah. I guess there's a group in San Francisco who want

to create a hippie museum," she said. "They'll use the bear as publicity to raise money. I'm happy for him."

"If this group is legit, you mean." It sounded hokey to me.

"They want to put the bear in Cleveland's Rock and Roll Hall of Fame first, in order to raise money, and then ship it to California." Maddie sounded morose. "So Kip wants to get back together, of course, and celebrate."

"Are you going to cave? I'm staying neutral, in case you're wondering."

"I can't do it, Sash. If I give in, I'll set myself up for more disappointment. I didn't like him pushing me the other night after the Polka Bear was ruined. Or how Kip yelled at me, telling me I was painting all wrong. Like I've never handled acrylics before! Please. I thought he was kidding, but nope. So that's another factor."

"You've worked in all kinds of media," I said, surprised.

"More than he has, although I never told him about my degree."

"What about all the classes at Cranbrook, the BBAC, and Pewabic Pottery."

"I know. But at least he's trying to apologize, in his own way."

I stopped Maddie, right in the middle of Archibald Street. Other pedestrians streamed around us. "Stick to your guns," I said. "You deserve respect for your artistic talent."

Her eyes filled with tears. "I like Kip, though. So much."

"I do, too, but—oops, there's Jay. Come on." I pulled her along the street. "Looks like Emily's band is playing tonight."

We rushed to join him. We both waved to Emily Abbott, warming up with the other musicians on the courthouse steps. Remyx, according to the large bass drum's printing, although I hadn't noticed their name at the pub; Emily wore her usual pale Goth makeup but with red lipstick. Her leather dirndl— as short as Holly's, but with dangling chains—flared out below a plain white T-shirt and spiked dog collar. The black felt top hat on her long, purple-streaked hair sported a long black-dyed ostrich plume. She pointed to the leather-jacketed silver teddy that sat atop a huge speaker to her left.

"Hey! How do you like Hairy Bear?" She waved him in the air. "Turned out so cool."

"Great," Maddie called back.

The lead guitarist plugged the soundboard in and then checked the volume levels of all their instruments. Maddie headed to the beer tent, while Jay and I headed to the roped-off section of Main Street. Five padded seats for the judges sat in front of the Regency Hotel.

"Folding chairs," Jay said. "Perks for volunteers."

I laughed. "I thought there were only four of us. Maybe there's five in case we don't agree? They must think it's better to have an odd number of judges."

"Not all of us will be around for every dance." Isabel French settled on a chair. "Kristen is supposed to judge, too, taking turns with her boyfriend, but she's also helping her dad pass out campaign flyers. Poor Mayor Bloom! I hear Holly Parker has a good chance to win."

"All because he's a murder suspect," I said bitterly. "Doesn't seem fair."

"Maybe you could do something. Don't you have an in with the detective handling the case?" Isabel asked. "That's what I heard, anyway."

I didn't answer, too annoyed. Instead I smiled at the dark-haired woman who perched on the last chair. "Hi, I'm Sasha Silverman."

"Lacey Gordon. I bought a graduation teddy bear at your shop, back in May," she said. "For my daughter. I'm glad I wore my sweatshirt today. It's good football weather."

"Sitting here all afternoon, even with the sunshine, I'll freeze," Isabel said. "It's not even getting to seventy degrees today."

"Too bad we can't dance," Lacey said. "This band is really good. So I heard you talking about Mayor Bloom. I thought he'd get re-elected easy next month."

"Things changed since the murder," I said.

"And Holly Parker is going gangbusters, collecting donations and setting up lawn signs," Isabel added. "I've heard some odd things. Is it true, Sasha, that you took out a PPO against her? So did Lisa Blake. What's that about?"

Wow. Word traveled fast already, and I wondered if Holly had spread it to gain more sympathy. "Yes, I did. But I can't explain right now. I'll be right back." I'd caught sight of my college friend Laura Carpenter, and rushed to overtake her. We'd been playing phone and text tag for over a month. "Laura! Hey, Carpenter. Wait up, girl."

Laura skirted the dancers standing by the registration table and then met me halfway. Two silver clips held her red hair in place. She wore a jean jacket over a floral minidress, black leggings, and leather boots. Laura hugged me with enthusiasm.

"Hey, don't you look like a million Deutschemarks! Euros now," she said with a grin. "We have *got* to catch up, Sasha. Looks like you're working today, though."

"Beer wench yesterday, dance judge today. How was Door County last month?" I'd been jealous hearing about her vacation. We'd once gone there together several years ago to take in the lighthouses and wineries. "You had great weather for it."

"We did. Greg and I had a blast. I posted a few photos on Facebook."

"I'll check 'em out. Haven't had a chance to do anything online with this event, the teddy bear tea party a few weeks ago, and the Bears on Parade."

"I saw some of the sculptures, how cool! I thought Maddie did one—"

"She did, but," I interrupted, and kept my explanation about the vandalism brief. I didn't hold back in sharing my suspicions, however, without actually naming my school rival. "Maddie worked so hard on the Polka Bear, too."

"Here I thought the hospital had backstabbing to an art form." Laura introduced me to a younger woman who joined us, with pageboy-styled dark hair and a slender figure. "Sharon Edwards owns a scrapbook and stationery shop over in Plymouth. She also teaches classes and weekend workshops."

"You both ought to try a class," Sharon said, and frowned at Laura's pained reaction. "Oh come on, don't give me the same excuse that you're all thumbs, or without a crafty gene in your body. Anyone can peel a sticker or arrange a few photos on a page."

"I guess you didn't see the pitiful one I made at a wedding shower."

"A scrapbook shop?" I caught sight of Holly Parker across the street, this time near the Time Turner, passing out campaign flyers. "Do you know that woman in the red miniskirt over there—the embroidered one?"

"Oh yeah, I know Holly Parker." Sharon's tone had swiftly turned acerbic. "A while back, we started a scrapbook store together in Elmwood Township."

I blinked. "Where's that?"

"Just north of Traverse City. We called it Scraps," she said. "I first met her here in the Detroit area, when Holly worked with me and my sister. We took several vacations together up to Petoskey, Charlevoix, and Traverse City. She was so friendly then. I had no clue about the tricks she could pull. I count her as an enemy now."

"Wow. That bad, huh."

Sharon hesitated. "Holly Parker ruined our scrapbook business. On purpose."

My blood pounded in my ears. I glanced several times across

the street to make sure Holly hadn't noticed us. I didn't want her to interrupt or make a scene like last night. That would be the last thing I needed right now.

"I'd like to hear how she managed that."

"It's complicated."

"Why did you choose Traverse City, if you don't mind me asking?"

Sharon shrugged. "We both loved the area, and visited the Cherry Festival several years in a row. It's always crammed with people, and in winter, the residents get so much snow people are housebound. Older women were our biggest customers at Scraps. They'd make it to weekly classes, no matter what the weather, except in blizzards when the roads were closed."

"Brr." Laura rubbed her arms. "I'm cold thinking about that one day I stopped by your shop, remember? Mid-July and only sixty degrees, raining like crazy. But I loved seeing the shelves of unique papers, stickers, the stamps and punches, and all the fancy embellishments. What didn't you carry?"

"It all fell apart," Sharon said, "a year and a half after we opened."

"So what happened?" I asked.

"You told me Holly stole a little bit of inventory every month," Laura said. "That she must have been selling it online."

"With a friend who was savvy enough with computers to help. I didn't have a shred of evidence, though. I think Holly cooked the books, too—"

"You're a liar!"

I twisted around in dread. Holly stood there, her cleavage straining her blouse, cheeks as apple red as her skirt. She carried a stack of *Holly Parker for Progress* flyers.

"You're calling *me* a liar?" Sharon faced her head-on. "How else could you explain all that missing inventory? You must have kept a second set of books. And profits went to hell, so we couldn't get a loan to pay our creditors. They zoned in like sharks in bloody water."

"I carried Scraps by myself, when you were *too busy* to bother."

"My brother's wife was going through chemo," she snapped back. "I had to help them. And he worked double overtime to pay their medical bills."

"I did the best I could, by myself, while you were off playing nursemaid," Holly said. "And then you claimed you never signed that change in our partnership—"

"I never signed anything! You talked one of your friends into notarizing that change after you forged my signature. You also slept with my lawyer so he wouldn't file a lawsuit against you. Perfect timing, I'd say."

"You're full of—"

Spewing profanity, Holly stormed into the crowd of the shocked onlookers. I breathed a sigh of relief. I definitely believed Sharon's story, despite the "she said, she said" aspect. What a mess to deal with at the wrong time in Sharon's life, too. And I could guess who the savvy but now deceased computer expert was, too—Gina Lawson. Another convenient piece of the puzzle. If only Mason would listen. Holly was now number one on my suspect list.

"So that little liar came back here," Sharon said. "Where she grew up."

"That's not the whole story," I said.

Sharon and Laura listened with rapt attention while I described Holly's competition with the Silver Bear Shop & Factory and The Cat's Cradle, plus how Gina Lawson's borrowing the "Think Pink" hoodie led to her tragic demise. I added my theory about Holly taking revenge, and how she may have destroyed the Polka Bear and poisoned my dog.

"Who else would target us," I said. "And she's running for mayor, too."

"I hope to God she loses," Laura said. "Imagine her getting into power."

"That's how Holly operates." Sharon shook her head. "I bet she has plans for a lot worse against you. Her MO is profiting from other people's troubles."

"I'm curious. You said things went missing from your store, right? How about a sample scrapbook that you could show customers," I added.

"One of our best, yes."

"I saw it," Laura said quickly. "Gorgeous. Pale blue pages with a beach theme."

"Bingo. The detective found it at Holly's shop, along with other stuff she kept. Like a trophy collection," I said. "Items to prove her victories."

"Wow." Laura glanced at Sharon. "Good thing you only lost your business instead of your life. Oh, sorry. Holly allegedly killed Gina Lawson, but I hope the cops find evidence to stick her with it. Then she can collect trophies in jail."

"We'll see." I glanced around, wondering where Holly had gone, but saw no sign of her. "Listen, I'd better get back. You two be careful."

Laura and I parted after promising to meet for coffee or dinner next month. Then I sat down with the other judges, apologized for missing the first few dances, and watched a darling ballet performance. All the young girls in pink tutus held silver teddy bears with pink ribbons. Shivering in the bitter breeze, I thought over Sharon's story about Scraps.

Jay slid his arm around my shoulders. "Cold? I brought a windbreaker." He pulled out a small nylon package, unfolded it, and then held it out. "Kind of dorky."

"Better than nothing."

I struggled into it, not wanting to stand up and draw attention to myself. A group of toddlers in miniature dirndls, white blouses, vests, and flower crowns careened on the street, prancing with little boys in lederhosen. They ended the dance by throwing kisses at the crowd.

"Look at this next group," Jay said. "Impressive."

Emily's band had started playing "All That Jazz" from *Chicago* while five teens, two boys and three girls, did a sultry rendition. Only Isabel noticed a few mistakes.

"Not bad, though. My daughters are in competitive dance," she said with a sigh. "All those costumes cost a fortune, but they love it."

To my surprise, Deon Walsh was up next with a tap dance, accompanied by a taped saxophone solo. His feet flew, his specialty shoes rapping in rhythm; no wonder he listened to music while he worked at the factory. Everyone clapped with enthusiasm when he finished. Jay caught my arm when the noise died down.

"So who were you talking to a while ago?" he asked.

I launched into Sharon's story about Holly Parker and the scrapbook store, keeping my voice low. "No different than here, playing the same game. However it profits her."

"No wonder she wants to run for mayor," Jay said. "I remember Kip telling me about Scraps. He lived up in Traverse City, and knew Holly. Kip called me last night. Said he wasn't going to let Holly hurt you or your sister again."

"She can't. Not with that PPO," I said. "Mike texted me that he filed it yesterday with the court. We can go straight to the police the next time anything happens."

"Let's hope that stops her cold. Oh, no!" Jay groaned and waved his cell. "Michigan fumbled the punt! Are you kidding me? Unbelievable!"

"What?" I peered at his tiny phone screen. "No way! They were winning."

We watched in disbelief. I hadn't been paying that much attention to the game's score, confident that the Wolverines would beat the Spartans. We'd planned to watch the highlights later that night. Now my heart sank as the replay showed a shocking touchdown in the very last few seconds of the game. UM's receivers had fumbled the punt, and bam. Game over.

That sent my mood into a downward spiral.

Chapter 25

"Wow, look at those kids move." Isabel French clapped when little boys in suits twirled girls in fancy ribbon-trimmed dresses around in a circle. "A quadrille, not easy to learn. And look at that adorable little blond boy. He must be four years old, if that."

Instead of paying attention, I'd been replaying past conversations with Holly Parker in my head. Oops. I snatched up a grading form and filled it out with the group's information, since Lacey had done the last one. But everything I'd learned over the last few weeks crisscrossed together. The theft of Mom's Minky Bear and Jay's carved bird, the scrapbook store fiasco, even Gina's bad habit of borrowing. It all fit. But did it add up to Holly being a murderer?

Maybe Gina knew too much, and Holly had to get rid of her.

The sun sank toward a bank of clouds on the horizon. Long shadows stretched to the east, across the paved street where the dancers twirled around one another. When I stood to stretch, Jay's light jacket slipped off my shoulders. I grabbed it, but it hit the ground with a loud clunk.

"What's in your pocket?" I draped it over my chair while Jay chuckled.

"My phone. Going somewhere?"

"I thought I'd stretch for a bit. Walk around."

"Isn't that your uncle? He's next up to dance."

Twisting around, my jaw dropped. I hadn't recognized Uncle Ross, not in a gray wool blazer, embroidered vest, green knickers, knee-high socks, and a feathered hat. Aunt Eve's blue-, green-, and beige-striped dirndl looked sweet beneath a buttoned corset, white blouse, and short wool jacket, plus she wore a knotted scarf around her neck. Her blond hair was pinned back in a severe bun, but she wore a pink flower above one ear. At their signal, Emily flipped a switch on a boom box. I was surprised again to hear the lovely strains of a waltz.

My aunt tipped her head back when Uncle Ross led her around, stepping gracefully, with fast twirling steps. They were marvelous to watch. Now I understood why they'd spent so much time practicing. I was sure it had also led to my uncle's proposal.

"They sure seem to belong together," I murmured.

"You're right." Jay slid an arm over my shoulders. "A unique pair, him with that vintage Olds, and her vintage fashion. She always looks terrific."

The music ended sooner than the audience expected. Their thunderous applause brought a pinker glow to Aunt Eve's face. She smiled and curtsied while Uncle Ross bowed. To the cries of "Encore!" he twirled her around again for another minute, but then nodded to Emily. Once they departed, she and the band played a traditional German song. Two men in faded lederhosen led a woman in a dirndl out, who was soon forgotten while the men circled each other, slapping their knees or feet, before they launched into a pretend fight. The crowd laughed and clapped.

Next up, I recognized Walter in a spiffy tux along with

Shirley, who wore a slinky black and white satin dress. They danced a rumba, although Isabel pointed out a few mistakes. I let her fill out the grading form. Uncle Ross led Aunt Eve to where I sat with Jay.

"That was wonderful, you two lovebirds! I've never seen a prettier waltz," I said.

"We've had great dancers today," Lacey Gordon said. "Oh, I love Irish step dancers. What great costumes, too, all green and white."

"Irish step dancers at an Oktobear Fest?" Jay shrugged. "Why not?"

"It's good exercise—"

Someone half-dragged me, up and out of the judging circle of chairs. "Sasha, I need your help." My cousin Matt looked frantic. "This way, come on."

"Hey, what's going on?" Jay asked, so I beckoned him to follow us.

We met Elle in front of Mary's Flowers. White-faced, she held Cara's hand in a tight grip. "I can't find Celia! I called the cops. They're looking all over the village."

I could tell she was on the edge of breaking down, but didn't want to scare her older daughter. "What happened?" I asked. "Did Celia wander off?"

"I kept both of them beside me, but stopped to chat with one of the room moms from Cara's class. One minute Celia was there, the next she was gone."

"She ran after a dog, Mommy," Cara said. "I couldn't stop her—"

"I know." Elle hugged her tight. "It's not your fault, darling."

I realized that Matt and Jay had left, without telling us. Not good, because we might end up overlapping in our search, but it couldn't be helped now. The streets were clogged with pedestrians, people drinking beer or eating all types of food, and observing the dance contest. Teens slipped in and out of the crowd, in groups or individuals; the chatter, music of the band, and dancers mingled together and sounded deafening. I couldn't see Jay or my cousin in all the mass of people surrounding us.

"What should I do, Sasha?" Elle's breath caught, and she trembled in panic. "What if someone snatched her? I looked away for a few seconds. Celia doesn't walk that fast."

I recognized her terror and squeezed her hand. "Before we search, let's take Cara to the coffee shop," I suggested. "That way we won't lose her, too."

"Good idea."

We race-walked around the crowd with the little girl, panting for breath, until we reached Fresh Grounds. A line snaked out the door. I pushed our way inside and waved frantically at Wendy Clark, who had ditched her costume; Mary Kate was busy in the hot kitchen putting a fresh batch of fat, salted, and twisted pretzels into the ovens. Two young workers slid cooled ones off wire racks and onto a tray, and then rushed them out to the food tent.

"Can you keep an eye on Cara in the back?" I asked Wendy while she cashed out a few customers. "It's an emergency, so keep her safe until we get back."

"Sure thing." She beckoned to Cara, who skipped around the counter. "Sit on that little bench, okay? Thanks, sweetie!"

"We'll explain later. Sorry we don't have time right now." I dragged Elle out the side door and ran smack into Maddie. My sister gobbled the last bit of an apple pastry. "Hey, Mads. We need your help searching for Celia. She's lost, and we—"

"Lost in this crowd? Oh, man!" Maddie swiped crumbs from her apron and hugged Elle, who shook from head to toe. "We'll find her, promise. Where do we start?"

"How about you two circle the Village Green?" I said. "That's where most of the dogs are. Cara said Celia ran after one. I'll head east of here and circle around. Have you got your phone? Call if either of you find her first."

Gulping hard, wiping tears that streaked her face, Elle sprinted across the street. Maddie ran after her. I wondered how the police put out an Amber Alert. I wasn't sure if they had to wait a specific length of time, or if they needed proof that a stranger had taken a child.

"Officer! Over here, over here!"

I hailed Hillerman's patrol car near the corner of Main Street and Kermit, but my cousin Matt raced to reach it first. He blurted out the story while the policeman took notes. When the dispatcher's tinny voice squawked over the radio, I strained to hear any update.

"Nothing yet," Matt said to me. "First I'm under suspicion of murder and get dragged out of my bookstore. And now my baby's gone missing."

"Stay positive. We have to find her, she can't have gotten far."

"Got it. Okay." Hillerman set the microphone aside and turned to Matt. "Your kid's missing, right? Fifth one today. We found all the others, so don't worry."

"She followed a dog into the crowd," I said. "Celia adores dogs."

Hillerman listened again to the quick report via the radio. "Okay, someone brought in a little girl to the station. Blue T-shirt, white shorts."

"No, she's wearing a dress and a yellow sweater." Matt described Celia's dark curls and brown eyes. "She's got a pink teddy bear with her. The one you gave her this week, Sash. I'm gonna check over by that Bling Bear. Maybe she found her way to it."

I spotted Jay near the Ham Heaven, where Mary and Tyler Walsh had a food stand, and hurried in that direction. A crowd of people lined up while the Walshes served thick sandwiches, fry pies, and nonalcoholic drinks. I met Jay in the middle of Kermit Street, trying to avoid the worst of the jostling mass who waited impatiently for their food and beverages.

"Elle told me she's wearing a dress and a sweater," Jay said. "Right?"

"And carrying a small teddy bear," I added. "Pink."

"Wait. I found a pink teddy bear. With a tag from your shop."

"Where?" My heart sank, and I felt sick. "On the Village Green?"

"No, over on Archibald Street."

"Great." I rubbed my damp forehead in dejection. One less way to find Celia, with so many other kids roaming around the village. "What did you do with the bear?"

"I gave it to Elle."

"I'll go check over by the vet clinic. She loves dogs, right?"

Jay headed off. I slowly turned in a circle, wondering which way to go. I couldn't imagine how someone would succeed in luring Celia away. Even by promising to let her pet a dog. Elle had taught her kids about "stranger danger." But what about Holly Parker? Celia might have trusted her, being a woman, if she'd offered the little girl candy or a toy. The idea seemed crazy. But I couldn't discount it, in case there was a remote chance.

I set off walking fast, my dirndl swirling around my legs, along the street toward the church. If she'd been frightened, Celia might have recognized the steeple and made her way to the familiar building. I checked behind every pillar in vain. Down Church Street, I saw several people admiring the Hippie Bear at the antique shop. The noise of the crowd from the Village Green's food and beer tents sounded dim this far away.

"Celia? Are you hiding, honey? Come on out! It's me, Sasha." I circled the church and raised my voice. "I'll take you to Mommy."

A little path led to a cemetery plot surrounded by an ironwork fence. I doubted that she'd come this way. Too scary, for
one thing. Celia couldn't squeeze between the narrow bars or
climb over the railing's pointed tips. Instead I returned to Kermit Street. A few cars rumbled past, so I kept walking. Past the
shuttered houses and then around Through the Looking
Glass's side yard, also fenced with the same type of iron bars
and railings.

Was Holly passing out her campaign flyers in the village
somewhere? Or was she holed up inside the shop, keeping
Celia quiet? The little girl would easily have been drawn to
the play structure—if she'd gotten this far. The butterfly chair.
I had to check behind it.

Noting the dense patch of shrubbery behind it, I rattled
the gate. It creaked open. "Celia? Are you hiding somewhere,
sweetie?"

A peculiar scent tickled my nose. What was it? I couldn't
tell at first, but headed toward the thick green bushes. Parted
the branches. Recoiled at the sight of a huge cobweb behind
it, and an overly large spider. I gave a shaky laugh. Spiders, ugh.
I thought I'd gotten over that fear long ago. Guess not. I
turned away, leaving the creature alone.

"What is that smell?" I muttered aloud. "Kerosene?"

I couldn't tell its origin until I approached the bookstore's
side door. It gleamed wet in the dim light. Someone had
splashed fuel over the door, the threshold, and the foundation.

"Holly, Holly Parker! Are you in there?"

I shook the doorknob. Locked tight. I heard a piercing
scream. I flew, heart in my throat, back through the open gate
and around to Theodore Lane. Without any fairy lights strung
along the eaves or around the porch supports, the steps were
dark. I stumbled to the door, the stench of kerosene nearly
gagging me. Had that been a child's scream? It was certainly
shrill enough.

Had Holly gone absolutely crazy? Was she that much of a monster to kill a child and burn her shop down? I pounded on the locked door, shouting at the top of my lungs.

"Open up! The police are coming—Holly!"

At a second scream, cut short, I wrapped my right hand in a fold of my skirt. Bashed the windowpane's corner, right above the doorknob. It took several tries, but at last glass rained down. Luckily inside, and not on the bare tops of my feet in flats. Careful of one jagged shard still sticking down, I reached in and unlocked the door.

And then pushed it wide open.

Chapter 26

"Holly? Are you in here?"

I crept forward, ignoring the powerful stench. My eyes finally adjusted to the darkness. Although I'd stubbed my toe, I managed not to cry out. A hissing sound from the back reached my ears. Not knowing the store's layout, I groped in that direction.

"Stay back."

"Holly, is that you? Is Celia Cooper here? A little four-year-old—"

"No, but Holly's here." The low voice puzzled me until the room flooded with light from an LED lantern. Kip O'Sullivan held it up. "Too bad Maddie's not with you, Sasha. But I'm glad you're here to witness Judgment Day."

I blinked in confusion. "Judgment Day?"

Holly, wearing her short dirndl and cleavage-baring blouse, struggled against cords that secured her onto a chair. And a gag tied tight around her mouth. Kip set the lantern on the counter, next to a metal tin of kerosene. I froze.

"Or Judgment Night. Everyone will see the fire, for miles around."

"Kip, have you lost your mind? Arson is a crime."

"So it is." He sounded so matter of fact, so determined, and splashed kerosene over my rival's bare legs and shoulders. Holly grunted. "So many people have tried to stop this witch, but nothing worked. Think of all the harm she's caused to so many people over the years. And then Holly destroyed Maddie's bear and poisoned your dog. So she'll burn."

"Two wrongs don't make a right," I said stubbornly. "Stop this. It's not too late."

"It needs to end. And it's a fitting end, too."

"You can't be judge and jury—"

"I wouldn't have to do this if she'd been wearing that pink jacket." Kip stared at me, his dark eyes narrowed in rage. "That was a mistake. I am sorry Gina was killed, but she wasn't all that innocent. She helped Holly up in Traverse City, stealing from people."

I swallowed hard. "Then go to the police! Tell them what happened," I said. "Holly will plead guilty, to vandalism and theft."

"She'll never admit anything. And why do you want to save her measly life? Holly's the last person you ought to care about."

I glanced her way, noting the terror and pleading in her eyes. "I do care. This is wrong. Morally wrong."

"As far as I'm concerned, this is the only way. Even if I have to spend the rest of my life in jail. She ruined me, Sasha. And she planned to do it again."

I inched closer to Holly's chair. "In what way?"

"She stole my oil painting, you know. Up in Traverse City." Kip grabbed her ponytail and pulled her head back so hard, Holly grunted in fear. "Maddie told me about that tro-

phy box the cop found here in the back room. I had a deadline
for a big commission, but Holly convinced the client to de-
mand changes. And then she stole my underpainting."

"How—"

"It doesn't matter! I'd already spent too much time, painting two or three versions. Isn't that right?" He knocked her
chair over sideways, and I gasped when Holly's head hit the
floor with a thud. "She gloated the day I left Traverse City for
good. Told me to go to hell. But that's where she's going now."

"Listen to me," I said, desperate now. Holly moaned against
the gag, so I knew she was still conscious. "Detective Mason will
help clear all this up."

"Sure, like the last time. Sharon Edwards found that out
the hard way. So what if people have family to take care of?
She doesn't care. Holly only cares about herself."

He stalked behind the long counter. Pulled open drawers,
as if looking for something. A match? While Kip was dis-
tracted, I punched 911 on my cell phone. Turned sideways,
hoping the dispatcher would answer without him noticing.

"You've taken advantage whenever possible, Holly. By
whatever means—"

I hissed the address into the phone. "Yes, it's a fire—oh!"

Kip had crept up behind me and grabbed my cell. He
threw it so hard against the wall, it shattered into pieces. "Maddie said you were resourceful, but come on. Don't bother calling for help. I'm not going to hurt you, Sasha," he said, his tone
coaxing. "I'd never hurt Maddie's sister. I'm doing this for you
both. I love her. I want to save her."

"She wouldn't want this."

"I'm saving her career," Kip roared. "And your family's
business!"

"By killing Gina?" I stepped forward, but he backed away.
"And now Holly?"

"You of all people ought to understand. It's come full circle," Kip said, "unless someone stops her. I will stop her. I'm the only one who can."

I took a deep breath and chose my words with care. "I learned something important a while ago. Letting Holly see how she affected me only fueled her satisfaction. And a sense of triumph, so I ignored her. She hates that most of all. Let her go, Kip. Let all of this go."

He shook his head. "No. She'll pay here and now. Here's proof of how she planned to ruin your Silver Bear Shop. I found this in the drawer."

He held out a sheet. Holly's eyes widened when I reached for it. Read the list of how winning the election would lead to rezoning Theodore Lane back to residential. I shrugged and waved the paper in the air.

"We're not the only business on the street."

" 'Number three, renaming the section where the tea room and restaurant are to a new street,' " Kip recited. "Only your shop would be on the rezoned part. And there's more."

"It reads like Holly's New Year resolutions. It doesn't mean anything."

"Like number four? 'Get Kip fired.' Holly persuaded some chick in one of my classes to file a harassment suit with the provost. I have an appointment Monday." His anger flared all over again, and he held up a wooden match. "He'll never listen that it's a setup. What college would hire me after that? Like I said, it's over. Judgment Day has come."

I stared in horror when he struck the match against the counter. It didn't flare, though. The moment Kip focused on finding a better surface or another match, I darted forward and tugged at Holly's cords. I needed a sharp knife.

I ran to the door and fetched a shard of window glass. Holly had loosened the gag and began screaming at the top of her lungs. I flinched, especially since I saw flames leap along the shop's back wall. I ran forward again and sawed at the cords. Cut my hand instead.

Black, greasy smoke billowed up, choking me. Tossing the shard aside, I dragged her, chair and all, toward the front door.

"No! You won't ruin this for me!"

Kip clamped an arm over my neck and chest from behind. That brought back Sandra Bullock's quick self-defense lesson in *Miss Congeniality*. SING—solar plexus, instep, groin—oops, forgot the nose part. Groaning, Kip fell like a rock. He toppled over Holly, who kept screaming. The fire roared, no doubt fed by all the books and toys.

"God help me—"

With a surge of adrenaline, I shoved Kip aside and tugged Holly's chair a few inches. But Kip had risen to his feet, a gun in hand. The ceiling above had caught fire. I coughed, sputtering hard. When the door crashed open, flames whooshed upward in a fireball.

"No!"

I screamed again when Jay wrapped strong arms around my waist. Dragged me outside and down the porch steps. We rolled onto the lawn, both of us gulping fresh air. My lungs felt seared. Two blasts rang out before sirens shrilled in the distance. I heard a huge crash inside the building and felt sick.

"You're safe," Jay said. "It's over."

"I know." My raspy voice surprised me.

"Come on, we'd better move." He pulled me to my feet and helped me hobble away from the burning house. "I should have guessed he'd try something—"

"Oh, Jay." I hid my face against his chest. "Don't blame yourself for this."

By the time I turned back to see the carnage, the township's fire engine sat in the middle of Theodore Lane. Firefighters in their gear streamed forward with hoses, passing us;

they aimed gushing streams of water, keeping the fire from spreading to the neighboring buildings.

People streamed down Kermit Street from the Oktobear Fest and congregated at a far distance. More stragglers joined them. I saw Sean Jones, one of the hefty volunteer firefighters, clearing fallen debris around the area. My throat burned. Floating cinders stung my eyes. When Bill Hillerman arrived, Jay helped me walk down to Kermit Street to meet the policeman.

"Celia Cooper—she wasn't in the shop," I croaked.

"She's been found, she's safe," he said. "Kirby, take her to the EMT truck for medical attention. It's over by the church."

Once the techs checked me over and watched me drink from a water bottle, I leaned against their vehicle's bumper. Static and buzzing from walkie-talkies hurt my head. Jay drew me away at last, back to Theodore Lane. I didn't realize we'd reached my porch until he sat me down on the swing. Grateful, I leaned back and closed my eyes. Kip had used his gun, so both he and Holly at least had been dead before the flames devoured the shop.

I'd failed to save either of them. That would haunt me for a long time. Jay sat beside me, silent but supportive. I curled my legs into my chest and rested my cheek against a knee.

"I had no idea Kip was that crazy," Jay said. "What kind of friend does that make me? Why didn't I call him, get him to talk things out?"

I wanted to console him, but couldn't find the words. Holly Parker had not wanted to die. She did care. Maybe she would have changed her ways, given a choice. A chance to redeem herself and set things right. Kip had been wrong to take that chance away.

I'd been wrong, too. Holly had not killed Gina. Three lives had been lost, one the victim of a simple mistake. "Kip should have gotten psychological help," I said, "but he made a choice. The wrong choice, but he wouldn't listen."

Vigilante justice, while a common plot in films, was not realistic in life. It only caused more suffering, more pain than Kip
would ever realize. Than anyone really understood. And he'd
hurt Maddie, too, despite his belief that he was saving her career and our family business. My sister would grieve his death.
Probably blame herself, to some degree.

"I need to find Maddie. Tell her what happened."

Instead I stared at the smoking ruin of the former Holly
Jolly Christmas shop. What a shame that all those wonderful
Alice in Wonderland collectibles had also perished. The Ital-
ianate structure was a burnt and blackened shell.

Uncle Ross and Aunt Eve appeared out of the smoky darkness. "Sasha, you're okay!" My aunt rushed up the porch steps.
"We were so worried."

"Where's Maddie?"

"With Matt and Elle. She's helping them get the kids
home. Maddie tried calling you, over and over again."

"My phone's in there."

I waved toward the ruined building. Took a few swigs from
the water while Jay explained what happened. Red lights continued to flash around, making me dizzy, but I managed to add
details until the whole story came out. By the time my parents
arrived, Jay repeated it all for their benefit. Mom shooed everyone inside the house and started brewing coffee and tea, while
Aunt Eve took Rosie out to the yard. My dog quickly returned and crept into my lap. Dad shook hands with Jay and
then eyed me in concern.

"Are you okay, honey? Kip didn't hurt you?"

"No, I'm fine."

"You don't sound fine," Uncle Ross grumbled, but shut up
at Aunt Eve's strict look. "They found Celia asleep behind that
big speaker on the courthouse steps. The band didn't realize
she'd gotten past them. Too busy playing their music, I guess."

"How could she sleep through all that noise?" Jay asked.

"She's four," I said. "That's why."

"A tired child can sleep through anything," Mom said. Somehow she managed to hug me and Rosie both. "How you ever get yourself into these situations, I'll never know."

I let her fuss over me and sipped the honey and lemon tea she'd made. By the time I'd finished, Maddie rushed into the house. Her dirndl was streaked with dirt, and her extension braids hung loose by their clips. She pushed them aside.

"Sasha, are you okay? Is it true? About Holly—"

"I'll explain," Dad said, and led her off to the comfortable armchairs in the next room. Jay and I followed. I carried Rosie with me and perched on the chair's arm, anxious about how Maddie would take the news.

"Oh, man. Kip really freaked out," she said, clearly dazed. "No wonder he sounded so crazy last night. He left a string of phone messages, promising he'd help us get free of Holly. But I had no idea what he meant."

"I'm sorry," I said. "I wish—"

"It didn't have to end like that? Yeah, I understand."

"Excuse me, you all have a visitor," Aunt Eve interrupted. She stepped aside. Detective Mason walked into the room, his face grimy with soot.

"Sorry to hear what happened, with the fire." He met my gaze and then glanced at his Moleskine notebook. "I heard part of the story from Officer Hillerman. I'd like to hear the whole thing from you, Sasha. Start with why you went to Ms. Parker's shop."

"To search for Celia Cooper." I took a sip of water from the bottle Jay handed me. With his help, I recited the events. Maddie kept silent, biting her lip whenever I had to mention Kip's name, and twisted her hands in her lap. "I never expected to find Kip there," I said. "Or that he'd be so determined to kill Holly."

"I'm sorry that other case took most of my time," Mason

said. "And I should have taken into account what you said about Holly Parker."

I sighed. "So case closed."

"And Mayor Bloom is also off the hook," Mom said.

"Officer Sykes regrets not reporting his knife as lost or stolen. You're right, by the way, about his brother Larry," Mason added. "He knows all the stats of every Detroit Tigers player from 1905, when Ty Cobb began playing for them."

"But he didn't touch his brother's knife," I said.

"No, but he told me who did take it." Mason flipped back in his notebook. "Larry saw Kip hiding it in his gear. My fault, because I didn't ask him the right question until last night when I saw him at the festival. I didn't have time to hunt O'Sullivan down today, either. By the way, I brought something."

Mason drew out something furry from inside his jacket. "Minky Bear," I said with a smile, and accepted it. "Here you go, Mom. It's your teddy bear."

"Thank you so much, Detective," my mother said, but patted my shoulder. "I want you to keep it now, Sasha. With Dad's old bear. They belong together."

"I'm surprised you're releasing it so soon," Dad said. "Figured it would take a while for all the paperwork to get processed. Having to file your reports, the interviews, the vandalism, and arson documentation."

"Technically, I hadn't processed the box from Holly's shop as evidence yet," Mason said. "It sat on my desk all this time. If you want that bird carving, Kirby—"

"Yes," I said. "For his sister."

Startled by a loud commotion from the kitchen, I rose to my feet. Mason pocketed his notebook and followed Jay, who followed me into the other room. The grand prize bear in its lederhosen and feathered felt hat filled the doorway. Flynn Hanson peeked around it, since he'd bumped the bear into the ironwork baker's cart while trying to bring it inside. Several heavy cookbooks fell to the floor with a loud thud.

"Hey, watch out," Uncle Ross growled. "What are you doing with that?"

"You won the dance contest," Flynn announced, but my uncle protested.

"No, no. We can't win—"

"Oh, Ross! Yes, we can." Aunt Eve clapped in delight. "We'll donate it to the women's shelter. All the kids there will love playing with that bear."

"Cheryl had to cancel our plans, so I stepped in as a dance contest judge when Sasha and Jay took off," my ex said. "The Viennese waltz came in first, and then I saw your names on the grading sheet. You won, fair and square, so what do you want me to do with it?"

"Take it to the factory for now, Ross," Mom said, "and you can deliver it next week."

"We'll donate a dozen small bears to go with it," I added, and Maddie agreed. "That way the kids at the shelter will have their own to take, whenever their moms find a new home."

"Great idea. Don't you think so, Ross?" Aunt Eve smiled at his sour look and poked him in the stomach. "I know you do."

"I saw the fire from the courthouse," Flynn said. He rested an arm on the giant bear's head and grinned at us all. "So. What did I miss?"

Unbelievable. I lobbed Minky Bear at his head.

Chapter 27

Ding dong. "Trick or treat!" Muffled laughter and giggles wafted through the door. The kids rang the bell again.

"Coming!" Daylight hadn't yet faded, but the clock showed six-fifteen. I handed every child a small packet of gummy bears plus a chocolate bar. "Happy Halloween!"

"Aww, look at the dog," they said, and pointed at Rosie.

"Count Dog-ula." I crouched down to hug Rosie, who barked. She looked adorable in her black silk cape with its red lining. The collar stood up around her ears and head. "Watch out for all the ghosts at the tea room down the street. They're scary."

"We will!"

The kids clattered down the porch and raced on their way. I carried my zero gravity chair down the steps and set it up on the sidewalk. Then I retrieved the two huge bowls of candy, the bag of extra treats in case I ran out, and Rosie on her leash. For the last night of October, the warm temperatures held and I could sit outside for a better view of the kids and their costumes. A hint of smoke from the fire that had burned down the corner shop, now razed to the ground, lingered in the air. Only a pile of rubble remained.

The owner of Flambé planned to buy the lot, as long as the Davisons agreed on a decent price, and build a new restaurant facing Kermit Street. I'd already heard rumors of a modern structure of glass and steel, but I figured Mayor Bloom would persuade them otherwise. It had to blend in with Silver Hollow's quaint architectural style, and if the village didn't already have an ordinance spelling it out, they'd vote on that soon and make it retroactive.

Rosie whined, so I lifted her onto my lap and swung my feet up. "No, you can't have any gummy bears. But here's a peanut butter treat. Good girl."

I opened a chocolate bar. Indulged, while the next batch of kids raced in my direction. "One per customer," I said with a laugh. "Yes, you can take an extra for your little sister."

Maddie had watched the shop for me earlier this afternoon. After meeting Jay for a midafternoon burger, I'd toured his studio and marveled at all the gorgeous carvings. Bear cubs, mama bears, grizzlies, and even teddy bears. My favorite was a small bear lying down, an open book in front of him, with glasses perched on his nose. Jay had finished our new Silver Bear Shop & Factory sign, but wouldn't allow me to peek under the canvas tarp. His dad would be delivering it in a few days, once the sealer dried.

Then I'd helped him finish packing. We took time for a proper good-bye, and after promising to spend Christmas together, I watched his truck drive north. I missed him already. But Jay needed to take every opportunity to enhance his résumé and portfolio.

"Trick or treat, smell my feet—"

"Give me something good to eat," I finished, and tossed treats into their bags before watching them run off into the growing twilight. "Maybe I'll make a batch of spiders."

"Ooh, with the chow mein noodles, chocolate chips, and peanut butter. Yum!" Maddie said, dragging a chair from the porch. She plopped down. "I love those. So, what do you think about the empty restaurant? All those floor-to-ceiling windows. Hmm."

"Hey! Your new design studio—what a great idea." I sat up, dislodging Rosie, who curled up on the ground instead beside my chair. "I thought you wanted to be in the village."

"Now that Mom and Dad are buying a condo, I won't mind sticking closer to the shop." She looked a little shamefaced. "I really didn't want Mom popping in every day, looking over my shoulder. She'll be busy decorating their new place."

"Are you sure? We haven't had a chance to talk about much."

"You had enough on your plate all month," Maddie cut in. "Now we can both sit back. Relax. At least for tonight."

"Until the holiday rush begins." I held out a packet of gummy bears. "Happy Halloween, and a merry beary Christmas."

Connect with Us

Visit us online at
KensingtonBooks.com
to read more from your favorite authors, see books
by series, view reading group guides, and more.

for sneak peeks, chances to win books and prize packs,
and to share your thoughts with other readers.

facebook.com/kensingtonpublishing
twitter.com/kensingtonbooks

Tell us what you think!

To share your thoughts, submit a review,
or sign up for our eNewsletters, please visit:
KensingtonBooks.com/TellUs.